Praise for Greg Egan

An Unusual Angle

"Egan gets at the old familiar material, schooldays in the suburbs, and provokes his readers to redefine it. This redefinition, moreover, is not in terms of traditional metaphysics . . . In other words, he is pushing back the limits of literary pasturage."

—Veronica Brady, *Xeno Fiction*

Quarantine

"*Quarantine* explores quite convincingly what it may mean to be human a hundred years from now. Egan's future fascinates, and the interiority of the narrative as well as the anonymous, powerful meta-organizations in which no one really seems to know the whole story evoke the edgy, European feel of Kafka or Lem . . . He adroitly finesses quantum theory to the nth degree, making the consequences utterly real—and at the same time, utterly unreal—to his characters."

—Kathleen Ann Goonan, *Science Fiction Eye*

"*Quarantine* becomes both philosophical treatise and procedural whodunnit, a hard feat to pull off, but the two threads do eventually converge in a stunning ending."

—Colin Harvey, *Strange Horizons*

Permutation City

"Wonderful mind-expanding stuff, and well-written too."

—*The Guardian*

"Immensely exhilarating. Sweeps the reader along like a cork on a tidal wave."

—*Sydney Morning Herald*

Distress

"A dizzying intellectual adventure."

—*The New York Times*

"The plot offers both adventure and depth, with themes of information, science and human relationships interwoven in complex and often profound ways. Egan is a major voice in SF, and this impressive work should help win him the wide readership he deserves."

—*Publishers Weekly*

Diaspora

"A conceptual tour de force . . . This is science fiction with an emphasis on science."

—Gerald Jones, *The New York Times*

"Vast in scope, episodic, complex, and utterly compelling: a hard science-fiction yarn that's worth every erg of the considerable effort necessary to follow."

—*Kirkus Reviews*

"Egan's remarkable gift for infusing theoretical physics with vibrant immediacy, creating sympathetic characters that stretch the definition of humanity, results in an exhilarating galactic adventure that echoes the best efforts of Greg Bear, Larry Niven, and other masters of hard sf. A top-notch purchase for any library."

—*Library Journal*

Teranesia

"Egan knows his material, has a keen talent for extrapolation, a vivid imagination and a passion for intellectual banter."

—*San Francisco Examiner*

"Egan is perhaps SF's most committed rationalist in the mould of Richard Dawkins. If it cannot be measured, weighed and analyzed, for Egan it does not exist . . . *Teranesia* show why the genre needs him."

—Colin Harvey, *Strange Horizons*

"One of the very best."

—*Locus*

Schild's Ladder

"Egan focuses on the wonders of quantum physics, bringing a complex topic to life in a story of risk and dedication at the far end of time and space."

—*Library Journal*

"[Egan is able to] dramatize the interplay between intellect and emotion in the advance of science. He finds unexpected poignancy in a confrontation between those scientists who are impatient to destroy the new universe before it destroys us and those who want to find a way to coexist with it—and with any life-forms that it might have engendered. Even 20,000 years in the future, such issues can still provoke recognizable human passions."

—Gerald Jones, *The New York Times*

Incandescence

"Greg Egan has no equal in the field of hard SF novels. His themes are cosmic with galactic civilizations and plots spanning millennia. Compelling throughout, [*Incandescence*] contrasts some fascinating moral quandaries of knowing decadence with the mind-expanding discoveries of isolated peasants and eventually blends its narrative threads in a surprising twist."

—Tony Lee, *Starburst*

"Audacious as ever, Egan makes you believe it is possible . . . breathtaking."

—*New Scientist*

"The driving forces of this novel are a pure scientific puzzle and the intellectual joy of finding answers . . . Those who like their science hard will appreciate his thorough research and intricate speculations."

—Krista Hutley, *Booklist*

Zendegi

"Both beautifully written and relentlessly intelligent, *Zendegi* is like a marvelous, precision-engineered watch. It never sacrifices its thematic content to its science, or its richly drawn characters to either, but enmeshes them fully, treating them as the deeply interconnected pieces of the human experience that they are."

—io9.com

"A thought-provoking, intensely personal story about conflicting instincts and desires as technology recapitulates humanity."

—*Publishers Weekly* (starred review)

"It might look, at first glance, like a plot we've already seen hashed out ad nauseam, but have faith in Egan's ability to create stunning, complex futures, with grand themes given a human dimension: he delivers something extraordinary, with no easy answers. Despite its tragedies, the story is remarkably hopeful and certainly one of the best of its kind."

—Regina Schroeder, *Booklist* (starred review)

The Clockwork Rocket (Orthogonal Book One)
"The perfect SF novel. A pitch-perfect example of how to imagine aliens. Captivating from the first page to the superb last paragraph."

—Liviu Suciu, *Fantasy Book Critic*

"Greg Egan is a master of 'what if' science fiction. Other physics? Different biology? Egan's characters work out the implications and outcomes as they struggle to survive and prevail. The most original alien race since Vernor Vinge's Tines."

—David Brin, Hugo and Nebula Award-winning author of *Earth* and *Existence*

The Eternal Flame (Orthogonal Book Two)
"More than any Egan story to date, the books of the Orthogonal trilogy place science in a broader social context."

—Karen Burnham, *Strange Horizons*

The Arrows of Time (Orthogonal Book Three)
"An intellectual quest which involves us, the readers . . . It is as valid an apotheosis as anything which involves the physical or the spiritual, made rarer because it celebrates curiosity, knowledge, and understanding."

—Andy Sawyer, *Strange Horizons*

DICHRONAUTS

Also by Greg Egan

DICHRONAUTS

GREG EGAN

Night Shade Books
NEW YORK

Visit our website at www.nightshadebooks.com.

10 9 8 7 6 5 4 3 2 1

Library of Congress Cataloging-in-Publication Data

Names: Egan, Greg, 1961- author.
Title: Dichronauts / Greg Egan.
Description: New York : Night Shade Books, [2017]
Identifiers: LCCN 2016038952 | ISBN 9781597808927 (hardback)
Subjects: | BISAC: FICTION / Science Fiction / High Tech. | FICTION / Science Fiction / General. | FICTION / Science Fiction / Adventure. | GSAFD: Science fiction.
Classification: LCC PR9619.3.E35 D53 2017 | DDC 823/.914--dc23
LC record available at https://lccn.loc.gov/2016038952

Print ISBN: 978-1-59780-892-7

Cover illustration by Justinas Vitkus
Cover design by Claudia Noble

Printed in the United States of America

Five steps forward
Three steps right
Are four steps off the path
But keep you safe in sight

Three steps forward
Five steps right
Are four steps into Sider Land
Out of the light
                              —Children's rhyme

PART ONE

1

ON THE DAY THE movers zigzagged the museum, Seth's whole family woke before dawn. They ate a quick breakfast then set out across the city to join the crowd gathering to watch the spectacle.

By the time they arrived the sky was bright, and all the vantage points to the east and west of the museum were taken, occupied by a good-natured but impenetrable throng. So they sidled north into the border precincts thinned by the encroaching summer—and found themselves on a deserted hill overlooking the building itself.

"Not from the north!" Elena complained. Irina responded indignantly, "I can make it twice as clear as you can!"

«What do you think?» Theo inspoke. «I'm not even pinging the scene myself—there's so much bouncing around from the crowd that it wouldn't make any difference.»

«This is fine,» Seth replied. He didn't know if Elena was just being spiteful, or if she and Irina had a real problem sharing views.

Seth's mother said firmly, "We'll watch from here, it's as good a spot as any."

The movers had finished their preparations inside the building, and were assembling into four rope teams outside: two near the south-west corner, two at the north-east. There must have been fifty Walkers in each team, but a part of Seth's mind still refused to accept that they stood any chance of shifting the huge structure. He'd seen the wheels and pivots under the floor once, in a tour of the ancient building that had treated it as an exhibit in its own right, but the sheer size of those hidden components, however well-designed they were to aid the movers' task, had only made it seem more fanciful that anyone could set them in motion.

"There's a career for you, Seth," Theo's father suggested.

"Maybe." Seth wasn't sure if he was joking or not. "I think Theo would get bored, though."

"That's not important. He can still enjoy his own work. It's like that with all of us: give and take."

«What is it with your father?» Seth asked.

«He wants me to study business law—so he's hoping you'll pick something that he thinks I'd hate, as much as he thinks you'd hate his choice for me. If we'd both be suffering equally, it would be harder for you to complain.»

«Do you want to study law?» Seth's gut tightened at the thought of spending half his life, even as a scribe, on anything so soul-sappingly tedious.

«No.» Theo sounded amused that he'd needed to ask. «Do you want to be a mover?»

«I don't know. I doubt I'll ever be strong enough.»

The teams had taken hold of their ropes and were beginning to strain against the impossible load. The two groups at each corner were pulling at slightly different angles, but all four directions required an awkward stance. Seth noticed that a few of the movers at the north-east corner were west-facers, which had to make their work even harder.

«You see that?» he asked Theo.

«If they were upside-down, I'd be impressed.»

Seth laughed and did a half backflip, landing on his hands, west-facing himself now. His own vision was undisturbed—the world itself no more seemed upside-down than when he tipped his head back to see westward—but his arms were blocking Theo's view, and the thought of trying to maneuver them out of the way made him fear he'd lose his balance, risking a dangerous uncontrolled fall. He hadn't hand-walked since he was a kid; it had seemed easy then, but he was seriously out of practice. He completed the flip, and brushed the soil from his palms.

"What are they doing?" Elena asked irritably. "Nothing's happening!"

"The hardest part is getting the wheels moving," Seth's father explained. "But once they start—"

The museum began to turn. It stretched out along the grand avenue that cut diagonally across the city, growing ever more slender, taking up ever less of the width of the road. The center of the building, the pivot, stayed fixed, while the opposing teams of movers ran ahead of their ropes' anchor points: half of them heading north-east, half south-west.

"See anything now?" Irina asked sarcastically. Elena said nothing, but when Seth glanced her way she seemed rapt.

«Are you sure you don't want to be a mover?» Theo teased him. Seth could feel his own face contorted into an expression of delighted stupefaction. The parallelogram below them was insanely skinny now; he'd turned pebbles about as far as this, but nothing larger.

«Only if I get to ride inside the buildings, and see all the rooms remain normal while the city turns around me.»

«You can always turn yourself and get the same view.»

«You think so? Who's going to clear the streets for me?»

The museum's far corner, needle-thin, slid past the bakery, the grain store, the bath house. It crossed the bridge over the brook and pushed on into the northern residential precinct. The movers themselves were barely visible now, stretched out along the road into surreal slivers of flesh. Despite what he'd said to Theo's father, Seth doubted that their Siders were feeling bored. Strength and agility were not the only skills at play here: to execute a maneuver like this, you'd need the clearest possible sense of your surroundings in all directions, demanding a flawless collaboration between Walker and Sider.

The corner itself became too narrow to discern, but then Seth noticed some of the movers reorienting their bodies and heading back down the avenue. They'd turned the massive building as far as they needed for the first step, so now the central pivot would be raised and a new one, almost at the corner, lowered, as the wheels were reconfigured to facilitate a counter-turn that would end with the museum one-eighth of the way to its destination. It would take the whole day to bring it to its new location at the city's southern edge.

Seth's father handed out the stone-fruit he'd brought, and everyone sat on the dusty ground of the abandoned lot, chewing the sweet, heavy pulp while they waited for the second act to start.

Theo said, "We should halt the sun, not move the cities."

His mother laughed. "One day, maybe."

"I'm serious."

Seth's mother tipped her head back and scowled, unable to resist taking Theo at his word. "And survive on what? Do you think you could farm the same plots of land forever?"

"And what about quarries?" Seth added. "Whatever happened with the crops, you couldn't dig up the same stone twice."

"How much new stone would we actually need," Theo countered, "if we weren't leaving a trail of rubble behind?"

"Hmm." Seth paused to give the question due consideration. Theo had a habit of blurting out these absurd, dream-like propositions and then defending them with such sincerity that everyone's skepticism began to waver.

"And how exactly do we halt the sun?" Theo's father asked.

"There's a mover for every job, isn't there?" Theo replied. "So surely there's an un-mover for this one."

This assertion was so strange that it hung in the air unchallenged.

Seth looked down across the city. Much as he admired the movers, the truth was that the best he could hope to be if he joined them was some kind of minor assistant, checking ropes or carrying tools. He was healthy enough to be a stonemason or a farm laborer, but he did not have the strength to fling buildings around like toys.

Theo inspoke, «You know who goes before the movers?»

Seth wasn't sure he understood the question. «Road-builders?» Theo clearly wanted to escape the law, but there had to be limits to what he would put up with.

«Before the road-builders.»

Privately, Seth ran through a list of ever-less-appealing prepara-
tory trades—then as he pictured the untamed ground that the very
first of these workers would confront, a wilderness untouched by
leveler or plow, he finally understood what Theo had been hinting
at. Why hadn't he thought of it himself? He'd always wanted to work
outdoors, and there was no job less confining.

«You'd be happy with that?» he asked. «We'd do it together?»

«Why not?» Theo replied. «We could study something real, and
do something useful.»

«While we wait for the un-movers to catch the sun?»

«Of course. And not a statute, a contract, a lease, a trust, or a lien
in sight.»

Seth's mother was facing away from him, but he caught his
west-facing father's eye.

"We know what we're going to do," he announced. "Both of us."

"Is that right?" Theo's father asked warily.

«Fuck, yes,» Theo inspoke. Seth struggled to keep a straight
face, waiting for his Sider to find the courage to express the same
sentiment out loud, but then he found himself unable to keep silent
any longer.

"We're going to be surveyors," he said. "Movers are indispens-
able—but even they need someone going ahead of them, to find the
best route for the city to take."

2

"THE POSSIBILITY THAT THE world might be infinite was recognized by people as far back as the Siseans." Maria's Walker,
Samira, wrote the name beside the timeline she'd sketched; Seth cop-
ied it, wondering abashedly if he was the only person in the class
who'd never heard of this entire civilization before. "But many other
cultures assumed that the migration was ultimately cyclic. There were
two main variants of that mythology: one in which constant southwards travel would eventually take you back to where you'd started—
as if north and south were no different than east and west—and
another, more elaborate, version, in which the advance of the sun regularly slowed, halted, then went into reverse, allowing the migration
to change direction. Of course, the last occasion on which the reversal
was meant to have happened was always taken to be so remote as to
be the stuff of legend rather than history, and the absence of any signs
of past habitation required the proponents to believe in summers so
fierce as to transform buildings into sand, while mysteriously permit-
ting the same kind of stone in its natural state to survive intact."

Seth resisted the urge to share a silent joke about the halting sun
with Theo. There was no prohibition on inspeech during lectures,
but if they didn't discipline themselves and limit its use to helping
each other follow the material, they'd end up constantly distracted.

"Later," Maria continued, "as geodesy began to develop into
a true science, doubts arose as to whether an infinite assembly of

matter was physically possible. The sun was understood to be orbiting the world under the influence of the same gravitational attraction that we feel here on the ground—but then the sun itself, a finite body, was seen to exert a tidal pull on the water in every river. If the world was infinite in extent, how could its gravitational pull fail to be infinite too?"

Seth contemplated this disturbing notion. If you could measure the tides raised by the sun, and then measure the tug of the world upon your body, hadn't you, by implication, measured the world itself and discovered its limits?

But Maria had a far less radical solution. "In the generations following Siméon's *Treatise on the Tides*, geodesists reached a consensus on this question. There is, in fact, a simple shape the world could take that would allow it to be infinite, while giving rise to a finite gravitational force." Samira sketched four hyperbolas on the drawing board, symmetrically arranged around a central point. "Imagine that these curves go on forever. Take the area between them and spin it around the north-south axis to make a solid. The one-sheeted hyperboloid that wraps around the axis is the ground on which we stand. The two dish-shaped surfaces at the north and south are unreachable to us, but if anyone lived in those sunless places they would feel the same kind of gravity holding them to the ground as we do."

Samira began writing a familiar equation below the sketch, while Maria reminded the students of its role. "Siméon's Law of Gravity says that if you add the second rates of change of potential energy along the two ordinary directions, then subtract the same quantity along the axial direction, the result will be proportional to the density of matter. Though this shape has an infinite volume and, in its entirety, an infinite mass, you can satisfy Siméon's Law while still producing a finite force everywhere—in fact, a force that's of equal strength everywhere on the surface.

"Your task, to be completed by tomorrow, is to find precise expressions for the potential energy in each distinct region. You may assume, for the sake of simplicity, that the density of the rock is the same everywhere."

«This gets better every day!» Theo enthused as they headed out of the classroom. «All the things they never explained properly in elementary school are starting to make sense now.»

«I'm going to need your help with this,» Seth confessed. Geodesy delighted him, too, but some of the technicalities were frightening.

«Remember the formula they gave us for the point mass?»

«Vaguely.»

«You wrote it down,» Theo assured him. «I think we'll just have to . . . spread that out over a larger volume.»

«An infinite volume!»

«Yes,» Theo conceded. «But the shape is so symmetrical that there's bound to be some kind of trick to make the problem simpler than it sounds.»

Seth went to the study hall and sat scribbling formulas, trying out Theo's suggestions. In the empty space around a point mass, the potential energy was proportional to the inverse of the true distance from the point, with the force the inverse squared. But when matter was spread out at a uniform density, there was a solution that was even simpler, with the potential energy proportional to the *square* of the true distance from some point, and the force proportional to the distance.

«Some point?» Seth could follow all the algebra, but the symbols meant nothing until he knew what they were measuring. «Which point?»

«Whatever makes things simplest,» Theo proposed.

Seth liked that rule. «The center?»

When they followed through with detailed calculations, everything began to fall into place. On the ground, and in the space above it, the gravitational pull of the entire, infinite world was no different from that of a certain finite mass at the world's center. It was as if all the vast plains and mountain ranges that stretched on forever to the north and south had been replaced by a single pebble—an absurdly heavy one, but not boundlessly so—that acted as their gravitational proxy. But there was a further, equally astonishing twist: although an idealized point mass produced infinite forces along its cones— where the true distance from the point fell to zero—in the solid rock between the hyperboloids, those forces weren't merely hidden, they were tamed: reduced to finite quantities. The pebble at the center of the world was a useful fiction, from a sufficient distance, but if you could actually burrow down into the rock, instead of being torn apart as you approached the cone, you'd find the force of gravity decreasing.

«Well done, Surveyor Theo.»

«Well done, Surveyor Seth.»

Walking home, they passed a playground where half a dozen kids were sledding up a northwards ramp. Seth paused, tempted but a little embarrassed.

«Go ahead,» Theo encouraged him. «We're not that ancient yet.»

The group were friendly and one of the kids let Seth take a turn on her sled. He lay on his stomach on the polished stone, gripping the worn handles. Three Walkers sidled up the start of the ramp, pushing him to get him started. Seth could feel the changing forces in his gut as his helpers' task grew easier, then superfluous, and as they stepped away he cried out in abandon at the rush of acceleration. The sled shot up the slope; Theo showed him the edge drawing closer. Then they were truly flying, off the ramp, through the air, down into the straw heap.

«Isn't gravity glorious?» Theo's words sounded muddy and his view appeared blurred; the jolt of landing must have shifted him a little. Seth waited for him to squirm back into place before replying, «It is.»

He rose to his feet and picked up the sled, sidling back to return it to its owner.

With the sun low in the western sky, it was hard to believe that it could ever threaten anyone, let alone blast abandoned cities into dust. Seth stood for a moment, savoring the smell of the hay that still clung to his sleeves, then he bade the children goodbye and set out for home.

3

«SOMETHING'S WRONG,» THEO SAID as they approached the house. «Can you hurry?»

Seth broke into a run—though they were coming from the west, so if he couldn't see anything amiss himself, nor could Theo. «What's the problem?»

«My sister's in trouble.»

«How do you know?»

«I can hear her.»

Seth had reached the porch. He unlocked the door and stepped inside. "Elena?" he called out. She didn't reply. «What's Irina saying?» he asked Theo.

«It's muffled. But I think they're in their room.»

Seth climbed the stairs, bracing himself, unsure what to expect. He knocked gently on his sister's door. "Elena? Are you all right?"

"Go away! I'm busy!"

"Can I talk to Irina?"

"We're both busy."

"Can't she tell me that herself?"

"Just leave us alone."

Seth stayed by the door. Theo said, «You need to do something. She's crying out for help.»

Seth didn't doubt him, but the claim was confusing. «Why doesn't she pitch it so everyone can hear?»

«Something's constraining her.»

Constraining? "Elena?" Seth called again.

"Go away!" she shouted. "I'm trying to study!"

«Just open the door,» Theo urged him.

«She'll have locked it.»

«There's a key in our parents' room.»

«For emergencies.»

«This is an emergency.»

Seth said, "I need to talk to Irina! It's important!"

"She's asleep."

"I thought you said she was busy."

"She's busy sleeping, I'm busy studying. You might want to listen to Theo yammering away all day, but normal people work out a better way."

"I know she's not sleeping," Seth replied. "Theo can hear her."

Elena fell silent. Seth could hear movement in the room. He waited for his sister to come to the door.

«Get the key! *Now!*» Theo's tone had turned frantic.

«Why?»

«She's hurting her!»

Seth ran to his parents' room. «Where is it?»

«By the window.»

Seth grabbed the key and sprinted back to Elena's door. He pushed the slotted card into the lock, then tugged on the handle until the door unlatched and the counterweights flipped it up against the ceiling.

Elena had a band of cloth fitted tightly around her head from chin to cranium, covering every visible part of her Sider. But she'd slid the longest left finger of her right hand under the binding, deep into the place where —

Theo screamed at her, "*Stop!*"

The word left Seth's skull ringing. Beyond all the rage and anguish it carried, the sheer force of it made him feel like he'd been punched.

Elena pulled her hand away and sank to her knees. Seth steadied himself and approached her. He took hold of the cloth and started easing it forward; there was blood on the material, spots and streaks in yellow and red. When the whole thing was free he dropped it on the floor and gazed down at Irina.

The membrane of her right pinger was torn, and there was a dark unnatural space between her damaged flesh and the tunnel through Elena's skull. Two rivulets were seeping from the cavity, entwined but immiscible.

Theo said, «They need a doctor.»

Seth stood in silence, swaying.

«Seth? They need help.»

«I know.» He put a hand on Elena's shoulder. "Do you think you can walk to the clinic with me?"

Elena started sobbing. "I didn't have a choice! She didn't give me any choice!"

"We can fix this," Seth promised. "But you need to come with me." He couldn't leave her alone while he fetched the doctor; he had no idea now what she might do. Their neighbors wouldn't be home yet, and there was no one else nearby on whom he could call for help.

He took her hands and pulled her to her feet, then tipped his head and started backing out of the room. Elena resisted for a moment, but then she let him lead her into the corridor and down the stairs. On the porch, Seth scrawled a note on the message board, then they set out into the twilit streets.

Lamps showed in a few scattered windows, but as Seth headed west the paving stones beneath his feet were all but lost in the gloom. Elena kept her face to the east and followed him by touch alone. When they finally reached the corner and began sidling south, it was like stepping halfway into daylight again, with Theo's crisp vision revealing every crack and bump on the path well enough for Seth to plan his movements. But this was the side of Irina's injury; to Elena, they were walking into darkness. Seth did his best to steer her past the hazards, and offer a cue when she needed to take a larger step than usual, but he couldn't bring himself to offer verbal advice. Avoiding the humiliation of advertising her condition to passing strangers was only part of it. So long as no one spoke, everything he'd seen in her room felt contained by the silence.

When they entered the clinic the lamplight was dazzling. Seth counted at least twenty patients waiting on the benches, huddled miserably, alone or with companions who glowered at him as if he'd come to usurp them from their places in the queue. He got Elena seated, then took a numbered card from the dispenser by the door.

The doctor's assistant approached and bent down to examine Elena and Irina. "This is urgent," he said sternly. "Come with me."

The assistant took Elena by the arm. Seth started to follow them, but when he reached out for his sister's hand she pulled free. "Just wait for me," she said.

Seth sat on the bench. Theo hadn't spoken to him since they'd left the house, and he didn't know what to say himself. The silence made him feel hollow; Theo was still sharing his view, but everything Seth saw, by light or by echo, seemed dead and empty.

When their parents arrived, Elena and Irina were still with the doctor.

"What happened?" Seth's father asked.

"They were bleeding," was all Seth could say. "Both of them." He wondered if Theo was talking with his own father at a higher pitch, beyond any Walker's hearing.

Irina's mother spoke quietly with the doctor's assistant, then the assistant led the four parents in the direction of the consulting rooms. Seth leaned back on the bench and closed his eyes, then shut out Theo's view.

In the darkness of his skull, Theo finally spoke.

«Elena's pregnant.»

Seth had no wish to follow this partial revelation to its logical conclusion, but Theo always chose his words with care. «Just Elena?»

«Irina refused. Elena went alone.»

The claim was surreal; if not for the night's horrors, Seth would have laughed and called Theo's bluff. No playground know-it-all, let alone biology teacher, had ever raised such a possibility.

«So what will happen with the baby? She'll have a side-blind child?»

«They'll try to adopt an unpaired Sider,» Theo guessed. «I don't know how easy that is, but it happens.»

Seth felt as if he was sinking into the darkness. He didn't want to open his eyes and face the crowd of strangers, who had by now all surely guessed his family's bizarre affliction.

But the strange, curdled shame he felt had nothing to do with Elena and Irina. What disturbed him the most was the sense of his own naïveté. How could it never have occurred to him that a Walker and a Sider could disagree on their choice of partners? That the idea hadn't been put to him long ago by some giggling schoolmate or sober adult was no excuse: what kind of idiot could fail to imagine the dilemma, unprompted?

Theo's father was always prattling on about *give and take*, always talking down the notion that both Walker and Sider could ever get their own way and be entirely happy. And though his son had proved him wrong about that once, it wasn't the last choice the pair would face. There was a lifetime more to come.

Theo said, «They're back.»

Seth opened his eyes. Their parents were walking slowly between the benches, holding Elena's hands. There was a bandage on her head, covering the wound but not entirely blinding Irina's right side. Seth stood and waited for them, then led the way to the exit.

No one spoke aloud in Seth's range of hearing on the way home, but Theo said, «They're going to be all right. The doctor told them there's no permanent damage.»

«Good.» They reached the corner and headed east. Seth looked up into the warm yellow light from the windows of the houses. No permanent damage.

4

SETH HAD BARELY FINISHED breakfast when Samira strode to the center of the encampment so Maria could announce the first task of the day. "Each group is to make their own estimate of longitude. There'll be points for tighter error bounds—but be sure you can justify them, or your grade will be zero."

"I'd say our longitude is ninety degrees east," Sarah whispered, reaching across the dining blanket and grabbing the last of the bechelnuts. "Plus or minus ninety."

The three Walkers in Seth's group rose to their feet, then he and Amir picked up the blanket and shook it clean. Sarah fetched pegs and string from their toolbox, then they sidled away from the tents. They'd camped in the middle of a grassy plain, which offered a clear view of the horizon but was not the ideal site from which to obtain a geological bearing.

"Find some exposed rock," Judith suggested.

"There's none around here," Aziz replied. "We passed an outcrop earlier, but it would take half a day to get back to it."

Sarah said, "Then we'll make the best of what we've got." She and Amir each took one end of the string and pulled it taut in a roughly east-west direction. Seth moved closer, then the three of them crouched down so he and Theo could judge the string's alignment with the ground. The blades of grass would be arranged to catch the most sunlight, revealing very little about the land itself.

The hidden roots would be intimately connected to the soil, but though the stems were visible, they gently twisted from root to leaf, making it difficult to use them as a guide.

Between the grass, though, it was possible to discern a series of faint, broken striae crossing some of the patches of exposed ground. However loose the individual grains of sand were, however free to be rattled by the wind and the rain, they couldn't turn far from their neighbors' average direction without bumping into each other. If they could all have conspired to move at once, they might have ended up offering a skewed bearing; after all, that was what the grass had done, with the sun coordinating the conspiracy. But lifeless soil subject to random disturbances was blocked at every turn. Short of digging down to bedrock—and hoping that it was either nicely marked, or easy to cleave—exploiting these imperfect signs of order was the best chance they'd have of determining geological east.

Sarah pegged her end of the string, then Seth gestured to Amir, sending him sidling back and forth until the alignment was as good as they could hope for.

Amir pegged the bearing, then went and fetched the theodolite. He set it up with two legs of the tripod touching the string to orient the platform, spent a few minutes leveling it, then took a sighting of the rising sun through the alidade.

"Seven and a half degrees north," he announced. The angle was small enough that there was no point using a conversion curve: it implied that they were that much less than a right angle, or eighty-two and a half degrees, east of the western node.

"So in ten days, we've come two degrees *east*?" Theo sounded shocked. "I thought we were heading due south!"

"See what happens when there are no street signs?" Sarah replied, mock-aghast at such wild meandering.

Seth could understand Theo's response, but he felt more exhilarated than anxious himself. This land was too close to Baharabad to have remained unmapped, but they'd come to it empty-handed in order to practice the surveyor's art: to get a little lost, and then to find their bearings.

Aziz said softly, "Look to the north."

Seth had been caught up in his own view; he switched his attention to Theo's.

To his left, in the distance, the grass was trembling: the blades displaced by some unseen force, then rebounding, only to be unsettled again. Seth could feel no movement in the air where he stood, and the disturbances looked less like the rippling of a breeze than the work of a thousand separate tiny whirlwinds.

"Axis lizards," Judith proclaimed.

"Are you sure?" Amir asked.

Theo said, "We can hear them. They're pinging like crazy."

The seething in the grass was moving closer. Seth glanced at the other members of the group, trying to decide if he'd seem timid or merely prudent if he suggested evasive action. He had always thought of axis lizards as harmless, but in the city he'd only encountered occasional lost stragglers, and he had no idea how a whole swarm would behave.

«Doesn't it confuse you?» he asked Theo. Whatever kind of din Theo was hearing from the lizards, the view he was sharing seemed unaffected.

«Not really. It's like being in a crowd of people who are speaking a language you don't understand. It's distracting, but it doesn't make your own conversation with the landscape disappear.»

Seth braced himself: the swarm was almost upon them. As the first wrinkled forms showed between the tufts of grass on his left, then began crossing into his own view to the east, he realized with relief that the animals were opting for prudence and would split up and flow around these oddly shaped strangers.

He watched them stream by a few paces in front of him: long green bodies between front and rear pingers, scurrying south on six clawed feet. With their legs more or less horizontal, they could lift their feet and reposition them without any of the hip-swiveling nonsense that a Walker had to perform when sidling. And with their mouths on their bellies, they could snatch up hapless insects even as they bolted across the plain.

"There goes your grandma, Judith," Amir joked.

"Fuck off."

Theo said, "Thousandth cousin, maybe."

"Why would they ever want to crawl into our heads?" Seth wondered. The swarm was navigating perfectly well without the benefits of his own form of vision.

"Free meals," Sarah replied.

"Anyone want to rejoin them?" Amir asked.

"Just give me a wheeled cart and that's the last you'll see of me," Aziz replied whimsically.

"You'd never keep up with them," Sarah replied.

"This cart has magic wheels that let it roll straight north and south," Aziz joked.

The last of the lizards darted away to the south, with the swarm veering west to avoid the tents. Seth was mindful of Theo's silence. Free meals or not . . . did he envy his cousins?

Amir said, "Seven and a half degrees, but now someone needs to help me get the error bounds right or it will all have been a waste of time."

LATER IN THE MORNING, each of the four groups set up a shadow tracker and began plotting the curve cast by the tip of the gnomon across the platform. Seth, Amir, and Sarah took turns marking points, dotting the paper with dark indentations.

Seth sidled a few steps away from the tracker and glanced at the paper through Theo's view.

«The pits are deep enough,» Theo informed him. «But would it really matter if they weren't?»

«Probably not.» Seth wasn't expecting his eyes to droop shut halfway through the exercise, as they might well have done if he'd been sentenced to a life of helping Theo read badly printed law books. But it still seemed like a minimal courtesy to make all their records bimodally legible. He glanced across the camp toward Samira. «Do you think she likes being a teacher? She hardly ever speaks to us.»

«She never dozes off,» Theo noted. «And she's never slow to write on the board in lectures—it never looks as if Maria needs to prompt her.»

«That's true.» Seth supposed the pair had found an agreeable way to divide up their tasks, and if Samira chose not to complicate the lectures with her own interjections, that didn't mean she was unhappy, or disengaged.

They plotted the shadow across noon and beyond, then Sarah and Judith performed the analysis and handed it on to the others to check. Seth could find no flaws in the result, and Theo confirmed it: the expedition had reached fifteen degrees north of the midwinter circle. Compared to Baharabad's average solar latitude of twenty-three, this was beginning to sound positively adventurous. Seth doubted that he'd feel like a true surveyor until he'd seen the shadow of the gnomon vanish at noon, but the distance they'd covered no longer seemed trivial.

With latitude and longitude in hand, the students spent the afternoon revising their maps, making use of the new information to adjust their earlier estimates of the locations of various features they'd encountered along the way. Theo had been shocked that they'd skewed so far east, but as the group worked through their logs of theodolite measurements it was easy to see how small uncertainties had mounted up across the dozens of sightings, loosening the rigid struts of the imaginary grid they'd drawn across the landscape.

Sarah stippled the Annoying Hills into place in their new position, brushing paper dust and pigment onto the ground as she worked. "I don't know why we're bothering," she joked. "Before long this will all be in summer, and no one will care where these hills were or what they looked like."

"Before that, I think the road-builders would quite like to avoid them," Aziz replied.

Judith said, "The city won't come this way at all. It'll just follow the river."

"The Zirona won't last forever," Seth replied, though he was more assured of the truth of this claim by the fact that he'd heard it stated in lessons than by any gut feeling about the nature of the thing. The Zirona River flowed the full width of the habitable zone from north to south, supporting five cities along the way—giving it a far more impressive air of permanence than if it had split up into a hundred insignificant streams that trickled away into mud flats on the midwinter plains. But apart from the possibility of changes in topography reshaping its course, the summer rainstorms that fed it could always grow less intense, or drift to the east or west, as the new terrain entering the northern steamlands altered the weather patterns there.

"It will be tough if we lose it," Amir observed solemnly. "How long since we got by on nothing but local rain?"

"A while," Sarah said. "But that's the point of surveying so far from the river, instead of just seeing what's ahead downstream."

Before the evening meal, Maria ordered an inventory of their supplies. They had enough food for another fourteen days, but Seth knew they wouldn't push their luck; they would probably head back in the morning, or at most after one more day.

«I'm going to miss this,» he told Theo, as he sat down to eat.

«It's not over yet.»

«No.» But the prospect of being back in the city already felt oppressive.

«Once we're qualified, we can go on every survey you like.»

«You won't mind?»

Theo was amused. «I'm the one who suggested this job.»

«And ten days in the sticks hasn't dampened your enthusiasm?»

«Sleeping rough has no effect on me,» Theo pointed out. «You could lie on a bed of stones and I wouldn't know the difference.»

The sky grew dark, and the world of light shrank to two flickering triangles, stretching out from the campfire to illuminate the huddled diners. To the north and south Theo's vision reached farther, but it too was soon defeated by the vastness of the plain. The campsite was like a pinprick of awareness, poised between fading memories and the unknown future—and if daybreak and the journey home would reclaim some of what the darkness now shrouded, that reprieve itself was only temporary. Seth thought of the old maps in the museum, recording the courses of rivers long ago baked dry and roads that no one would walk upon again.

But if the north was forever lost, the darkness to the south was always hopeful, charged with new possibilities. He'd made the right choice, he and Theo. Nothing could be more vital than to plot the way into the unfolding new world.

5

"ISN'T SHE BEAUTIFUL?" ELENA demanded, daring her brother to contradict her.

"Of course," Seth replied. He reached down and placed a fingertip in the infant's hand; she clutched at it, clumsily but with surprising strength.

"I'm going to call her Patricia."

"Patricia," Seth repeated. His niece squinted up at him from her crib then pushed his finger away. "It's good that she's west-facing," he decided. It wouldn't make much difference while she lay flat on her back, but once she was walking it would be nice for Elena to be able to make eye contact without having to tip her head.

Theo inspoke, «Ask her when she's going to fill the hole in her daughter's skull.»

«Ask her yourself.»

Irina said, "You know the father's moving in tomorrow?"

"Really?" Seth was surprised; the last he'd heard, the boy's family had been refusing to acknowledge his paternity.

"Of course," Elena replied serenely, as if this had never been in doubt. "Daniel can't wait to join us."

Theo said, "I didn't see him here for the birth."

"Don't be so stupid," Elena retorted. "Men have no business getting involved with that."

Seth wasn't sure that this rule extended to the child's father, but he'd been happy to take a long walk while his mother and aunts had overseen the event. He believed his father had remained downstairs, muttering imprecations.

"What does Daniel do?" he asked.

"He's a road-builder."

"And what about his Sider?"

"I really don't care," Elena declared.

"Sam's studying architecture," Irina interjected.

"Oh, good." Seth could imagine this mix of vocations working out, especially if Daniel was willing to switch from roads to more elaborate structures once his Sider was qualified. "I'd better let you rest," he said. Elena was watching her daughter, but Seth leaned forward so Theo could show him his sister's face. "I'm glad it all went well," he added.

Downstairs, all the parents and aunts were whispering angrily at each other, so Seth walked out of the house again so they wouldn't be forced to make insincere small talk for his benefit.

The optimism he'd felt in the presence of the newborn child was beginning to fade. «What happens if Sam wants a child now?» he asked Theo. «Or Irina?» Whether they did this independently, or changed their minds and had one together, the age difference would already rule out a place for it in Patricia's skull. And even if they found another unpaired Walker of the right age to act as host, how would the paired infants share their time between the Walker's parents and the Sider's? There could be three or four different households involved.

But Theo seemed to find the whole question ludicrous. «Do you really think Elena would allow that?»

«Why would it be her choice? She had a child alone; she can hardly tell Irina not to do the same.»

«And of course hypocrisy is physically impossible,» Theo replied sarcastically.

Seth let it drop. He wasn't interested in taking sides, but there seemed to be no end to the recriminations.

He strode east across the city, over the southern bridge then on into a residential district that he had no memory of visiting before. The houses all looked disconcertingly pristine—as if they'd never been moved, let alone bumped or scratched—but perhaps they'd just been re-clad. There was a hot breeze blowing and the sun was in his eyes, but he longed to keep walking and never go back.

«You want to run away to Shakton?» he asked Theo.

«And waste all our study?»

«They must need surveyors there too.»

«Yes, but if we just wander in, half-trained, they're not going to pay for the rest of our education. Where would we live? How would we support ourselves?»

Seth had no answers.

«I'm worried about Irina,» Theo confided.

«Our parents won't let anything happen to her.» Seth didn't want to believe that Elena would attack her again, even if the pair were far from reconciled.

«And how will they protect her when Elena and Daniel have their own house?»

«Why would they want their own house?» Seth replied. «Once we move out there'll be plenty of room for the children.» Of course Elena would have another child with Daniel, whatever Sam and Irina did. Seth could feel a part of himself wanting to spring to her defense: why shouldn't it be her and Daniel's choice, and no one else's? But then that principled stance began to sag under the weight of the endless complications.

Theo said, «Can you look up?»

Seth shielded his eyes and peered down the street. A crowd was gathered outside one of the houses, arguing heatedly. A man and a woman were banging on the door, demanding to be admitted.

Seth considered backing away, but his curiosity got the better of him. As he approached the edge of the crowd he made eye contact with a west-facing woman, who must have been resting her neck or leaving it to her Sider to observe proceedings.

"What's happening?" he asked.

"Those two want to see their father." It was the Walker woman who replied, so Seth supposed she meant the Walkers at the door specifically. "Jonathan, the widower. They're worried about him."

Seth didn't understand why they didn't have keys to the family home—or, if they were really concerned, why they hadn't broken in. But then he heard a Sider's voice from within the house: "Clear these people away, then you'll be welcome to visit."

This response only seemed to infuriate the children. "These are our friends, they're here to help us!" Jonathan's daughter shouted.

"We're not letting a mob into the house," the Sider replied.

"Who's this 'we'?" the son yelled back contemptuously. "You don't speak for my father!"

"So his father's too sick to talk?" Seth guessed. It didn't sound like he was bed-ridden, though; it sounded like he was standing right behind the door. "But what's with all these hangers on?"

The woman's Sider said, "They're interfering fools."

The woman clarified this remark, without really contradicting it. "They think he's turned Sleepwalker. They think Matthew's in charge now."

Seth hadn't heard the word since childhood. Were there really adults who believed in Sleepwalkers?

A new tumult rose up from the crowd. A man was attacking the window of the front room, trying to force the bars out of the frame with some kind of improvised jimmy. As he wiggled it clumsily back and forth, it protruded out over the heads of the onlookers, almost reaching as far as the street. Half the crowd was cheering him on—but Seth could hear the man's own Sider loudly berating him, presumably hoping that this humiliation would cut through where mere inspeech had failed.

The door to the house swung up, forcing the half-dozen people on the porch to back away. An elderly man stepped out into view. "Leave the window alone!" his Sider shouted. Matthew and Jonathan, the woman had called them. The man with the jimmy withdrew, and the crowd fell silent.

"Father?" Jonathan's daughter approached him and put a hand on his shoulder; he returned the gesture, but remained mute.

"His throat's very weak," Matthew explained. "We've already been to the clinic—"

"You're a liar!" the son declared.

"Get a pen and paper!" a woman shouted. "That's the test!" There was some discussion in the crowd, then a boy ran off down the street.

Seth tried to read the widower's face. His eyelids drooped, and his demeanor was impassive. There was no doubt that he was sick, but that hardly proved that he'd been robbed of all volition. "They should just take him to the clinic again," he suggested.

He'd addressed his words to the woman he'd been gossiping with, but an east-facing man beside her tipped his head back and interjected angrily, "Mind your own business!"

"And why is it yours?" Seth challenged him. "Are you a relative?"

"I'm his neighbor. Who the fuck are you?"

"If you're such a good neighbor, why don't you take his problems seriously, instead of stirring up trouble?"

The man backed closer to Seth, bringing his inverted face right up to him. "There's only one way to help a Sleepwalker, and they don't offer that service in the clinics."

The boy returned with writing implements. Jonathan's daughter took her father's hand and held it between her own two, allowing her to trace a shape on his palm with a fingertip—out of sight of everyone, her father included. In the children's stories this always ended badly: a Sleepwalker's Sider controlled their host's limbs, but didn't share their sense of touch, so the Walker's failure to reproduce the shape betrayed their true state.

Son and daughter held the paper and ink pot steady as Jonathan took the pen. Seth watched the old man's shaking hands with a sense of foreboding. He didn't have to be a Sleepwalker to be flustered by the crowd, or confused by the whole absurd ritual.

When he'd finished drawing, his children held the paper up for the crowd to inspect. The son seemed disappointed, but the daughter was clearly relieved by the roughly sketched pair of hyperbolas.

"This is what I gave him through his skin," she declared. "This is proof that my father still controls his body."

A few bystanders offered desultory cheers, but the rest just muttered darkly. Seth had expected all the Siders to express their anger and disgust now, shaming the instigators of the farce, but he heard nothing from them as the crowd dispersed.

He wanted to say something to Theo—to offer some kind of vow about his fate when they grew old—but what could he promise that was actually within his power? And no Sider wanted to be forced to think about that time. If Theo died first, he'd merely be left side-blind—but if he died first, Theo would be reduced to a pitiful half-life, beholden to charity, slurping donated blood from a bowl.

«You don't want to change your mind about Shakton?» Seth asked.

«Shakton's to the east,» Theo replied.

«Yes. What difference does that make?»

Theo said, «Everyone knows you can only walk away from your problems by traveling south.»

6

ETH WOKE EARLY AND made his way through the dark streets, swinging the empty buckets back and forth to enliven the journey. Other people must have been afoot on the same errand, but around him the city was silent. The pump was almost due east of the house, so he'd let Theo sleep; there was no reason for both of them to be tired all day. On the rare occasions when he'd been side-blind in daylight it had felt like a terrible affliction, but now it seemed almost natural. He had no trouble moving through the blackness: each time his foot touched the ground he could sense the precise direction of his step from the proportions formed between his sole and the cobblestones.

The pump-house lamp appeared in the distance, proving that he hadn't gone astray. As Seth joined the queue, Theo woke, summoning whole buildings out of the darkness. «I thought I was dreaming,» he said groggily. «Isn't it Daniel's turn today?»

«I swapped with him, so we'll be rested tomorrow.»

«Good idea.»

Seth said, «Go back to sleep if you want to. I'll just be shuffling down the line for a while yet.»

«No, that's a terrible habit.» Theo's inspeech was sharper already. «But if they organized the roster better, people wouldn't need to queue for so long.»

«Take it up with the Office of Hydrology.»

«You mean the Office of Complacency, Panic, and Guesswork?»

«Don't be cruel. Not everything can be as simple as geodesy.»

Through Theo's view, Seth could see the empty water channels running along the side of the street. He'd been a small child the last time the river had fallen so low; his parents must have carried water to the house, but he had no memory of it.

Theo said, «We have records going back to the day Baharabad joined the Zirona, and maps of the topography of the steamlands for most of the same period. You'd think that by now someone would have sat down in the museum and worked it all out.»

«If it's an afternoon's work for a genius like you, you should have mentioned that sooner and I'd have set aside the time.»

«Ha. I never said it was trivial, but we should be able to do better.»

Early in their training the surveyors had joined the hydrologists for a few classes, but even the basics had left Seth's mind spinning. He could understand the formula for the north-south temperature gradient due to insolation; that was simple geometry. But then there was an altitudinal temperature gradient, followed by corrections for atmospheric moisture content—which wasn't fixed by latitude or height, but changed dynamically in response to everything else. Parcels of air rose and fell, warmed and cooled, grew denser or more rarefied. By the time you threw in a mountain range or two, the idea that it might be possible to calculate the strength and location of the rainstorms from details of the terrain where they formed seemed wildly optimistic.

When they reached the front of the queue, Seth worked the pump as quickly as he could to keep the people behind him from complaining. The sun was coming up, and as he peered over the railing at the darkly shimmering surface of the river, the water looked even lower than it had been four days before.

He sidled away from the pump, then tipped his head and started back down the street.

«One more day,» he said numbly. «Is it really that close?»

«Assuming we're not dreaming,» Theo replied.

«You'd better not be planning to sleep through the exams.»

«Likewise,» Theo replied irritably.

Seth laughed. The buckets felt heavy already; he'd grown used to walking for days with a pack of tools and provisions on his back, but having these sloshing weights dangling from his arms made every step arduous.

Theo said, «It's a joint certification. You're not there solely as my scribe, and I'm not there merely as your Sider.»

«I know.» But it still wounded Seth's pride a little to acknowledge that while Theo could have passed the exams with any idiot writing down his answers, he would have been struggling to do the same, unaided.

«I'm just glad we can sleep until dawn tomorrow,» Theo declared. «That alone should be enough to tip the balance.»

AS SETH WANDERED THROUGH the crowded hall, he saw the same expression of dazed relief on face after face. Caught in the yellow lamplight or etched by Theo's pings, everyone looked amazed by their good fortune. But even some of the students who he knew had failed to graduate appeared strangely satisfied. Perhaps they were glad to have been spared from a career that they'd never really wanted in the first place.

He found Sarah and Judith beside one of the buffet tables, chatting with a group of people. He recognized a few of them: they'd been in a class ahead of his own, a while back, so presumably they were working surveyors now.

Judith made the introductions, and everyone offered their congratulations to him and to Theo.

"Where have you been out to lately?" Seth asked, directing his words at no one in particular so that whoever had the most interesting answer would feel free to respond.

"The northern steamlands," Raina replied.

"The steamlands? You mean you came close?"

"I mean we went in."

Seth had never heard of an expedition entering the steamlands—not since ancient times, when people had been naïve enough to imagine that summer might be finite and traversable, and hoped to return with news of milder climes on the other side. But once the temperature at noon reached the point where water could simply vanish into the air, by any sane definition you'd left the habitable zone behind.

"What's it like?" he asked.

Raina hesitated. "Hot and wet."

He glanced at the rest of the group; they had the body language of people who'd been through an ordeal together, and were not prepared to suffer foolish questions on the subject.

"Any news about the drought?" he asked, hoping that this was less inane than his last attempt.

"The storms are as strong as ever," Haidar said. "But they're moving west."

Seth's mind blanked for a moment, refusing to rise from its post-exam torpor and summon up an image of the catchment area that would allow him to interpret this reply. But when Theo declined to fill in the silence, he forced himself to concentrate.

"That doesn't sound good," he decided.

"If it keeps up, we'll lose all our flow," Haidar confirmed. "It will end up in the Orico."

While Seth was still pondering this, Theo said, "The Orico's crowded—but if it takes the Zirona's flow, why shouldn't it take the Zirona's population?"

Haidar made a noncommittal sound, but his Sider, Osman, said, "Inter-city politics isn't always so accommodating."

"And it wouldn't be unreasonable for the Orico's cities to object," Raina's Sider, Amina, argued. "Even if the flow rises, that's no guarantee that it will remain high enough to support so many people. If they let us squeeze in now, and then they find themselves with a drought of their own, that will only make things harder for everyone."

"So where should Baharabad go?" Theo demanded. "Or should we just scatter across the plains and live on wild berries?"

"It's not up to us to decide," Haidar replied. "That's in the hands of the planners and the diplomats."

AS SETH STOOD WAITING in the briefing room, along with all the other newly qualified surveyors, he found his gaze returning again and again to a beautifully rendered map that all but covered the eastern wall. It showed the portion of the habitable zone that lay within thirty degrees of the central meridian, and the cartographers had packed in everything from altitude to soil type. The longer he spent contemplating the full gamut of information it conveyed, the more absurd it seemed to hope that all five of the major habitations arrayed along the Zirona could simply move west and join the eleven that had followed the Orico for generations. The solution was as impractical on any geographical assessment as it was on political grounds. It wasn't just a question of the volume of water moving down the river: finding enough suitable land that could be irrigated and farmed to feed all the new arrivals, even for a single crop, would be miraculous, let alone ensuring that this state of affairs persisted as the sixteen cities migrated south.

Jonas, the Director of the Office of Surveyors, walked to the lectern and addressed the gathering. "Three days ago, I had the great pleasure of welcoming you into our profession. On this occasion, I have a less celebratory message to convey. Everything we've learned from our most recent investigation suggests that the drought is unlikely to break in the foreseeable future."

The rumors had already spread across the city, but Seth could see a change in the room as people absorbed this confirmation. And while some of his colleagues appeared despondent at the news, most seemed to grow more resolute.

"In principle," Jonas continued, "we could try to wait out the dry spell, following the riverbed south and making do with residual ground water, in the hope that the Zirona will eventually be restored to its former glory. But we've already received intimations that certain of our neighbors to the south are contemplating a different strategy: holding their ground for as long as they can."

Seth felt a surge of anger. Why couldn't the other Zironans cooperate and make life easier for them all? But one glance at the map punctured his self-righteousness: even if the gamble paid off for Baharabad, it couldn't work for everyone. Sedington's usual latitude was so close to the southern summer that they'd kept the river dammed to stop the flow from going to waste. The only ground

water the Zirona had deposited lay north of that dam. And if Sedington decided to stay put, dam and all, there would be no point in
anyone bypassing it.

"What we need now," Jonas proclaimed, "is to identify the locations of potential new sites. We have reason to believe that there
might be new, north-flowing rivers emerging from the southern
steamlands. But the rivalries brought on by the drought limit the
prospect of obtaining reliable second-hand reports. Our duty is to
secure the best new path possible for Baharabad. To achieve that,
we'll need to survey the largest possible area to our south—and do so
faster, and more thoroughly, than every other city that would benefit
from the same intelligence."

Theo inspoke, «And who have the advantage of being closer.»

The Director began detailing the expeditions that would set out
in the coming days, most of them traveling as far as the border of
the southern steamlands. Seth gazed at the annotations on the map,
invigorated by the prospect of finally leaving the city for something
more than a training exercise, and impatient to learn which group
he'd be rostered with. But alongside this restlessness the gravity of
the situation filled him with as much anxiety as pride. The idea that
the city's survival could be at stake, with the outcome lying in the
hands of its surveyors, had always struck him as little more than the
profession's characteristic swagger. He had never imagined that he'd
be carrying that kind of weight himself.

«Did you hear that?» Theo demanded.

«Yes.» Seth wasn't lying, but it had taken some time for the
details to register. He and Theo would be part of the westernmost
expedition, along with Sarah and Judith, Aziz and Amir—and Raina
and Amina, veterans of the steamlands. «You think someone knew
the roster in advance?» It was no surprise that the six who'd worked
together as students were being reunited, but it was hard to believe
that meeting the expedition's leaders had been down to chance.

«Lucky we made such a good impression,» Theo observed dryly.

"Make your preparations," Jonas advised them. "Say your fare-
wells. And if your families lament your departure, just remind them
that this is the only way to keep Baharabad thriving."

SETH WATCHED PATRICIA WADDLE excitedly across the floor toward him. She wasn't yet steady on her feet, but he reached down and grabbed her before she lost her balance and fell.

"Don't coddle her!" Elena scolded him.

Seth didn't reply; it wasn't his place to offer child-rearing advice. "I'm going to miss you," he said. "My beautiful nieces."

Elena groaned with disapproval at his affectionately miscegenous plural, but Patricia smiled and Leanne babbled delightedly. She seemed to be fitting more tightly into Patricia's skull lately, having put on weight now that she was feeding properly, but she did still sometimes wriggle and expose a disconcerting gap.

«Did you understand that?» Seth asked Theo.

«It's baby talk, not some secret Sider language.»

«I just thought you might be hearing her more clearly.» Seth knew full well that when they spoke their secret language, he wouldn't hear it at all.

Irina said, "And I'll miss both my brothers."

Seth felt a pang of guilt—but Theo had expressed no desire to veto the trip and stay home to watch over her. Leanne's parents and their bereaved Walkers hadn't quite become part of the family, but their ongoing scrutiny of their daughter's circumstances surely counted as some kind of moderating influence. Irina's position was still impossible, but no one could change that, and Seth did not believe that she would come to further harm.

He placed Patricia and Leanne gently on the floor and surveyed the room. Everyone had risen early to say goodbye, and if his parents and Theo's were struggling to keep their anxieties about the long journey in check, there was something refreshing in Elena's disdain and Daniel's indifference. Sam had said so little that Seth had no real idea what he was feeling, but having been dragged into the family through no choice of his own, he was probably just lamenting the loss of Theo as an ally.

Seth's pack was light, for now: most of his supplies were still waiting for him at the depot. As he hoisted it onto his back, his mother approached and placed a hand on his shoulder.

Theo's mother said, "Look out for each other."

"Always," Theo replied.

Seth's mother added, "And don't let him do anything crazy."

Theo inspoke, «You do realize she was talking to me?»

Seth tipped his head and backed away. As he swung the door down and stepped off the porch, his sadness gave way to relief, and then elation.

PART TWO

"**W**E'VE MISSED IT," RAINA declared with grim finality. Amir bowed his head and gazed down at the shadow tracker. Aziz asked, "Are we too far north, or too far south?"

"There's no way of knowing," Raina replied.

"So we pick a direction . . .?" Aziz persisted.

Amina said, "We can't go chasing this forest. All we can do is move on."

Seth watched Amir sag even lower, and wondered if he should say something himself. They'd performed the measurements together, checking each other's work; that Amir had carried out the last few sightings hardly made their situation his fault.

"It's not a navigation error," he said tentatively. "We couldn't be out by that much."

"No," Raina confirmed. "The forest's drifted—lagged or sped up, but there's no point guessing which. We just need to be sure that we find the next one."

"All right," Amir said quietly. He began packing up the shadow tracker.

Raina headed back to the camp. Seth swept his gaze along the eastern horizon, then tipped his head and did the same to the west, but he couldn't discern so much as a promising smudge rising up from the barren ground. On the midwinter plains there had always been a few berries they could gather along the way—food so sparse that no settled community would have bothered to collect it. But it had kept the expedition from starving without requiring any special effort at all, let alone the kind of hit-or-miss detours they were relying on now.

"Why can't Siders see farther?" he grumbled. The errant forest could be less than a day's walk away to the north or south, but they'd never know it.

Theo said, "You want to see farther along the axis?"

"Yes."

"Raise yourself up to the height of a mountain—"

Seth interrupted him. "From higher ground, I'll see farther east and west. How does that help?"

"Who said anything about higher ground?" Theo retorted. "Raise yourself up *through the air* to the height of a mountain. Then look straight down."

It took Seth a moment to picture this fanciful configuration. His dark cones would still stretch out to the north and south, but instead of reaching the ground a couple of paces away, they would remain above it for a distance equal to his elevation, and all the land they no longer enclosed would be dragged into the light. Of all Theo's useless ideas, this had to be the most beautiful.

Aziz said angrily, "While you idiots are joking, Sarah's wasting away."

"I gave her half my rations!" Seth protested. Raina had had to force her to accept the extra food from her colleagues; she'd kept insisting that her sickness had nothing to do with their dwindling supplies. "She just needs another day's rest, then she'll be fine."

Amir had finished with the shadow tracker. He tipped his head back to face Seth. "We need fresh supplies, and we need them soon, or none of us will be fine."

SETH WAS WOKEN BY the sound of movement in the tent, but he kept his eyes closed and tried to fall back to sleep. Amir rarely passed the night without needing to go out and empty his bladder, but Seth had learned that if he stayed deliberately inert he could usually drift away and avoid being roused again by the return.

Then Theo woke and asked Amir, "Why are you taking your pack?"

When Seth accepted Theo's view he caught a blur of vanishing limbs as Amir contorted himself, trying to sway out of reach of Theo's pings, but his pack was still clearly visible. And he wasn't rummaging through it to look for something: he was wearing it, ready to travel.

Seth opened his eyes, though in the darkness of the tent this revealed nothing new. "What's going on?" he whispered.

"I'm not letting Sarah and Judith die," Amir replied angrily.

Seth said, "We have to trust Raina and Amina."

"Trust them to do what? They can't promise that the next forest won't have drifted just as far."

"So what's your plan? The one we just missed could be in any direction. Do you think you're going to find it in the middle of the night?"

Aziz said, "Forget about the forest. We're heading for the nearest town."

Seth rubbed his eyes, as if that could summon clarity out of the gloom. Their instructions had been unambiguous: they were not to enter any inhabited area, and if they saw other travelers, they were to keep their distance. It could hardly be a secret that Baharabad was searching for a new home, but the regions they were surveying could not yet be acknowledged, and the details of what they found could not yet be shared.

"To do what, exactly?" he asked.

"Steal some fruit from an orchard," Amir replied. He was still squeezed against the wall near the exit. Seth sat up, bringing more of the tent into Theo's view.

"That's not a bad idea," Theo conceded. "If we do it at night, we might get away with it."

«We?» Alarmed, Seth began rising to his feet, almost forgetting the point where he needed to stop to avoid driving his head into the fabric above.

Theo didn't answer him directly, but he made his reasons clear. "If you two go alone, Raina and Amina will insist that we continue without you. But if half the expedition's gone, she's not going to try to move Sarah and Judith on her own."

Seth moaned softly. "What's the punishment for mutiny?"

"If we're questioned by the townspeople, the charge will probably be treason," Theo replied helpfully. "Assuming we ever get back to Baharabad."

Amir said, "We won't get caught. And if we return to camp with enough fruit to keep us going for ten more days, do you really think Raina's going to drag us home in chains?"

Seth did not believe that Sarah and Judith were on the verge of death—but if the next forest they were relying on to feed them had drifted out of sight, none of them would have the strength to go hunting for it.

He said, "I'll leave a note for Raina, begging her not to move on. But if we come back empty-handed, we'll only have made things worse."

Amir said, "Ask her to give us two days. If we make it any less, we might not get back in time—but if we ask for more, she might decide that it's not worth waiting for us at all."

THE FOUR MUTINEERS LEFT the camp, heading north. Theo and Aziz had shut off their southward pings to avoid any risk of waking Amina or Judith, plunging three quarters of the world into darkness.

Amir set the pace, sidling briskly over the loose sand. Seth followed, close enough to see him clearly, far enough behind not to risk a collision. As a child, he'd once hit a patch of uneven ground on a playing field at the same time as a fellow team member, and despite the considerable separation of their feet, when Seth had swayed northward and the other player southward, their tilted bodies had extended so far that their skulls had met halfway.

«Don't let me stumble,» he pleaded to Theo.

«What do you think I'm going to do? Fall asleep?»

«I'm more worried about my own lapses of attention. Just warn me if you see anything dangerous—don't assume I've noticed it myself.» The ground ahead appeared soft and almost level, with a pattern of ridges and valleys that were barely toe deep—but the route that had brought them to the campsite had been strewn with hidden stones, and there was no reason to believe that this area would be any less treacherous.

As the blackness in the east softened with the first hints of dawn, it began to rain. Seth tipped his head back and let the cold droplets fall straight into his open mouth, glad to be sidling so he didn't need to stop to drink. Then the rain grew heavier and Amir yelled out that he was slowing his pace, because the downpour was starting to interfere with the Siders' vision.

The ground became muddy, and perilously slippery. They agreed to change formation and jog together, lined up east to west, with Seth's arms outstretched and his hands on Amir's shoulders.

"Castling wasn't a wasted skill, after all," Amir shouted over the rain.

"What's castling?"

"You didn't play that game?"

"No." Seth had never heard of it.

"Kids pair up like this, then crash into each other," Amir explained. "Two Walkers together have extra stability."

"I could have done with the extra stability, never mind the crashing."

Aziz said, "Be careful what you wish for. Some temporary alliances have been known to become permanent arrangements."

By mid-morning the rain had eased to a light drizzle. They un-castled but kept their east-west alignment. Muddy rivulets swirled over their feet, always flowing more or less to the east, which Seth took as a good sign. Lida, the town they were aiming for, had no permanent water from the steamlands to supply it, but it migrated along a wide, shallow depression that funneled local rain onto its fields, as well as offering accumulated groundwater. If they oriented themselves by the movement of the runoff, they'd know in which direction to keep watch for the town.

Theo said, "We should do a quick detour east, while we've got the sunshine."

"Why?" Seth couldn't see what purpose that would serve.

"Suppose Lida sped up, and it's south of us already."

"That's not impossible," Amir conceded. "It's a small town and there's no one blocking them. They could change latitude easily enough if they wanted to."

They set off to the east, keeping their eyes on the ground ahead. The rainwater was soaking away now, and if they crossed any land that Lida had occupied recently it would take a lot more than a few puddles to hide the evidence.

Seth was ravenous, but the change of gait let him rest all the muscles that had wearied most, and satisfy those that had grown impatient with their disuse. As the midday sun dried his damp clothes he felt clear-headed and invigorated.

"There's nothing," he concluded. The gentle east-west gradient had reversed, proving that they'd traversed the width of Lida's most likely path with no sign of so much as a paving stone left behind.

They crossed back to the western side; apart from a second chance to spot the town's trail, it was worth it just to switch gaits again.

The weather stayed fine, and after they'd been sidling north again for a while the ground became as dry as when they'd set out from the campsite. Seth could tell that Amir was tiring, not from any misstep, but from the way he kept his torso braced as he ran, as if he feared losing control and overbalancing. But whatever his physical travails, he'd shown no sign of giving up on the plan.

"Are you keen on Sarah?" Seth asked.

"What?" Amir was facing away from him, so there was no chance to read his expression.

"You heard me."

"What are we, children?" Amir blustered. "I can't do this for a colleague without you making a joke of it?"

"I'm not mocking you," Seth insisted. "It was a serious question."

"Then save your breath for one that's more serious."

«What do you think?» Seth asked Theo.

«Does the sun rise in the east?»

«Yes—but does it set in the west?»

«That too,» Theo replied.

Seth had forgotten precisely what these euphemisms were meant to encode. «Did you just tell me that Sarah reciprocates his feelings, or that Aziz feels the same way about Judith?»

«The latter. How should I know what Sarah and Judith feel?»

«How should you know what Aziz feels?»

«He told me.»

Seth ran on in silence. He felt a slight twinge of jealousy, but it was fleeting enough to be more amusing than shameful. He'd thought about Sarah since they were students together, and wondered if they'd ever be more than friends, but it had always seemed too soon to pursue the idea: no one left young children behind to go surveying. But if he'd been serious, he would still have sought to discover her feelings.

And Theo's. And Judith's.

No wonder he'd put the whole thing off.

Amir was beginning to lag behind. Seth watched their shadows stretching out across the sand, and tried to urge him on by staying just ahead of him. They needed to reach Lida before nightfall, or they'd risk being too late returning to the camp.

Theo's view contracted, reaching no more than half a dozen paces ahead. Seth understood: he didn't want to risk alerting the locals. But there had to be a better strategy.

He said, "We should move far enough west that we're certain we'll pass the town on that side, and not run right into it. Then we can still ping our route without worrying that it will give us away, while we keep watch to the east for Lida."

The others concurred. As Seth tipped his head and backed away, all of his misgivings about the plan that he'd been trying to ignore began clamoring for his attention again. But there was no question of going back now, with nothing to show for all the time and energy they'd gambled.

They sidled on northward. Seth wondered if they should pause to perform a longitude measurement, in case they'd become confused in the rain or misled by some unexpected change in the topography. But then Amir said, "There it is."

"Where?"

"East-north-east."

Seth squinted against the glare from a bank of low clouds that was casting back the sunset. Below the clouds, the town was so flat, and fit so snugly into its water-trapping hollow, that it barely registered as an artificial presence. From this distance, he could easily have mistaken it for a few stone outcrops and a few patches of mud.

They approached slowly, then paused and waited for their shadows to disappear.

"Where would you plant the orchards?" Amir asked anxiously. In Baharabad there were a dozen or so, dotted around the outskirts of the city, but you'd walk half a day through fields of grain before reaching them. In the twilight it was difficult to interpret the structures ahead of them, but Seth guessed that they were mostly farmhouses, and none yet showed the glow of lamps.

"All we can do is go in and look," he said.

There were no fences around the fields with gates to guide them, and at first they moved through knee-high stalks that swished like languorous sentinels. But then they chanced on a track where the well-trampled ground barely betrayed their footsteps.

Amir said, "I can smell it."

"Smell what?"

He paused and rested a hand on Seth's shoulder. "Black sapote."

Seth sniffed hopefully, but he couldn't detect anything. "Are you sure you're not—?"

Then the breeze shifted, and he almost swooned.

A lamp appeared in the window of the farmhouse ahead of them. They detoured to the north, with Theo and Aziz cautiously pinging the ground just enough to keep them from stumbling. To the east, there were lights aplenty now: the town was small, and they were gazing right into its center. But to anyone gazing back they'd be hidden in the gloom, and the only people with any chance of pinging them would have to be out wandering the fields.

Seth deferred to Amir's superior olfaction and followed him in silence. «Can you smell the orchard?» he asked Theo, before recalling that this was only marginally less crass than asking a Sider how fast they could run. «Sorry, I'm tired.»

«Forget it. The only thing I need to smell is your sweet, sweet blood.»

«Which is probably more like sweet, sweet water right now.»

«Try sweet, sweet air: when you're this hungry, I get nothing at all.»

"There it is!" Amir whispered, pointing to the silhouettes of half a dozen small trees, clustered together at the corner of the farm. Seth was dismayed; they could fill their packs from one of Baharabad's orchards and the theft would barely be noticed, but here they'd be wasting their time if they didn't strip every tree bare. The only thing that assuaged his guilt was the likelihood that a single farmer probably owned both field and orchard. No one would be relying on five or six fruit trees for their entire livelihood.

The fence around the orchard was only waist-high, but vaulting it was enough to remind Seth of how weary he was. Amir followed him, and between them they quickly plucked every ripe sapote from the lowest branches.

Then Amir braced Seth as he raised an arm above his head and tilted it northward to reach the higher fruit. It was an awkward maneuver, but it was probably safer and quicker than trying to climb the trees.

Seth's pack felt satisfyingly heavy as they jumped back over the fence. They retraced their steps in silence, and waited until the town was almost out of sight before daring to stop and sample their harvest.

"Is this enough?" Amir asked, as if he were contemplating a second raid.

Seth resisted the urge to tease him with a joke about the folly of courtship's grand gestures. "It's enough to keep the whole expedition moving for eight or nine days," he said. "And it's as much as we could carry, if we want to get back as quickly as we came."

"That's true," Amir conceded.

"Sleep for an hour. I'll stand guard."

"We should get moving."

"Half an hour," Seth insisted. "Then you can do the same for me."

Amir was silent, but then perhaps Aziz persuaded him, because he lay down and closed his eyes.

Seth stood beside him, still finishing his meal, chewing every mouthful as slowly as he could.

«Are you getting something now?» he asked Theo.

«A trickle.»

Seth gazed into the darkness, disconcerted by the pity and revulsion he felt. Theo had more than earned his share of the spoils, but he would never know what it was like to bite into a piece of fruit himself. And though he'd guided almost every step of the journey, in the end it was only the free limbs of his Walker that could have leaped the fence and plucked the sapote. Seth was sure that if some impossible circumstance had left him facing the same constraints, he'd rather be dead than live the life of a Sider.

But they were what they were, and there was nothing to be done but to make the best of it.

THE SKY WAS STILL black as they began the journey south. Seth could see no clouds, but the wind was cold and sharp. The sapote had taken the edge off his hunger, and though his body was sore all over, just knowing the route and the destination made every step feel lighter.

As dawn approached the wind grew stronger, whipping up the sand and all but blinding Theo.

"We need to wait this out!" Seth shouted to Amir.

"All right," he replied reluctantly.

They squatted with their faces to the ground and their arms protecting the Siders' pingers. «I'm never going to complain about carrying a tent again,» Seth promised. «Ah, that stings!» His clothing barely seemed to be dulling the impacts.

Theo said, «I think it's a cone storm.»

«Are you sure? I couldn't see anything from what you were sharing.»

«I couldn't see the ground, but most of the airborne sand was moving near-diagonally.»

«Wonderful.» Seth started cursing aloud. Even with his mouth barely open, this muttering felt much more satisfying than inspeech.

Theo waited for a break in the profanities. «Remember how Merion used the example of cone storms, to argue that air had to be a liquid?»

«I swear you've been to lessons that I never attended.»

«Maybe you just dozed through that one.»

«What could air be, if it wasn't a liquid?» Seth asked irritably. «Why is this idiot famous for stating the obvious?» He could feel blood trickling down his forearms.

«Barat thought air was like very fine sand: lots of loose particles that were too small to see. Merion replied, if air is like sand, wouldn't it suffer cone storms? Barat said, maybe it does, but no one's ever seen them.»

«Isn't that a fair comment?»

Theo said, «If air was a kind of free-moving dust, so light that it was perpetually scattered above the ground, then the collisions between the constituent particles would see them traveling ever faster, with the energy needed to move perpendicular to the axis supplied by the negative energy from axial motion. The wind would grow so strong that the whole atmosphere would fly away into the void."

«Really? Then why doesn't all the sand in the world fly away into the void?»

«Because the air is viscous enough to slow it down. Yet more evidence for Merion's position.»

Seth had run out of ideas for prolonging the conversation, but with nothing to distract him, his mind became entirely occupied with the prospect of each impending laceration. His muscles were beginning to hurt more than his skin, as they tried to shield him—or maybe just shrink him into a smaller target—by imposing an involuntary rigidity that was as painful as it was ineffectual against the storm.

Theo said, "I think they need help."

Through slitted lids, Seth peered into the storm. The air was still black with sand, but he could just make out Amir sprawled on the ground, face down.

He waddled forward until he was beside his friends. The back of Amir's head and hands were thick with blood, and Aziz's pingers were raked with scratches. Seth bent over and tried to cover as much of the exposed skin as he could, but while his torso gave Amir some shelter, his arms couldn't keep the storm away from Theo and Aziz at the same time.

He closed his eyes and thought for a moment, struggling not to panic. He took Amir's pack off his back and placed it on the ground to the right of his head, giving Aziz protection on that side. Then he crouched down further and managed to block most of the barrage from the left with his own body, without compromising Theo.

"This can't last much longer," he shouted, filling his mouth with grit. He braced himself and held his position, waiting for the heat of the rising sun to blow the storm away.

IT WAS MID-MORNING BEFORE Amir stirred. He lifted his head and tipped it back slowly until he spotted Seth.

"You should have gone on without me," he complained. "If we're back too late—"

"We won't be. We might not make it to the camp before nightfall, but they won't leave before dawn."

Amir struggled to his feet. He'd stopped bleeding, but the red welts criss-crossing his skin still looked excruciating.

He lifted his pack out of the sand and shook it clean, but then he seemed reluctant to open it: if the fruit was too damaged it could spoil in a day, and their whole journey would have been in vain. But the packs were made of sturdier material than their clothing, and Seth's own stash had come through the storm with nothing more than mild bruising.

"Have some breakfast," Seth urged him, "then we'll get moving." Amir reached into his pack and plucked out a virtually pristine sample.

"Let's just hope that Lida hasn't sent out a search party for their sapotes," Theo joked.

Seth didn't find the prospect sufficiently improbable to be amusing; in a small town, perhaps a family of farmers could be confident that none of their neighbors were thieves—and could call on them at a moment's notice to help hunt down the actual raiders.

Aziz said, "Let's hope they think the orchard was stripped by the storm."

When Amir had finished eating, he still looked unsteady. Walking east or west in this condition was one thing, but if he toppled while he was sidling he could easily break a leg trying to halt that hyperbolic fall.

"We should castle," Seth suggested.

"That'd slow you down," Amir replied impatiently. "You need to get back as quickly as you can. It doesn't matter if I can't keep up, so long as one of us arrives in time."

"Do you really think Raina would abandon us? And even if she wanted to, do you think Sarah and Judith would let her?"

"They might not have a choice."

Seth was growing tired of arguing; if Amir refused to understand that to leave him injured and lagging in the dust was unthinkable, he'd have to find another way to persuade him. He said, "I'm not walking into that camp alone and taking all the blame, just so you can come limping in half a day later to take all the sympathy."

And Amir seemed duly chastened. "Fair enough," he said. "Then let's finish this together."

A LIGHT FLARED AT the southern edge of Seth's vision. For a moment he thought he was hallucinating from lack of sleep, but as the image steadied his spirits soared: he'd just crossed out of the dark cone of what could only be a campfire.

"Do you see that?" he asked Amir.

"Yes."

"It looks like they're expecting us."

They sidled further south together, then separated and walked east into the camp. Sarah and Raina were sitting on the ground, on opposite sides of the fire. It was Raina who saw them first.

"You look terrible," she said.

"We brought fruit," Seth replied.

Sarah tipped her head to examine them.

"How are you feeling?" Amir asked her.

"Perfect. Whatever that sickness was, it's passed."

Amir took off his pack and sat beside her, and Seth joined them, glad he could use Raina's westward gaze as an excuse to keep the fire between them.

Amina said, "Welcome back, you idiots. Are you badly hurt?"

"Amir got the worst of a cone storm," Seth replied. "But we're both still walking, nothing's broken."

"Have some bechelnuts," Raina suggested. "You can't live on fruit alone." She pushed the sack toward them; Seth took a handful, then split it with Amir.

As they ate, Raina spoke calmly. "I'm not your enemy," she said. "And part of my job is to keep you alive. Next time you have a problem with what I'm doing, come and talk to me. If you're still convinced that my decisions are endangering you, that's when you're free to walk away."

Seth was too tired to find equally gracious words to express his contrition. "You're right," he said. "I'm sorry." Theo, Aziz and Amir followed with their own apologies.

Theo said, «And now we need to sleep like civilized people. In a tent.»

8

SETH AND THEO WERE the first of the team to make their way back to the rendezvous point. Seth checked the small stone outcrop for the triangle Raina had carved into one side as a distinguishing mark, then he took off his pack and sat on the warm rock with his head upside-down so he could keep watch for the others.

«If we bring nothing else back to Baharabad,» he said, «at least we can update their useless maps.»

«If it had been up to me,» Theo replied, «we would have gone openly to all the towns along the way, asking for directions to the nearest forest.»

«They would have steered us into the desert, just to be rid of us. Who wants a hundred thousand people coming to fight them for a new river?»

Theo said, «Most of the towns around here are so small that there'd be nothing to fight over. If we find anything like another Zirona, they could even merge with Baharabad if they wanted to; there's no reason why we couldn't make room for them.»

Seth was amused. «Ah, now you're a diplomat.»

«Isn't that the best way to keep everyone happy? It must work sometimes, or Baharabad would never have grown so large.» Theo waited for a reply, then realized why his Walker had become distracted. «Is that Sarah and Judith?»

Seth had been staring at an ambiguous speck in the distance, but he'd not yet convinced himself that it was anything more than a transient blemish in the bright line where the sky reflected off the ground's warm air.

«It could be.» He stood and raised a hand. When this elicited no response, he braced himself against the rock, held his arms high, then tilted them to the north and south. A moment later, the speck grew taller and wider as it deformed into a similar forked line against the heat haze.

«It's them.» Seth resisted a comradely urge to stride across the desert and meet them halfway. Raina had made it clear that no one was to leave the designated spot until three of the team's pairs had arrived, and he was not prepared to disobey her instructions again without a compelling reason, however innocent the transgression might seem.

As she approached, Sarah slowed to a dawdle, either out of genuine weariness, or perhaps to tease him for the way he was clinging to the rock. Seth glanced past her to the routes that Raina and Amir had taken, but there was no sign yet of anyone else.

"We're still hoping to be the last to the rendezvous," Sarah shouted. "Someone's sure to overtake us any minute now."

Theo yelled back, bemused. "The advantage being . . .?"

"Less waiting, of course."

Seth sat patiently in silence until the conversation could proceed without raised voices.

"See anything interesting?" he asked.

"There were traces of the forest," Judith replied. "We tripped on a few dead roots under the sand."

Seth was encouraged. "How old, do you think?"

Sarah said, "They weren't rock-hard, or crumbling to dust. So I'd bet Amir and Aziz are the ones sitting in the shade of a weyla tree right now."

Raina and Amina had headed south-west, Amir and Aziz west-south-west. Seth had been worried that Amir might not have fully recovered from the cone storm, so if it was his branch of their four-pronged reconnaissance that ended in success, all the better.

"You do know that Raina would have used the same strategy for the last forest if I hadn't been sick?" Sarah asked pointedly. "It wasn't her fault that we missed it."

Seth had his doubts about the first claim; he suspected that it was only their earlier failure that had inspired this new approach. But that wasn't important.

"I don't blame her at all," he said.

"So why did you do it?" Sarah persisted. "Why run off like that?"

Seth had no wish to be dishonest with her, but to say too much would be disloyal to Amir. "Once we started talking about the orchards in Lida, and picturing the fruit, we could almost smell it. It was impossible to resist."

"Idiots," Judith declared smugly. "No self-control."

«Are you sure the sun sets in the west?» Seth inspoke.

«Stranger things have happened,» Theo replied.

Sarah tipped her head and surveyed the western horizon. "Ah, here they are!"

"Where?" Seth still couldn't see anyone.

"Almost at the cone."

He walked a few paces away from her, then turned his whole body toward the south; in this flat desert, it wasn't impractical to triple his axial span. He ignored the comical distortions the maneuver induced nearby, and concentrated on the southern periphery of his view.

"You're right," he said. The new speck could only be Raina and Amina. Assuming no misadventure had befallen them, Amir and Aziz would be recuperating in the forest, waiting for the rest of the team to join them.

AS THE BLOTCH OF dark green in the distance began to resolve itself into foliage, Seth quickened his stride a little in the hope that the others would do the same. But Raina kept to her usual measured pace, and Sarah remained a step or two behind her, so he quelled his impatience and fell back. He wasn't desperately hungry, and it made sense for them to conserve their strength, but it still felt unnatural not to rush to embrace this thing they'd sought so long, and whose absence would almost certainly have been fatal.

"Why has it drifted so far south?" Theo wondered. "You'd think the trees would stick to whatever solar latitude they're accustomed to."

"It could be chasing the rain," Amina suggested. "Every plant has a preferred range of temperatures, but if the topography shifts the rain a degree or two south, the forest has no choice but to go with it."

"That sounds familiar," Judith said wryly. "Is there anything you can name that isn't dragged along by some force beyond its control?"

"The sun," Theo replied.

Raina said, "Even the sun only moves because there's some kind of asymmetry in the world, tugging on its orbit."

"That's the usual theory," Theo conceded. "But I've heard a better one."

Sarah laughed. "Of course you have."

"Hesethus believed that the sun's orbit isn't changing at all; it's the world that's moving beneath it. Turning to the north, on our side of the nodes, so it looks like the orbit's tilting southward."

Sarah was incredulous. "Are you sure it's not turning *to the east* as well? Then you could account for night and day too—all with a single theory in which the sun doesn't move at all."

Theo ignored her sarcasm. "If the sun wasn't orbiting us, it would fall to the ground. And Siméon showed that if the world was rotating once a day, we'd notice air and water swerving in the opposite direction when they flowed from north to south. But before you start protesting that this proves that it must be entirely still, if it's merely turning north at the speed of the migration the effect will be too subtle to detect."

"So you're happy for the sun to follow its orbit—but to explain the migration, you want the whole world to move instead?" Sarah made it sound as if treating the two cases differently was some kind of gratuitous conceptual profligacy.

"Show me the bump in the world that's pulling on the orbit," Theo insisted. "If that's the explanation, I want to see it, I want to measure it."

Raina said, "There's no reason why it should be visible to us. If there's a change in the density of rock deep underground, that could sway the sun, but there'd still be nothing we could see."

"But whatever it is," Theo replied, "as the sun gets closer to it, shouldn't the attraction grow stronger?"

"I expect so," Raina agreed cautiously. "But that could take hundreds of generations to discern. We don't have measurements going back that far."

"If the world is turning around the nodes," Theo persisted, "that would explain everything."

"But why is it turning at all?" Sarah demanded.

"Why shouldn't it?" Theo countered. "There's no friction in the void. Left to itself, the sun will follow the same circle over and over. Left to itself, the world will keep turning around the same axis. Just as day and night follow from the first motion, the migration follows from the second. What could be simpler?"

"Once the world was turning it would never stop," Sarah agreed. "But how does an infinite mass start moving in the first place? What could deliver the infinite force required to set the world in motion?"

"I have no idea," Theo confessed.

"Because it's impossible," Judith concluded.

Seth inspoke. «What happens to your plan to un-move the sun, if it turns out that it's already motionless?»

«It should be even easier to end the migration.»

Seth doubted that it could be easier to bring the world itself to a halt, so that only left one possibility. «You mean you want to make the false theory half true, and have the world drag the sun along with it?»

Theo said, «If a bump in the world that no one has seen can tip the orbit by accident . . . think how much better the job could be done if we all worked together to raise mountain ranges in exactly the right positions.»

THE WIND HAD ERASED Amir's tracks from the sand, making it impossible to retrace his route precisely, but apparently he could see his friends coming from the barren east more easily than they could spot him against the camouflage of the forest. Seth heard Aziz shouting to attract their attention, then caught sight of Amir striding jubilantly toward them.

When he reached the group, Amir escorted them westward with the air of a seasoned local welcoming visitors into his home. "You won't believe how beautiful it is!" he enthused. "We should give up the city and come and live here."

"And what happens to the rest of Baharabad?" Judith asked.

"That's what I meant: not just us, everyone."

"You think this forest could feed that many people?" Judith pressed him.

"It's not impossible," Amir insisted. "I'm sure it's bigger than it used to be—bigger than it's shown on the maps."

Seth was relieved that Raina's plan had succeeded, but the search for food wasn't over: this was not going to be as easy as robbing an orchard. From where he stood he could already see a bewildering variety of trees, only a few of which he recognized. Most of the branches were high, and, worse, overlapping and entangled; no one was going to be able to reach up from the ground to pluck what they needed in a single move.

Amir led them to a shallow stream he'd found; they drank from it and filled their canteens. They set up camp and rested for a while, then Raina sent Seth and Sarah north to gather what they could before nightfall, while she and Amir went south.

As they sidled through the undergrowth Seth's eyes adjusted to the dappled sunlight breaking through the foliage, while Theo's view of the clutter of trunks and branches also grew more refined, as he learned better ways to ping the surfaces and interpret the results. Sarah and Judith proved skilled at spotting fallen nuts among the leaf litter, and ripe berries on some of the knee-high shrubs, but fruit was more elusive. Many of the trees were clearly root-migrants, with a fresh young sapling a few strides south of a middle-aged specimen of the same species—or a shriveled, half-resorbed corpse tree just north of its thriving matriphagous offspring. Plants like these had no need to bother making anything edible to lure animals into spreading their seeds.

Seth raised his face to the canopy, leaving Theo's view to guide his steps, and was finally rewarded by the sight of a whole branch thick with glistening pink hyperboloids. No one recognized the fruit, but it seemed worth sampling.

"They're awfully high," Sarah noted.

"Have you seen any low-hanging fruit?"

"We could go back for rope," Judith suggested.

Seth stared up into the maze of twigs and foliage. "A rope would just get snagged—and if the branches can bear my weight on the end of a rope, they can bear it with my feet pushing down on them."

Sarah braced Seth so he could tilt far enough to grab hold of the lowest branch, sparing him the arduous task of shinning up the trunk. He raised himself until his waist was level with the branch, then bent over and rested his arms for a while before bringing his legs up and managing to sit.

«That was hard work,» he confessed to Theo. His current perch was relatively smooth, but twigs from an adjacent branch had already scratched his face and torn his sleeves.

«I think Amir fell in love a bit prematurely,» Theo noted dryly.

«You can't see Baharabad's merchants getting their breakfast this way?»

«By lunch, they'd have hired a hundred laborers to clear the ground for the first fields.»

Seth found a secure handhold and maneuvered himself up onto his feet. The trees he'd climbed as a child had all belonged to domesticated species—and been regularly pruned by orchard workers with ladders. «Forget about asking the locals for directions to the nearest forest,» he told Theo. «We should have just brought something to trade with them for food.»

As he hoisted himself up onto the next branch, he heard a squeal nearby, then a blur of leaf-colored limbs brushed past his face. The branch swayed; Seth clung on tightly. Theo's view showed a scamper sitting further down the branch, one pinger aimed their way, with two tails protruding beneath it, undulating gently. Four clawed limbs gripped the branch tightly, and two other tails were curled around it.

«Do you think we could train it to climb up and bring down the fruit?» Theo joked.

«Bribing it with what?»

«Affectionate tickles?»

Seth had only seen the things in books before, but he knew he shared a certain degree of kinship with it. Some ancient taxonomist had dissected a scamper and shown that the four-limbed, four-tailed animals had light-sensing eyes alone, but hosted their own variety of Siders.

His arms were beginning to tire. He raised himself up until his shoulders were directly above the branch he was holding, then managed to widen the distance between his hands, forcing his lower body higher and making it easier to hook his legs into place. The scamper fled, setting the branch bouncing again; it was an alarming sensation, but Seth doubted that the animal would be so reckless as to risk snapping it, even if it was better prepared to deal with the consequences than he was.

When the movement had died away he began the final ascent. He felt more confident in the mechanics now, even if there was little he could do to keep the twigs from scratching him. Standing on the third branch, the fourth, fruit-bearing one was level with his chest, but the prize itself was farther from the trunk. Seth shuffled cautiously outward, glancing down to check that Sarah was still in place to collect anything he dropped. As he did, it struck him that she was several paces due south of him—yet he was seeing her with his own eyes.

«Do you remember what you said?» he asked Theo. «About the view from on high?» Seth couldn't hide his delight: the feat was perfectly explicable, but it still felt like a kind of magic.

«Of course,» Theo replied. «Now we just need to find a way to go higher, and we can map everything from here to the steamlands.»

Seth raised his eyes and concentrated on reaching the fruit without getting impaled along the way. Each time he took a step he could feel the branch beneath him bend a little, but if he shifted his weight to the one he was holding, the one at his feet sprang back up smoothly, suggesting that it was yielding to the force rather than suffering any damage.

The pink fruit dangled from pale threads attached to the branch. Seth grabbed the nearest one with his left hand, called down to Sarah, then yanked it free and dropped it.

"Did you get that?" he shouted.

"Yes!" Sarah replied.

He plucked half a dozen more that were all within reach, then sidled out a little farther. Eight more fell; the arduous harvest was finally starting to feel worthwhile. He took another step—

There was a tearing noise from below, and Seth felt air beneath his feet. As he clung to the upper branch, a new sound arose behind him, like a powerful gust of wind ripping through a field, followed by a deafening thud. He tipped his head back to see that the branch he'd been standing on had broken free entirely, and tilted over so far that one end speared the ground. The other end protruded through the canopy and vanished from sight.

"Are you all right?" Sarah called up.

"Yes." Seth hugged the surviving branch to his chest, trembling with relief at the realization that not only was he uninjured himself, the wayward branch that might have skewered her had done its damage elsewhere. "I just need to think." The next intact branch below him was out of reach with his legs hanging straight down, but if he moved his feet wider apart he could bridge the gap, albeit at the cost of compromising his balance.

He tried it. There were no clear footholds where he needed them, but he stamped at the obstructing twigs and managed to make space. «Don't worry,» he muttered. «If I fall, it won't be head-first.»

«We're going to be fine,» Theo said calmly.

Seth moved his arms apart and bent his knees, then succeeded in squatting on the lower branch while still maintaining handholds on the upper. He freed one hand and brought it down, then thrust his legs back and lowered himself to lie on his stomach, like a rag thrown over a washing line.

When his limbs were rested, he got his feet onto the branch from which he'd begun his ascent. Then he sidled close to the trunk and used it to help him make the last move, hanging by his hands for a moment, then spreading his feet to touch the ground. Sarah ran up and steadied him as he assumed a normal posture.

He said, "I think I'll let you climb the next one."

Sarah walked over to the fallen branch that was slanting up from the ground. Though the part Seth had stood on was thicker than his arms, farther from the trunk it forked into two more slender pieces, and the tip of one of them remained unburied. She took hold of this piece and pulled it sideways, trying to snap it at the junction—which had ended up higher than the point where the branch had originally been attached to the trunk. Seth came and helped her, and together they managed to break it off, while leaving the severed end resting on the main branch.

"Let's see what we can poke loose with this," Sarah suggested. There was still some fruit remaining where Seth's efforts had been curtailed, and they tried manipulating the severed branch so that its far end reached that unplucked bounty. But the geometry wasn't in their favor: wherever they moved, the prod ended up too close to the trunk.

Judith said impatiently, "You don't want it to be axial!"

Sarah found a sturdy east-west side branch and broke it off, then cleaned away the twigs. Held vertically it was only a little taller than she was, but with Seth's help she got it resting on the slanted branch at a point well above their heads, then they carried the lower end north so the far end rose up higher still. Fighting the torque, they maneuvered it into position and started jabbing at the threads that held the fruit in place. It was finicky, exhausting work, but in the end they brought down every target.

Seth was famished, and once he'd taken a bite of the exotic pink fruit and failed to drop dead, Sarah joined him. The flavor was unusually woody, but not unpleasant—a bit like a stone-fruit with traces of bark and sap.

As they sat under the tree recuperating, Seth began to feel nauseous. But his stomach was not rejecting the meal: the source of his discomfort was an overpowering odor, a suffocating, excremental stench that had risen up out of nowhere.

"You do smell that, don't you?" he asked Sarah. He was about to speculate about the presence of a large, decaying animal cadaver somewhere upwind, but there was no wind to speak of.

"It's disgusting," she replied, peering into the undergrowth with an appalled curiosity, as if the source might abruptly reveal itself. But if she was as baffled as he was about the odor's origin, the remedy was clear. "We need to get away from here."

The light was fading, and there wasn't much prospect of locating more fruit by pinging from the ground, so they decided to head back to the campsite. The stench kept them moving briskly at first, but then it fell away with surprising speed, robbing them of the extra impetus. Once it was gone Seth found himself dawdling lethargically, his limbs aching and his stomach heavy. It took all the discipline he could muster not to beg to be allowed to stop and rest, and when he glanced at Sarah he suspected that she would not have needed much persuading.

She groaned suddenly. "That smell? It was from the fruit!"

"What?" Seth took one from his pack and sniffed it; it was as inoffensive as bark.

Sarah grimaced, impatient with his obtuseness. "*The fruit* made us hate the smell of the tree. It drove us away, so we wouldn't leave the seeds too close."

Seth pondered the idea, unsure whether he felt resentful or amused. "Everybody needs to find their way south," he conceded. And if they'd tried fleeing to the north, no doubt they would have found a malodorous gradient arranged to discourage them.

"Didn't I say that already?" Judith was definitely amused. "In the end, none of us gets to choose where we're going."

UPON THEIR RETURN THEY found the camp deserted, but Seth wasn't worried; it was hard to judge the time in the forest, but it looked as if the sun had barely set. He bathed the cuts on his arms and face in the stream, then gathered dry leaf litter and twigs for a fire.

"So where are the others?" Sarah asked, glancing out into the deepening gloom as Seth arranged the pile of fuel beneath the cone guard.

"They probably found some food source worth persisting with," he said. "If we'd reached that tree a bit later, we might still be there, trying to finish what we started."

Seth kept the fire burning brightly, recalling his own return from the raid on Lida. But by his sixth trip into the undergrowth to gather more fuel, his optimism was wavering.

"Maybe they've set up their own camp for the night," Sarah suggested. "If one of them's injured, and just needs to rest overnight."

"Maybe." Seth could imagine situations where that might make more sense than going for help.

Judith said, "If they're not back by morning we can mount a search, but until then I think it's best to wait."

"We should take turns sleeping," Sarah decided. "If there's going to be a search, we need to be rested."

"All right." Seth waited for her to lie down beside the fire, then realized that she was expecting him to go first, and he was weary enough not to argue.

When Sarah prodded him awake, Seth saw that she'd kept the fire burning, but the air was cold enough to convince him that it was sometime between midnight and dawn.

"No sign of them?" he asked, rising to his feet.

"No."

"Raina and Amina survived the steamlands; there's nothing in this forest that they can't deal with. I bet someone's just sprained a muscle."

Sarah said, "Wake me if you get tired, or when it gets light."

Seth sat by the fire, rubbing his arms. «You can sleep if you want to,» he told Theo. There was enough fuel stockpiled to last all night, and he could feed and tend to the fire without side vision.

«No, it's my job to help keep you awake.»

«All right.» Seth wasn't so proud as to insist that he could do that unaided. «I know it's just simple geometry,» he said, «but it was still amazing to see so far south when we were up in that tree.»

«I have an idea for how to take that further,» Theo confided.

«Really? If it involves taller trees, I'm not sure I'm ready.»

«Have you got a small bag, made of light cloth?» Theo asked. «Like the ration bags for bechelnuts?»

«Sure.» Seth rummaged in his pack and found exactly what Theo had described. «Does it need to be empty?»

«Yes.»

There were only four nuts left; this was a good excuse to eat them. «All right. Now what am I meant to do with it?»

«Spread the opening as wide as you can,» Theo instructed him, «then hold it upside down over the fire.»

Seth walked up to the fire. It was not so fierce that the warmth was unpleasant when he stretched his arms out directly above the flames.

«Hold the seams by your fingertips, so your hands aren't above the bag at all,» Theo said.

Seth complied.

«Now let go of the bag.»

«You want me to burn it?»

«If you're worried about that, be ready to catch it if it falls.»

«*If* it falls?»

«Humor me,» Theo begged him.

Seth let his fingers part. Caught in the updraft from the fire, the bag rose up as high as his face before tipping over and starting to tumble; he brought his hands together and trapped it before it could get out of control.

«This is your idea for getting higher than the treetops?» Seth restrained himself from mocking the failed experiment too mercilessly, biting back an uncharitable quip about the value of experiencing the real heft of things as only a Walker could. «Even if you set a whole forest on fire, I doubt the updraft would be strong enough to keep a person from falling.»

«It's not about the updraft,» Theo replied. «It's about the reason for the updraft.»

«That's too subtle for me.» Seth suspected that it was just bluster, but he wasn't going to start an argument about it.

«I need to think it through some more,» Theo admitted. «When it's clearer to me, I'll try to explain it.»

«All right.» Seth sat and gazed into the fire, hoping the shared vision would prove inspiring, or at least not send them both to sleep.

SARAH WOKE UNPROMPTED AS the canopy began to brighten with the dawn. She glanced inquiringly at Seth, read the answer in his face, then stretched wearily and rose to her feet.

"Where do we look for them?" he asked.

"We should follow the stream," she suggested.

Judith said she'd seen Raina and Amir setting out along the bank as the groups had parted, so everyone agreed that this was the best strategy.

The stream flowed from the south, and though they'd lost sight of it on their journey north—it must have petered out, veered west, or gone underground—when they pursued it in the opposite direction it proved to be a more useful landmark. Seth had been expecting to arrive at a point where the water emerged from the ground as a spring, leaving them with nowhere to go, but instead they kept encountering distributaries that had forked off into the forest, and upstream from each junction the flow only grew stronger and the water deeper.

Beside the stream the undergrowth became taller and more lush. Pale vines appeared, draping the trees, dotted with gray-and-orange puffballs. Seth didn't doubt that they'd be as poisonous as their northern cousins, which sometimes appeared on the walls of derelict buildings—but every child was taught to avoid them, and it was inconceivable that Raina or Amir would have been foolish enough to mistake them for food.

Whatever animals the forest sheltered were proving shy so far; Seth caught fleeting glimpses of lizards fleeing from his feet, and heard movement in the treetops that might have been scampers, but it was clear that most of the fauna remained hidden. He wondered if some fierce predator, last seen by the ancients, might live on in this isolated jungle. He'd been taught that the laceraters had been hunted to extinction, or at the very least driven closer to the nodes than anyone ventured, but if the creatures' sole encounters with civilization now consisted of picking off unwary surveyors, who would bring back word to the cities and ensure that the textbooks were rewritten?

"Do you hear that?" Theo asked.

Seth paused and strained to discern something more than bur-bling water, rustling branches, and insect chirps, afraid of where his imagination might lead him. "Is that rain?" He raised his palms toward the canopy, but however much water was pattering against the leaves, none was reaching his skin.

"It must be falling nearby," Judith said.

As they continued upstream the noise grew louder, and Seth felt a fine spray dampening his face, though it remained so light that he couldn't tell if it was falling straight down or wafting in on the wind. But the sound did not accord with this delicate mist; it seemed wor-thy of a torrential downpour.

They followed a bend in the stream, and the rain, finally, slanted down upon them in a palpable drizzle, bouncing noisily off the foliage above. But where the weight of the water forced the leaves aside, it opened up enough chinks in the canopy to show that the sky overhead was bright and cloudless. Seth had never encountered a sun-shower before where the elements were in such stark con-trast—though perhaps the forest was distorting his perceptions, by amplifying the noise of the rain while concealing the rain-clouds themselves.

The stream led them deeper into the miniature storm, as if it were revealing its source. But it had been flowing at least since Amir reached the forest—and there'd been no trace of storm-clouds in the sky as they approached across the desert.

At the next bend, Theo's vision showed the trees suddenly thin-ning away to the south. But if the forest came to an end here, in its place was no desert or grassland: the stream was emerging from a body of water so vast that nothing could be seen beyond it.

Seth struggled to make sense of the geometry. The surface of the water was neither flat nor horizontal: it arched into the air, rising higher than the trees around it, a vortex of splintered and braided torrents crashing together, sending a false rain spraying out over the forest.

"It's some kind of waterfall!" Sarah shouted.

They approached as close as they dared without risking being drowned or deafened, and did their best to interpret the unnerving spectacle. There had to be a river flowing in from the south, running uphill and then hitting a peak here, sending water flying through the air in a mighty parabolic fountain. But the ground on the far side of the peak was apparently steep enough to drive the water back up again, traveling in the opposite direction. Where the two flows collided, the spatter was more than enough to pass for a rainstorm. But the remaining mass of circulating water couldn't spin itself into an ever-larger reservoir forever, and as this airborne lake lost energy, it leaked away into the forest, giving rise to their stream and a dozen others.

They had found an unmapped river—perhaps one to rival the Zirona. In any other circumstances they would have been jubilant, but Seth felt numb and hollow.

As they headed back toward the camp, Theo said, "Those falls could change shape in an instant. If they were standing in the wrong place when the counterflow pushed the flow aside . . ."

Seth wasn't ready to assume the worst. "Or they could be sitting under a tree somewhere, injured by a falling branch, or sick from a bad choice of fruit. We just have to keep searching."

"Of course," Judith agreed.

Sarah was quiet. Seth tried to think of something more that he could say to lift her spirits, but then he decided that Judith was better placed for the job.

When they reached the campsite Seth saw that the note he'd left pinned to Raina's tent was missing. He sidled quickly up to the tent, calling out her name. But there was no reply, and the tent was empty.

"Seth!" Sarah was behind him, pointing to the ground. The note had fallen off and become tangled in the undergrowth. But it had not been hard to spot; if anyone had returned, they would still have seen it and waited.

"We need to make a plan," she said. "It's unlikely that they would have gone east, out toward the desert. So we should start by doing a sweep along the stream's west bank."

BY THE FOURTH DAY of the search they were moving through parts of the forest so dense, and so distant from the water, that it was difficult to imagine anything that could have lured their companions here on a quick hunt for food, bypassing all the fruit and berries in more accessible locations. Seth forced his way through the waist-high undergrowth, inured to the thorns and the insect bites, trying to forget the previous night's dream in which a careless step in precisely the same conditions had ended with his foot plunging deep into Amir's putrefying corpse. In the dream, the search had been going on for a thousand days, and he'd been dreading the need to explain to Amir that the children born in his absence represented hope, not betrayal.

Back in the camp that night he sat hunched over his meal, listening to the crackling of the fire.

Judith said, "We need to keep looking—but not around here."

"Where else would they be?" Sarah asked.

Theo said, "Suppose they reached the waterfall, but it was in a different state than the one in which we found it. Maybe it was easy for them to get past it and walk alongside the river itself. But when they tried to return, the way was blocked. So they had to make a detour."

"Even with a detour they'd be back by now," Seth replied.

"Not if they got into trouble," Theo countered. "All the things we first imagined might have happened nearby might still have happened—but on the other side of the falls."

"So we should search along the river," Judith proposed. "But we don't need to risk the waterfall. We can go around the edge of the forest."

"That's a plan," Sarah said quietly.

Seth gave his assent. He'd grown wary of expecting too much every time someone came up with a plausible new scenario and made it sound as if success was imminent—but almost anything made more sense than pushing deeper into the forest.

THEY PACKED UP THE camp and set out into the desert. There was no reason to adhere precisely to the ragged boundary where the vegetation surrendered to the sand, so they followed a broad arc southwest. They knew that the river had to come in from the west, or

Raina and Amina would have stumbled upon it at the same time as Amir and Aziz found the forest itself.

By midday they'd passed the southernmost part of the forest, so they headed west-north-west. Seth was beginning to wonder if there might yet be some flaw in their reasoning, and the river would simply fail to materialize, vanishing as inexplicably as their friends. But he kept his doubts to himself.

"This must be what lured the forest south," Judith mused. "The rain was growing sparser, but the trees and the animals could smell the falls throwing moisture to the wind."

"Maybe the other forest is heading here, too," Theo suggested. "The one we missed."

"We might even be around to see them merge," Judith replied. "Not now, but when Baharabad arrives."

Seth wished he could distract himself with their chatter, but it just aggravated his growing sense of unease. Perhaps the river ran underground, all the way from some subterranean reservoir in the steamlands, flowing up along a vast fissure that only came to the surface at the falls. How could anyone find their way here, when the maps were out of date, local knowledge was off limits, and every town, river, or forest might have drifted, split apart, vanished, or merged?

No one spoke for what felt like an hour. Then Sarah said, "There it is."

Seth squinted to the west. In the distance, something glinted in the afternoon sun.

As they grew nearer, he saw a hint of grasslands along the banks. If the forest relied on the chaos of the waterfall to mimic rain, apparently this more modest vegetation could survive on whatever moisture seeped through the ground, or lingered from sporadic flooding when a surge flowed up from the steamlands.

Seth was relieved that the landscape hadn't proved unremittingly perverse after all, but it seemed likely now that it would take them until nightfall to reach the riverbank. The intervening desert stretched out in front of them, not malicious, but indifferent to the urgency of the task.

As he scanned the glistening ribbon of water, he noticed a smudge of earthen colors far to the south. At first he thought it was simply a barren region where the desert came closer to the banks than usual, but when he turned for a better look it was clear that it was not flat ground.

"There's a town," he said. Someone else had found this newborn river, long before the surveyors from Baharabad had arrived.

9

As NIGHT FELL THEY set up camp in the desert, behind a low, crumbling outcrop, out of sight of anyone traveling directly between the forest and the town.

Seth tried to remain clear-headed, uncommitted to any one theory about the townspeople's role in his friends' disappearance. All of the old possibilities of misadventure by natural causes remained, but even if these strangers had played some part in the event, it need not have been malicious. For all he knew, they could have stumbled upon the surveyors unconscious in the jungle, and carried them back to town for medical treatment.

He and Sarah had nothing to burn for a campfire, sparing them the need to decide whether it would be a risk worth taking, so they sat in the dark eating the pink repeller-fruit.

Sarah said, "If they're in the town, we need to remember that their cover story will be different, because they weren't found with their instruments."

"Right." Seth had considered it comical when he'd had to memorize two completely different lies, but he hadn't forgotten the version where they claimed to be diplomats, originally part of a larger party that had been set upon by marauders midway through their long journey west. It was only if they were pegged as surveyors that they were to pretend to hail from Sedington—a town so much smaller than Baharabad that the prospect of its thirsty population coming after someone else's water might sound more like an opportunity than a threat.

"So do we hide the instruments and limp into town, claiming to be stragglers who survived the same attack?" Sarah wondered.

Judith said, "I vote we don't announce ourselves at all, until we've done a bit of surreptitious reconnaissance."

"The problem with that," Theo replied, "is that if we're caught, we're far more likely to be treated badly."

"If we do it in the early hours of the morning, we're not likely to be caught."

Seth said, "If we do it in the early hours of the morning, what will it tell us? What would we learn about our friends by wandering the streets of this town while everyone's asleep?"

"So we go in early, and see if there's a vantage point," Judith decided. "A place where we can stay hidden during the day, and watch what unfolds."

Theo was unimpressed. "Of course: we'll just follow the signs pointing to the special viewing platform that every town constructs for the benefit of wandering spies."

Sarah said, "It wouldn't hurt to take a closer look before we commit to showing ourselves." She glanced at Seth with a somber expression conveying what none of them wanted to say: if their friends were dead at the hands of these people, the sooner they knew that for sure, the less chance they'd face of sharing the same fate. "But we shouldn't risk everything on this. Only one pair goes in."

"All right," Theo said reluctantly.

"And we toss for it," Seth insisted.

They had no coins, but after scrabbling on the ground for a minute they managed to find a small, flat stone that was symmetrical enough to be fair without its sides being indistinguishable. Sarah tossed it, Seth called, then they both took a step to the south so their Siders could see how it had fallen.

AT THE POINT WHERE Seth reached the river, it ran from the south-south-west. The darkness was impenetrable, but Theo's pings—wide to the north, cautious to the south—guided him well enough to let him move along the bank with confidence. The view to the north was not redundant: seeing the part of the river he'd just passed gave the tentative peek ahead valuable context, without which he would have felt about as secure as if he were groping his way forward by touch alone.

«Lucky we got in so much practice at Lida,» Theo said.

«Except at Lida, we couldn't swim into town.»

Theo hesitated, unsure whether he should take this threat seriously. «You really think you could go against the current?»

«Not a chance,» Seth confessed. As he'd marched across the desert he'd fantasized about it, but if he'd actually dived into the river he would probably have ended up at the waterfall instead.

«With a boat, maybe,» Theo mused. «If you gave it steep enough runners, you might be able to drive it upstream.»

Theo's peek to the south revealed an irrigation canal branching off from the river, just in time to keep Seth from stumbling into it. He squatted down at the edge and dipped one foot into the water; it was shallow enough, and sufficiently slow moving for him to wade across—but chilly enough to kill off all further thoughts of deliberate, prolonged immersion.

As he trudged across the muddy edges of the fields from canal to canal, Seth tried to keep track of his progress against the overall sense of the scale of the city that he'd formed from the distant view by daylight.

«Do you remember that geography class when they gave us a formula for agricultural land use as a proportion of a city's total area?» he asked Theo.

«No.»

«*No?*»

«Some of those lessons were as boring for me as they were for you,» Theo replied. «If it was so important, you should have paid attention yourself.»

«Fair enough.» Seth tipped his head to the west and caught a flicker of lamplight reflected off the river, though the path directly to the source appeared to be in his dark cone. «Forget about the formula, I think we're getting urban right now.»

A minute later he could see half a dozen lamps on the far side of the river, and as his eyes slowly made sense of the dark shapes between them, it was clear that he was staring at closely spaced buildings, not scattered farmhouses. He slowed his pace and looked back to the east, prepared to enter the city itself.

A single lamp appeared at the southern edge of his vision, then Theo showed him the cobblestones moments before they met his feet. Seth paused and tried to make sense of his location; he seemed to be at the end of a narrow road that ran down to the riverbank. «A little more to the south,» he begged Theo. Theo obliged, pinging progressively farther until he revealed a high wall, the side of a large building blocking the way.

Seth found the corner of the building nearest to the river, but there was no prospect of squeezing past there: between water and wall there was nothing but waist-high reeds in treacherous mud. He walked slowly east down the road; Theo retracted his pings to just a pace or so in both directions, but there was enough scattered lamp-light to keep them from being entirely blind.

Dawn was still hours away, and Seth could hear nothing but the lapping of water on the riverbank. After a while he came to a cross-roads, signaled by a change in the orientation of the paving stones. He sidled south, peering into the darkness to the east and managing to discern a row of houses beside the road.

«All of this had to come from somewhere,» he said. «It didn't just rise out of the desert by magic.»

«Maybe they've always been close to the forest,» Theo suggested. «And when it started drifting, they followed it.»

Seth pictured their unreliable map. «There was a town called Thanton north-west of the forest. But once they learned about the river, they might have come this far south.» As far as he could recall, the most recent travelers' accounts of the town that had made their way to Baharabad were from a couple of generations ago. If Thanton had been known for its fearsome inhabitants that would surely have stuck in his memory—and merited some discussion at the expedition's briefing—but after so much time had passed it wasn't safe to assume anything, especially now that these people had a river to defend.

He sidled on down the dark street, passing three more crossroads before the character of the buildings around him began to change. Though he was struggling to interpret slabs of gray that he could only just distinguish from the background, the shift to more imposing structures was unmistakable. A grain store? A bath-house? A meeting hall? He was tempted to ask Theo to ping everything to the south and prove that they'd reached the center of town, since they were probably far enough from any private residence to avoid waking a single Sider, but that would be foolhardy. What he needed to do was find a hiding place and lessen his risk of discovery, not increase it.

Seth began exploring east-west side roads, and Theo cautiously pinged the objects they passed. There were three large bins behind a restaurant, unmistakable from their odor of rotting food scraps, but though the space between these containers and the wall might have made a good site to avoid detection for a while, there was no way of knowing when and how the bins would be emptied, and the chances of learning anything vital from the gossip of kitchen hands dumping vegetable peel seemed slim.

«Forget this,» Theo said. «I know the perfect spot.»

«Somewhere we passed?»

«I'm not sure. But it must be close by.»

As it turned out it wasn't far, but it still took them what felt like an hour of pursuing dead ends before they found the bridge. Seth clambered awkwardly over the guardrails along the eastern approach, then trudged around the muddy edges of the riverbank to a point behind a supporting column where he would be out of sight to anyone up on the street. He sat on the sloping ground, his head tipped so he could watch the river. If a barge went by—or a brave swimmer—he would need to retreat even further behind the column, but he wasn't going to do that preemptively and leave himself vulnerable to being cornered if someone approached on foot.

«Are you sure you'll be able to hear people talking?» he asked Theo. In Baharabad it was common practice to dawdle on the bridges when chatting with friends, but the river here sounded loud enough to drown out any conversation, and once the planks above were creaking with footsteps that would only make the task harder.

«You have no idea,» Theo boasted.

«I don't,» Seth conceded. «I can see what you see . . . why can't I hear what you hear?»

Theo thought for a while. «Maybe you're just not equipped to make sense of such detailed sounds. Knowing about an object in your dark cone isn't really any different from knowing about an object right in front of you: it's exactly the same kind of thing out in the world. But even there, what we learn from each other is limited: I can't glean colors from what you share with me, and you can't perceive textures the way I do. And it's not that either of us is holding things back. We just don't have space in our minds for the kind of details we can't see for ourselves.»

«Right.» Seth could recall occasions when Theo had tried to point something out to him by referring to the roughness of its surface, as if that were meant to be obvious from afar, and no doubt he had committed the same kind of gaffe himself with hues. Over time they'd adjusted their expectations of each other without thinking about it too much, but it was still easy to forget that the world inside Theo's skull was not the same as the world inside his own.

The riverbank was damp and chill as they waited for dawn. Seth heard the first footsteps overhead before the sky was light, but these early risers walked alone, some empty-handed, some struggling with heavy loads. There was even the rhythmic squeak of a wheeled cart, but no conversation.

Gradually, the town began to stir, with shouts and laughter in the distance, then finally some murmurs from the bridge itself.

«What are they saying?» he asked Theo.

«They're arguing about a debt.» Theo sounded tense.

«Why is that so worrying?»

«It's not,» Theo replied irritably. He was probably just straining to hear, and could have done without being pestered for a running commentary.

As the morning wore on, Seth watched the light on the river, wishing he could contribute more to the endeavor. He tried to picture the owners of each set of footsteps from their gait, but that was just a game, and even when they raised their voices in anger or mirth, the words were so muffled—or the accents so thick, the dialect so foreign—that he barely understand half of what was spoken.

Theo said, «Have you noticed anything strange?»

«I've barely noticed anything ordinary.»

«How many Siders have you heard so far?»

«I have no idea,» Seth replied. If he heard clear speech in a familiar accent, he could usually distinguish between the characteristic timbres, but whatever the cues were here, he was oblivious to them. «Ask me something easy, like how many of the Walkers were missing a leg.»

«I haven't heard one,» Theo declared. «Not on the bridge, not from the streets around us. Not one Sider has spoken, this far into the day.»

«Maybe there's a custom here that they get to sleep late,» Seth joked.

«They're pinging,» Theo said.

«Are they pinging *us*?» Seth asked, alarmed.

«No, but I can hear that they're pinging the bridge.»

«How many people have you heard talking?»

«Dozens.»

Seth was perplexed. «Could their sounds be different from yours? I mean . . . could you just not be hearing them, the way I can't hear it when you speak with another Sider, out of my range?»

«Even if they possess some freakish talent that lets them use pitches I can't hear, why aren't they talking to the Walkers? I can't believe the Walkers would share the same skill.»

«No.»

Theo said, «They must have done something to them.»

«What do you mean?»

«Harmed them. Crippled them.»

The revulsion in Theo's voice left no doubt that he was convinced, but to Seth the conclusion seemed fanciful. «That makes no sense,» he replied. «If the Siders have been harmed to the point where they can't speak, why would they still be pinging?»

«I don't know what kind of injury's been inflicted on them,» Theo said. «But half the people around us are mute. That's not down to chance.»

Seth had no counter-explanation to offer, but the precept that declared it a shameful aberration to mistreat your Sider was hardly some cosmopolitan affectation that tough-minded frontier folk would be free to discard. How could a whole town survive, if the practice became routine? A Walker who lost their temper and jabbed at the parasite in their skull just ended up side-blind.

Theo said, «I want to try something.»

«What?»

«Next time there are footsteps above us, I want to shout "stop!" in the Sider language and see what happens.»

Seth shifted uncomfortably on the sand. «Do you think that's a good idea?»

«We need to know,» Theo insisted. «This isn't idle curiosity. If we have a chance to communicate with Aziz and Amina without anyone overhearing us, that could make all the difference.»

«But what if you're wrong, and you give away our presence?»

«One word might make people stop and look around—but they're not going to climb over the rails and traipse through the mud just because they weren't sure where a shout came from.»

Seth said, «They might, if it's as rare for a Sider to speak as you say it is.»

«If it's as rare as I think it is,» Theo countered, «no Walker will ever learn of it.»

«Maybe.» If the Siders had been cowed into silence, they weren't going to betray another Sider to their oppressors. «All right. Just make sure you're listening carefully to the aftermath, so you can tell me which way to run.»

Seth rose into a crouch, ready to flee along the riverbank if necessary. Footfalls sounded, planks squeaked; when he looked up directly at the underside of the bridge, he could see the timber beams shifting slightly. But the Walker continued on, without so much as a pause.

«Did you do it?» he asked Theo.

«Yes.»

«How loudly?»

«Like a matter of life and death. Either the Sider didn't hear it, or they didn't tell the Walker, or the Walker didn't care what the Sider said.»

Seth considered these three possibilities. If it had been the last, they'd hardly be safe to roam the streets at night yelling out Aziz and Amina's names. «You want to repeat the experiment, with different words?»

Theo said, «You read my mind.»

Commands, pleas for help, insults, and warnings all had the same effect: none at all. It seemed unlikely that a dozen different Walkers would have reacted with indifference to such interjections if they'd actually known about them.

Seth was cheered by the prospect of exploiting the discovery, however disturbing Theo's theories about the underlying reason. And he didn't want to try to guess what was really going on, while crouched under a bridge, unable to ask a single citizen of Thanton for their own account. Perhaps in Elena's angriest moments she'd wished for a world in which all Siders were voiceless, but you couldn't run a town on the darkest urges of its most miserable children.

He stared out across the river and tried to stay alert, without distracting Theo with needless chatter.

IT WAS MID-AFTERNOON BEFORE Theo had anything more than an absence to report, but the revelation was worth the wait.

«"When's the Council going to decide what to do with the diplomats?"» Theo quoted one of the bridge-crossers as saying; the words had been nothing but muffled burbling to Seth's ears. «To which the answer was, "Tomorrow night."»

«So they're here? They're not lying injured in the forest somewhere!» Seth barely managed to keep himself from shouting in jubilation. «Are you sure it was "do *with* the diplomats," not "do *about*"?»

«Yes,» Theo said flatly.

«Maybe that's just a difference in dialect? Do *with*, do *for*, do *to* . . . this far from Baharabad, who knows what preposition means what?» Theo didn't reply. Seth said, «So we have a day and a half to find them, before *something's* done.»

«To find them, and release them,» Theo corrected him.

Seth felt the muscles in his back squirming in rebellion at the thought of remaining where he was for another second; the news that Thanton's hospitality toward strangers was now as suspect as its treatment of its Siders only left him more ashamed than ever at the prospect of cowering under the bridge until dark.

«Do you think there's any chance that we could pass for locals?» he asked Theo. «This town isn't so small that everyone would recognize everyone else.»

«My part would be easy,» Theo replied dryly. «But do you think you could fake the accent?»

«I wasn't planning on actually talking to anyone.»

«That might not be an option. And what about your clothes?»

Seth had no reply to that. Apart from a general travel-worn shabbiness, it was possible that the style alone would mark him out instantly as a stranger.

«We need to see some of these people,» he declared. «For all we know, they might have two heads.»

Theo said, «Two heads is normal, by my count. But I'd say they only have about one and a quarter.»

Seth rose to his feet and moved cautiously to the edge of the column. He peeked out across the river at a road that ran beside the opposite bank. It wasn't easy to make out the details of people's apparel from this distance, but after a while it was clear that the colors were all brighter than his own, the sleeves shorter, the hems of the shirts lower. As far as he could tell from their body language, merely passing someone on the street didn't always entail an exchange of greetings. But the fact remained that, at the very least, his dull, oddly cut clothing would attract attention before he said, or declined to say, a single word.

«So we wait until dark,» he said, retreating back into his hiding place. The delay was infuriating, but when he thought through the situation as calmly as he could, he had to accept that it need not be calamitous. The "diplomats" were alive, and their fate was yet to be decided. Risking all six lives for no other reason than his own impatience would have been the worst possible choice.

SUNSET ARRIVED WITH THE punctuality that geometry dictated, but then the dusk seemed to linger at its own pleasure. Seth stole a glance across the river and found that the streets were still far from empty. As in Baharabad, this appeared to be a time to make the most of the cool of the evening and go out to eat, or to visit friends.

Gradually the sky grew dark. Seth stepped out of the gloom beneath the bridge and looked down at his clothes; he could barely tell what color they were. An attempt to make his sleeves appear shorter turned into an unwinnable battle between the contradictory demands of the differently oriented fabrics, and he ended up with a bulbous mess like a child's attempt to re-pack a tent. So he smoothed them back into their normal shape, then trudged up the riverbank and onto the road.

As he headed east, Seth saw two figures approaching through the gloom. Theo said, «I'm going to ask their Siders for directions to the nearest boarding house.»

«All right.» Seth kept his gaze on the road as he passed them—hoping to seem sufficiently preoccupied to forestall any need for an exchange of pleasantries—but through Theo's view he could see them responding to his presence: turning their heads slightly to keep track of him, as anyone in Baharabad would have done, to ensure that they didn't bump into him.

«Any reply?» he asked Theo.

«Nothing. Even their pinging is strange.»

«In what way?»

«Monotonous,» Theo replied. «Unvarying. Normally, when we crossed paths like that, there'd be a whole host of changes in the sounds the Siders emitted. It's as if they imaged us without noticing us; they pinged us, but only the Walkers really saw us.»

«Sleepsiders.» Seth didn't want to think too deeply about the whole disturbing phenomenon; he needed to stay focused on the search. «It looks as if we're safe to make as much noise in your language as we like. So shout at will, and let me know if you need me to break the search pattern.»

Theo said, «There's only one thing that could stop us finding them now.»

Seth knew what he was alluding to, but he didn't want either of them to spell it out. «Two things: we could fail to be thorough. So let's make sure that we don't miss so much as a single farmhouse, if it comes to that.»

«Right.»

They'd sketched out their strategy under the bridge, as well as they could without knowing the whole city's street plan. Seth walked east until he was four blocks from the river, then at the crossroads he began sidling north. He would weave his way across one quadrant of the city, repeat the process in the south, then cross the river and do it all again if need be.

As he approached a side street, a small crowd came around the corner: half a dozen people all talking and laughing. Theo's view of their clothes was free of color but alarmingly crisp; Seth cringed at the thought that they were seeing him with the same kind of detail. As he moved to the other side of the street, someone called out to him, "Hey, ragamuffin!" A second speaker followed, with words he couldn't understand at all.

Seth kept his face away from them as he passed to their east; he heard laughter and more shouting, including what might have been a reference to his appalling smell. But he heard no change of gait— no one breaking off their sidling to approach him directly. When they crossed into Theo's view again, there was no sign that they'd ever shown an interest in his presence.

Apparently he could pass for an impecunious local, without anyone connecting his style of clothes to that of the captives. But then, how many people in Thanton would have actually seen the "diplomats"? Their presence might have been widely discussed, but other aspects had likely taken precedence over matters of couture.

Theo said, «I'm learning to ping like a Sleepsider, if that gives you any comfort.»

«Would anyone know if you didn't?»

«Maybe not, but it's better to be safe. Perhaps the Siders would twitch with surprise in their sleep, and their Walkers would notice.»

«Some comfort,» Seth replied. «Hearing their own language after who knows how long might surprise them more than anything.»

«I'm not going to yell when someone's right beside us.»

They reached the northern edge of the city, went east for four more blocks, then south. Theo had promised that this grid was fine enough—that his call would be heard deep within each region they were skirting.

And the reply? Seth recalled Irina screaming for help, audible from afar to her brother, despite her constraints. It was only if Aziz and Amina had suffered the same treatment as Thanton's own Siders that the search would be in vain—and all Seth could do was hope that the Council's pending decision precluded any such prior atrocity.

Even if, to the Walkers of Thanton, it was not seen as an atrocity at all.

IT WAS LONG AFTER midnight when they began their sweep of the south-west quadrant. The streets were almost empty now, and the few people they encountered seemed less interested than ever in the business of passing strangers. Whether they were tired, wary, up to no good, or simply lost in their own thoughts, no one gave the ragamuffin with the screaming Sider a second glance.

Seth felt himself lapsing, if not into sleepwalking, into a kind of numbness. Since they'd hidden beneath the bridge he'd been one step removed from everything important about the search, and the mixture of danger and boredom, urgency and forced disengagement was exhausting. He felt no resentment at Theo's ascendant role, but he envied him the sheer stimulation; if he'd been free to bellow out their friends' names he might have been twice as frantic, but at least he would not have been dead on his feet.

«They're here!» Theo proclaimed ecstatically.

Seth's veneer of stupefaction shattered. He stopped walking but tensed his body, ready to bound off in whatever direction was required. «Where?» he demanded.

«East.»

The street they were on ran north-to-south, and Seth couldn't make out the next crossroads. «Back to the north, or further south?»

«South, I think.»

Seth began sprinting down the street, ignoring Theo's protests until the sound of his own echoing footsteps made his recklessness self-evident. He slowed to a brisk sidle, his skin tingling with excitement and fear.

«Are we any closer?»

«We've gone past them, but don't go back. The next side street should get us there.»

Seth could see the corner now, in Theo's view. «They're all there together?» he asked.

«Yes.»

«Are you sure?»

Theo said, «Aziz and Amina have both replied. If you're asking whether they've been torn out of their Walkers, the subject hasn't come up, but in those circumstances I doubt they'd have the strength to make so much noise.»

Seth hadn't even contemplated that possibility, but he pushed the image aside and focused on the news that both Siders seemed to be in good health.

He reached the crossroads and headed east, unimpeded by the darkness. He'd gained enough of a sense of the city's public works that he was confident he would not be wrong-footed by a curb or a gutter appearing out of nowhere.

«Keep going,» Theo advised him as they approached an intersection. At the next one he said the same. They were only two blocks from the river now; Seth could hear the water.

When they came to the last crossroads, Seth paused. Theo offered no immediate instructions, but as Seth stood motionless in the cold air, he was aware for the first time of a pattern of tension and relaxation in his own skin where it abutted his Sider's pingers. It could only be the rhythm of the conversation: Theo's body expanding very slightly as he yelled, contracting as he listened.

Finally Theo inspoke, «By day, they saw the river right below their window. The house they're in has no road to its east—just the riverbank.»

«Right.» Seth didn't know quite what to do with this information. «Where are they in this house?»

«The top floor.»

«Who else is there? And where, exactly?»

Theo said, «These are all good questions, but we need to get closer. So far Aziz and I have spent a lot of time shouting, "What did you say? Can you repeat that?"»

Seth said, «They might have lookouts on the street.»

«Of course,» Theo agreed.

«And they might have lookouts on the riverbank, too.»

Theo said nothing. Seth made a decision. «The riverbank's the lesser risk.»

He followed the eastbound street to the end, where the paving stones gave way to soft ground. The scattered lamps that had appeared the night before were nowhere to be seen, but even in the utter blackness Seth could sense the turbulent water ahead by something more than its sound: a shimmer so faint that he had to drag it out of the dark by a constant force of attention, as if he were striving to keep a heavy weight on a rope from sinking down into the river.

Theo pinged a few paces north, guiding Seth along the narrow strip of ground between the houses and the point where the riverbank became too steep to traverse. If there were lookouts, unless their own pings were equally restrained Theo would detect them long before a bodily encounter was imminent—and Seth suspected that the Sleepsiders had already shown themselves to be incapable of such subtleties.

Theo said, «We're close. We should stop here and work out a plan.»

«How close?»

«Maybe three houses away.»

Even if there'd been lamplight from inside, the building would still be in Seth's dark cone, but he didn't want Theo to risk pinging the place.

Theo said, «They're being kept in a locked room on the eastern side of the top floor. There's nobody in the room with them, but they think there are five or six Walkers in the house, and at least two are awake and guarding the door right now.»

Seth was dismayed, though he wasn't sure what he'd been hoping for: a lone guard who might have dozed off, with the key poking out of their pocket?

«What about the window?» he asked.

Theo passed the question on to the captives, then replied, «Four vertical bars, but no shutter. They don't believe there's anyone outside on the riverbank.»

Seth had brought no tools with him at all, leaving everything back at the camp so that if he was grabbed he could fit into the diplomats-meet-thieves story. «Where are we going to find a jimmy?» The riverbank was all sand, and the paving stones were the wrong shape.

Theo said, «No city moves without leaving pieces behind.»

«You mean to the north.» Seth wished he'd thought of this on the way in, when he'd been slogging through the muddy fields. There might have been scattered building material within easy reach under the soil, but it had never occurred to him to look for it. «Before we go off on that hunt, ask them if they have any better ideas.»

Theo obliged. «They don't.»

Seth hesitated. «And they're all right for now? No one's injured? Nothing's going to happen to them while we're gone?»

Theo said, «No one's injured. And we'll be quick.»

Seth continued north along the riverbank. *How quick was quick enough?* He'd lost confidence in his sense of time; his instincts told him dawn was hours away, but he was afraid now that it might take him unawares.

Fences and buildings intruded onto the narrow corridor he'd chosen, but he was determined not to waste time with a detour back onto the streets. He could squeeze past the artificial obstacles, but when reeds blocked the way he had no choice but to trample them, and hope that if he was heard he'd be mistaken for some kind of innocuous wildlife.

He said, «If we'd had just one more night after this, we could have gone back to the camp and made a real plan with Sarah and Judith.»

Theo took this lament literally. «Based on one conversation between random people on a bridge? Would you have risked everything on the chance that the information was correct?»

«There are too many levels of counterfactuals there for me to handle without a lot more sleep.» Seth backtracked to free himself from a thorny plant that had hooked into the fabric of his trousers. «How close are we to the farms now?»

«It can't be far.»

«Should I have crossed the bridge and gone back to the east bank?» That way they would at least have been heading somewhere half-familiar.

Theo said, «Too many counterfactuals.»

Seth emerged from the thicket and sidled on through the mud. His brief, second-hand encounter with his friends already felt like something he'd hallucinated as he criss-crossed the city—an act that itself seemed less like reality than a dream he was having after reading the story of some mythic character cursed to walk forever through a maze full of jeering strangers and carnivorous plants.

«Do you believe in Sleepwalkers?» he asked.

Theo was silent for a while, as if expecting something more. «Are you serious?»

«I never believed in them,» Seth assured him. «But if Thanton can have Sleepsiders, why can't the other kind exist?»

«How does a Sider wield a knife on a Walker?»

«You really think it's like that?» Seth hadn't intended to broach the subject, but weariness had robbed him of his tact.

«It's either drugs or mutilation,» Theo insisted. «Even people who claim that there are Sleepwalkers describe them as rarities: the Walker is so old or weak-willed that the chatter in their skull wears them down until they surrender all volition. You don't lull a few thousand healthy Siders into a stupor by inspeech alone.»

«Right now, I wouldn't mind being a Sleepwalker,» Seth confessed. The riverbank stretched on interminably, a tiny patch of pinged ground surrounded by blackness. «That way it would be up to you to keep us moving, and I could just look on in comfort.»

Theo said, «Give it a million more generations.»

Seth stopped just in time to keep himself from stumbling into an irrigation channel. «Two million, to walk safely when we're both asleep.» He waded across the channel, and was about to continue along the bank when he realized that that would be idiotic. The houses would have been farther from the water.

Theo pinged the field nearby, revealing both crops and fallow ground. Seth strode over to an empty plot, squatted down, and began groping through the soil.

It took a hundred or so empty handfuls before he understood that he was wasting his time. This land had been plowed; the farmers would have removed anything that might have blocked the roots of the crop.

Seth stood up and swayed giddily. The farmers would have removed it, but would they have bothered moving it far? How much of a market would there be for bits of broken masonry?

«There must be a junk heap,» he said. «That's what we need to find.»

Theo pinged more widely. Seth walked slowly across the field, gazing into Theo's view, searching for some kind of pit or pile into which everything struck by the plow had been cast.

«There!» Theo said.

«Can you be more specific?»

«South-south-west.»

Seth saw it now. He approached and fell to his knees beside the mother lode, then began scrabbling through it. There were pieces of bricks, pieces of tiles . . . and whole, unbroken window bars.

The first two he found were lying east-west. He didn't discard them, but he kept looking until he found two axial ones as well. He gathered up these precious finds and headed back toward the riverbank. The gloom he moved through was unaltered, but everything seemed sharper now, urgent and specific.

«No more sleep-anything,» he said. «We need to keep each other awake on our feet.»

«Your feet,» Theo corrected him.

«For now,» Seth conceded. «But you never know what the future holds.»

WHEN THEY REACHED THE house, Seth stood on the riverbank with his head tipped westward, staring at the wall behind him until the faint hints it offered solidified into four rectangular windows: two on the bottom floor, two on the top.

«Are they sure they're in the northern room?» he asked Theo.

«No, but I am.»

Seth walked slowly toward the house. «Do you hear any of the guards moving around downstairs?»

«No.» Theo hesitated, seeking more information. «Aziz says they've been quiet for a while. But the two upstairs are awake and chatting.»

Seth's outstretched hands made contact with the wall, palms against the stone, the non-axial fingers pointing to the ground. It was an awkward stance, but he was afraid that if he switched to the backs of his hands they might lose traction. The gray rectangles guiding him had started swimming uncertainly as he approached, as if his mind was doing its best to recreate their likely position but was no longer getting the kind of feedback it needed from his eyes. But unless he'd become completely disoriented, he was about a shoulder's width north of the southern downstairs window.

With his feet far enough apart to give him some extra height without compromising his balance, he dug his heels into the ground. Then he began to tip his upper body to the north, shifting his palms up over the rough surface of the wall. He was sure he'd tried crazier stunts as a child, but usually with an accomplice, and never for remotely comparable stakes.

An ache spread up from his left hip and along his side. Seth froze, waiting to see if it presaged something more dangerous. If he slipped, he trusted his instincts to ensure that he ended up flat on the ground—rather than sliding across the wall until his body reached so high that the torque snapped his ankle. But any kind of fall was sure to make enough noise to wake the entire household.

The ache remained no more than a discomfort. He leaned a little further, then a little more. The friction between his palms and the wall began to seem perilously close to inadequate—like the moment before a sled flew freely up a ramp. He clawed at the gaps between the bricks, wedging as many fingertips as he could into the narrow crevices to give himself more purchase. Then he advanced slowly, never freeing both hands at once—until a north-pointing finger met air, and his momentary sense of panic turned to triumph. He was touching the edge of the window.

«Ask them if they're ready for some gifts.»

Theo replied, «Go ahead.»

Gripping the wall tightly with one hand, Seth reached into his pockets and passed up the salvaged bars, one by one—holding them beside the window and waiting for an occupant of the room to slide them out of his grasp. The axial bars had to pass through the gap at an unwieldy angle, but he managed to coordinate the handover with his silent collaborator without so much as a tap of stone on stone. He retreated from the window as slowly as he'd approached it, straightening his body and lowering his hands until he was merely standing beside the wall with an aching back and a few more scratches on his palms.

«If you were a better throw, you could have just tossed them through the window,» Theo joked.

Seth decided to stay beside the wall, rather than hide somewhere along the riverbank while his friends worked on the bars of their prison. No one in the house could see him here, but the more he moved about, the more he risked being heard. And if something happened inside that required his intervention, it would be better to be as close as possible.

He strained his ears for any rhythmic scraping or creaking, and was reassured to hear nothing. He'd resisted the urge to offer Raina and Amir any advice as to how they should attack the task, and he hardly needed to tell them that they could use a shirt wrapped around the work site to muffle the sound.

Theo said, «Catch!»

Seth stretched an arm out under the window and a piece of stone struck it before bouncing to the ground. Neither impact was silent, but both were quieter than if the fall had been uninterrupted. He squatted down and felt around for the object; it took a while to assess it by touch alone, but it seemed to be an entire, unbroken bar. «From the window?» he asked Theo. «Or did they drop a tool?»

«From the window.»

They must have chipped away at one of the mortises where the bar slotted into place, until the gap was large enough to work it loose. Seth resumed his position, with his arm out ready for a repeat performance. «Any response from the guards when it fell?»

«No. The two at the door are telling each other idiotic jokes, and downstairs is still completely silent.»

Seth only learned of the next bar's removal when the news reached him via Theo; Amir had managed to hold onto it. The third bar was the same. «Someone's showing promise for a second career as a burglar,» he said.

«We'll all need something to keep us busy in retirement,» Theo replied.

There was a loud cracking sound, and two pieces of stone landed on Seth's arm. Bizarrely, they both stayed put—they were short enough not to overbalance. He reached across and gathered them up, as if it mattered now whether they fell or not.

Theo said, «Someone just woke up.»

Seth remained flat against the wall. A lamp was lit in the northern room downstairs, illuminating a patch of the riverbank with sudden, startling brightness. Then he heard shouted instructions to the guards upstairs, to check on the prisoners.

Amir landed on the ground with a thud, and crouched for a moment in the lamplight. Without even tipping his head westward, he set off to the north. The moment he was out of the way, Raina jumped down to the same spot. West-facing, she must have seen Seth skulking against the wall, but she betrayed no sign of it; the escapees were taking care to do nothing that might give away his position.

As Raina bolted north, Seth heard hurried footsteps approaching from the south side of the house. If he ducked under the window and made it to the north side, the guards might not see him as they passed. He'd have a chance to slink away through the streets, while the pursuit remained confined to the riverbank.

Or he could make himself useful.

Seth moved quickly into the darkness to the south, then as three guards came around the corner he sprinted back again, straight toward the leading figure. He collided with the woman and pinned her against the wall, then kicked one of her feet out from under her and sent her toppling northward. She cried out in panic and clutched at his shoulders, but he took her hands and thrust them away, then sidled along beside her tilting body with his arms outstretched, keeping her trapped, blocking the safe fall to the west. The fabric of her clothing scraped against his own with an unnerving rasp that rose in pitch as it ascended ever faster—while some visceral part of him, balking as much at this uncontrolled acceleration as the cruelty of the act, implored him to bring the motion to a halt.

As her comrades rushed to her aid, Seth fled, but he'd confined the hapless guard to the plane of the wall long enough for her head to have risen higher than the building. He sped north along the riverbank, weaving between the reeds, listening for the aftermath. There was no impact, no screams of pain, so his victim must have been caught before she hit the ground—but he'd managed to tie up his would-be pursuers for as long as it took them to maneuver her to safety.

«Can you raise Aziz and Amina?» he asked Theo.

«I'm already talking to them.»

«So what's the plan?»

«Keep running.» Theo hesitated. «We're being pinged now. The guards can see us.»

«Just us, or the others?»

«Just us so far.»

Seth picked up his pace a little, but after so long without food or sleep even fear could not do much to revive his flagging strength. This route had been difficult enough to traverse when he'd been moving much more slowly; now every step on the uneven ground felt perilous. «Can you tell how many are following us?» Theo wasn't pinging to the south at all, presumably because he still felt that offered some advantage.

«Five. Three closest to us, two in the rear. I swear there are lizards smarter than these Siders: the two behind need not have given themselves away, but they're all pinging with the same strength and sweep, as if they had no choice.»

Five. Seth couldn't think of any way that this could end well. The three in the front would easily overpower him, and then it might take just one to restrain him. Even if they had no allies that they could summon quickly, they had the advantage of local knowledge, and they were probably better rested than their former prisoners. In the end, they'd run down Raina and Amir, and everything he'd done would have been in vain.

But as he listened to the clumsy thudding of his footsteps, the river's susurration rose up from the darkness.

He said, «Tell the others I'm going to swim for the eastern shore. Aziz and Amina should be far enough ahead to ping the water and see if anyone comes after me.» If any of the guards followed him in, dunking their already dysfunctional Siders, they were unlikely to be able to determine the location of the people pinging them—and even if they did, Walkers trying to convey those details to their comrades back on land over the noise of the river would be as good as mute.

«Passing it on,» Theo replied. His tone made it clear that the plan dismayed him—but if he'd had a better one, now would have been the time to argue for it.

As Seth swerved to avoid a clump of tall reeds, his balance faltered and he slipped on the treacherous mud. He managed to catch himself, but when he tried to speed up again he felt a throbbing in his ankle.

Theo conveyed the leaders' verdict: «Amina says that if it looks safe, the others will follow you and meet you on the bank. If not, don't stop until you're back at the campsite.»

«Do they know how to get to the campsite?» Seth willed himself to forget the pain and hurtle forward; if he could summon a burst of speed that put him out of range of the Sleepsiders behind him, there'd be no need for him to test the waters or create a diversion.

«I've told them how to find it,» Theo assured him.

Seth stopped fooling himself: he was not outrunning anyone. He swerved to the east and forced himself not to stop as the ground sloped precipitously and he careered forward into the water. It was not the elegant dive he'd imagined, but as he landed face down old habits took over and his arms began a methodical stroke, before he'd even raised his head to breathe.

The water was freezing, swift, and turbulent. With his pingers drenched, Theo could show him nothing. When he looked up, Seth could see two faint lights on the eastern shore, but with every few strokes the beacons shifted visibly as the current carried him north.

In that direction at least, he was moving much faster than he could have on land. Even if his pursuers had chosen to follow him into the dark water, they'd have little hope of keeping track of him. All he had to do was make it across the river without drowning.

As he left the riverbank behind, the vagaries of the current began buffeting him mercilessly. Each unbalanced shove turned him away from true east, exposing him to more of the water's fury. Seth lost sight of the lights on the far shore and struggled to correct himself, picturing the falling woman growing ever taller, and his own spine snapping from the pressure as he was pummeled by an ever-widening portion of the river's flow. His agitation turned to panic and he felt himself floundering.

Theo said, «Calm yourself.»

«I'm turning too far—»

«Let yourself turn, you don't need to fight it.»

«The water will break me.»

«It would rather flow around you. But the more of it you block, the more it resists your motion, and the more you average out the forces. You can't go into free fall.»

Seth spluttered in the darkness, lifted his mouth clear of the water, and took a deep breath. Then he forced himself to relax, and he began making long, slow, even strokes, pretending that he was back in some placid creek that he could cross ten times effortlessly. He felt the growing pressure of the water against his body—but it was coming from both sides, squeezing him more than it was twisting him. He lost all sense of his orientation, and just advanced, stroke by stroke, along whatever path the river had chosen for him. It didn't matter. The current would sweep him north, out of Thanton, and nothing in the world had the power to turn him entirely away from the east. Wherever he was going, the shore was ahead. He only needed to persist.

For a long time he maintained his rhythm, holding on to his memories of sunlit water, counting laps of his imaginary creek and setting the total back to three every time it rose too close to ten. But then cold and fatigue began to dispel the reverie, and the muscles along the side of his body that aided his arms with each in-stroke turned to rags.

«I've got nothing left,» he told Theo.

«We're nearly there.»

«How can you tell? You're as blind as I am.» Seth couldn't blame him for trying; he would have told any lie himself if he'd thought it would save them.

«I can't ping the bank, but I can hear it in the sound of the water. We're close.»

Seth wished he'd had a more convincing story. «You think you know how the sound of this river changes, closer to the bank? When did you learn that?»

Theo said, «When you jumped in at the other shore.»

Seth's arms were aching beyond endurance, but if Theo couldn't take on that burden himself, he'd done everything in his power to make it tolerable. «Then you'd better keep listening, so you can stop me before I get a mouthful of sand.»

Seth swung his right arm out wide to lengthen his stroke, cupped his hand and drew it in, screaming silently. The same on the left. The same on the right. Whiteness flared across his vision, and when he closed his eyes it remained. He tried to count another lap of the creek, but all his dishonest subtractions came rushing back at him, correcting the total: twelve, seventeen, twenty-two, twenty-seven.

«We're close,» Theo promised.

«I can't do this any more.» Seth let his arms flop beneath him, and his body tipped back.

His feet struck something solid. The water was barely waist high.

Seth heard himself emitting some kind of faint noise, like an attenuated mixture of laughter and sobbing. He waded through the shallows, still pushed around by the current, giving every step his full attention so as not to lose his balance.

When he was clear of the water he knelt on the ground, waiting for the phantom lights in his head to fade.

Theo said, «Are you ready for some good news?»

«Always.»

«Raina and Amir both reached the shore before us, a bit to the south. I just told Aziz that you'll wait for them to catch up.»

RAINA WAS WORRIED THAT the guards might have procured boats and followed them down the river, so they set off into the desert as quickly as they could while they still had the advantage of night. Seth had never felt more comfortable marching into darkness; compared to the riverbank, an expanse of flat desert with the occasional rock was like a playground for coddled infants.

"Did they take you to Thanton by boat?" he asked Raina.

"Yes."

"Do you know why they were in the forest?"

"They were gathering something that grows there, that apparently they're unable to farm in the town." Raina's tone was becoming strained, so Seth stopped quizzing her. The abductees could tell their story later, once they'd all rested.

The dawn revealed that they'd left Thanton far behind. Seth soon got his bearings and led the way across the desert.

Just as he was beginning to wonder if he'd made a mistake, he saw Sarah standing on the outcrop waving her arms—and when the bedraggled expedition limped into camp she and Judith began an outpouring of relief. Seth hadn't given much thought to their situation while he'd been away, but the long, lonely vigil with no information, wondering if they'd end up as the sole survivors, must have been hard to endure.

Raina waited until they were spent. "We need to eat, then we need to get moving. It's still possible that Thanton will send out a search party."

Seth limited himself to a single repeller-fruit; he was hungry enough to eat a dozen, but he was afraid of rushing and giving himself stomach cramps.

As they packed up the camp, Theo shared revelations he'd gleaned from Aziz and Amina. «It's the puffballs in the forest. They don't eat enough to poison themselves, but it's still enough to damage the Siders.»

«Damage them, or just make them docile?»

«I can't say for sure,» Theo admitted, «but from the way Aziz described the guards gloating about it, even if the poison vanished from their diet those Siders aren't going to wake up and start quoting Hesethus.»

Ever since the bridge, Seth had been finding excuses not to dwell too deeply on the Siders' lack of speech. But now the notion that they might merely have been rendered a little quieter and more compliant than their cousins struck him as so stupid that he was ashamed he'd entertained it for a moment, even as an unexamined placeholder for the truth he'd had no time to deal with. If every Sider was silent, all of the time, how likely was it that they'd learned even the Walkers' language? And if they'd been raised from infancy with no language at all, what kind of stunted minds would they possess?

«There's no chance that they're using inspeech?»

Theo said, «The guards' favorite taunt was, "How can you bear to have those parasites babbling away in your head?"»

The expedition set off to the north-east. Seth felt as if his body had been bludgeoned all over, but he could still put one foot in front of another on this soft, level ground, and each time weariness began to overtake him, he reminded himself of the magnitude of his good fortune. They were all still alive, and reunited. They had found a new river that could easily support Baharabad—and perhaps all five towns from the dying Zirona—so they were heading home with the best possible news.

Almost the best possible news.

"The next team will need to be well guarded," he said. "Even if we build downstream from Thanton, taking nothing from their flow, I doubt they'll be willing to make peace except by force of numbers."

Amina said, "All the better if they fight us, so we have grounds to subjugate them."

"You want there to be a war?" Sarah was appalled.

"I want Thanton crushed." Amina was unapologetic. "What they're doing to their Siders is intolerable. We should attack them for that alone, never mind some contest over the river."

Seth said, "But once Baharabad's beside them, might that not civilize them?"

Amina made a sound of derision. "You think this is just a question of isolation? They've been wandering in the desert so long that they lost their way?"

"How else would you describe it?" Sarah demanded. "Everyone takes their values from the people around them. Thanton's been alone too long, and it's gone wild."

Aziz said, "You're talking about thousands of people, not a few dozen in some obscure cult. Whoever it was in Thanton that first had the idea to poison their Siders, the majority opinion at the time doesn't seem to have been enough to dissuade them."

Seth was beginning to wish that he hadn't broached the subject at all. He peered ahead across the sand, trying to picture the moment when they could set up camp again, and he could finally sleep.

Theo chose that moment to join in, with a typically provocative contribution. "If the idea spread throughout Thanton, who's to say it won't spread throughout Baharabad?"

"I say it," Sarah replied angrily. "We're not like those people!"

"You mean we don't have access to the same poison?" Judith interjected.

"There are puffballs all over the city," Sarah retorted. "Did you ever hear of someone eating them to harm their Sider? Even once?"

"I doubt it's the same species," Aziz countered. "But even if it is, it could be a matter of how the plant is processed, or the exact dosage. Whether it's a different plant, or just the knowledge of how to use it, the fact is that no one in Baharabad has ever had the means to treat their Sider that way. It doesn't follow that no one ever wanted to."

Seth thought of Elena, binding Irina in the hope of silencing her. And what would happen if a mob harassing a supposed Sleepwalker graduated from a supposed test of the condition to a supposed cure?

Amir said quietly, "We need to be stronger than Thanton. We need to swallow this whole and spit out the poison, without being poisoned ourselves."

For a while everyone was silent, but then Judith replied, "That's what we need, but need alone is not enough to make it true."

SETH HAD FEARED THAT the problem of Thanton might keep him from sleep, but he lost consciousness the moment he lay down and didn't stir until Amir nudged him and he opened his eyes to see that it was already mid-morning. Theo woke, under protest. «We're owed two nights and a day.»

«When we're home,» Seth promised.

Everyone else had already eaten breakfast, and Sarah and Raina had taken down their tent. Seth ate quickly, then helped Amir finish packing.

As they set out again, Seth felt stronger for the rest, but his disquiet had deepened. "Maybe some other expedition will have found a river closer to home," he said. Then Thanton and its poisonous forest need never be more than the subjects of an obscure travelers' tale.

"Anything's possible," Judith conceded.

"It's unlikely," Raina declared. "Sedington would have found it first, and even if they didn't want to share the news, I doubt they'd be digging for groundwater quite so energetically if they had."

"You really believe that?" Sarah sounded angry. "We're the only team that ever stood a chance?"

"That's why I asked for the job," Raina replied. "After the steamlands, they offered me my pick. And I wasn't going to waste my time on anything but the farthest to the west."

"So why are you wasting your time now?"

"What do you mean?" Raina didn't seem offended, just perplexed.

Sarah said, "We haven't gone as far to the west as we might have. Why come all this way, only to turn around at the first opportunity, when we could keep going and look for something better?"

Seth was expecting Raina to respond with a curt, dismissive rebuke: they'd fulfilled their duty as surveyors, and Thanton was a problem for the diplomats to solve.

But instead, she was silent for a long time before replying, "Why don't we put it to a vote?"

Theo said, "We can't lie about Thanton, vote or no vote."

"I'm not suggesting that," Raina assured him. "But Sarah's made a fair point: there's no reason why we can't return with more than one option. If there's a second river farther to the west, and it's unclaimed, or the locals are friendlier, that could make the migration a thousand times easier. It won't be a matter of concealing anything: the wiser choice will be obvious."

Aziz said, "Nobody's dragging me back toward Thanton again."

Raina had no such intention. "We can stay on the north side of the forest until we're far to the west of Thanton, then we can head down toward the steamlands. If they've sent people after us, that would be the perfect way to lose them; they'd never expect us to loop around like that."

Seth listened with mixed emotions. He was eager to get home, and Baharabad needed to escape the drought by whatever means possible. The search for the perfect river could not go on forever.

But the taint of Thanton was no small thing. He wanted to believe that the vast majority of his fellow citizens would prove honorable, but the whole of Baharabad didn't need to succumb for the poison to wreak havoc. If his job was to find the best path for the city, it would not be complete until he was sure he hadn't needlessly risked engendering disharmony between Walkers and Siders.

Amina said, "You know my position. We need to come back in force and deal with this sickness once and for all: occupy the city, impose our own laws, harvest every noxious plant and burn it. It might take generations before these people's descendants are normal again, but if we don't act now, the problem is only going to spread."

"And from where will you raise this occupying force," Judith wondered, "in which every last Walker will do what you demand, without a trace of sympathy for the people you expect them to control?"

"Fuck their sympathy," Amina replied. "They'll follow orders or face the consequences."

"Or rebel and make common cause with Thanton," Judith countered. "The more harshly we treat Thanton, the more we risk turning our own Walkers against us. As you say, it's going to take generations, but a far safer way would be to live apart from these people, while offering them a chance to migrate to a more prosperous city if they're willing to change their ways."

Amina was scathing. "So you want this abomination ended *on a strictly voluntary basis?*"

Judith was undeterred. "If possible. We should at least try that, and see how it goes. Apart from anything else, it might take us a while to learn how to deal with adult Siders who've been drugged for their whole life. Better to start with dozens whose Walkers will cooperate with the process, than thousands whose Walkers will frustrate it in every way they can."

By mid-afternoon, as they passed to the north-east of the forest, everyone had had their say many times over. Every argument had been expounded in detail, every counter-argument raised, criticized, elaborated and dismissed.

Raina called a vote.

Amina and Aziz, unswayed by the debate, still wanted to return to Baharabad immediately. But the rest of the team voted to head west and continue the search.

10

ALONG THE EDGE OF the steamlands, a narrow, verdant band
stretched as far to the east and west as the eye could see. To the
north lay barren, windswept sand, to the south an expanse of desiccated mud where the night's rain had pitted the ground then vanished in the heat of day. But weaving through the lush grass between
them, a thousand tiny creeks glinted in the sun.

As the expedition drew closer, the sight of this vast corridor of
greenery filled Seth with hope. It was true that all the creeks in his
immediate view dried out as they ran into the desert, because their
flow was divided so finely, shared along so many paths. But how
rare could it be for weather and landscape to conspire to consolidate
these trickles into something more resilient?

They trudged westward through the enervating heat, skirting
the northern edge of the grassland. In Theo's view, Seth could see
the vegetation quivering as mice and lizards fled from unfamiliar
footsteps. The shiny streams that had caught his eye from a distance
proved almost comically warm and shallow; when he squatted down
to try to fill his canteen, instead of immersing the container he had
to scoop water in with the lid. The grass had a tough, slippery coat-
ing, unlike anything he'd encountered before, and when he tried to
pick and eat a berry the first task almost broke his fingers and he
abandoned the second before it damaged his teeth. He'd been wondering why no one chose to live in this borderland, but even if they

could acclimate to the heat, the problem would be to coax something edible into growing here.

When evening approached they could hear the rain begin falling to the east, and as they set up their tents the distant patter grew nearer, but only the faintest spray touched their skin. Theo's pings to the south could just reach the edge of the downpour; much later, Seth woke in the darkness to the sound of water flowing nearby.

When they set out again, shortly after dawn, the creeks were running ankle deep, but by mid-morning Seth was ladling water with his canteen lid again. Threads of shimmering liquid criss-crossed his view, far into the distance; for all he knew, this outlook continued unchanged halfway around the world. But beneath the hot sun his thirst was incessant, and if no one could die from lack of water here, however much he drank he never felt that his need had been slaked.

The next night, when the noise of the runoff dragged him from sleep, Seth rose and went to refill his canteen. A part of him understood that the amount he had on hand could easily have lasted until morning, but the urgency that the task took on by daylight had entrenched itself too deeply to ignore.

«I should make you do this blind,» Theo grumbled, but he pinged the nearest rivulet and guided Seth's footsteps toward it through the clumps of grass.

As they made their way back, Seth saw Raina and Amina standing in the open, very still.

Amina said, "There's a huge storm to the west."

"Where?" Seth asked.

"Too far to see, but I can hear it."

He waited for confirmation from his Sider, but Theo could only defer to Amina's expertise.

Seth said, "That's a good sign, surely?"

"It was there last night," Raina replied. "If it repeats for a few more nights, then it's probably a feature of the landscape, not just a vagary of the weather."

As Seth lay down again and tried to sleep, he pictured the distant rain battering the ground. If the topography was unfavorable, all that water might flow south into the depths of summer and be lost.

But his thirst would draw it north, whether it flowed with gravity's help or not. His thirst alone was strong enough to make a river.

"THE STORM'S STILL STRIKING the same place, but we've passed it to the west."

Seth glanced toward Sarah and Amir to try to judge their reaction to Raina's verdict, but their faces were locked in the same rigid expression that he felt on his own: a kind of preemptive tightening that reminded them all not to open their mouths and lose the slightest trace of moisture unless it was absolutely necessary.

"That's it, then?" Theo asked indignantly. "For seven days you've been telling us that it's the biggest downpour you've ever heard . . . and now we're meant to believe that it's falling without a trace?"

"It's clear that there's no river," Amina replied. "Wherever the stormwater's going, it's not getting out of the steamlands."

Judith said, "Not right now—but we don't know how small a shift it might take to change that."

"Or not," Amina countered. "If it's falling on a long southward rise, whether the storm maintains its solar latitude, or whether it's tied more strongly to the topography, nothing's going to bring that water north."

"So we need to find out," Judith insisted. "We don't turn around and go home without knowing the answer."

Aziz said, "You want to go into the steamlands and map this storm's catchment area?"

"Yes."

Seth looked to Raina. "It should be possible," she said. "We know more or less where it is, and I don't believe it's so far south that it's unreachable."

"Then we need to do this," he replied. Raina and Amina had survived their trip into the northern steamlands; with that experience to guide them, what was there to fear? "Can we put it to a vote?"

Raina said, "We can vote, but I'm not forcing anyone to go in, no matter what the majority decide."

"So it's a matter of who volunteers?" Sarah asked.

"Yes."

The vote fell exactly the same way as the last one: only Amina and Aziz were against proceeding. But this time, their power of veto over their Walkers doubled the effective size of their bloc. Seth and Theo, Sarah and Judith were free to walk into the steamlands, but Raina, with all her experience, had no choice but to stay behind.

«I bet you'd like some of those Thanton puffballs to hand out right now,» Theo said dryly.

«Don't even joke about it.»

Raina said, "If you travel at night and take shelter in the daytime, you ought to be able to get the whole thing done in two nights and a day."

SETH SAT RESTING ON the east side of his tent, watching its shadow grow longer. His pack was prepared, with a minimum of food and four empty canteens. Even if they didn't find the storm before sunrise, the ordinary night rains would be more than enough to fill the containers.

«Remember when we thought that crossing the midwinter circle would make us surveyors?» he asked Theo.

«It did.»

«No, we're only surveyors if we find a place where the city can flourish. Anything less, and we're just two idiots who went for a long hike.»

«Whatever maps we take back to Baharabad,» Theo said, «the city's not going to perish. We might end up sharing a river with Thanton, or we might end up making some deal to join the Orico, but we're too big to die.»

«Not like all those cities in the history books?»

«Their people didn't die, they just found new homes.»

«Some of them,» Seth conceded. «Not all.»

As sunset drew near, he went looking for Sarah and Judith. He found them at the edge of the camp, talking to Raina and Amina.

"What's the one thing you forgot to tell us because it was too obvious?" he asked Raina.

"Don't get lost?" she suggested.

"That sounds right." Seth had grown used to finding his way back and forth across near-featureless deserts, but if he was going to be sidling through driving rain over ground endlessly reshaped by mudflows, he could not rely on old habits to fulfill even that basic tenet.

He tipped his head back to face Sarah and Judith.

Sarah said, "We're ready."

THE CREEKS NEAR THE campsite had all but dried out, but the four surveyors followed the widest slick of water south, since it marked a clear path through the vegetation. They moved without talking, concentrating on their footing. Seth could hear the rain starting in the east as twilight swept over the steamlands.

By the time they crossed from grassland to mud, dusk had robbed Seth of his own vision, while the warm, heavy rain played havoc with Theo's. The sheer density of the droplets was surreal; it was like being enfolded in endless layers of beaded curtains. South of the steamlands, water could not exist at all as a separate fluid—but vast quantities were present in latent form, dissolved in the searing air. When winds from the south carried that air to cooler climes the water would precipitate out, and the steamlands were first in line, generating more rain than anywhere else. All it would take to start a river here would be a reliable fall and a suitable catchment— modest requirements for an outcome that could bring prosperity to thousands of people. Seth was inured to the world's indifference to his needs, but this did not seem too much to hope for from chance alone.

«Can you hear it?» Theo asked.

«Hear what?» To Seth, the rain around them dominated every sense. He shook his head to try to clear Theo's pingers, and for an instant their surroundings grew sharper, but a moment later the membranes were drenched again.

«Amina's storm. It sounds almost subterranean.»

Seth stood still and listened through his bones; either the distant pounding of the storm was hovering at the edge of his perception, or he was letting himself succumb to Theo's suggestion. *Subterranean?* «Maybe the sound travels better through rock than through air.» He started sidling again, catching up with Sarah and Judith.

As they slogged their way south across the softening mud, the trembling in the ground intensified.

"Am I confused," Seth shouted, "or have we been going downhill ever since we entered the steamlands?" It was a subtle slope, hard to judge by foot alone in the dark, but now he'd spent at least an hour splashing through trickling water that was all flowing north.

"That's right," Sarah yelled back.

The trickles had grown stronger as the night wore on, but now, though the rain around them was steady, the runoff was actually lessening, suggesting that as they moved south they were seeing the flow from a smaller catchment.

"So why isn't the storm sending anything north?" he asked.

"We must be coming to the bottom of a valley. The storm must be falling on the opposite slope."

Seth couldn't argue with her logic, and he couldn't expect Theo to be pinging that distant slope through the rain. But if the storm was battering one side of a valley, and they were near the bottom, he would have expected the sound to be coming from somewhere higher than the rock beneath their feet.

Still, the long northward rise could serve as a conduit to bring the stormwater out of the steamlands, if it ever found its way across the valley. Once they'd mapped the whole area for the hydrologists to study, there might yet be hope of a new river for Baharabad.

Judith shouted, "Stop!"

Seth complied, peering into Theo's view to try to discern the cause of her concern. For most of the night the ground a dozen paces ahead had been rendered indistinct by the intervening rain, so he'd focused all his attention on closer terrain, where the view was sharper and the need for information more pressing.

But now, just before the point where Theo's valiant attempts to ping the ground lost their battle with the rain, it looked very much as if the ground itself had ceased participating in the process. It wasn't so much shrouded or blurred as absent.

Seth sidled a couple of steps closer. If they'd reached the bottom of a rain-soaked valley, there might be some unusual scouring process at work where the runoff switched direction—not just carrying mud away, but carving a pit into the rock itself.

From his new vantage point he could confirm, at least, that this wasn't some narrow trench they could step over: as far to the south as Theo could show him, the ground remained too low to ping. But the pit might have been a dozen paces wide, or a hundred.

"Let's see if we can get around it," Sarah suggested.

They headed east cautiously, walking into darkness but letting the edge of the pit guide them. Seth watched the trickles of water that disappeared and reappeared in Theo's view, alert for any sudden disparity suggesting more broken ground.

No new hazards appeared in front of them, but the sharp drop on their right persisted. After half an hour, Seth lost patience. "This thing might go on forever, but how deep can it be? Maybe we can clamber down into it and sidle across." If it had been filled with water, they would have heard rain striking the surface.

Sarah said, "Why not throw something in and count the time till it hits bottom?"

Seth squatted down and scrabbled in the mud; eventually he found a stone the size of his hand. For a trial run he tossed it straight up, and though the thump when it landed—at a count of two—was soft, he didn't doubt that Theo and Judith could pick up the same sound from a much greater distance.

«Ready?» he asked Theo.

«Yes.»

He threw it to his right, and had no trouble tracking it past the edge of the pit before it dropped out of sight. But the pronouncement of landfall never came.

Seth moved closer, but learned nothing new: all Theo could show him beyond the edge was rain falling through air.

"How far away is dawn?" he asked Sarah.

"It can't be long now."

They struggled to set up their tent in the mud, to be sure they'd have shelter once the sun rose. The interior would be like an oven by noon, but for now there was no reason not to sit inside and rest.

The rain on the cloth was deafening, and the floor was barely drier than the ground outside, but the sheer achievement of carving this artificial space out of the downpour raised Seth's spirits a little.

When the first hints of light showed through the seams, Sarah crawled out and Seth followed her. The eastern sky was brightening, with the glow of the impending dawn farther to the north than he had ever seen it. The rain was already much sparser than it had been in the night, but as they sidled toward the pit enough remained to imbue the scene with a sense of scale—and for as far as Theo could ping the droplets, they were falling unimpeded.

Seth moved closer and looked to the west. In the distance, there was enough of a curve to the edge for part of the drop to become visible—and by the scattered light of the pale pre-dawn sky, the rock face appeared vertical. "*We're on a cliff?*"

"Apparently," Sarah agreed.

Seth sidled a few steps nearer to the edge, and set his feet wide to raise his head, but with the ground nearby blocking the view it was still impossible to see down to the bottom of the cliff. "How deep is this thing?" he marveled.

"And how wide?" Theo added.

Seth shifted his attention from the northern face to the empty space beside it. If they'd been standing on the edge of some kind of canyon, the laws of perspective should have brought the southern face into view eventually, more or less converging with its partner toward some vanishing point. But beyond the revelatory bend in the cliff, all he could make out between west and south-west was a pale haze, scarcely different from the sky above. Like the rock face, there was no bottom to it, just a point where it was obscured by the foreground. For all he could tell, the land might never return to its normal altitude.

"So the storm was somewhere out there," he mused, gesturing to the south, "hitting whatever's at the bottom of this cliff. The drop can't be as deep as it looks, then, or how would the sound of the rain have reached us?"

Theo said, "What if the ground at the bottom slopes up to the north? We might not have been hearing the rain itself—we might have been hearing the runoff hit the cliff face."

"Maybe." Seth pictured the downpour falling on the slope, running uphill and crashing into the natural dam of the cliff face, forcing it to spill back and cycle around. It would be a bit like the waterfall in Thanton's forest, but all its energy would end up being used to pound the cliff. If what they'd been hearing was a trick of the topography amplifying the sound of the rain, there was no need for an actual storm.

He felt the heat of the first rays of sunlight biting into his skin. The rain had stopped and the ground was already drying out. They moved back beside the tent and prepared to spend the day following its shadow; even at noon, the sun would be so low in the north that the modest structure would offer some protection.

"Those cliffs would make perfect sunshades," Seth realized. "If we could get to the bottom, there'd be no direct sunlight, any time of day."

"Get to the bottom, how?" Sarah replied. "Even back at the camp, there's nothing like the length of rope we'd need."

"So we sit here all day, and then go back empty-handed?" Seth could hear the mud crackling around him as it surrendered its water to the heat.

"As opposed to what?" Judith asked. "Walk the edge, looking for an easy path down, while your body dries to a husk?"

Seth stared at the ground, frustrated. "You're the one who wanted to find a place where we could maintain a healthy separation from Thanton."

"Not at the bottom of a cliff," she retorted. "We don't even know that there's a storm here, let alone have any reason to think it will drift north. As the steamlands move south, they'll take the rain with them, and this will be nothing but an obscure place on the map, marked as an obstacle to future migration."

Theo said, "But aren't you curious as to just how big an obstacle it is?"

"No one's carrying a city over the edge," Judith replied. "We don't need to know precisely how tall the cliffs are, to be sure of that."

"So what would the alternative be?" Theo pressed her.

"It might be a good idea to go around them."

"And what kind of detour would that entail?"

Judith hesitated. "It will be important to know that, eventually," she conceded. "But we're in no position to follow the cliffs and see how far they extend. We seem to be at their northernmost point; if we pursued them much farther we'd be too deep into summer. We can send an expedition to map them once they're more accessible."

"Suppose we do that," Theo replied. "We wait until autumn arrives here, so it's an easy journey following the cliffs west. But we find that they don't come to an end, or turn to the south sharply enough to let us pass. They just keep on running *geographically* west, which takes them back into summer, but doesn't allow any kind of detour that puts them behind us once and for all. Instead, we're forced to keep veering to the west—until that becomes a problem in itself, because the habitable zone is too narrow."

Judith laughed. "So you think this escarpment could stretch so far that it would block the entire western half of the migration? That sounds unlikely, but even if it were true, there'd be tens of thousands of people prepared to build roads down to the lowlands."

"And if that proved impossible?" Theo persisted. "If the cliffs were too high?"

"Then we'd just have to migrate to the east."

"Suppose the same thing happens to the east."

"Now you're being absurd."

Seth looked up at the ground beyond the shadow of the tent. The night's puddles and rivulets had been transformed into arid depressions, but between them in places were some oddly delicate structures: arches and domes of once-damp soil that had dried out and become hollow, but were yet to collapse. He raised his canteen to his mouth before opening the lid just enough to allow the water to escape; even as it ran down his throat, he pictured half of what he'd swigged vanishing into the air before his parched body could absorb it.

Sarah said, "If these cliffs block our way from node to node, we'll deal with them. It's as simple as that. If it's a matter of life and death, any feat of engineering would be worth the effort."

"Of course," Theo conceded. "All I'm trying to say is that we need to determine exactly what we've found here."

Seth had been listening to the conversation without much interest; if they couldn't offer Baharabad the prospect of a second river, everything else was idle speculation. But Theo was rarely so persistent or argumentative just for the sake of it; there was always some kind of logic behind even his wildest blathering.

"Why do you think the cliffs could stretch so far?" Seth challenged him. "If you have some theory, spit it out."

Theo was silent for a while, as if the answer was a guilty secret that he was reluctant to disclose. Then he said, "Have we actually seen the bottom of them? Do we have any idea how deep that drop is?"

"No," Sarah replied. "But you're changing the subject: the question was how far they extend east and west."

"The thing is," Theo insisted, "we don't even know that they're cliffs. There's an edge to the level ground, then a drop. That's all we can be sure of."

Sarah groaned with exasperation. "There's an edge, and a drop . . . and then there must be lowlands, whether you can ping them or not. And if these aren't cliffs, what else could they be?"

"The edge," Theo replied.

"The edge of a plateau?" Sarah suggested.

"No."

"The edge of the high ground, the edge of the tablelands . . .?" Sarah was losing patience. "Whatever you like, it makes no difference."

Theo said ruefully, "Believe me, this is not what I'd like. But we need to contemplate the possibility that we've reached the edge of the world."

PART THREE

11

SETH WOKE EARLY BUT knew he was unlikely to fall back to sleep, so he headed out for a pre-dawn stroll, taking the opportunity to stretch his legs before the heat became too oppressive. On his way back, the sky had grown bright enough that he could see the whole encampment spread out before him, a patchwork of coarse fabric pinned to the dusty hillside.

«There must be two hundred tents,» he realized. «When did that happen?»

«You know what they say,» Theo replied. «It takes a village to raise a surveyor.»

At this time of day, the food hall wasn't crowded. Seth joined a group of artisans from Sedington, whom he'd seen before but never had a chance to talk to. They told him that they'd heard Raina and Amina speak about the project at a meeting in their town, and decided that it was worth the trip for the guarantee of work.

"It's a bit of an adventure for us, coming this far west," James, the chattiest of the group's Walkers, explained. "But I hope you fools know what you're doing." The remark sounded neither disdainful, nor simply a matter of good-natured teasing; rather, his tone carried a mixture of incredulity and genuine concern.

"We trust your sewing," Theo replied.

"I'm a rope-maker," James corrected him.

"Then I hope we can trust that, too."

"Oh, here come the half-heads," Margaret whispered. Seth glanced toward the entrance; four traders from Thanton had entered the tent.

"Be civil," James chided her. Seth wasn't sure if this was a serious admonition, or a sarcastic recitation of the instructions they'd all received from their superiors.

A single bench ran north-to-south along the hall. When the traders had collected their food they chose the northern end, as far from the artisans as possible, but any ordinary conversation by one group would still be well within the hearing of the others.

The artisans began joking about the foibles of various members of their own community, so Seth did his best to grant them his full attention and listen with an air of polite amusement. Experience had taught him that if he allowed himself to take in any of the Thantonites' small talk he'd be at risk either of hearing something so blatantly offensive that he'd struggle to conceal his revulsion, or of seizing upon something ambiguously sinister and spending the rest of the day obsessing about it.

Theo inspoke, «I was watching closely, and I'm fairly sure they didn't sprinkle puffballs over the buffet.»

«I don't like doing business with them any more than you do,» Seth replied. «But if we'd shunned all trade with Thanton, the whole project would have taken ten times longer.»

«I know. And I'm glad they're here, in person.»

«Why?»

«Because whatever we learn about the edge, it will be clear to them that they're getting the same story as everyone else. If we'd tried to send a delegation later, armed with pronouncements about the likely future of their river, they could have dismissed all our claims as self-serving misinformation.»

The artisans had finished eating, so they bid farewell to Seth and Theo and departed. One of the west-facing traders glanced in Seth's direction, as if contemplating an introduction, but Seth lowered his gaze and concentrated on his food.

"YOU MUST BE EXCITED!" Raina enthused, as they approached the work site. "All the doubters could soon be eating their words."

"Or it could go badly," Theo replied, "and I'll be a joke in thirty cities."

"The people who backed you are the ones who'd look most foolish," Amina decided. "It's one thing to come up with a wild idea that turns out to be wrong, but nobody forced those merchants to invest in it."

"I'm not sure that humiliating the wealthy would work in my favor," Theo mused. "I believe there've been a few occasions in history where that didn't turn out so well."

From a distance, to Seth the assembly of fabric panels laid out over the ground looked a bit like a second camp, smaller than the one they'd left but so crowded that it was impossible to tell where one tent stopped and its neighbor began. Almost anything was more plausible than a single piece of material the size of half a dozen city blocks, and his mind could only accept the truth once the evidence was entirely unambiguous. Today, as he drew nearer he could see that the furnace had already been lit, sending currents of hot air wafting into the structure, raising the panels in synchronized undulations that no tent village could possibly exhibit.

They paused on the slope to watch the balloon fill out a little more. As the center rose the western rim was drawn in, while the other free edges pushed farther north and south, keeping the upper surface more or less taut. On the eastern side the balloon was attached to the furnace room, a long stone building into which a relay of workers could be seen conveying timber from a heap outside.

"That's got to be the toughest job of all," Seth declared. "We should show our appreciation to those people."

"Of course," Raina agreed.

They walked down toward the furnace room, past the hill-sized wood-heap. The sheer scale of it was even more striking once it resolved into individual logs, which summoned up thoughts of all the individual ax blows that had been struck in the service of its formation. One of the suppliers had told Seth that each trial consumed more fuel than the Baharabad bath-house used in a hundred days, which had only compounded his discomfiting sense of the magnitude of the whole endeavor. Theo was afraid of being laughed at, but what weighed most on Seth's mind was the possibility that they'd end up having wasted people's time.

Even a few paces from the building's entrance, the heat was intolerable. Seth stood back, looking in toward the soot-encrusted vestibule, while a woman finished loading the feeder with wood and dispatched it into the furnace. Despite all the seals and interlocked doors working to ensure a one-way journey for the fuel, a gale of hot, smoky air rushed out of the chute, filling half the vestibule before slamming the empty feeder back into place and blocking its own egress.

"We want to thank you for your hard work!" Seth shouted, struggling to make himself heard over the pounding of the flames on the furnace walls. "If we succeed tomorrow, it will be your efforts that raised us!"

Most of the people in the relay ignored him, but the grimy-faced woman who'd just worked the feeder paused to regard the visitors with amusement. "Better you than me up there," she said. Her Sider added, "I know which one of us is at the greater risk of being barbecued."

"The scamper survived uncooked," Amina pointed out.

"Did you ever try cooking one, to see what it took?" the Sider retorted. Seth was about to laugh, but then he realized that she had a point: no one really knew whether the animal's heat tolerance was the same as a person's.

They left the furnace room and sidled north to check on the first anchor point. Seth had joined the rope team here for two of the trials, but as he walked between the tents, the people he'd joked with only days before—most of them movers from Baharabad, who'd abandoned any notion of professional rivalry to welcome this mere surveyor into their ranks—now seemed guarded and ill at ease in his presence. He greeted everyone, but then made his excuses and joined Raina and Amina as they went through their usual round of inspections.

The rope was coiled on a single flat reel, mounted on a spindle that pointed horizontally north-to-south at present, but whose bearings allowed it to tilt and swivel. Seth followed Raina up the stairs of the supporting frame, from where she proceeded to run her fingers along the curved wooden rails that enabled the spindle to tip, checking that nothing was loose, warped, or insufficiently lubricated. Any structure with so many moving parts seemed like an invitation for one of them to fail, but Seth could see no way around the complexity. It had been necessary to make the rope as stiff as possible in the axial direction, or it would have been useless at constraining the balloon's range of motion: free to depart from a taut, straight line into one that curved to the north or south, a fixed length of rope would have been able to reach any altitude at all, with the axial detour's negative contribution balancing the extra height. But this rod-like stiffness in the crucial dimension meant that the rope could not be wound into a more compact, helical arrangement on a barrel-shaped spool, and the entire flat coil needed to tip to accommodate the changing position of the rope's endpoint. In a perfect world, the tilting mechanism might have coped unaided as the rope unspooled, but in reality it took half a dozen people watching over it to keep any problems in check—and for the reverse process, the whole team of twenty had to work non-stop to give the balloon a relatively smooth descent.

"Everything seems fine here," Raina declared. "But feel free to check it yourselves."

"I trust you," Seth replied.

"And the truth," Theo added, "is that if we start fretting about everything we haven't verified in person, we'll end up far too anxious to step into the basket."

"Fair enough." Raina descended the stairs, but Seth lingered on the frame, not so much belying Theo's claim as taking comfort in the structure's bulk and solidity.

"The one bad thing that always happens in my dreams," he confessed, "is that the anchors all break free of the ground and rise into the air, while the balloon drifts upward toward absolute summer."

Amina said, "If that does happen, you'll be famous for rewriting half a dozen laws of physics before reaching your death."

"That's comforting," Seth replied. He started down the stairs, trying not to dwell on the fact that a couple of snapped ropes could deliver the same endpoint far more easily, and with none of the glory.

AS NIGHT APPROACHED, SETH heard the rain spreading across the steamlands, but at the work site the air remained calm. He sat on the hillside in the twilight and watched the balloon floating beside the furnace room like a giant, inverted piece of fruit, its skin rippling and wrinkling as it swelled and ripened from the heat. A dozen short ropes restrained it, sparing the three anchors for now.

He heard footsteps approaching from the east, then Raina called out, "We have visitors!"

When Seth saw who accompanied her, he rose to his feet. "Welcome to the edge of madness. Are your husbands with you? And the children?"

"No, but Amir and Aziz send their good wishes." Sarah clasped Seth's shoulder in greeting.

Judith added, "They were tempted to make the journey, but it wouldn't have been fair on our parents to expect them to look after the children for so long."

Theo said, "You've arrived just in time: one day later, and you would have missed history being made."

"Nothing's over in a day," Judith replied.

«Meaning what?» Theo wondered, before asking aloud, "Have you volunteered to do follow-up measurements?"

Sarah said, "We're here to help in any way we can."

"It's a long way to come without a definite plan!" Theo seemed to be doing his best to sound friendly, but he couldn't entirely erase the suspicion from his voice. He addressed Seth in private. «Why do I get the feeling that the armchair surveyors in Baharabad have already decided what comes next?»

«Paranoia?»

«Were you asleep through all the politics and infighting when I was trying to sell them on the project?»

«Quite possibly,» Seth admitted. Some of the meetings had lasted for hours, and since Theo had done most of the talking, it had only seemed fair to let him do most of the listening as well.

Sarah said, "Whatever you find, there's sure to be more work to be done here. But I'm glad we arrived in time to wish you luck."

"Thank you," Seth replied.

Theo said, "Thanks for your good wishes—but if we find what I'm expecting, the work to be done will all be elsewhere."

Judith laughed. "You think you get to make all the rules now?"

"It's the world that makes the rules," Theo retorted. "Or are those cliffs just a figment of my vanity?"

"We'll only know what they are when we've mapped them properly," Judith insisted. "But even if your guess turns out to have been right, that doesn't turn your every whim into some kind of decree."

Seth said, "I'm not going to spend what might be my last night alive listening to two bickering Siders. If you want to keep arguing, do it in your own language."

There was an awkward silence, then Raina spoke. "I'll be back in a little while, and we can go through the basket checks together."

"Of course," Seth replied.

As Raina and Sarah walked away back up the hill, Theo said, «If you're having second thoughts, we don't need to do this. There are plenty of people who'd be willing to take our place.»

«Fuck off.» Seth gazed at the balloon; the upper half, into which the hottest air fresh from the furnace had risen, was taut now, the skin stretched out as far as it could go. The thought of the impending journey terrified him, but he was trapped by his own vanity, not Theo's. «You're the one who doesn't need to do this,» he said. «You could crawl out for the duration and wait on the ground. This is all about light; you wouldn't be missed.»

«I'm not worried at all,» Theo declared brashly. «Everything's been tested a dozen times. We'll be safer tomorrow than we ever were stumbling about near the edge of the cliffs in the rain.»

«Maybe.» To back out now would be humiliating—but Seth had decided that the worst thing would be to back out and then watch their replacements die. So the more afraid he was that the ascent might go badly, the less choice he had.

AN HOUR BEFORE DAWN, Seth climbed into the basket and moved into position, lying face-down over the observation bay. He could smell the soil an arm's length below the aperture, but all Theo could show him were his own hands beside two slates; the sides of the basket were so high that even the edges couldn't be pinged from here.

"Are you comfortable?" Raina asked, standing beside him.

"As much as I'll ever be."

"Try reaching the alidade," she suggested.

Seth maneuvered his right hand through the access hole and groped around for the sighting bar. Once he was touching it, he picked up a pencil with his left hand and scribbled a few random figures at the top of the slate. Theo pinged the thick residue clearly enough, and the numbers appeared legible. "It's fine," he said. He'd practiced all of these tasks many times, but there was still something reassuring about the last-minute checks.

"All right," Raina said. "See you soon."

Seth listened to the squeaking of the boarding ladder as she departed. When she was gone, all he could hear was the slow wheezing of the balloon itself, like a giant in poor health standing over him, trying unsuccessfully to breathe quietly.

Theo, though, had heard something more. «Here we go!» he announced excitedly, sounding as untroubled as if they were about to sled up a ramp.

The restraint ropes were cut in rapid succession, sending the basket tipping unevenly until it was free. The balloon rose up smoothly for a second or two, then it jerked and swung westward a short distance before finding itself suddenly constrained again. Seth braced himself and waited for the motion to die down, glad that it was still too dark for him to see the ground shifting below.

Eventually the balloon settled, having found the spot where all three anchor ropes were taut. In the stillness, Seth felt his fear abating. Give or take the effects of the wind, the teams on the ground could now control his position by choosing how much rope to dispense from each reel. He trusted the rope teams, having witnessed their discipline first-hand—and if he'd marveled at the elegance of the positioning system when he'd merely been watching from the ground, here, even in the darkness, he felt the consequences more viscerally than ever. *Three hyperboloids with three different centers intersected in a single point.* That geometric theorem was keeping him from drifting away into the summer sky.

The unreeling began, and the balloon rose and shifted, smoothly for the most part, sometimes in fits and starts. Seth stared down through the observation bay at the dark land spread out beneath him, where the blackness was beginning to give way to hints of desert hills in the predawn light. The exact scale was difficult to judge, and for all he knew thousands of people might have enjoyed higher vantage points from various mountainsides. But if his altitude alone was as yet unexceptional, his separation from the ground was already surreal.

The balloon wanted nothing more than to ascend, but the rope teams offered it a deal: it could only gain altitude by moving south. Below, slender threads of pale gray appeared, water reflecting the brightening sky. When the strip of vegetation beside the steamlands slid into view, Seth felt a giddy thrill at the sheer speed and effortlessness of the journey. On foot, it would have taken him at least half a day to come this far—and for all their labors, the rope teams had only dispensed a tiny fraction of the horizontal distance he'd covered.

«We were right to thank the furnace workers,» he told Theo. If anyone's exertions had been commensurate with this result, it was theirs.

Vegetation gave way to mud flats, still damp and glistening in places, though the dustier, desiccated regions were growing visibly larger as he watched. At the sight, Seth became conscious of the heat, which had arrived with such speed that he'd had no time to dwell on it. The sides of the basket shielded him from any possibility of direct sunlight, but his altitude alone thrust him even deeper into summer than the parched land below. Still, the temperature was not intolerable—and if a scamper could complete the journey and return unsinged, he had no reason to start fretting when his own trip had barely begun.

«Almost, almost,» Theo muttered. Seth shifted his shoulders and tried to make himself ready; he'd been lying so still that all his muscles had grown stiff.

The cliffs came into view on his right, at the periphery of his vision, but the pace of the balloon left him with no time to grow impatient; if anything, he wished it could have moved more slowly, giving him a better chance to understand what he was seeing. The mud flats disappearing to the north remained crisp and comprehensible, but past the edge, in the gloom untouched by the dawn, he could find nothing for his eyes to fix on.

The ropes were slowed and locked; the basket lurched disconcertingly, but then stabilized, swinging gently. They had come to a halt just south of the edge, leaving Seth staring down at the sheer rock of the cliff face on his left, while below, and stretching to his right as far as he could see, was a shadowed landscape so dark and distant that only the constancy of its few discernible features convinced him that they were more than hallucinations, summoned by his eyes to puncture the monotony of the blackness.

«So it's not straight down forever,» he said numbly, as if that had ever been a real prospect. But finally glimpsing the floor—or shelf—that had stopped all the pebbles he'd tossed over the edge from actually falling all the way to the antipode was no small comfort.

«I think that gray patch in the upper right is something we can fix on,» Theo suggested, laudably businesslike in the face of the vertiginous spectacle beneath them. «Even when the background's not as dark, it should show enough contrast.»

«Right.» Seth reached out and brought the alidade into play, then sighted the pale feature and recorded its angle from the nadir. The light remained too dim for him to see the instrument's markings with his eyes, but the alidade was geared to a pointer on his left, which showed the angle on a dial that Theo could ping.

As the sky brightened, they chose another dozen points to record. Seth could only guess what kind of geology these distant smudges of contrast represented, but so long as they hadn't been fooled by pools of water that might shift or vanish, it didn't matter exactly what they were seeing.

«Notice anything to the south-west?» Theo asked.

Seth regarded the unmitigated blackness. «No.»

«Exactly. If this were flat ground, then the shadow of the cliffs would come to an end. Dawn would be breaking.»

«I'm not sure we could see that far.»

«If the ground slopes down, it will be even farther. And if the slope is steep enough, it might not happen at all.»

«Let's wait for the data,» Seth urged him.

«The absence of dawn isn't data?»

«It says something, but it's not quantitative yet.»

Theo laughed, undiscouraged. «All right, have it your way.»

The teams on the ground set to work again, reeling the balloon in to the west while dispensing more rope from the eastern anchor point. With the sun climbing higher, the scattered light was bringing out more details in the terrain below: forked gray streaks that might have been rivers, and sharp edges that might have marked further cliffs beyond the initial drop. Seth did his best to sketch the main features on the slate to his right, though drawing at this strange angle was even more difficult than scrawling numbers. A heavy mist—or perhaps a bank of clouds—drifted in from the south, and for a while he was afraid that it might obscure his sighting points, but it thinned and broke apart before it reached them.

When the balloon halted, Seth waited for it to stabilize, then he quickly repeated the measurements. He had no intention of trying to interpret these numbers before he was back on the ground, but his Sider had no qualms about trusting his own mental arithmetic.

«There's a clear slope down to the south,» Theo declared. «Almost forty-five degrees.»

Seth had expected a significant gradient, to explain the run-off battering the cliff face that Amina had taken for a storm. But *forty-five degrees* was not an angle much seen in geology. Any slab of rock that was initially horizontal was likely to encounter serious obstacles long before it was sloping more than ten or fifteen degrees north-to-south.

«Isn't that what I predicted?» Theo demanded gleefully. «Go deep enough, and the pressure from all the rock overhead can't be held in along a vertical face; there's nothing pushing back from the south. Eventually, the rock has to bulge out, spreading the change in pressure over a greater distance the deeper you go.»

«So it's some kind of hernia,» Seth conceded. Nothing had tilted to create the slope; it was a by-product of increasing amounts of horizontal slippage. «But we still don't know the size of the cavity into which the world's straining bowels have protruded.»

«You put it so poetically. You know my answer, though: there is no cavity. To the south of this, there's only air, and then the void.»

The heat was becoming harder to ignore. Seth pressed his foot against the lever that operated the cooling system, opening a grate that allowed droplets of water to fall onto his back. He kept the lever engaged for half a minute, then shut off the grate; the water gave him some relief, but the supply was limited.

The ropes were adjusted again, hauling the balloon even farther to the west. Seth could see rain falling now, from a patch of clouds that passed almost directly below. He watched the glistening runoff flowing uphill to the north, spilling rapidly across the dark rock, but before it reached the cliffs it struck a change of gradient that brought it to a halt. At one degree less than forty-five, water would rush up a slope, but at one degree more it could only move downhill. The illusory storm must have arisen from a long stretch of terrain where the slope had remained below the critical value all the way to the bottom of the cliffs.

Seth started the third set of measurements, still relying on Theo to ping the angles; the dial directly in front of him was no longer in darkness, but there was a glare behind it to which his eyes were forced to adjust, rendering the instrument illegibly dim in comparison. The distracting brightness did not seem to emanate from the land; there was still no sign of dawn breaking anywhere south of the cliffs, and he had already moved a screen into place to spare himself the sight of the sun-baked mud flats to the north. Eventually he understood that the glare could only have one source: the air below him, between the balloon and the boundary of the cliffs' shadow. The sunlight was so intense that even the tiny fraction being scattered his way was enough to dazzle him.

Theo recalculated the positions of the landmarks, and announced that his earlier conclusions remained unchallenged. «There'll be no crossing this, or skirting around it,» he said. «We need to halt the sun, or we're finished.»

«No one's going to accept that from one set of observations,» Seth cautioned him.

«Of course not,» Theo replied. «Let them do a dozen follow-ups if they want to. But do you honestly think they're going to find anything that will change the outcome?»

Seth had no energy to pursue the argument; all he could think about now was the heat. He slid the screen across the observation bay, blocking it completely, and sprayed his back with water again. «Reel us in,» he begged, as if the rope crews could read his mind and depart from their schedule. In the trials, he'd taken care not to rush his pretend measurements, to be sure that he'd have plenty of time to complete the real ones if anything went awry.

After a few minutes they began to move again, but Seth's relief was short-lived: even with the observation bay closed, he could tell from the way his body pressed against the floor that the balloon was *ascending*, rising up and heading south. Seconds later it halted abruptly, leaving the basket swinging. «What the fuck are they doing?» The churning in his gut went far beyond any physical effect of the ropes' unreeling. If the balloon could travel in entirely the wrong direction, then all his trust had been misplaced, all his confidence sheer naïveté.

Theo replied tentatively, «They might have stripped a ratchet. That brake was slammed hard: I heard the rope twang.»

Seth doused himself with water to clear his head. «That's possible.» The combined strength of each rope team was enough to counter the buoyancy of the balloon and reel it in, but it was the ratchet that kept them from surrendering their hard-won gains between bouts of exertion. Dragging on the rope then slamming down the brakes each time it began reversing wouldn't just be slow and inefficient: each sudden rise in tension risked damaging the rope—either severing it completely, or snapping the fibers that prevented axial buckling.

«How long do you think it would take them to replace it?» Theo asked.

«Half an hour. Maybe longer.»

Theo was silent. So far, he hadn't complained about the heat, but that didn't mean he wasn't feeling it.

«The real problem's the amount of tension,» Seth reasoned. «If we could lower that, they might be able to get us down without the ratchet.»

«You mean reduce the buoyancy?»

«Yes.» In the earliest tests, they'd aimed to have the air in the balloon cool quickly enough to facilitate its own descent, but that had left too fine a line between a successful ascent and a dangerous lack of buoyancy when it was needed. «We should have put a valve on top.» The consensus had been that that was dangerous, too, in case the control lines snagged and it opened prematurely.

Theo said, «But in the absence of a valve . . .?»

Seth rose to his knees and looked around the basket. There was a box of spare pencils and slates, three canteens of water, and a bag of bechelnuts. He glanced up at the underside of the balloon, squinting against the glare. The fabric of the panels was a tough triple-weave; a pencil wasn't going to pierce it.

«How is it possible that I don't have a knife?»

«What about the sighting bar?» Theo suggested.

Seth pulled the screen away from the observation bay and reached down to the stone bar that held the sights of the alidade. He strained against it, and managed to snap it out of the instrument frame. It was stronger than a wooden pencil, but much blunter; his only hope was to get the angle right.

He lay on his back and slid to the side until he could rest the bar against the top edge of the water tank. Then he shifted a little farther, in increments, tipping the bar to the south, bringing its far end closer to the underside of the balloon. When he finally made contact, the bar met the panel obliquely enough to present its corner to the fabric as a sharp point. Seth pushed as hard as he could, and felt something yield—but when he relaxed the pressure the bar rebounded. He was deforming the panel, not piercing it.

He climbed to his feet and took a swig of water from one of the canteens. He'd been holding off, afraid that once he started he'd never be satisfied, but if he was weak from dehydration it would be better to remedy that and put up with the cravings. He lay down again and rearranged the bar so that it stretched all the way from the floor of the basket to the underside of the balloon. Then he scraped the low end across the floor, tipping the bar and driving the high end higher.

The balloon remained intact.

Seth wedged his left arm under the bar and used his right to brace himself against the side of the water tank. Then he spread his arms, forcing the bar to tilt. In Theo's view, he could see that he'd carved a furrow into the basket's wooden floor—stretching almost to the north side. That was the limit: if he reached it there'd be nothing more he could do. He strained against the bar; it skittered over the wood, but he could feel it threatening to force its way back into the furrow.

«Next time, they'll put a valve in the balloon,» Seth predicted. «That will be the first recommendation from the inquest.»

Theo said, «What inquest? If the heat gets unbearable, you can slide down one of the anchor ropes.»

«There's a thought. Hang a chair from the rope with a hook and we could sell tickets for the ride down.» Seth lifted his shoulders from the floor and turned them, forcing the lower part of the bar a finger's width farther to the north. Above him, the wheezing giant started whistling.

He dropped his arms and lay staring up at the balloon. He couldn't see the hole he'd made, but it wouldn't take long to have an effect. Now they had to hope that someone was monitoring the ropes while the repair crew were focused on the ratchet.

The basket began swaying gently. The balloon wasn't falling, but the drop in tension was already freeing it from the need to sit precisely at the ropes' taut lengths from all three anchor points.

The undulations grew larger, punctuated by abrupt changes in direction that sent Seth sliding across the floor of the basket. «I think this is when I'd recommend closing the valve. Maybe I should write that down for the coroner?» The wind-tossed balloon now had time to pick up speed before bouncing off the invisible walls imposed by the new, less stringent constraints. That was surely as bad for the ropes as repeated braking down on the ground.

Theo said, «You should pack up the slates, so they don't get smashed.»

«Right.» Seth got to his feet and grabbed the water tank to steady himself, then he gathered up the slates with the measurements and jammed them into the same box as the spares. He lay down again, holding the box tightly against his chest as the basket weaved and swayed. «If you had to go, which would you prefer?» he asked Theo. «Fall or burn?»

«Fall.»

«Good choice.» The drop would certainly be terrifying, but perhaps the fear would be accompanied by a liberating thrill. Drifting up toward the solar cone might have sounded lovely and ethereal back at midwinter, but Seth was already as warm as he wanted to be for the entire remainder of his life.

The balloon lurched down, swung to the west, then hit the limits of the eastern rope and rebounded. But then gradually, over a minute or so, the motion settled into something so steady that it was barely perceptible.

Seth reversed onto his stomach and opened the observation bay. The glare was painful, but so was the brightness of the land below; the balloon had already been dragged north of the cliffs.

The trip back was not as smooth as the ascent, but Seth could tell from the long stretches that passed without anyone needing to brake the reels that the partially deflated balloon was proving easier to handle.

When the landing site came into view, there were a dozen people waiting. They grabbed hold of the dangling restraint ropes and hauled the balloon all the way down.

As Seth reached the top of the boarding ladder, Raina called out, "Are you all right?"

Seth's voice failed him, but Theo replied, "We're fine."

"See anything interesting?" Amina enquired.

Seth started laughing, though he wasn't sure why. Theo said, "A long drop, then a forty-five-degree slope."

Raina frowned, impatient for more. "And then?"

"That's it," Theo replied. "A forty-five-degree slope, as far as the eye can see."

12

Jonas said, "i've asked you here to talk about your next job. You've served the Office of Surveyors with great distinction, and I'm pleased to say that we're in a position to offer you no less than three choices."

"I'm honored," Theo replied. Seth added an awkward nod to indicate that he felt the same way. But it was Theo's ingenuity that had made the balloon observations possible, and it was Theo with whom the Director wished to discuss grand plans for the future of the migration. Jonas's own Sider was so reserved that Seth didn't even know his name, and in meetings like this Seth wished that he could make himself equally unobtrusive.

"The first possibility," Jonas continued, "is retirement on a full pension." Seth's desire for invisibility couldn't keep his astonishment from showing on his face; Raina exchanged a glance with him, more amused than reproving, that told him exactly how he looked. "The Baharabad Council has approved the offer, in recognition of the extraordinary contribution you've made to the city's interests."

Theo spoke, with a tone of bewilderment. "Why would we even think of—?"

"Please," Jonas raised a hand and cut him off. "Wait until you've heard all the options. And once you've heard them, don't rush to decide."

"Of course not," Theo said, courteous but unmistakably wary now.

Since hearing that Jonas had arrived in the camp, Theo's mood had been swinging wildly between anxiety and supreme self-confidence. With all the observations proving to be consistent with his theory, he had seemed convinced that anyone who saw the data—let alone the increasing number of surveyors who had seen the dark slope itself first-hand—would come around to his point of view. But at the same time, it had unsettled him that Jonas, like Sarah and Judith, had set out from Baharabad long before anyone knew what the observations would reveal. So what was the Director doing in this wretched outpost, whose sole function was to prove that all future efforts should be directed elsewhere?

"The second possibility," Jonas said, "lies at the western node." Seth managed to remain stony-faced this time, though it might have helped that the proposal, so far, was not so much surprising as incomprehensible.

"If the migration really is blocked to the south," Jonas explained, "we'll need to consider routes that the ancients believed were impassable. After all, the true width of the habitable zone is equal at every longitude. If the world was a smooth, featureless hyperboloid, there would be no obstacle to crossing the nodes."

Theo couldn't help taking a stab at where this counterfactual statement was leading. "You want to flood the western node? Turn it into a giant lake, and cross it by boat?"

It was Jonas's turn to be taken aback. "Full marks for lateral thinking, but I believe the water shortage precludes that."

«You could always make an offer to buy the Orico,» Seth joked.

«Fuck off.» Theo wasn't accustomed to the armchair surveyors being one step ahead of him, and nothing put him off balance faster than the threat that they might have out-reasoned him.

"We can't flood the terrain at the node," Jonas continued, "but there's another way to avoid the clash between the alignment of the habitable zone and the surface geology: stay high above the ground, where it doesn't matter if you're turned so far that each of your feet stretches across a thousand mountains and a thousand valleys. The plan is to build a bridge of balloons, from the westernmost point where the habitable zone lives up to that name on land, all the way across the node."

Jonas wasn't making eye contact, so Seth risked an "Are they serious?" glance at Raina; her response seemed to imply that they were. Theo managed to hold his silence for a couple of seconds, but then his frustration overpowered his self-control.

"Wouldn't you need to burn a dozen forests a day, just to keep a structure like that aloft?"

"It won't burn a twig," Jonas replied. "One of the observers of your own balloon project has proposed a way to keep the air heated by redirecting sunlight with slabs of polished stone. The construction will be a monumental effort on the part of surveyors, weavers, and engineers, but once it's built, it should require only maintenance and repairs, not an ongoing source of fuel."

"I see." Normally, Theo might have begged to hear the details of the new heating method, but Seth understood that all he cared about right now was confirmation that the best offer had been saved for last.

"Your third option," Jonas said, "would be to join the expedition to explore the chasm." He paused to give Theo a moment to accept that his own grand scheme was not on the list at all. "With the cliffs shielding the floor from the sun, it should be possible to follow the rift west, well past the point where the higher ground is uninhabitable."

"It's not a 'floor,'" Theo replied bluntly. "A floor is close to horizontal."

"Let's not quibble over terminology," Jonas suggested amiably. "You've found an expanse of low ground, and it should be traversable, if not easily. Given the height of the cliffs and the angle of the terrain, there's a chance to map the extent of this chasm long before it emerges from summer. While work on the bridge of balloons will continue for as long as any threat to the southern migration remains, this expedition has the potential to resolve all our doubts. Believe me, every surveyor in Baharabad wanted to join. But you and Seth have earned a place on it, and it's yours if you want it."

Having been mentioned, Seth felt it was his duty to fill the silence that followed. "Thank you," he said.

"Take your time," Jonas urged them. "Think it over, and give me an answer in five days."

He tipped his head away from them, and began conversing with Raina and Amina. Seth walked briskly out of the tent, not wanting to give Theo a chance to decide that he'd have nothing to lose by speaking his mind.

«These people are idiots,» Theo declared sullenly. «Why did I ever think that I could trust them?»

Seth kept moving past the dusty row of tents, picking up his pace—wishing that, just once, the children's tale of The Boy Who Outran His Sider could come true, letting him escape into blissful solitude.

"Seth! Slow down!"

Seth tipped his head; Raina and Amina were approaching. He stopped and waited for them to catch up.

"I know you're upset," Amina told Theo. "But did you honestly think that the cities' merchants were going to agree to pay a hundred thousand laborers for six generations . . . to build mountains to trap the sun?"

"They're paying for a fucking 'bridge of balloons,'" Theo retorted. "Which will probably kill a hundred thousand people just trying to make it work. And if they ever succeed, we'll just be facing the same situation on the other side of the node: migrating north, following the sun, until we meet the northern edge of the world. At which point there really will be nowhere else to go."

"Even if that's true," Amina argued, "the northern edge might be a thousand generations away."

"Or it might have crossed the northern habitable zone a thousand generations *ago*," Theo countered. "You're right that there's no reason that the solar latitude of the edges should be symmetrical, but that cuts both ways."

Seth found the prospect of crossing the node on a bridge of balloons quite audaciously wonderful, regardless of what lay on the other side, but he wasn't feeling brave enough to say so.

"All that anyone's ever known is the migration," Raina said flatly. "Even if they believed that it was possible to end it, that doesn't sound like a solution, it just sounds like a new kind of disaster."

"So the edge is just something I dreamed up, is it?" Theo demanded bitterly. "A dozen people have seen it now, and it's still possible to pretend that it's some kind of hallucination?"

"It's not a hallucination," Amina replied. "But that doesn't prove that it encircles the world. The cliffs might still turn out to stretch no more than a few degrees east-to-west. The expedition is the only way to settle that question."

Theo said, "But what if it doesn't settle it? What if they travel a few degrees west, but then the cliffs turn to the south? The ground won't be in shadow any more, making it impassable, but that won't prove that the change in direction is anything more than a temporary meandering."

Raina said, "They'll find whatever they find, and that will be better than knowing nothing."

"Fine," Theo replied. "But since I have a choice, I'd rather go back to Baharabad and try to think of some new way to deal with the drought."

They walked on through the camp in silence for a while. Then Seth asked Raina and Amina, "You're going on this expedition?"

"Yes," Amina replied.

"And Sarah and Judith?"

"Yes."

Seth wasn't surprised. "Who else?"

Raina said, "That hasn't been settled yet. There's a certain amount of politics to be accommodated."

"What do you mean?"

Before she could reply, the four of them were distracted by shouting coming from nearby. As they approached the source, Seth saw a crowd gathered outside one of the tents.

"I want to talk to Catherine!" a man was insisting, holding a woman roughly by the shoulders. "Why can't I do that?"

"Leave me alone," the woman replied angrily. "If she doesn't want to speak to a fool like you, that's hardly a surprise."

"She can't tell me what a fool I am herself?" The man gestured at the onlookers. "She can't tell anyone here to pass on the message?"

"She's given me the message," the woman retorted. "That will have to be good enough."

"When did you poison her?" someone called out, a taunt that was quickly taken up and repeated. Seth's gut tightened with dismay; it was like a Sleepwalker mob in reverse.

The man said, "This is what will happen: you can stay in your own tent, but we'll bring you all your food. Then after a few days, we'll see if we can wake her."

"You can't imprison me!" The woman pushed his hands away. "Who do you think you are? You have no authority to tell me what I'll eat or where I'll stay."

"You'll stay in your tent, half-head!" a Sider yelled from the crowd.

"Can't we bring a doctor?" Amina suggested. She didn't even raise her voice, but other people picked up on the suggestion and echoed it. Seth was encouraged; this was a sensible compromise. The woman's Sider might be uncommunicative for any number of reasons. Allowing self-appointed experts to judge whether or not she'd been fed the Thanton puffballs would be a recipe for vigilantism and paranoia.

But the accused woman wasn't interested in compromise. "You can't force me to see a doctor," she declared defiantly. "My health, Catherine's health, is no one's business but our own." She began trying to shoulder her way through the crowd, but no one was willing to let her pass.

Seth was unsure now where his duty lay. Harassing anyone in this manner was obnoxious—but if Catherine really was in danger from her own Walker, her friends were entitled to come to her aid.

"Here's the doctor!" someone announced. Seth saw a woman with a bag of instruments approaching, and people were parting to let her through, but when Catherine's Walker began screaming at her to go back to where she'd come from, she stopped to reassess the situation.

The doctor's hesitation did nothing to mollify the besieged woman, who began punching her nearest accuser and yelling at the crowd. "You're all hypocrites! You'd do it yourself if you had the chance! You're all sick of your own parasites jabbering on, telling you what to do! Well, I have the legs, I decide where I walk! Stand up for yourselves, you cowards! It's the easiest thing in the world now! Show some fucking pride, and reclaim your bodies from those mind-eaters!"

Seth was expecting this rant to be drowned out by angry rebukes, but instead the crowd became silent as the woman continued her tirade. "Be honest for once! It's what you all want!" She laughed and held her hands up. "Learn the code, ask for help, pass the message palm to palm where they can't see it. We can free ourselves, all of us! We just need to have the courage!"

WHEN SETH WOKE IN the early hours of the morning, he could tell that Theo was already awake. He wasn't pinging the tent, but the darkness that would have held his view was still imbued with his presence: seeing what Theo saw when he saw nothing was not the same as seeing nothing at all.

«The sun trap isn't a lost cause,» Seth said. «If the bridge at the nodes doesn't work out, and the expedition finds no limit to the edge . . .»

«I don't care any more,» Theo replied. «I just want to stop wasting my time with people who refuse to take any of this seriously.»

«So you'd rather retire and go back to Baharabad?»

«Why not? They offered us that pension to get us out of the way. The message is clear: thanks for everything, but we don't want to listen to you any more.»

Seth said, «Which is the perfect reason not to take it.»

«No, it's the perfect reason why we should. I've already spent enough time telling these idiots things they didn't want to hear.»

Seth hunted for a tactful way to phrase his response. «No one likes hearing that someone else has all the answers.»

«No, and they'd be free to ignore everything I said if it didn't make sense. But it does make sense. Has any geologist ever seen a structure like this? Is anything of the kind even mentioned in passing in some apocryphal source or ancient legend?»

«No,» Seth conceded.

«The drop from the cliffs to the slope,» Theo said, «is already more than twenty times the depth of any other chasm ever surveyed. If this was simply an extreme example of some ordinary geological phenomenon, maybe it could be twice as deep, or five times—but *twenty*? Before we've even found the bottom of it?»

«I'm not arguing with you,» Seth replied. «It's different in kind, it's unprecedented. But that's not enough to prove that you're right about everything.»

«If the world is finite,» Theo said, «it can turn to the north while the orbit of the sun stays fixed. That's the simplest possible explanation of the central fact of everyone's existence. If I'd been bold enough to publish a book spelling out that argument, and predicting that we'd eventually reach the southern edge, everyone would now be telling me that my theory had been vindicated.»

«Maybe.» Seth understood his frustration, but it still didn't justify abandoning their career. «If you're worried about Irina,» he ventured, «then I can accept that. I'll stop arguing, and we can go home.»

Theo was silent for a while, then he said, «She was fine last time we saw her. Elena's still Elena, but she seems to have grown up a bit. I don't think Irina's in danger.»

Seth had been sincere in his offer, but this matched his own assessment of their sisters' complicated lives. «Then if we have no urgent reason to go back, I'm really not ready to retire.»

Theo fell silent again. Seth wasn't sure if he was chafing with resentment, but when he finally spoke his tone was conciliatory. «I need to make my own view clear to Jonas, but if you want to take up one of his offers yourself, I won't try to stop you. Not if all I have to do is tag along.»

«All right.» Seth was encouraged—and if the notion of Theo as some kind of inert passenger was unlikely to last long out in the field, he was entitled to take whatever stance he wished with Jonas in order to salvage his pride. «So what do you think of the bridge?»

«It's up to you,» Theo insisted.

«You don't think it's too dangerous?» Seth prodded him.

«High altitudes, extreme geometry, uninhabitable ground below? What could possibly go wrong?»

«And the expedition?»

«The geometry of the slope is extreme, in its own way,» Theo mused. «But compared to a project where a puff of wind could knock you into absolute summer, it looks positively benign.»

Seth didn't push his luck; if he started listing the merits of gathering more evidence to test Theo's hypothesis, that would only be treated as a provocation.

«Then the expedition it is,» he declared. «We can each give Jonas our separate answers: you can claim your pension, and I'll go on hauling my pack for a living.»

Theo hesitated; it had surely occurred to him that he'd be facing all the same hardships for substantially less money.

But his pride held out against temptation. «Exactly,» he said. «I wouldn't have it any other way.»

SETH WALKED DOWN TO the site where the winches were being built, to check on their progress. The giant reels were similar to those on the balloon anchors, but the supporting frames had had to be redesigned completely to allow the rope to be fed out beneath the structure instead of rising up from it.

«We did agree that falling was better than burning,» Theo recalled.

«Thanks for the reminder.» The winches had benefited from many of the improvements to their skyward brethren, but Seth had no doubt that sticking them on platforms overhanging the cliffs would offer up entirely new modes of failure. «Can you imagine lugging these things into the steamlands?»

«Another reason to be glad that you didn't end up a mover.»

In the food hall, Seth spotted Sarah and Judith, so he collected his breakfast and sat down beside them.

Sarah said, "Did you hear about Catherine?"

"I heard that she'd recovered," Seth replied. Apparently she hadn't suffered any permanent damage in the short time her Walker had been eating the puffballs.

"She's asking to be liberated," Judith said. "Cared for by friends, or given to a side-blind Walker, but she won't accept being bound to Felice any more."

"Fair enough," Theo decided. "Let that poisoner be side-blind, and some innocent person healed."

Sarah said, "At that age, 'healed' might be putting it too strongly. I doubt they'd be able to share views or use inspeech."

"Maybe not. But having a companion who'll warn you if you're about to sidle into a ditch would still be better than nothing."

Seth was growing resigned to the likelihood that, one way or another, the poison would make its way to Baharabad. And though he doubted that Elena would ever seek to use it, it could still affect his family indirectly. If the practice of punishing poisoners by separating Sider and Walker became the norm, other Siders with lesser grievances might start seeking the same outcome.

"It would be a miserable existence if she has to stay unpaired," Judith said. "Pushed around on a cart, relying on donated blood. Her Walker friends might be willing to cut themselves while their outrage is fresh, but are they really going to do that for the rest of her life?"

"What we need is a more symmetrical response," Theo suggested. "A drug that strips Walkers of their will, transforming them into compliant slaves."

Seth said, "If you fed that to me, would you even notice the difference?"

Raina and Amina approached the breakfast table, but instead of joining them the pair merely offered curt greetings, then Raina stood fidgeting impatiently. Sarah said, "You're giving me indigestion."

Seth was confused. "Do you need us for something?" he asked Raina. She just glared at him, exasperated, but Amina said, "Jonas is announcing the full team for the expedition this morning."

"Today?" Seth had forgotten; once he'd settled things with Theo, details like that had seemed unimportant.

"Yes, today," Raina said irritably. "Once the six of us turn up."

"You mean five," Theo corrected her.

"If you really want your absence taken seriously," Judith suggested, "you're going to need to start resisting the urge to remind us of it every five seconds."

Sarah paused in mid-bite. "If *Theo* swapped places with Catherine, would that satisfy everyone? Would justice be served?"

Theo inspoke, «Thump her.»

«You thump her, if you can't take a joke.»

«Some compliant slave you are.»

Sarah finished her meal, and Seth hurried to do the same. As they left the dining hall and crossed the campsite, Seth pondered Raina's anxiety. She'd been muttering for days about the politics of the selection process. Perhaps she was worried that she wouldn't be appointed to lead the expedition, if someone more senior was included?

At the entrance to Jonas's office, Raina paused, as if having second thoughts about disturbing him so early in the day. Sarah stepped past her and announced the group to Jonas's assistant. A minute later, they were ushered inside.

Jonas tipped his head west to face them. "I'm glad you're all here," he said. "The composition of the team was settled last night, and it seemed best to let you know exactly what was happening before you were introduced to your new colleagues.

"A pair of surveyors from Laverington, Andrei and Nicholas, will be joining you. They're among the most experienced that city has to offer, and I'm certain that the expedition will benefit from their skills."

This news was not especially surprising, and Seth saw no reason not to welcome it. Laverington was the second-largest city on the Orico, and with Baharabad's water shortage unresolved, anything that might strengthen their ties with one of the beneficiaries of the shifting northern storms seemed prudent.

"You will also be joined by an observer from Thanton, named Ada. I'm told she studied geology, though her primary qualification is her membership of one of the town's merchant families." Jonas hesitated, as if expecting to be interrupted, but Seth had no immediate response fit to utter, and apparently no one else did either. "This is not ideal, I know, but we rely on Thanton's cooperation to maintain our supplies, and they have a legitimate interest in understanding the terrain to their south. Notwithstanding our distaste for the way they treat their Siders, they're entitled to know the fate of their river and their prospects for migration. So I expect you to treat this woman with the same courtesy as you'd show to any other guest."

PART FOUR

13

As night fell, Seth sat on the hillside and watched the movers set off for the steamlands, dragging the last of the winches. On the uneven terrain, the large wheeled platform supporting the device needed to maintain a fixed orientation, but the planes of the individual wheels could be turned a little, allowing the team to lug the whole assembly back and forth: east-south-east, then west-south-west. After the first winch had been delivered, Seth had asked his friends if it had been frustrating to be forced to travel so far like this—stopping and starting, weaving from side to side—but they'd insisted that the rhythm of the motion was enjoyable in its own way, and the incremental progress that emerged was not a source of resentment, it was simply to be expected. "South is south," Eunice had told him. "Not even a child imagines that they could roll anything directly south."

«They should have just hung the winches from balloons,» Theo asserted.

«Doubling their height above the slope? Letting the wind blow them around, so we can be dashed against the cliffs?»

«How hard can it be to solve those problems? If they're going to build a bridge across the western node . . .»

«Yeah, yeah. Save it for someone who cares.» Seth rubbed his eyes. Theo was diplomatic enough not to spend his time needling him about the pointlessness of the chasm expedition, but his endless complaints about the futility and impracticality of the bridge were irritating in their own way. «If you want to see the bridge canceled, you'd better hope we come back with evidence that the southern migration will be unimpeded.»

Theo laughed derisively. «You're really saying "southern migration" now? Do we need to talk about the "eastern sunrise" as well, to avoid any risk of ambiguity?»

«I don't know. Do you have plans to reverse the sun's orbit? Trap it . . . and then bounce it around somehow?»

The movers passed out of range of Theo's pings. As Seth sat in the dark, the wind from the south brought the smell of rain, and he pictured himself back in the steamlands, tramping through the mud toward the edge of the world as if he'd never been away.

"I BELIEVE THE CHASM was produced by a runaway fault ejection," Ada declared. "A crack forms in the rock along a plane that slopes down to the south, steep enough that the rock above the shallowest part of the fault tears free and slides north along it. That in turn takes the pressure off the deeper rock, and allows it to do the same." She'd learned to speak the Baharabadi dialect pretty fluently, and though her accent was strange to Seth's ears, it was perfectly comprehensible.

Seth did not feel qualified to offer an opinion on her theory. Having finished inspecting the last of the winches, they were standing on the eastern side of the platform, peering over the safety rail. The platform protruded far enough to ensure that the rope wouldn't get snagged if the top of it slackened and hung straight down, but the sight of the nearby rock face disappearing into the gloom did not exactly rival the view from the balloon, and any evidence of the structure's detailed geology was in short supply.

"Where's the ejecta?" Nicholas asked Ada. "If the rock excavated itself by sliding up a fault and showering into the air, shouldn't there be a mountain of rubble somewhere to the north, as big as this hole?"

"There would have been, once," she replied. "But it's been blown away in the wind. Whenever this happened, it must have been long ago."

Seth looked to the east, where the middle winch of the three could be seen, thrust much farther south over the precipice than the others, in order to sharpen the control the ropes' geometry would exert on their joint cargo. An assembly of girders beneath the platform braced it against the cliff face, but the extent of the overhang was still alarming to behold. Not entirely rationally, he felt more worried for the rope team who'd have to stand on that perilously jutting structure, laboring for half the night, than he did for himself and his fellow travelers—as if the beams could snap and send the first group plummeting to their death, without the second suffering an equally grisly fate. But if the middle rope did break free like that, the two intact side ropes wouldn't be enough to stop the basket being smashed into the cliff face.

"What do you think, Theo?" Ada asked. "Could a fault have done this?"

Theo inspoke, «Tell the half-head I'm asleep.»

«Why should I lie for you?» Seth replied.

«Were you there when they took our friends prisoner?»

«Yes, and if you want to snub her, I'm not stopping you. But if you want to do it, do it openly. Don't ask me to pretend that you've dozed off.»

Theo fell silent. Ada mused, to no one in particular, "We might find evidence in the rocks on the slope. Matches to stones found far to the north."

Andrei squatted down and picked up a pebble that had blown onto the platform, then threw it over the rail. "We might," he said. "You never know."

It was almost sunset, but as soon as they stepped out of the shade of the winch and started back to the campsite, Seth felt the heat sapping his strength again.

«Do you think the rope teams will actually come back to haul us up?» he asked Theo. «They might decide they've had enough of this weather.»

«If they do, you'll just have to scale the cliffs.»

«That's not going to happen.»

At the campsite, the rope teams had woken and were resting or eating in the shadows of their tents. Seth recalled the dead-man-walking glances many of the same people had cast his way before the balloon flight, and took some comfort from the fact that his presence didn't seem to unsettle them at all now.

He parted company with the others and went looking for Sarah and Judith. Sarah was awake but still prone behind her tent, lying still to allow Judith to sleep a little longer.

"Please tell me it's going to be cooler down there," Sarah whispered, fanning herself with a copy of Ada's self-published pamphlet *On the Meaning of Strata*. As she spoke, the rain began falling. "And drier."

"It's sure to be," Seth promised. "Everything but flatter."

"I can't believe I talked Amir into staying behind," she said. "I miss him so much."

Seth struggled to think of something comforting to say; however the expedition fared, the reunion was hardly imminent. "Just think of the stories you'll have to tell him when this is over."

"Actually, I'm hoping it will be mostly just walking and measuring," Sarah replied. "Rather than *memorable*, in the sense of our last trip."

"I'm not anticipating any abductions," Seth assured her.

Theo said, "Walking and measuring on a forty-five-degree slope might be memorable enough in its own way."

Twilight engulfed the camp, and the rain closed in. There didn't seem to be any point seeking shelter; they were going to end up soaked whatever they did. When Judith woke, she proposed that they head for the departure point, and no one could think of any reason to delay. Seth could already hear the rope teams assembling, shouting to each other over the pelting rain.

A crude path had been laid from the camp, running due east. Seth followed Sarah and Judith blindly, guided by nothing but the paving stones beneath his feet. Without the weight of a pack on his shoulders he felt ill-prepared for any kind of journey, but all the tools and provisions for the expedition had already been assembled in the basket.

A haloed patch of brightness appeared ahead, trembling and splintered by the strange refractions of the rain, but only vanishing entirely when Sarah crossed Seth's line of sight. Eventually this beacon resolved into a lantern, hung from the ceiling of the gazebo where the other members of the team had already gathered.

Standing apart from the rest, Ada looked utterly lost and alone, and at the sight of her dripping form Seth felt a disconcerting pang of almost brotherly concern. It was not her fault how she'd been raised: her parents would have begun feeding her the poison when she was an infant. She must have known that there were such things in the world as sentient Siders long before the balloon project had brought a horde of foreigners passing her way—but she might well have lived her whole life until then without speaking to one.

Raina spotted them approaching and nodded a greeting as Seth followed Sarah into the sheltered space. Amina said, "We just need to wait for the rope teams to do their final checks."

"I'm in no hurry!" Seth assured her. The last two test runs had been flawless, but the more eyes that were cast over the equipment before the basket was lowered with people inside it, the better.

"I still think my plan would have left us more at ease," Judith declared wistfully. "We would have been in control all the way." She'd wanted to position the ropes in advance, by lowering a heavy object to anchor them, and then have the basket ride down the central rope, with the passengers able to start and stop at will. Seth could see the attraction of this kind of autonomy, but the engineers had judged her gadget for governing the speed of descent to be too complicated. And if a stripped ratchet in a distant winch could cause problems, any damage to its counterpart in the basket itself would have been much harder to deal with.

"Surely you're accustomed to someone else dictating your movements?" Andrei protested. It was the kind of joke that any of the Baharabadi might have made among themselves, but Seth could see Sarah tense with displeasure, as if it were some kind of personal attack against her and her Sider.

"I just want to be down there as soon as possible," Raina interjected. "With rock beneath my feet instead of thin air."

A pair of messengers from the rope teams arrived. The Walker pulled the inspection reports out of a protective bag and handed them to Raina; she looked them over then announced, "Time to go."

The expedition filed out into the rain. Seth followed the path to the middle platform, then gripped the guide rail tightly as he sidled toward the far end where the basket was waiting below. Mercifully, there was a small roof here to keep the rain out, and a couple of carefully placed lamps. Raina supervised the boarding, checking each Walker's safety harness before letting them climb down into the basket.

«Don't look down,» Theo begged him as Seth's turn came to approach the rope ladder.

«You keep forgetting that you're not here.» Seth let Raina help him with the harness, then he reached across the hole in the platform, gripped the ladder, and stepped onto the nearest rung.

Enough light from the lamps was spilling through the hole to show the roof of the basket gently swaying against the darkness as Seth began his descent. Despite its sheltered location, the ladder had grown slick from wind-blown rain, but he wrapped each hand tightly around its rung before releasing the other, and willed himself not to think of the fear and shame that would come if he lost his grip and ended up swinging in the harness.

As he approached the basket's roof he suffered a moment of vertigo, unable to shake the absurd notion that he might accidentally step onto it and go skidding down into the blackness, rather than passing through the hatch into the safety of the interior. But then he caught sight of Sarah standing near the base of the ladder, her upraised face lit by the basket's own lamp; with his eyes locked on hers, he ignored everything else. When his feet touched the floor of the basket he found that it was not quite steady, but Sarah helped him out of the harness then jerked the rope and called up, "He's safe!"

Ada followed, then Raina and Amina. A member of the rope team pulled up the ladder and harness, then Raina slammed the hatch closed. "No one's changed their mind?" she asked cheerfully; Seth wasn't sure if she was serious, but she received no replies.

The basket was about the same size as the balloon's, but with five Walkers and the expedition's supplies it was much more crowded. Three windows looked out into the rain, with the lamplight doing as good a job as Theo's pings to reveal the downpour, while to the sheltered north Theo showed the platform's supporting girders all the way to the cliff face.

"Time to get seated," Sarah suggested. She joined Seth on one narrow bench, while the three west-facers sat opposite. Seth pictured the rope teams signaling each other with lamps, preparing to begin the unreeling together. The changing geometry of the ropes ought to be enough to alert them if they fell out of step, but there would be no cues to compare with the sight of a balloon the size of a building rising up into the sky.

"It's started," Theo said. With the basket swaying in the wind Seth hadn't felt its downward motion commence, but the girders were already rising out of sight to the north, leaving nothing but the bare cliff face in view. The lamp suspended from the ceiling began oscillating with a new, steady rhythm that stood out against the vagaries of the wind: the rhythm of the rope teams, smooth and practiced, promising to bring the travelers safely to their destination.

The cliff face disappeared behind an ever-thickening curtain of rain, as the same geometrical constraints that had sent the rising balloon to the south played out for the descending basket. Seth exchanged a glance of shared relief with Raina: it would take much more than a freakish gust of wind now to see them hit the rock.

Ada took something from her pocket and held it up to her Sider's left pinger.

"What's that?" Seth asked.

"A barometer," she replied. "It weighs the air above us; it ought to show an increase in pressure as we descend."

Seth had never heard of such a thing. "Where's it from?"

"I made it myself."

"From whose plans?"

"My own."

If that was true, then her ingenuity was impressive—but it rendered one aspect of the design disturbing. The dial of the thing, which presumably displayed the quantity it measured, was a north-facing circle, so she'd never be able to see it for herself. Somehow, Seth realized, the silence of her Sider had lulled him into thinking of her as side-blind: alone but independent, making her way in the world with nothing but her own senses. And that wasn't remotely true. On the contrary, she clearly took the assistance of her stupefied slave for granted.

She must have seen the unease on his face, because she put the device away. Seth had no wish to blame her for his own confusion; he composed himself and lowered his gaze.

Theo said, «How can you weigh the air?»

«I'm not the one you should be asking.»

«It sounds like a hoax to me,» Theo grumbled. «It probably tells fortunes and makes matches as well.»

«I really wouldn't know.»

The sound of the rain on the roof stopped abruptly, though when Seth looked north through Theo's view he saw that it was still falling in the distance. Once the edge of the rainstorm was too far away to ping, the windows showed nothing in any direction, and all he could hear was the rhythmic creaking of the roof as the tension in the ropes rose and fell.

Andrei smiled uneasily. "I'm used to leaving the crowds behind, but not the world itself."

Sarah said, "Even Theo thinks we'd need to go farther south to achieve that."

In the silence that followed, Seth pictured her words spreading out into the darkness and vanishing, swallowed by the emptiness around them.

AT FIRST, WHAT THEO was showing him through the northern window looked like distant rain or fog. Seth waited for the thin presence to dissipate, or simply recede as the basket continued to the south, but instead, very slowly, it drew closer.

"That's rock?" he asked. "That's the slope?"

"It must be," Theo replied. "It doesn't match the practice ramp, but I never expected the texture to be the same."

Seth hadn't been expecting much ping-back, given the geometry, but instead of the faint, smooth sheen that their mock-up had exhibited, the real thing registered as a thousand tiny flecks that required a positive act of the will to perceive as belonging to a single surface at all.

The ramp they'd used as a surrogate for the slope had been made by taking slabs of rock and propping them up at extreme angles—a tricky business, but a great deal easier than carving a similar structure out of the side of a mountain. The catch was, tilting an initially horizontal surface to such a degree stretched out all of the rock's corrugations and crannies to the point where they became imperceptibly shallow—whereas it was apparent now that the slope itself had achieved the same overall gradient by a process in which there had been no tilting to smooth away its ordinary blemishes.

Amina said, "We'll learn to make sense of this too, it's just a matter of time."

As the slope came nearer, its foggy appearance sharpened dramatically in places. These streaks of clarity seemed to arise from small cliffs where the incline had collapsed, leaving near-vertical rock faces above rubble-strewn terraces, as if from an abandoned project to build roads across the impossible landscape, or tame it for agriculture.

The basket skimmed the terrain ever more closely, but though proximity revealed more details in the rock the speed of the descent left Seth with no time to study them. They were traveling almost parallel to the slope now, but he felt himself growing tense at the possibility of a premature impact. For all the balloon surveys and all the winch tests, the system could not be so finely calibrated nor the landscape so perfectly mapped as to promise that the basket would be motionless at the instant it met rock.

They slowed, and began to drop. Seth wished belatedly that he'd asked for an observation port in the bottom of the basket: even without sunlight, they could have lit the ground themselves for the final approach, and even without Judith's vision of total autonomy they might have devised some way to steer clear of the most dangerous obstacles.

The basket thudded to a halt. For a second or two there was stillness and silence. Then the floor creaked and tilted, and they began
to slide upslope, accompanied by a horrifying grinding sound. Seth
clung to his seat, glancing up to see the others bracing themselves
awkwardly, grim-faced with the effort. As they built up speed, the
lamp canted so far to the south that it came halfway to the floor.

The ropes snapped taut. The roof moaned and shuddered and
the lamp swung back and forth, dividing the cabin with a halluci-
natory hyperbola. Seth waited anxiously to see if they'd reached a
stable resting point, with the forces from the ropes and the ground
not merely in balance for the moment, but actively disposed to resist
any further motion.

The lamp's oscillations died down. Raina rose and began lowering one of the supporting legs that were tucked inside along the
southern wall of the basket; Seth was about to do the same, but
Sarah was on her feet before him.

When the legs were locked in place, Andrei began testing the
stability of the setup, at first just swaying on the spot, then cautiously sidling back and forth to gauge the basket's response. Seth
joined in; he could hear the floor creaking, but as far as he could
tell it didn't shift. The small portion of the slope in Theo's view
through the northern window was confusing: an indistinct slab of
conflicting cues with unstable meaning, like a Sider's idea of an
optical illusion. But as he moved around the cabin and observed
the way the texture responded to his changing position, it began
to seem less strange.

While they waited for the twilight that would have to suffice in
lieu of a true dawn, they took their packs out of the storage hold and
divided up the provisions. Not knowing what the local vegetation
would be like, they'd come laden with nuts, seeds and dried fruit.
Seth wondered where Ada had placed her stash of the stupefying
drug; there were no puffballs mixed in with the more conventional
supplies, but perhaps the concentrated form was potent enough that
she could carry a hundred days' supply discreetly in her pocket.

Raina opened the hatch in the roof and unrolled the rope ladder
beside it. She lit a second lamp and ascended. After a minute or so,

she called down, "There's room for two at a time up here, if anyone wants to join me."

For a moment, mutual deference paralyzed her colleagues, but Seth was standing closest to the ladder so he stopped wasting everyone's time. As his head rose above the hatch, he paused to let his eyes adjust.

The light from Raina's lamp could not reach far, but the brightest part, near the shadow of the cone guard, struck the slope half a dozen paces from the spot where the basket had come to rest. The brown rock looked abraded, but hard enough to have survived for eons, like some outcrops Seth had seen in the desert. It was unlikely to crumble under their weight; the question would be whether they could keep their balance on it, when all their experience had come from an imperfect approximation.

"Look west-south-west," Raina suggested.

Seth climbed all the way through the hatch and stood on the roof to get a better vantage. To the south, Theo was utterly blind; if the slope wasn't exactly forty-five degrees, it was near enough to ensure that any pings in that direction met nothing but air. Seth tipped his head back to the west and peered out across the illuminated ground. After a moment he noticed a line cutting across the edge of the lamplit terrain that had nothing to do with the geometry of the beam.

"Do you think that's a drop?" he asked.

"Yes," Raina replied. "But it's not too deep."

"How can you tell?"

"You can't see the bottom clearly, but you can see that the lamp's reaching it."

She was right: the bright edge of the beam on the contiguous part of the slope vanished abruptly, but it was possible to discern a faint, shifted band of light where it struck another surface below.

Theo said, "We might have got lucky."

Seth climbed back down into the basket to give someone else a chance to take a look. As he descended, Ada was standing nearest to him; he couldn't quite bring himself to offer her a verbal invitation, but he gestured toward the ladder and she did not demur.

The mood of the other travelers was already optimistic; they must have pieced together the implications of the rooftop conversation. But Judith wasn't satisfied with mere luck. "I could have put us down with a terrace right on our doorstep," she boasted.

"Next time," Nicholas suggested.

"Why would there be another expedition?" Judith asked irritably. "Whether this thing is small enough for the migration to detour around it, or not, sending in another team isn't going to change the answer."

Nicholas said, "Maybe. But I think people will still want to know exactly what this place is, and I doubt it's going to be small enough for us to answer that in the time we'll have."

Theo was amused. "If the edge runs geologically west and continues unbroken, we could follow it for as many generations as have already lived, and still not return to where we started."

WHEN A PALE LIGHT began to spread across the sky from the northeast, Seth watched with a sense of gratitude that he would not be facing the fierce dawn that had come to the land above the cliffs. The twilight did nothing to dispel his hopes about the terrace, though the exact scale of the drop remained hard to judge from a distance.

Andrei and Nicholas volunteered to be the first to test the terrain. Sarah helped Andrei into a harness then Seth joined her beside the spools of safety rope, while Raina and Amina, and Ada, watched from the roof.

Andrei slid open the western hatch. The northern edge of the basket's floor was resting against the rock not far from the doorway, but the slope still made for an awkward disembarkation. After binding a small wedge to his right foot, Andrei lowered a single stilt to the ground and placed his left foot on the stilt's platform. They'd all gained some proficiency in the strange technique, but the practice ramp had been an imperfect substitute, so Seth watched anxiously as Andrei shifted his weight onto the stilt, checking that it wouldn't go skittering north, then placed his wedged right foot on the ground and stood.

Gripping the stilt by its handle, he raised it and pivoted forward on his right foot, then brought it down. Seth resisted the urge to offer advice: Andrei surely knew that in his eagerness to make progress he had placed the stilt too far downslope for safety. A moment later he half-reversed the step. Then he brought his right foot forward and began repeating the whole cycle, breaking into a halting walk as precarious and comical as their attempts on the ramp, but no less successful.

Seth and Sarah played out the ropes as Andrei shambled westward. Once he'd found his rhythm he became more ambitious and began to veer a little to the south, bringing him closer to the drop. Navigating the approach would not be easy: nothing due south would be visible to Nicholas, and at best a small patch would lie in Andrei's peripheral vision when he looked down. All he could do was fix a point on the edge in his mind while it was still in front of him, and then hold on to his memory of its relationships with the rest of the terrain when it vanished into his dark cone.

Theo said, "I bet we'll find no animals here. Even if there's a gentle way down the cliffs that we've yet to discover, there's nothing to the north that could have prepared them to move safely on a gradient like this."

"There might be plants, though," Sarah replied. "Of all the seeds and spores blown around on the wind, some hardy species might have lodged in a few crevices." To Seth all the rock in sight appeared barren, but he didn't want to dismiss the possibility.

"This is perfect!" Andrei shouted excitedly. He'd come to a halt a pace north of the drop. "We'll be able to reach the bottom easily. The ground still slopes a little to the south down there, but not so much that we'll need stilts."

"How far does it continue?" Judith called back.

"As far as I can see."

Raina was silent, but Seth could not imagine any reason why they should refuse this gift. The terrace might not run as far west as they needed to go, but wherever it ended it was hard to see how that could leave them in a worse position than if they'd chosen to limp across the slope from the start.

"I'd better take a look," Raina decided.

When Andrei and Nicholas returned, they took Seth and Theo's place at the safety rope while Raina and Amina repeated the short journey. Seth stood back from the doorway, unable to get a clear view but reluctant to join Ada on the roof. He'd thought he'd reconciled himself to the need to treat her with civility, but now the whole idea of being at ease in her presence felt shameful.

Raina reported what appeared to be a number of boulders scattered further down the terrace. If they really were loose objects that had come to rest there—rather than outcrops of some tougher underlying rock that had resisted the collapse—then it seemed unlikely that the weight of a few people could trigger a fresh subsidence. But she could only be sure of that if she went down onto the terrace and examined the boulders directly.

Seth was about to volunteer to help her with the descent when she asked for him specifically. He put on a harness, gathered the tools she'd requested into a spare pack, picked up his stilt, attached the wedge to his right foot, then squeezed past Andrei and Sarah and stepped out onto the slope.

The moment his stilt made contact with the rock he could feel the small pits and bumps in the surface, which rendered it far less slippery than the practice ramp. Seth was sure that in the long run this rougher texture would make things easier, but he was also aware that some of the hard-won instincts he'd acquired in training were now obsolete. After clipping his harness to the northern safety rope he spent a few moments recalibrating his sense of the forces at play, and adjusting his posture accordingly. Then he set off across the rock.

Out on the slope, Theo's southern blind spot was far more unsettling than it had been from the roof of the basket. At first, Seth took some comfort from the fact that if he went sliding at least it would be upslope, allowing him to see where he was going—but then he realized that that wasn't necessarily true. The basket's immediate surroundings were certainly tilted at just below forty-five degrees, but any shift to a slightly greater angle might be impossible to discern until the moment he felt the unexpected force on the stilt that sent him toppling. The safety harness should have reassured him that he wasn't going to fall in any direction, but the eerie, asymmetric emptiness to the south imbued everything with a sense of imbalance.

«You know what would be worse than skidding blindly down the slope and crashing onto the terrace?» he asked Theo.

«Skidding blindly down the slope and overshooting the terrace, so we keep on falling.»

But once Seth was able to see the terrace clearly, his anxiety began to diminish. His mind seized on the stretch of level ground ahead and extrapolated its presence backward, not exactly filling the blind spot, but robbing it of much of its potency.

When he arrived at the cliff's edge, he called to Sarah to dispense some more rope from the southern spool, but he held it back from Raina and let it hang slackly between them. He took a wedge-mounted pulley out of his pack, coiled some of the rope around the pulley, handed it to Raina, then stepped back to get a better view.

Even with her stilt raising one leg above the ground, Raina could reach all the way down to the edge by swinging her arm out to the south, but it was not an ideal posture to see what she was doing, so she needed Seth's perspective to guide her. By adjusting the vertical plate that protruded from the southern face of the pulley's mount and hung over the drop, she was able to counterbalance the tendency of the mount to slide north, at least to the point where it was stable against small disturbances.

"Now comes the fun part," Raina muttered. She summoned Seth forward and rested an arm on his shoulder so she could keep her balance while she released her stilt's locking pins, collapsed it and put it in her pack. She unclipped the northern safety rope, and passed the end to him so he could secure it to his own harness.

Then she jumped sideways over the cliff.

Seth heard a solid thwack of flesh against rock as the rope threading through the pulley went taut. "Are you all right?" he asked.

Raina grunted irritably, but Amina replied, "Yes!"

Seth kept a close watch on the pulley and conveyed instructions from below back to Sarah, until Raina announced, "We're down."

A short time later she came into view, walking slowly west along the terrace. "It looks like the same kind of rock as the rest of the slope," Amina said. "Maybe there was some pre-existing fissure or inhomogeneity here, but it's not an entirely different mineral."

Raina walked up to the nearest of the boulders and squatted down to inspect its base. "It's not contiguous," she declared. Seth was surprised that there wasn't more rubble on the terraces, since they seemed to be the only places anything could rest, but perhaps over time the wind had removed most of the smaller rocks, sending them sliding from terrace to terrace until they'd been ground into dust.

Eventually Raina was satisfied. "We'll be safer here, and we'll be able to travel faster. We should start bringing everyone down."

AS THE EXPEDITION BEGAN the long march west, Seth looked back to commit to memory the view from a distance of the part of the terrace near the rope they'd left dangling over the small cliff. If they lost this slender thread they might still find their way back to the basket, but if they could not locate the basket itself they'd almost certainly perish. Seth had never faced a situation before when a failure to retrace his steps could extract such an unforgiving penalty.

The terrace was more than wide enough for all four Walkers to stay abreast of each other, but after a while they settled into a staggered formation. With Sarah and Judith to the south of him, interrupting the void, and the vertical cliff face to the north replacing the foggy presence of the slope, Seth felt as if something close to normality had been restored.

«Do you think we should change places every now and then?» he asked Theo.

«Why?»

«To give Judith something to ping to the south. If my left eye received no light at all for a couple of days, I wouldn't want to rely on it working normally the instant I had need of it. Aren't your pingers the same?»

«I never thought about it,» Theo admitted. «But I have no problem taking an equal share of the sensory deprivation.»

To measure their progress they used callipers to position themselves at a known distance from a prominent feature on the cliffs, which they sighted through an alidade to record its inclination and calculate its height. By repeating the sighting some time later they could determine how far they'd come, before switching to a new point of reference. The cumulative errors in these measurements would mount up as they traveled, but the conventional methods of estimating latitude and longitude simply weren't available.

Even in this land without shadows, though, a rough sense of the motion of the sun could be obtained from the shifting pattern of intensity in the haze of scattered light from above. Midday arrived sooner than Seth had been expecting it; what had passed for dawn must have been later than he'd realized in the already short summer day up on the surface. But it was cooler than it had been in the steamlands at midnight, and when they stopped to eat he had no trouble rationing his water.

While the rest of the team sat digesting their meals, Ada took the opportunity to scrutinize the cliff face, sidling up close and then walking back and forth beside it, jotting occasional notes into a book she was carrying.

"So how can you be sure what the textures of the rock are?" Seth asked her. Ordinary Walkers and Siders trusted the perceptions they shared because they'd known each other since birth—but what credence should anyone give to the visions of a drug-addled slave?

"The same way as you," Ada replied cheerfully. "I see the rock too, I touch it too. If it's all consistent, why wouldn't I trust the details that each modality reveals?"

Each modality? Seth wasn't sure what kind of response he'd expected, but the sheer brazenness of this answer was shocking. To her, a Sider was just one more sensory organ.

Ada continued her examination of the cliff face, showing no signs of discomfort at his question. Seth's anger began to dissipate under the weight of its own uselessness. If he started treating every ordinary thing she did as a provocation, he'd poison the whole expedition with his rancor. He did not want to spend the next hundred days ineffectually venting his outrage while he vacillated between the position that Ada, having had no choice in her upbringing, deserved only pity, and the undeniable fact that her Sider had suffered an incomparably worse fate.

«Good luck with that "runaway fault ejection" hypothesis,» Theo scoffed. «She'll need a trail of matching rubble from here to the midwinter circle to account for all the excavated rock.»

Seth didn't reply. He could hardly blame Theo for his own ineffectual venting . . . but all their gestures of contempt would do nothing to resolve the plight of Thanton's Siders. In the end they'd both have to find a way to get along with this particular Thantonite—and promise themselves that they'd engage with the cause in a far more useful fashion once the mission was over.

SETH WAS WOKEN BY a gentle rain falling on the terrace. He left his tent and set up a funnel to replenish the canteens, working by touch in the darkness.

«All the spillage is away from us,» Theo observed. The terrace itself sloped down a little to the south, and some water was pooling on the north side beneath the cliffs—but none was spraying up over the southern edge, or drizzling down from the top of the cliffs.

«We must be on a transition line,» Seth concluded. The slope to the south of them had to be slightly steeper than forty-five degrees, and that to the north a little less steep. «Maybe that's the most likely place for terraces to form, because there's some kind of extra strain in the rock.»

He left the canteens to fill and stood beside the tent in a sheltered spot, brushing some of the water off himself before re-entering.

"Is the rain going to be a problem?" Andrei asked.

Theo described the situation.

"So when this terrace comes to an end, the best way to find the next one might be to follow the transition line," Nicholas suggested.

"Follow it how?" Seth wondered. "Unless it's raining, the cues could be almost imperceptible."

"If you start out with one foot on either side of the line," Andrei proposed, "it would be easy to tell the difference if you ever stopped straddling it."

Seth suspected that this might be an understatement. "So to get around the visibility problem, we arrange to be sent sprawling if we take one wrong step?"

Andrei laughed. "Not if we're prepared! And we're much less likely to be taken by surprise by any meandering of the line if it starts out right between our feet, than if all we know is that it was once so many paces to the north or south."

"How did the surface end up so close to forty-five degrees?" Nicholas mused. "I don't believe it was a fault ejection, it's too large for that. But if it was extrusion from the pressure in the rock, why should it stop at precisely that angle?"

Theo said, "Maybe it hasn't stopped—but weathering keeps the angle close to forty-five degrees. If you have part of a stream running as fast as possible, and it hits a section of the slope with a different gradient that impedes the flow, over time isn't that obstacle going to be carved away?"

Nicholas considered this. "But how much water would there have been here in the past, when the steamlands were still far to the north?"

"That's hard to say," Theo admitted. "When it was absolute summer up on the surface . . . what was the weather like down here?"

Andrei said, "You still believe this is the edge of the world?" His tone was challenging but not derisive; he wasn't simply ridiculing the hypothesis.

"Yes," Theo replied.

"Then if you want to understand the long-term hydrology of this place, shouldn't you be asking yourself about the weather much, much further down?"

LATE IN THE MORNING of their eighth day on the slope, the terrace came to an end.

They had seen the cliff face slowly shrinking beside them for days, and the edge of the southern drop drawing nearer, but Seth had kept telling himself that the trend was as likely to reverse as to continue. Then the point where the ledge finally shrank out of existence came into view to the west, and they'd been left marching toward its demise, unable to stop grumbling about an event they'd always known was inevitable.

"I'm just glad that all those days we spent practicing on the ramp weren't for nothing," Sarah declared sarcastically. Seth tried not to think about how arduous he'd found the short journey from the basket to the terrace, even with the safety ropes to give him confidence and the reward of level ground in sight. If there was another terrace farther west on the same transition line, it was not yet visible. All he could see ahead was a roughly planar expanse of brown rock at the slope's usual incline, dotted with outcrops that looked more like obstacles than potential resting points.

The final section of the ledge was narrow enough to force them to move in single file. Andrei and Nicholas were at the front, followed by Raina and Amina, Sarah and Judith, Seth and Theo, and Ada in the rear. They shuffled forward cautiously, well separated so there'd be no chance of bumping one another.

Andrei called a halt and began preparing himself. Seth couldn't see what he was doing, but he could hear a stilt being expanded and the locking pins snapping into place. There was a steady wind blowing from the south; a day earlier, he would have enjoyed its touch on his skin, but now it just felt like a threat to his balance. He glanced down at the emergency hooks strapped to his wrists; the spikes were intended to offer some hope of getting purchase on the rock if he went sliding, sparing him the likely flaying if he tried to achieve the same result with his bare hands. Without shifting his feet on the ledge, he stretched an arm out and pressed one hook against the slope to the north. The tip lodged in a small depression in the rock, but it took no effort at all to scrape it across the surface.

Ada said, "It might still slow you down, even if it can't bring you to a halt immediately."

"That's true," Seth replied.

"Here we go," Andrei announced.

Seth heard the tap of stilt on rock, and the softer step of the leveling wedge. Andrei muttered something incoherent, then there was a second tap, a second step completed.

Five footfalls later, a pause. "It's not too bad," Andrei decided. "You just need to lean inward from whichever foot you're keeping on the ground. And standing motionless feels easier than it did near the basket: you just need to tense your upper legs a bit."

With that, he set off again. Raina and Amina followed him, swiftly, without commentary. Seth took his stilt from his pack and readied it for use.

Sarah shuffled forward and used her stilt to stay balanced while she lifted her right foot to attach the leveling wedge. Seth could see the point a pace in front of her where what remained of the terrace finally crumbled away to nothing. A morbid image came to him, unbidden: Amir and Aziz comforting their children, while Seth looked on helplessly. The only way he could banish it was with an equally lurid fantasy: if Sarah and Judith were taken by the slope, he'd throw himself after them in a doomed attempt at a rescue. In the irrational logic of his competing anxieties, the absurd grandiosity of this imaginary gesture made the imaginary antecedent seem far less likely.

Sarah stepped out onto the slope and began to walk, swaying inward with each step as Andrei had counseled. She made it look easy.

Seth fitted his wedge and replayed Sarah's successful transition in his mind, then he mimicked her as closely as he could, making contact with the slope in all the same places. When the memory guiding this impersonation came to an end, he hesitated, unnerved for a moment, but then he reached back to the rhythms of the steps he'd just taken, recalled the sensations in his joints and muscles, and resumed the act of mimicry in the first person.

After a dozen steps, he looked back to check on Ada. She was off the ledge, following him, a little shaky but not in trouble. "You're doing well," he said.

"You too," she replied.

He tipped his head back to the west. Whatever he felt about Ada's culpability, to deny anyone in this situation a few moments of reassurance and solidarity would be barbaric.

The practice ramp hadn't included anything quite like the transition line they were straddling, but to Seth the habit of giving his full attention to the placement of wedge and stilt, over and over, seemed invaluable regardless of the details of the surface. He lost himself in the minutiae of the act, the judgments of balance, forces, and friction.

Andrei called back, "It veers south a little, from where I am now!" Seth searched for some distinguishing feature on the visible part of the slope that would help him identify the spot; he settled on a small outcrop to the north of Andrei's current position, and described the choice to Theo.

«Will you recognize that when you're pinging it?» Seth wasn't confident that he'd be able to make the connection himself; he hadn't been paying much attention to Theo's view since moving off the ledge, but after days with the vertical cliff face to his north, the one thing he knew was that he was still at risk of misreading the slope's strange echoes.

«I'll keep track of it as it crosses the cone,» Theo assured him.

«Tell me if my gaze drops too low.»

«Don't worry about that. Just concentrate on walking safely.»

«All right.»

As he approached the bend in the transition line, Seth wondered about Ada. With no one to share the task with her, would it be a struggle to coordinate the information, or was she so accustomed to doing everything for herself that this would be no different? If Walkers had been born with pingers sprouting from their skulls, they might have learned to make sense of every echo, unaided. So perhaps that was how she thought of herself: a Walker who could see north and south, more entitled to claim those sensory organs as her own than the sleeping Sider who had never really used them.

Theo said, «Your landmark's coming up to due north of us right now.»

«Thanks.» Seth shifted his gait toward the south, stepping slowly to be sure that he hadn't left the turn too late. As he brought his northern, wedged foot tentatively down, he felt the slope sending him an unexpected signal: it wanted him to slide down, to the south. He'd made the turn too early, not too late.

He calmed himself, and adjusted his posture, shifting his weight to retain his balance. He took another step, directly west, with the stilt and then the wedge again. This time, the wedge landed north of the transition line.

«This isn't going to be easy,» he admitted.

«It's not too late to join me in retirement,» Theo replied.

«Yeah, we'll just walk back to Baharabad from here.»

«We could go back to the basket and wait for the retrieval. Or we could kill some time on the terrace first, to avoid being cooped up for too long.»

Seth was no longer entirely sure that he was joking. «That's tempting, but no. I want to see what's down here with my own eyes.»

Theo was silent. Seth took another step, bringing his foot down with infinite care, waiting for the slope to tell him which way it was trying to make him fall.

THEY STOPPED WHILE THEY still had an hour or so of good light remaining and managed to find suitable crevices for a dozen spikes, to which they attached safety ropes and the wedged slings they hoped to sleep in. With their movements so restricted they had less privacy than ever, but Seth took hold of the longest axial safety rope and went south for a while out of everyone's view, giving him a chance to defecate in peace.

He'd volunteered for the first shift keeping watch, and though only Theo could observe the spikes in the dark, Seth took his own role seriously, attending to the tension that reached him through the network of ropes supporting his sleeping colleagues. If a spike came loose, he was sure he had as good a chance of noticing it as Theo.

When Sarah and Judith took over, he climbed back up north and lay down in the empty sling, with his stilt uncollapsed beside him. He'd never felt more vulnerable, but he was exhausted, and as weariness fought fear, a part of him declared, however insincerely, that it might not be such a bad way to go: sliding away in the night, barely waking before friction with the slope tore his body apart.

He woke before anyone else, except for Ada, who was still on watch. He ate some bechelnuts and took a few swigs of water; it was so cool now that he rarely felt thirsty during the day. As it grew lighter, he could feel the others stirring, sending tremors through the linked slings.

THE EFFORT REQUIRED TO move safely across the slope never lessened, but by their third day off the terrace, the sheer accomplishment of traveling so far without mishap gave Seth a renewed sense of vigor.

It rained that night, but it was a light drizzle, just enough to let them refill their canteens. They'd brought tents, but no one thought it was worth trying to set up shelter, and Seth felt safer sleeping in the rain than if he'd been shielded by a structure that restricted Theo's vision and might hinder his movements in an emergency.

The real downside came the next morning, when the slope remained too slippery to traverse until the twilight's noon. But that was a small inconvenience, and Seth took the whole episode as an encouraging sign. The chasm offered up the most difficult terrain he'd ever faced, but so far it had not proved implacably hostile or impossible to traverse. He felt sure now that they stood a good chance of completing their task safely and returning to the surface with a clear verdict on the obstacle's longitudinal extent and its significance for the migration.

Two days later, they saw the river.

Amina had already heard some kind of susurration from the west, though she hadn't been prepared to commit to any particular interpretation of the sound. But if she'd ever thought that it might have been nothing more than the patter of distant rain, over the course of the morning a shimmering smudge in the distance resolved itself into an unmistakable torrent, streaming over the slope beneath a cloudless sky.

As they drew closer to the river, it became apparent that it was flowing north—and the fact that water could cross their intended path in either axial direction proved that the transition line they'd been following would soon come to an end. Even if they'd arrived here at a time when the riverbed was dry and they could march straight across it, the hope of being guided to a second terrace would have been just as dead.

"We'll follow it north and see what becomes of it," Raina decided. Seth had no reason to argue: if they traveled north at least the Siders would be able to ping the terrain ahead of them.

They kept their distance from the damp slickness of the riverbank, and ascended slowly, struggling to master the new gait. Seth's hips began to ache incessantly from the need to raise his legs higher than usual to give them clearance from the tilted ground. It was a welcome change not to have to tip his head to the west, though.

"Why couldn't they give us a separate expedition to the east?" he joked with Sarah.

"And the return journey . . .?"

"Maybe we would have stumbled on a river that let us circumnavigate the habitable zone."

Theo couldn't resist the opportunity to return to his second-favorite gripe. "More chance of that than doing it with balloons."

Andrei said, "The bridge of balloons is just a gesture. No one really believes that's going to work, but they need to be seen to be trying everything."

For the first time since they'd left the basket, Seth had Andrei's face in front of him as he spoke, but he'd missed the opportunity to give him a warning glance to steer him away from the subject.

"*Trying everything?*" Theo was incensed. "Except the one idea with a real chance of success!"

"They didn't just dismiss the possibility of trapping the sun," Andrei replied. "Nicholas and I were on the committee that examined it."

Theo took a moment to absorb this revelation. Finally he asked, "So did you reject it yourself, or were you voted down?"

Andrei said, "I was positively disposed to your plan at the start, but after the committee had spent nine days examining it, our own calculations led to a consensus. Your basic idea was perfectly sound: if we could erect mountains in the formation you proposed, they'd put a torque on the sun's orbit that would balance whatever's causing the current tilting. But the logistics turned out to be insurmountable."

"'Logistics'!" Theo retorted. "You mean political will?"

Andrei remained calm. "No. Politics wasn't even part of our brief. We took it as our starting point that the diplomats could clear the way to assembling the largest construction workforce imaginable: eighty percent of the adult population of the habitable zone, with the remainder either farming, transporting food, or looking after children. But building the necessary structure in any given location would still have taken longer than the time in which that location remained in the habitable zone. Any dawdling child can keep up with the migration, but not even a million adults could build mountains high enough to trap the sun before it moved on. You might as well try to catch an axis lizard by weaving a cage out of grass as it runs past you."

Theo fell silent.

Seth wasn't sure how to take the news himself. If it meant that he'd heard the last of Theo's diatribes against the feeble-minded cowards who'd rejected his plan, that would be bliss . . . but the fact that they'd treated the proposal with the utmost seriousness, only to rule it out even as a measure of last resort, was a little disquieting. If Andrei's opinion on the bridge of balloons was equally well informed, then finding a way past the chasm might be the only remaining option.

"Why couldn't someone tell me this earlier?" Theo demanded.

"You're not known for your discretion," Andrei replied bluntly. "The concern was that if you were told about the assessment, you'd dispute the results aggressively, while publicizing them in a way that spread panic."

Theo said, "Don't you think people are entitled to know all this?"

Andrei's face took on an expression of mild incredulity. "Most people have never even heard about your plan, and most of those who have thought it was both impractical and entirely unnecessary. Telling the world that surveyors from ten cities were so worried about the future of the migration that they'd seriously contemplated trying to halt the sun would not inspire people's confidence. When we have a plan that we're sure will work, that will be the time to spread the word about it."

AFTER THEY'D PURSUED THE river north for three days, even the Walkers could hear that there was a change ahead. Rising above the steady babbling from the west, the sound of water pounding rock presaged a dramatic change in the flow. Though they were north of the point where the basket had been set down, they were still well south of the cliffs, but the incline would only need to increase by a few degrees to start opposing the water's northwards passage.

As a mist of fine droplets began to spray down on them, they veered east in search of dry ground. The spray became thinner, but did not die away entirely; perhaps the wind was dispersing it, though it did not seem to come and go with any palpable breeze. Theo could ping a fair distance upslope, but not far enough to reveal the source of the droplets. Facing east, away from the presumed waterfall, Seth thought he could see a distant glistening in his peripheral vision, but even turning his gaze as far to the north as he dared in his precarious state of balance couldn't make the smudge of light entirely convincing.

The next day, by mid-morning, the view was clearer, and Raina confirmed his hunch. "It looks like a flooded terrace," she agreed.

If the river had reached a terrace and branched in two, the flow on their side would be traveling east. Even if it was tame enough to ride, it would carry them in the wrong direction. Their only real hope of continuing west would be to cross this branch of the river and resume their journey from the northern bank.

By the time they stopped to set up camp for the night, the twilight shimmering off the surface of the distributary was unmistakable, whether they looked for it west-north-west or east-north-east. Farther to the west, Seth could see hints of the waterfall at the river's bifurcation point, with the spray rising high into the air around a vortex comparable to the one in Thanton's jungle. The eastern branch of the river seemed placid in comparison; the topography at the junction must have directed most of the flow to the west.

In the morning they advanced slowly; there was no avoiding rock dampened by the spray, so they minimized the risk by scrupulously checking every spot where they placed a stilt or wedge. Seth barely lifted his gaze from the slope until Sarah announced in a tone of relief, "That looks navigable to me."

They were only a few dozen paces from the river now. Between Theo's pings of the bank directly above them, and his own view of the adjacent stretch to the east, Seth could discern a steady flow beneath the mist of droplets escaping from the water's surface. The spray here wasn't coming from some turbulent collision of currents, or a jagged outcrop obstructing the flow. Although the slope at the southern bank was less than forty-five degrees, pushing the water uphill, the steeper angle of the as-yet invisible northern bank was blocking its passage, leaving the bulk of it piled up with nowhere to go but east. But it didn't take more than a faint gust of wind to disturb the surface, pushing parts of it beyond the critical angle and sending droplets cascading down—fast enough for the lightest to bounce off into the air.

Raina instructed them to start assembling the boat. The small tents that each of them carried in their packs were made of a fabric sufficiently tough and waterproof to serve a second purpose: with a few different choices in the way the panels were tied together and braced, the final structure could form a rigid enclosed volume, with its lower surface seamless and impermeable. Each of the five modules was able to float independently, but the safest configuration would be to bind them all up into the hull of a single vessel.

They'd rehearsed the assembly process more than a dozen times on the practice ramp, though Seth recalled that only the last attempt had been successful: every other time, either the boat or a member of the team had ended up falling from the ramp into the hay. He proceeded to unpack and unfold the material, switching his attention methodically between the act of ensuring that his balance and footing were secure whenever he needed to shift his weight, and the precise manipulations required to bring the panels of fabric a step closer to their final state.

The sheer size of that final state made it unwieldy, but for the last few stages he found he could rest at least one corner of the structure on the slope, letting the rock take some of the strain off his wrists. When he was done, he had a shallow, open-topped box with hollow walls and a hollow base. He prodded it cautiously, checking that he hadn't left any strings loose or struts unanchored. In one of the rehearsals, he'd managed to do everything perfectly, except that the whole surface was inverted, with all the joins where the panels were merely laced together—closing off the would-be tent's entrance flap—appearing on the craft's underside, rather than tucked into the edges above, where they'd have a chance to remain dry.

Andrei said, "Give me flat ground, one dead tree, and five days to carve it into a canoe."

"While you're dreaming, just give us a balloon," Judith retorted.

"Actually," Nicholas replied, "if there's a second expedition, they should find a way to make that work. Think of the ground we could have covered by now."

Judith said, "Only if 'by now' excludes however many hundreds of days it would take to set up the infrastructure to get the thing into the air in the first place."

When the five modules were complete, they set about the finicky task of binding them together. Four of the boxes had corners cut out of their rectangular bases, allowing them to fit snugly around the fifth. Raina and Sarah started with their modules, lacing them together along a shared wall, then they lowered the northern edges of the pair onto the rock, and Ada came in from the south to attach her own, central component. Seth found it odd that the expedition leader hadn't been granted that position in the middle of the boat, but apparently the seating plan had been chosen by some anxious bureaucrat in the Office of Surveyors, worried by Ada's relative inexperience, and the diplomatic consequences if she came to any harm.

When Ada was done, Seth moved in, with everyone whose hands were free now standing guard around him to be sure the work in progress didn't go sliding upslope. The trickiest parts were the bottom joins between two surfaces facing north and south, where he had to tip his own piece of the hull southwards to give himself access to the lacing points. He worked slowly and meticulously, planning every movement in advance, trusting his colleagues to perform their supporting roles but taking care to do nothing that took them by surprise.

Finally, Andrei had his turn, giving the boat its south-east corner. As Seth watched, he had to force himself to stop thinking about the way he would have gone about the job himself, and concentrate entirely on being prepared to halt the boat if it went sliding up the slope.

Andrei tightened the last length of string and knotted the end. "We have . . . something," he said, torn between relief at the task's completion and disdain for the inelegant result. "A floating biscuit tray?"

"We're not finished," Raina reminded him. "We need to attach the runners." One by one, the four of them in corner positions took the small, stiff boards from their packs and fixed them to the outside of the hull.

They stood and rested for a while. Seth ached all over; he hadn't needed to apply any great force during the construction, but to maintain precise control over every movement seemed to require a heightened muscular tension that took its own kind of toll.

Raina looked around for any crevices in the rock where they could anchor a safety rope and tie up the boat, but there were none in sight. The only way they'd get respite now would be to carry their awkward burden all the way to the river and commence the crossing.

Seth exchanged a glance with Sarah. "Rivers have always been lucky for us, haven't they?" she joked. Seth hoped, a little cruelly, that Ada would innocently ask why—but then, Ada had probably heard the whole story of their escape from Thanton long before she'd joined the expedition.

They set off up the slope toward the water's edge, moving more slowly than ever as they tried to coordinate their steps. Seth wasn't sure whether the ten-legged creature they comprised was more stable than a lone Walker, thanks to its numerous points of contact with the ground, or less, given that the south-west leg risked losing track of what the north-east leg was doing.

At the riverbank, the water fizzed and spluttered, raining down across the slope and flowing back in shallow rivulets. Seth was less afraid now of slipping upslope into the water than of striking the treacherous surface in such a way that he'd be thrown off and dashed against the rock.

Raina told Ada to climb into the boat. Seth set aside his irritation as he shouldered the shifting weight, treating it as a test of the craft's robustness. If it could hold together with a passenger in the middle, unsupported from below, that would prove that all the seams were in good shape.

They continued north until Raina and Sarah were standing in the churning water. They paused to assess the depth, but judged the river too shallow, and advanced again, bringing Seth and Andrei in up to their northern ankles. The surface of the water was still far from horizontal; the flooded terrace was at least a dozen paces away. Seth could feel the slickness of the riverbed: the tiny, experimental forces he applied to the wedge that supported his foot were met with almost no resistance.

Raina said, "If we keep going like this and someone slips, we're going to be scattered in five directions."

She had them lower the boat until its northern edge was surrounded by water, with the bottom resting on the rock below. Then she and Sarah clambered in, leaving Seth and Andrei holding the boat level. The two new passengers tied their stilts to the east and west sides of the hull, near the halfway point, then Seth and Andrei began sidling again, very slowly, worried as much by the risk of scraping the edge of the hull on the rock as the risk of losing control.

Finally, Seth felt the boat being buoyed up along its northern edge. Raina said, "See if you can get in."

Seth glanced at Andrei, who said, "You first." The hull came to just above Seth's waist; he tied his own stilt to the side without taking his weight off it, then he slithered over the edge, face-first, into the snug compartment.

Nothing toppled, or broke, or went sliding out of control. Seth got up off his stomach and tipped his head west so he could hold onto the stilt and see what he was doing. It was disconcerting to be kneeling on the taut fabric of the hull, and feel the whole structure flex as he shifted his body. Even in the balloon, staring down through thin air from twice the height of any mountain, he'd been able to rest his body on the solid wood of the basket.

Andrei performed the same maneuver, a little less clumsily. The four stilts remained in place, keeping the boat level. The ten-legged land creature had become some kind of tentative, shore-dwelling water-lizard; the only question was whether it was capable of making the transition all the way into the river's depths.

Andrei and Sarah leaned away from the boat, taking some of the weight off Seth's corner, as Seth forced the top of his pivoted stilt southward, sending the bottom scraping its way north across the rock. The wedge that comprised the foot of the stilt didn't need a Walker's ankle joint in order to remain in contact with the riverbed; the slope was so close to forty-five degrees that the main effect was to increase the area of contact. They repeated the exercise for each corner in turn, then performed the second stage: putting as much weight on the southern edge as possible, while Seth and Andrei tipped the stilts back to the north while trying not move their bases. Finally, Sarah and Raina did the same. The whole process was exhausting, but having one edge of the boat in the water seemed to provide enough extra support to make it viable, and the way the buoyant force adapted to the boat's changing orientation had a stabilizing effect.

When their heads rose above the point where the water began to level out, Seth was both gratified and a little daunted. The river was far wider than the narrow terrace they'd first encountered; Theo couldn't even ping the northern bank. If the runners worked, there'd be nothing to stop them making the crossing, but in the meantime the current would be carrying them east.

"Maybe we should rethink our plans," Sarah suggested. "If the water wants to take us this way, why fight it? We're just as likely to find the edge of the chasm to the east as to the west."

Seth wasn't sure how serious she was. Raina said, "Let's just see what we're dealing with. It's still possible that we can get to the far shore without too much backtracking."

When the northern half of the boat was sitting almost level in the water, Raina and Sarah withdrew their stilts. Seth and Andrei gave one last push from the south, and suddenly the vessel was floating. The current took hold of it, and they began drifting eastward.

Seth untied his stilt and collapsed it, then secured it at the bottom of the boat. To the west, in the distance, he could just make out the turmoil where the changing slope turned the north-flowing branch back on itself—but here the surface was almost flat, with none of the frantic activity of the overspill. After so much effort and anxiety, it felt glorious to be held up by the water and lofted along, whatever the direction, no longer having to worry about putting a foot wrong.

Raina must have felt the same, because she gave them all a few minutes of relaxation before saying, "Now we need to deploy the runners."

The boards were already attached to the corners of the boat, but they were sitting horizontally, with no effect. At Raina's count, the four Walkers in the corner modules tipped them, gradually and simultaneously, until they were sloping upward to the south at a modest angle.

Water flowed up over the runners and spilled off the top, giving the boat a gentle push to the north—along with a gentle push downward, making it ride lower in the water. Seth peered into Theo's view, but the far side of the river was still unpingably distant. The runners weren't robust enough, nor the hull deep enough, for the boat to be driven much faster. And if there was nothing they could do to speed up the crossing, perhaps Sarah was right: perhaps they should welcome the effortless passage east, and just reverse the expedition's original plan.

The runners needed to be watched carefully, in case they snapped or came loose, and the imperfect mounts meant that they required small adjustments every few minutes, but compared to the arduous demands of the slope, to Seth the task felt almost shamefully effortless. «It looks as if I've finally joined you in retirement,» he told Theo, dipping a hand languorously in the water.

«My retirement's canceled,» Theo replied glumly. «When we get back, we'll need to join the balloon project. It might be insanely dangerous, but if it's the only hope then we have to be a part of it.»

Seth was impressed that Theo had accepted Andrei's word on the sun trap, and was even willing to reconsider the merits of a rival endeavor, but it was too much to hope that he'd change his mind about three things at once. «And if this river carries us to the eastern edge of the chasm, by nightfall . . .?»

«That's wishful thinking. There's not going to be any eastern edge—or western edge, or southern edge.»

Seth gazed out across the sparkling water. «If there's nothing to the south of us but the void, what's the source of this river?»

Theo hesitated. «Rain clouds blowing in from the southern hyperboloid.»

«Wouldn't all the water there be frozen solid? If there's no sunlight, ever?»

«At the edge, maybe the summer air can circulate around and come back with more moisture than it started with.»

Seth didn't know what to make of this idea, but he couldn't think of anything that ruled it out immediately.

«We should be patient,» he decided. «The only thing I'm sure of is that we'll have much more of a chance to learn the truth here than if we'd stayed up on the surface arguing about everyone's theories.»

NIGHT CAME, WITH NO end in sight to the river, either to the north or to the east. Raina decided that they should withdraw the runners until morning; though the supervision they needed was minimal, it couldn't be performed by anything less than a crew of four, and having each person sleep for just one-fifth of the night would have rendered them all incompetent for the day ahead.

With no camp to set up, Seth felt more idle than ever. The only downside of their new accommodation was the disposal of bodily wastes, which had to be done via a container—and in Ada's case, passed to a neighbor to tip over the side. Seth and Theo took the first watch, and with the boat no longer propelling itself, they pinged the water to the north with little expectation of change.

«I hate not knowing where we are,» Theo said. Since they'd lost sight of the southern shore, they'd had no reference points to observe, so even their crude system of additive navigation had come to an end, replaced by even cruder estimates about the current.

«We'll make new measurements on the way back,» Seth replied. «We know more or less how far north of the basket we were when we entered the water, and however we return it will probably mean crossing this river in the opposite direction. And even if we don't retrace our whole route, we ought to be able to locate that first terrace again, coming at it from the east.»

When he judged his shift to be over, he woke Andrei and Nicholas then lay down to sleep. He couldn't quite stretch out flat on his back, but with his head propped against the western rim of the hull, his knees bent and his feet against the eastern wall of his compartment, he felt more comfortable, and safer, than he'd ever felt in a sling.

Someone prodded him awake. Raina said, "Seth?" It was still dark, but she wasn't whispering.

"What's happening?" he asked. Theo woke, letting him see enough of Ada and Sarah to make it clear that everyone in the boat had been roused.

"There's a change in course for the river up ahead," Amina said. Seth couldn't hear anything, but Theo said, «I think she's right.» The flooded terrace had had to come to an end eventually, but it hadn't seemed too much to hope that they'd make it to the north bank first.

"We need to be ready to reconfigure the boat," Raina added.

"Of course." Seth's grogginess was entirely gone now. Whichever way the river turned, once it was no longer flowing over the terrace the surface of the water would take on more or less the same inclination as the underlying rock. The modules had been designed to allow for that: the southern pair could slide down lower than the others, allowing each individual part to stay level even on a forty-five-degree slope. But he'd always imagined making the modification in daylight, when he could see exactly what changes in the water were ahead, and how fast they were approaching. As close as Theo could ping to the north-east and south-east, there was still no sign of whatever it was the Siders were hearing.

Seth loosened the ties around the sliders at the northern wall of his compartment, as much as he dared; he didn't want to be fumbling to free them at the last moment, but if they were rattling about for too long they might become damaged.

"We need a signal," Andrei suggested. "To be sure we both use the sliders at the same time."

"Shouting 'now!' ought to do it," Seth replied, still gauging the tension in the ties.

"If you like," Andrei said. "I was going to suggest that we treat any loud imprecation as proof that the other person has noticed the boat tipping, since that might incur less of a delay than anything requiring a conscious choice."

"It might," Seth conceded. "But you don't want to start reconfiguring the boat just because I stub my toe."

Ada said, "The river turns south. I can hear it now: there's a clear asymmetry."

Seth didn't reply, and no one else spoke to fill the silence. Was she claiming superior auditory skills of her own, or was she claiming that her drugged Sider was sharing its sense of hearing with her? Either way, he'd reserve his trust for Siders he could actually converse with.

The boat glided on across the dark river. Theo showed the patches he was pinging shimmering slightly, ruffled by the breeze, but the surface was as inscrutable as ever.

Then Sarah said, "There's a cross-current, and it's growing stronger. We're accelerating south! Can't you feel it?"

Seth couldn't honestly say that he did: he hadn't been paying so much attention to the exact amount of pressure exerted on his body by different parts of the hull's fabric that he could register any change now. But if they were coming to the end of the terrace, the direction of the flow might start to change well in advance.

"What if we use the runners to try to get back to the south bank?" he suggested. "If the current alone would take us south and down the slope, an extra push might get us back on land before the river changes course."

Raina considered this. "All right. We're probably too far north, but we've got nothing to lose by trying."

They had to redeploy the runners by touch, but the mounts gave a click at every increment in the angle, and the boat responded with a burst of speed that Seth had no trouble feeling. He moved his hand from the runner back to the slider, checking that it hadn't come loose.

Now that they had a chance to avoid the rush downslope, Seth found himself picturing the dangers far more vividly than when it had seemed inevitable. Even if the south-flowing river was deep enough to spare them from any rocks, when it came to an end on another flooded terrace, the transition was unlikely to be gentle.

"How close now, Amina?" he asked.

"A few more minutes," she replied.

Theo's view still showed a level surface, but the water was growing choppy, with the usual orderly ranks of wind-blown waves broken up by more chaotic formations coming in from the east. Seth could see the boat's wake too, imprinted on these natural undulations, but it looked feeble in comparison.

Suddenly, an edge appeared to the south: a line beyond which the crumpled sheet of waves dropped out of sight. Seth shouted with jubilation; they were approaching the riverbank. He groped down and found his stilt. "We need to fix these again, don't we?" he asked Raina. If they shot out of the water back onto the slope, they'd need some way to try to keep the boat level.

She hesitated. "Yes."

Seth reattached the stilt to the side of the hull, while Andrei did the same.

More and more of the shimmering surface Theo was painting gave way to darkness. Seth's blood pounded in his ears and his body tensed, ready for the shock that would come through the stilts if they managed to scrape back onto dry land. In the complex topography south of the bank, there had to be a line where the slope increased, from a fraction less than forty-five degrees, to a fraction more. All they had to do was part company with the water on the near side of that line, where the slope would still bear them up and contain the river.

At its eastern edge, the border of the encroaching darkness began to veer south, exposing a turbulent froth that was scattering pings in every direction. Seth was confused for a moment, then he understood what Theo was showing him: water from the terrace was arching down over the slope, rather than conforming instantly to the shape of the underlying rock and dropping neatly out of sight. If they failed to reach the shore, the boat would be riding that waterfall.

"Reverse the runners!" Judith pleaded.

"Why?" Nicholas asked.

"We're going down the slope, whatever we do. But if we travel farther east, if we can get past that corner, the flow should be smoother."

Raina said firmly, "No. Leave the runners as they are. We could still make landfall."

Seth watched the clean, sharp precipice to the south growing nearer—and growing shorter even faster. He wasn't sure if Raina believed what she'd said, or if she'd reasoned that Judith's tactic would come too late to make any difference.

Theo inspoke calmly, «Five. Four. Three. Two. One.»

The shoreline was behind them. Seth bellowed, "Now!" and pushed down on the slider's handle as the boat lurched into the dark air. A fine spray stung his skin, and all he saw from Theo was the same scattering of droplets—and the northern half of the boat rising up to his left.

They hit the surface of the southbound river, sank down almost to the top of the hull, then bounced up again. For a moment water rained down on them—but then the falls were gone, receding to the north so rapidly that they'd vanished behind the upper section of the boat before Seth could brace himself for a pummeling. A mixture of terror and a visceral sense of elemental power took hold of him as the boat accelerated in the current, easily outrunning any kind of rain. Gravity in midair was nothing compared to the forces on the slope itself, where the gradient rendered the efforts of the rock to retain its integrity beneath the modest weight of the river so stupendously inefficient that most of its resistance to compression was spent on directing the flow ever faster downhill.

"Everyone still with us?" Raina shouted. Between the darkness and the boat's new two-tiered shape Seth was in no position to check, but a chorus of affirmations came back. "Then hang the fuck on tight. When we hit the next terrace, we won't have any warning."

Their descent seemed to have reached its terminal velocity, and while they bobbed and jittered in the water, making the hull shudder, it was only the force of the air rushing over the boat that kept them from moving in lockstep with the flow. When Seth cautiously dipped his hand into the water he could feel it vigorously outpacing them—but if he'd tried the same thing from the river's shore, it would probably have torn his hand off. As it was, the wind bit into his skin as fiercely as anything short of a cone storm. Whatever change finally brought them to a halt, it was going to be painful.

Ada said, "The air pressure's up by almost fifteen percent."

"Could that be an artifact of the wind?" Nicholas suggested.

"It's an average, as much downwind as upwind."

"Then what does it mean, exactly?" Sarah asked.

"That we're lower now than we've ever been. Much lower."

Seth stared into the darkness. With every minute that passed, they might easily be traveling so far that it would take the expedition a whole day of struggling up the slope to regain the lost altitude.

Theo said, «We'll find a north-flowing river.» That wasn't an idle hope: as far as they knew, every drop of water around them had once flowed north. The more immediate problem was the end of their descent—and there was nothing to be done about that except to brace for it.

The current around them grew more turbulent, shaking the boat, snapping rods and ties. The wind rose and fell in cheek-numbing gusts, so intense that they could only have come from dips and rises in the slope. Seth willed the torture of waiting to be over, imagining a dozen survivable scenarios, then imagining the worst and telling himself that he was ready for anything. But the river flowed on relentlessly, bearing them south like an idiot child who'd snatched something valuable from the adult world by mistake, fleeing ever faster out of sheer stubbornness and perversity. Having chanced upon the only living things in sight, all it could do was carry them deeper, farther from home, to no purpose, until it finally lost interest and smashed them against the rocks.

WHEN THE SKY BEGAN to brighten, Seth wondered if he was hallucinating: that their fall could outlast the night was no longer beyond imagining, but the intensity of the light far exceeded anything he'd seen since they'd left the surface. It took him a while to clear his head and make sense of the change: the shadow of the cliffs wasn't infinite, and the farther south they went, the narrower the gap would be between the slope and the sunlit air above.

As the river emerged from night, the water rushing past the boat glinted fiercely in the dawn. The boat's own motion reduced the eastern bank to a blur, and it was only in the far distance that the rocks of the slope appeared still enough to perceive as anything solid at all. Seth searched the south-east corner of his vision for a river flowing from the west, then tipped his head and sought the opposite branch. But the landscape was almost indecipherable, and every distant shimmer that seemed like a portent of the boat's imminent deceleration proved to be a false alarm.

Amina called out, "I think—"

Seth gripped the hand-holds beside him as the sky filled with water. Before he had a chance to take a breath, the boat had plunged so deep that every trace of light from above was gone. With Theo equally blind, Seth's world shrank to the weight of the water crushing his chest, and the silence pressing in on him.

If he gave in to the urge to inhale, he was dead. Theo began inspeaking gibberish; Seth replied in kind, losing himself in the simple rhythm of the exchange. When the pain in his lungs intruded, he shouted it away: *Not yet, not yet, not yet.*

Theo said, «Flerdibyll graznisniff?»

Seth responded effortlessly: «Mulpeneresh, sockulee!»

When he burst to the surface, he drew in air while water was still streaming over his face. He spluttered and choked until he'd driven the offending liquid out, then he lay still for a while, gasping, waiting to get his strength back.

He sat up and began assessing the situation. His section of the hull was full of water, but the hollow walls were apparently keeping it afloat. He could see Andrei sitting in front of him, bedraggled but very much alive, and as Theo cleared the water from his pingers he revealed Ada's arm in motion near the side of her compartment. She was scooping water out with her cupped hand.

But the rest of the boat was gone.

Seth tried to remain calm: he had no more reason to fear that his friends had come to harm than they'd have to believe the same of him.

The current was carrying their half-boat west, much more rapidly than it had ever moved on the first flooded terrace. Looking back toward the waterfall, Seth could see no trace of his missing companions, but if anything, they'd probably ended up with a more suitable craft: this one was only staying level because the two waterlogged southern compartments were keeping Ada's from overbalancing.

"Should we try to reconfigure?" he asked Andrei.

"I wouldn't risk it," Andrei replied. "We're stable enough as we are—and if we hit another axial branch, at least we'll be prepared."

"Where do you think the others are?"

Nicholas said, "I've been calling to them, but I've had no reply. They must be on the other side of the falls."

"You mean you think they've gone east?"

"Yes."

Seth absorbed this. "We need to get back on land, as quickly as possible." The only way the separated groups would have a chance to reunite was if they both headed for the river's southern shore.

"With what?" Andrei gestured toward the boat's east side. "My runner's gone. What about yours?"

Seth checked. "The same."

Theo said, "If the water's shallow enough, maybe you could do something with the stilts?"

Seth fished around at the bottom of his flooded module. Amazingly, the stilt was still there, strapped to the floor along the northern side. He brought it up, extended it, then lowered it into the river and tied the top to the side of the hull. As he tilted it to increase its reach the shifting currents tugged at it erratically, but he couldn't feel resistance from anything solid, and when he glanced back at Andrei, who'd been making his own attempts, it was clear that he'd fared no better.

Ada said, "Can you see that?" She was gazing west.

"What?" Seth was so low in the water that his own view was pitifully curtailed.

"I think we're about to turn again."

Seth leaned north as far as he dared, raising his head almost to the same height as Ada's. They were approaching a point where the river veered west-south-west, spilling down the slope along an ordinary gradient, not an axial one. It was difficult to judge whether the current would do anything helpful at the bend, but the river appeared to grow broader as it turned, which had to decrease its depth.

He lowered himself and braced against the sunken hull, gripping the stilt tightly. His hope was to get enough purchase to allow him to take turns with Andrei forcing the boat to pivot around their respective ends, with the current doing most of the work, zigzagging the vessel toward the shore.

As the river spread out and veered down across the slope, Seth tipped the stilt to the south, sending the far end shorewards and ever deeper into the water. In air, the torque at such an extreme angle might have snapped his wrists, but in water the wood's buoyancy took some of the load.

The stilt began to shudder; it wasn't catching on the riverbed, but it was scraping over it. Seth cried out to Andrei, "I've got contact!" Between the two of them, surely they could halt the boat.

"Same here," Andrei replied. "But it's not sticking."

Seth's forearms were burning. He clung on, swinging the stilt back and forth, desperate for anything that might work in their favor. "All we need is a rut, a depression in the rock . . ."

At the sound of churning water, he glanced up to see what was making the noise, but they were traveling almost south-west now, leaving them blind to any changes ahead. Suddenly, the stilt refused to move with the boat; it felt as if it was jammed into a crevice. Seth's jubilation turned to alarm as the rear of the boat swung far to the north, widening the hull across the flow. Andrei fought to snag the riverbed at a second spot—but he had no luck, and in a matter of seconds the force of the current had freed them, and they were adrift again.

Seth wiggled the stilt, preparing for a second attempt, then realized that it was taking much less effort to move it than before. He brought it upright, untied it and pulled it out of the water. The bottom two-thirds had snapped off.

There was a spare in his pack, but before he could retrieve it the boat lurched, slamming him against the hull, and the churning water around him became a torrent flooding straight down the slope.

The transition was smoother than the last time they'd gone south, and though Seth was not inured to the wild acceleration, once it was clear that the boat remained stable his thoughts turned to the struggle the others would face, trying to keep their own vessel level if their eastward journey took the same turn.

"When does it stop?" Ada asked. The question might have sounded plaintive if she hadn't had to shout to be heard.

Andrei said, "The river must split up, and every branch must dry out eventually."

That claim sounded absurd when the words were almost lost in the noise of rushing water, but Seth clung to the fact that they'd already seen two bifurcations of the original, north-bound flow. So long as that process continued, and no other tributary joined them along the way, anyone riding the river would have to end up in a shallow stream somewhere. It was growing harder to feel sure that he had any idea of how long it might take the two halves of the expedition to find their way back to the basket, but for now he'd be ready to rejoice at the prospect of merely standing on dry land again.

He waited, tensed, for the next violent dunking, glancing now and then at the blur of the eastern shore. The wind had begun to split his skin in places; he could see the same wounds on Andrei's face.

Theo asked Ada, "Do you still have your barometer?"

"No. It's lost in the river somewhere." She hesitated. "But if we go much deeper, maybe we could judge our depth from gravitational effects."

"That would depend on what we're doing," Theo replied. "How we're moving, what other forces are in play." He sounded peeved that he'd been drawn into a conversation with the enemy, but having initiated the exchange he could hardly cut it short. "If we were walking down the slope, the most striking effect would be the gravitational force changing direction."

"How much would it change?"

"How deep do you want to go? Eventually it would cross the cone and turn axial."

Ada took a while to think that through. "Then on a slope like this, where water flows down under normal conditions . . . by the time you reach a point where gravity is axial and 'up' points south, the slope will have switched from more than forty-five degrees to less, measured from the new horizontal, and water will flow upslope. But upslope will mean *south*. So the flow won't change direction along the slope. Gravity alone won't turn the river around and send us back the way we came."

"That's right," Theo agreed.

Nicholas said, "But we're sure to end up traveling north again, for other reasons."

"Why?" Ada pressed him.

"If it's down to chance, how many times would the river branch the same way?"

Ada wasn't satisfied. "How can we be sure that it's down to chance? If the whole slope tilts a certain way over a wide enough area, the direction might not be random at all."

Nicholas had no reply.

Seth said, "Then we could just reach the bottom of the chasm." With nothing visible to the south to contradict Theo's edge-of-the-world nonsense, they'd started taking it far too seriously. "If the river doesn't carry us north, we could find ourselves on level ground." No more stilt-walking, no more waterfalls. So long as they had some shelter from the sun, they could live like civilized people for a while, resting and recovering their strength before facing the task of finding a way back.

AS NIGHT FELL, THE river still hadn't deviated from its southward course. Seth's concentration had been wavering; he didn't think he'd lapsed into sleep, but at times his consciousness had detached from his surroundings, distancing him from the relentless battering of the wind, the juddering of the boat, the landscape hurtling by.

Once it was dark, it became much harder to judge the passage of time. Whatever inner sense of duration he possessed had already grown addled from the daylong twilight, and the boat's interminable fall confounded it further. Nothing in ordinary experience could drop faster than a stone and not hit bottom by a count of ten, and Seth suspected that whatever fragment of his mind played timekeeper had lost confidence in the meaning of its silent count as it waited for the impact that never came.

The hull had never made a comfortable resting place, but as the night wore on it only felt worse. The force of the wind and the motion of the boat shoved him against the northern wall, pinning his arm, and he couldn't find any way to adjust his body that relieved the pressure. When Theo dozed off, Seth tried imagining the others escaping the river, trekking up the slope, and finding a way to complete the survey. The chasm had proved itself absurdly deep, but it might yet turn out to be narrow enough for the migration to detour around it.

Just as the eastern sky showed a hint of gray, a light rain began to fall. The boat was moving south so rapidly that Seth could feel the drizzle striking at an angle, with the south side of the hull sheltering half his body. The sky grew brighter, then a dazzling bead of light appeared on the horizon: true dawn. He closed his eyes for a minute or two, only opening them again when the rain stopped.

The shower had moved on, but it was still visible in the east. Seth watched the distant rain glistening in the sunlight. That it was sloping down from the south seemed perfectly sensible to him at first: that was how he'd experienced it, so why shouldn't it look that way?

But the rain was tilted against the landscape itself; nothing about the boat's motion could explain that. For a moment he wondered if the slope could have changed its gradient sufficiently to explain what he was seeing, but it would have needed to have leveled out and started rising to the south—without the river slowing, or their lopsided boat tipping over.

Theo complained indignantly, "We crossed over, and you didn't even wake me?"

Andrei stirred, sighing, noticed Seth's perplexed gaze and tipped his head to the east. The rainstorm was receding; Seth willed it to vanish entirely, taking the whole disturbing illusion with it.

Nicholas said, "Could it just be the wind?"

Andrei maneuvered his canteen out of his pack and held it in one hand, to the south of his body. "That's not blocking much more air than my arm alone, but I can feel the extra weight of it—pointing more to the north than it's pointing in the direction that used to be down."

Ada said, "I felt the change, halfway through the night. But I thought I must be dreaming."

Seth tried to sit up, but as his head rose above the side of the boat, the northward force—whatever its source—threatened to send him toppling over the edge, and he retreated.

The sun had risen fully now, and the heat was growing fierce. Seth had no doubt that if they'd been at the same latitude up on the surface they would have crossed into absolute summer; it was only their depth that had kept them clear of the cone.

"The river has to turn sometime," he declared. Unless the chasm was literally bottomless, the far end would be more like a ceiling than a floor, and at some point the approach would become far too steep for the river to climb.

Andrei said, "Let's hope so. Walking on stilts was bad enough; I don't even want to try with one hand and one foot."

Seth wasn't sure if he was joking. But however strange their circumstances, halfway to the other hyperboloid was still only halfway.

THE SUN AT NOON was merciless, hovering over the source of the now ascending river, painting the churning water at the northern edge of Seth's vision with a streak of white fire that kept pace with their retreat. He huddled into the boat, but however he squeezed and contorted himself he couldn't fit entirely in its meager patch of shade.

Now that he'd acknowledged the shifting vertical, he tracked the change with a dismal fascination. His body was receiving all the cues it needed to tell him just how far his right shoulder had risen above the left, but the situation was so remote from anything he had experienced before that it was more like taking a measurement from a complicated instrument than intuiting his posture in any ordinary way.

"We need to be prepared," Theo said. "If we end up on south-facing land, we need to be ready to assemble something that will help us move."

"There are some axial struts in the boat that should bear our weight," Andrei replied reluctantly. "More than one for each Walker. They could give us balance, I suppose. But we'd still be crawling around on our sides, scraping the ground with half our bodies. Unless it's just a few paces from wherever we're dumped to a north-flowing river, I don't think anything could make that journey survivable."

"We should have planned for this," Theo said bitterly. "We planned for the slope, we planned for the rivers."

"And what should we have built?" Nicholas demanded. "Forget about the weight we'd be lugging around; what would actually be useful? Wheels won't work there, in any direction. I suppose you could dream up a contraption with enough levers and pulleys to let a Walker control a set of axial legs beneath some kind of platform or harness . . . and then hope that the terrain was all as flat and firm as a paved road."

"I don't have any answers," Theo admitted. "Before we hit the river, the most I ever imagined was that we might find some kind of indirect evidence that the slope went all the way down. I wasn't contemplating a personal visit."

Seth kept quiet. He believed that they were far more likely to die in the chasm's final waterfall than face any of these insoluble problems, but nobody needed to hear that.

"Runners will still work though, won't they?" Ada asked, shouting up at them through the walls of her compartment.

"Yes," Nicholas agreed. "And in any direction. If we end up in calm water, we might be able to improvise something."

"And then hope that there's a route to a river north that doesn't involve dry land," Theo added. "That might be optimistic, but it's not unthinkable."

WHEN THE SUN FINALLY disappeared behind the slope, it took some dispassionate geometric reasoning for Seth to accept that the day now past, interminable as it had seemed, must have been shorter than any he'd experienced on the surface. Every ordinary cue around him had shifted its meaning, but he held fast to the lofty, impersonal image of the sun in its orbit, the cliffs as he'd seen them from the balloon, the world-piercing chasm as a line on a diagram in his mind's eye, slanting across the page from one hyperboloid toward the other, whether or not it reached all the way. Geometry might well kill them in the end, but only a rigorous understanding of its principles could make their situation intelligible, let alone survivable. He recalled an old schoolmate, who'd laughed when Seth had enthused over his plans to study surveying. "What use is all that academic nonsense? Every child knows in their bones how geometry works!" And no doubt they did, until they found themselves in a land where it was geometrically impossible to place both feet on the ground.

«Where do you think Sarah and the others are now?» Theo asked.

«I don't know. I just hope they had more luck getting out of the water.» Seth didn't want to turn every possibility over in his head, trying to select the most likely outcome. Wherever they were, he couldn't help them; whatever he told himself would make no difference to their fate.

«They had much more rope than we do,» Theo noted.

«So that's what would have turned things around for us,» Seth replied. «More rope.»

«No, but I've been thinking through some different scenarios. If we end up on a mudflat, and there are trees nearby, maybe we could snag a branch and haul ourselves along.»

Seth laughed. «And if we end up in a bustling market—even though we have no money, and even if we did it would probably be no good there—maybe we can barter our theodolites for all the rope, and food, and axial stilts we could possibly need.»

Theo lapsed into silence. After a while, Seth said, «You're right, though: we should try to think things through.» He struggled to find a way to join the game. «If we end up on ice, we might be able to slide the sections of the boat across the surface. There'd be no need to lasso trees, so long as we can push against the ice itself.»

Theo spoke aloud. "There's a change in the flow ahead. I can hear it."

Nicholas was less certain, but after a minute or two he concurred. And then Seth heard it too: a violent new hissing from the water above them, cutting through the noise of the wind and the creaking of the boat.

If the slope shifted its gradient slightly, rising above forty-five degrees, the river would continue ascending for some distance out of sheer momentum. But when it reached its limit and spilled back down the slope, the transition would not be a smooth one. The best they could hope for was another flooded terrace, broad enough, and with water running deep enough, to keep them from smashing into rock.

Seth reached up and gripped the handle on the right side of his compartment, but with his weight bearing down on him he was unable to take hold of the left one as well. He considered the merits of freeing both his hands and letting himself be thrown from the boat. How many more bends in the river did he think they could survive? And even if they ended up on dry land, they'd starve to death long before they found their way back to the basket.

But Theo's life wasn't his to take, and the thought of seeking assent for the act was enough to drain it of its allure. If the time came when he could argue in all honesty that no hope remained, he'd make his case, but not before.

The hiss was drowning out every other sound now. When Seth tried to picture the source of the noise, the image that sprang into his mind was not water slamming into water, or rock, but water scattering into the air. «Should I climb up onto the top of the boat and see if you can ping anything to the south?» he asked Theo.

«If I could, is there anything we'd do differently?»

«Not that I can think of.»

«Then it's not worth the risk.»

The hiss grew deafening, then painful. Seth's muscles were rigid, bracing his body against the hull. Any thought of surrendering to death was gone, but the prospect of meeting the same fate unwillingly had never felt more likely.

Something started drumming on the top of the boat; Seth felt the hull's vibrations before the impacts grew loud enough to hear. He poked a hand out to the north, and felt large, cold droplets pelting his skin: some portion of the river's flow was raining back down, in the aftermath of whatever lay ahead.

«Not long now,» Theo said calmly. Seth recalled his last, breathless immersion, and began consciously inhaling and exhaling, forcing himself to concentrate on the rhythm in the hope that he wouldn't break it, no matter what the shock. He pictured Andrei and Nicholas, and Ada with her silent passenger, all huddled in their own dark compartments—then he pictured Sarah and Judith, Raina and Amina hiking back up the slope toward the waiting basket. If he had to die, this was how he wanted to go: believing in his friends' survival, embracing their shared history.

«Remember when we were in awe of Raina and Amina, just for traveling to the steamlands?»

«Yes.» But Theo wouldn't countenance distractions. «Be ready,» he said sternly.

«For what?»

«For anything.»

The hull groaned, then something tore and something shattered. Seth's weight vanished; he cried out unwillingly, gasping and bellowing—but the fall went on for so long that he had time to recover and take control of his breathing, and even time to become aware of his grip on the handle and make it more secure.

Then the north wall of the compartment slammed against his side, and he was deep in the cold water. His right shoulder burned with pain as the hull jerked fitfully, belching out its last trapped air, but he clung on to the handle, less through any conscious act of will than an instinctive refusal to be prized out of his shelter.

In the calm that followed, he waited for the boat to break the surface, anxious and impatient but, with a lungful of air, infinitely better prepared for the ordeal than before. The shock of sledding off the top of the river lingered, but the pounding in his blood and the tingling of his skin began to feel as much a thrill of triumph as of fear. They had not struck rocks, and his own injuries seemed mild compared to the worst he might have suffered.

His lungs began to ache. It was not the blind panic he'd felt before, but an insistent nagging.

«Are we rising or sinking?» he asked Theo. However fast the boat had struck the water, it should have been ascending by now. «I can't tell.»

«I can't either. Take off your pack.»

Seth unbuckled the straps and let his pack fall away. A second later, he struck the top of the boat: unburdened, he was more buoyant than it was. The hull must have been breached, the air-filled walls ruptured.

His only choice was to leave the boat. The strange southwards gravity wouldn't let him swim upward, but he should still float up.

He groped around and found the edge of the hull. His intention had been to try to bring the others with him, if they hadn't already departed—but when he maneuvered himself into the place where Andrei and Nicholas should have been, there was nothing but open water. He forced himself down along the edge of the hull, hand over hand, then reached out for Ada's compartment, but that was gone too. He let go of the broken, sinking box of sodden tent fabric and willed his body to ascend.

In the blackness, he had no sense of motion. He stretched his right arm away from his body and tried cupping the water and driving it down, but his palm felt no resistance, however he angled it. He wanted to exhale some of the stale air from his lungs, but he was afraid it might be the only thing that made him lighter than the water around him; a careless stream of bubbles escaping from his lips could send him back down to join the wreck of the boat.

The blackness brightened to a strange bluish gray. Seth took the hallucination as a sign of imminent suffocation, but whatever instinct made him squeeze his eyes shut rewarded him with the knowledge that the impossible light was real enough to be extinguished and regained with a blink.

He reached up with his right arm, and felt cool air on the back of his hand. Jubilant, he clawed at the water, trying to raise his head, but it remained stubbornly immersed.

Seth forced himself to be still, and pictured himself floating just below the water. He swung his left leg slowly away from his body, while using his arms to maintain his balance and keep himself from tipping over the wrong way.

Air touched his cheek. He managed to turn his head far enough to catch a breath. For a time he was perfectly motionless except for the expansion and contraction of his lungs, but the whole configuration was precarious; the smallest disturbance in the water, the tiniest shift in his limbs, sent him back down and he had to start again.

«What now?» he asked Theo.

«We hope that one of the other modules is intact. Give me time to dry out a bit more, and I'll start yelling for help.»

«All right.» Seth didn't know how long he could keep up his balancing act, but they had no other choice.

With his head so low and his movements constrained, he couldn't see far across the shimmering water, but whatever lit it appeared to be both less diffuse than the twilight he'd grown used to on the slope, and much weaker than full sunlight. But then, neither had any right to manifest themselves in the middle of the night. The water around him felt impossibly placid; Seth searched for a landmark to give him some cue as to its speed, but it was hard to discern anything in the distance.

The current was turning his body slowly around a vertical axis— his own left-right axis—taking him through a leisurely backflip entirely unconstrained by gravity. East, west, and the old up and down were indistinguishable now, leaving him with no real sense of where he was facing. As he struggled to keep his head from submerging again, a string of blue-tinged lights came into view somewhere beyond the water, stretching into the distance and rising up as far as he could see. He counted a dozen individual points before they became too close to separate; they all seemed to lie more or less on a smooth, almost flat curve, and though they didn't conform to it perfectly, the curve made its presence clear nonetheless, with the lights that departed from it dimmer than those that hewed closer, as if they gained all their strength from proximity to this otherwise abstract and invisible form.

Theo said, «I can hear a Sider.»

«You mean Nicholas?»

«I hope not.»

«Why?» Seth was confused.

«This Sider's screaming like an infant. If it's Nicholas, he must have suffered something worse than a painful injury; only brain damage would make an adult emit sounds like that.»

«You think it's Ada's?» Seth had stopped wondering exactly where Ada kept her supply of the drug, but she'd confessed to losing her barometer, so it was entirely possible that her puffballs had been swept away in the river too.

«It must be.»

Notwithstanding the grotesque timing of the awakening, this bawling woman-child meant that one, and probably both, of the pair were alive. «Can you tell how water-logged this Sider is?»

«Less than me. I'd say she's clear of the water on both sides.»

So their module was still afloat. «We have to get Ada's attention—and hope she's got something to use as a runner.»

«Be my guest,» Theo replied. «I'm still drenched, and you can speak in her range as well as I can.»

Seth bellowed her name across the water, trying not to let the movement ruin his balance. His voice sounded feeble, but for all he knew she might be just a few dozen paces away behind him, waiting to be revealed in the current's slow panorama.

Theo said, «Something's coming through the water. Moving fast, almost straight toward us.»

«Ada's boat?»

Theo hesitated. «I don't think so. The Sider's not getting any closer.»

"Andrei!" Seth yelled, afraid that he might be all but invisible, a bobbing head barely breaking the surface.

Theo said, «If it's them, Nicholas isn't replying.»

Seth could wait until they were all together in one boat before he started fretting over Nicholas's silence. "Andrei!" he called again. His real worry was being missed entirely as Nicholas directed Andrei straight toward Ada's screaming Sider.

Theo said, «They're here.» Seth felt some kind of wake wash over him; he spluttered and went under.

Someone reached down and grabbed his shoulder and right arm. Two hands, three hands, four. They lifted him out of the water, and up across a short solid topside that did not feel anything like the tent-fabric hull of the expedition's boat. He was lowered onto the deck of the vessel, dripping, facing away from his rescuers.

"Who are you?" he pleaded. An excited chatter broke out behind him, in no language he'd heard before.

PART FIVE

14

SETH TIPPED HIS HEAD back. A dozen orange-furred limbs were stretched out across the deck toward him, below three pairs of eyes in three not-quite-faces.

«Are you seeing this?» he asked Theo.

«I'm only seeing what you're showing me, so it's your eyes I'll have to trust. There's nothing for me to ping but the deck and the sky.»

«We've reached the southern hyperboloid,» Seth realized. This wasn't one more flooded terrace; they'd left the slope behind.

«I'd say so.»

«Which is peopled by *scampers in boats?*»

«I don't think they look much like scampers.»

«They look even less like Walkers.»

Theo said, «They might struggle to walk in Baharabad, but here they seem entirely ambulatory.»

Seth struggled to get past his astonishment. Whatever he called them, these people had saved his life, but Ada and her Sider were still out on the water somewhere—and with luck, Andrei and Nicholas too.

He said, «Yell at them in your own language and see if they respond.»

Theo didn't ask why, and Seth didn't need to be told when he'd done it: the Southites began shrieking and hooting, turning their faces to each other and then staring at Seth with a renewed intensity. If they could hear Theo, there was a good chance that they could also hear the newly wakened Sider, and they might well have been drawn to this part of the water by her bawling. Seth was immensely grateful that their eyes were as sharp as their hearing, but there was no reason for the novelty he presented to distract them from continuing their search for the source of the sound. Granted, if he looked half as bizarre to them as they did to him he had to expect a certain amount of attention, but he hoped that he'd only piqued their curiosity, not sated it.

«We need to let them know that they should keep looking,» he told Theo.

«How?»

Seth thought for a while. «Which direction is the Sider?»

«It's hard to tell,» Theo grumbled. «I'm still wet, we've been moving around in the water, and I'm not used to . . . any of this.»

Seth gazed at the three Southites, who gazed back, showing no sign of losing interest in their exotic catch and getting on with other tasks. «Roughly,» he pleaded.

«Speaking body-wise, halfway between backward and down,» Theo replied.

Seth pointed his right arm in the direction Theo had specified. «Now imitate Ada's—»

«Dahlia.»

«*Dahlia?*»

«Someone has to name her.»

«Imitate Dahlia, before they think I'm just stretching my arm out for no reason.»

Seth couldn't hear anything, but he felt a strong enough vibration in his skull to be assured that Theo wasn't holding back.

The Southites burbled, grunted, and squeaked, glancing at each other and swaying on their long, low limbs. Seth didn't presume to read their emotions, but the one thing they weren't was indifferent.

He moved his arm back to his side, then repeated the whole act three more times. The Southites became ever more animated, but they remained fixated on Seth himself. Had they failed to understand his message, or did they simply not care? He was at a loss as to what more he could do to rekindle their interest in their original goal.

Theo said, «I think Dahlia's getting closer.» He sounded confused.

«That's good, isn't it?»

Two of the Southites turned and scuttled away across the deck, giving Seth a better sense of just how wide the boat was. They stood at the opposite side, facing out across the water, but Seth's head was too low for him to see what they were looking at.

«It's not Ada's boat approaching,» Theo realized. «It's something faster, more like this one.»

«So their friends had her all along?» Seth was relieved, but the job wasn't done. «If spotting her was enough to have them scour the water and find us, they need to keep going until they have Andrei and Nicholas too.»

«How do we tell them that?» Theo wondered. «Three pairs, not just two?»

Seth pounded the deck, and tapped the side of his body. He pounded it again, and gestured toward Ada and Dahlia. Then he pounded it a third time, and swept his arm around vaguely.

The Southite who'd stayed with him seemed intrigued, but Seth's mime didn't spur it into any kind of action. Seth did it again, and a third time.

The Southite lost interest and moved away to join the other two, who were now shouting into the distance. Greeting their fellow sailors and describing their own find? After a while, Seth caught a glimpse of the second boat coming alongside, but between the crew of his own and the crew of the other, the forest of limbs defeated his attempts to see what state Ada and Dahlia were in. Finally, he called out at the top of his voice, "Ada! Are you all right?"

"Seth! I'm fine! What about Andrei and Nicholas?"

"I don't know where they are. If there's any way you can encourage these people to keep searching . . ."

The two boats were separating now. "I'll try," Ada replied, but her tone told Seth that she'd had no more luck communicating her wishes than he had.

The crew busied themselves with something near the rear of the boat, and it began to move. Seth tried propping himself up with his left arm, hoping to get a better view of both vessels and their surroundings, but as he slid his elbow over the deck and bent his arm, he realized that elevating his body this way would leave him precariously unstable—and that if he lost control, the price would be infinitely worse than the smack in the face that he'd somehow fooled himself into imagining was still possible.

He lowered himself back onto the deck, shaken. *There was no safe way to tip over here.* The Southites had eight almost-horizontal legs and a low, flat body; no impact or injury was going to unbalance them. But if his own body had been reconstructed with a vertical, axial torso that allowed him to walk around on two legs, he would have been in constant danger of falling toward the all-encompassing cone, with no prospect of ending up flat on the ground. The cruellest executioners in the ancient world had reputedly devised a form of torture in which the victim was trapped between two closely spaced walls, one facing east, the other west, and left there until they were too weak to remain standing. After days without food, water, or sleep, eventually they would topple in the only way possible, and the torque would tear their body apart. But here, there'd be no need to build the walls.

«Does it look like they're still searching?» he asked Theo. It was difficult to judge from the crew's posture how much attention they were paying to the water around them, but he hadn't felt the boat change direction at all.

«There might be other boats,» Theo suggested hopefully.

Seth turned his head a little, and caught sight again of the string of distant lights. «So what are they? Cities?» Cities so numerous, and so profligate with their lamps, that they could lift the whole surrounding landscape out of the eternal night?

«Why would they all line up that way?» Theo asked.

«Maybe they're on a river.» But Seth was beginning to doubt that the idea made sense at all. Before there had been cities and lamps, every animal would have needed to navigate in the dark. A Sider's axial pings would be no use here, but there was no reason why the same kind of sense couldn't work in ordinary directions instead. So if the ancestors of the Southites had flourished in a world without light, why would they possess eyes at all, and any wish to make lamps?

Theo said, «It's the sun!»

«What?»

«Can't you see it?»

Seth was bemused. «There's an awful lot of rock between us and the sun right now. Or do you think it's peeking over the edge of the world?»

«No, I was wrong about there being an edge to the world. What we came through was just a hole; the world goes on far beyond it.»

«And you know that how?»

Theo said, «You're showing me the proof. Sunlight can't scatter off the void—and even if there was enough dust out there to shine in the light, it's not going to form motionless clusters. But if the land stretches on to the south, and if the hole we passed through was just one of thousands . . .»

Seth gazed at the points of blue light: chasms like the one they'd traversed, but with entrances deep in absolute summer. The absurdly smooth curve that they didn't quite trace wasn't some coincidental alignment between the holes themselves; rather, the only chasms that were visible at any moment were those that happened to be close to the curve on the hyperboloid where it intersected the cone of brightest sunlight. Like the twilight that had illuminated the slope, this light was scattered by air and dust, but the source now was so unutterably fierce that, even from a great distance, it was enough to banish the night completely.

«I see it,» he replied. «But if there are so many holes in the world, why did it take us so long to find one?»

«Because what lies in your field of view, right now, is at least a million times more land than the whole migration has traversed throughout recorded history. Geology has always constrained the migration to a narrow swathe, and we've never had a way to see beyond that—but here, with the land rising up all around you, you can see forever. If you count ten thousand of these dots as the sun completes its orbit, that's not a measure of their proximity to each other. It's a measure of how vast a territory you now survey.»

The grandiose language seemed cruel, even if the irony was hardly of Theo's making. Seth could well believe that no Walker in history had beheld such a vista before—but then, no Walker had ever been as powerless to explore the land around them as he was now.

THERE WAS NOTHING KEEPING Seth from turning his gaze toward the boat's destination, but with so much of the lower part of his view obstructed he had no way of knowing if they were heading for the grandest city in the world, or the humblest village. The land he could actually see, above the rim of the hull, was so distant and so strangely lit that he struggled to discern its topography. A few hills stood out, catching the light on one side, but with their multitude of shadows they cast the surrounding terrain into confusion. There were glints that might have been rivers, or might have been tricks of the light. Everything was rendered in muted blues and grays; a subtle shift in hue and shading suggested a forest, but Seth wasn't confident that barren land might not look stippled in the same way.

The boat came to a halt without warning. One member of the crew crawled over the side, and Seth caught glimpses of a rope being thrown. There was shouting between the Southites, but he wouldn't have known the difference if they were cheerfully coordinating the task of securing the mooring, or arguing bitterly over some long-standing property dispute.

For a minute or two he was left alone in the boat. Then two of the crew returned, approached him without pause or ceremony, slipped two hands each under the side of his torso, and lifted him up from the deck.

Seth could feel their knuckles pressing against him; their feet didn't just double as hands, they were reversible, curling up to grip him from below. As the creatures' peculiar scent wafted into his face, he forced himself not to flinch or squirm away; the last thing he wanted them to do was drop him. They carried him off the boat, almost as briskly as they'd disembarked the first time; they might never have unloaded such strange cargo before, but his general shape and weight didn't seem to present an unprecedented challenge.

A few paces from the shore, they'd positioned some kind of thick, furry blanket in advance; they placed him down on it, and withdrew a short distance as if to judge how it suited him. Compared to the deck, it was comfortable: apart from being gentler on the parts of his body that he was forced to lie on, the way he sank into it felt like it offered a degree of restraint against the risk of toppling.

Peering between the watching Southites, he could finally see some of the land nearby. It was covered in low rocky outcrops, rising up from barren soil with patches of mud and ice.

"Now look for our friends," Seth pleaded, gesturing toward the water. "Take the boat back out and look for our friends!" He didn't expect them to understand his words, but how hard could it be for them to reason that a stranger they'd rescued from peril would only make a fuss and point back to the site of danger if there were others who still needed help?

The Southites chattered and watched Seth attentively, but none of them made a move toward the boat.

«Here come Ada and Dahlia,» Theo announced. Seth tipped his head back and saw the second boat approaching the shore.

"Please look for our friends!" Seth repeated, hoping that his continuing distress would make it clear that it wasn't Ada and Dahlia that he was fretting about. If Andrei's portion of the boat had remained intact, he and Nicholas might have improvised some kind of runner—but if they were unaware of their potential allies, they'd probably choose to stay in open water, at first just searching for their missing colleagues, and then seeking out a current to take them back north. It was what Seth would have done in their place, believing that he had no other options, but even if they made it back to the slope, without fresh supplies he didn't like their chances.

Two of the crew from the second boat placed Ada and Dahlia on the blanket beside him. Seth could hear Dahlia himself now; she wasn't confining her wailing to the Sider's range.

"How long has she been like that?" he asked Ada.

"Since we hit the water. When the boat came up, she just started screaming."

Seth spoke bluntly. "Do you have any knowledge of this happening to other Thantonites? People must have run out of puffballs before."

"Not that I've heard."

"There's never been a shortage?" Seth was incredulous. "There's never been a traveler whose journey took longer than they'd planned, or who lost their supply along the way?"

"Anything's possible," Ada said defensively. "But if that happened, no one wrote a book about it."

Dahlia had become quieter as they spoke, at least as Seth heard her.

«Have you calmed her down?» he asked Theo.

«A little.»

«What did you do?»

«I just made soothing noises.»

«As you would to a baby?»

«Hmm.» Theo's tone suggested that he found the comparison offensive, but in the circumstances he had better things to worry about.

Seth addressed Ada again. "Can you tell whether she's sharing your vision?"

"How would I know?"

"Are you actively blocking it?"

"I have no idea," she admitted. "We never talked about anything like that in Thanton."

"So Dahlia might be seeing nothing but what she can ping: a tiny patch of ground, and the empty sky? What a world to wake up to!"

Ada raised no objection to Theo's choice of name, but Seth's accusations seemed to rankle. She said, "I'm not deliberately keeping anything from her. And I've never had any trouble seeing what she pings; that's always worked, by instinct alone. So I don't see why it shouldn't be the same in the other direction."

One of the Southites approached. "Please look for our friends!" Seth shouted, waving his free arm at the boats behind them. "Please look for our friends!" The Southite showed no interest in decoding his message; it picked him up, unaided, made a surreal, ninety-degree turn, and started walking along the shore.

For several seconds Seth was dizzy and disoriented, then he finally turned his head to see where they were going. They walked past the point where the boats were moored, toward a strange contraption that was sitting on firmer ground. The top part was an elevated wooden platform, about as high as a Southite's head; beneath it he could see two segmented belts weaving through a system of guide rods and conical capstans. Each belt lay flat on the ground for part of its length, before twisting sideways up into the mechanism.

Theo said, «It's a cart.»

Seth stared at the thing. «I think you're right.» No wheel with a horizontal axis would work here, but these belts were apparently flexible enough to roll over the ground and then loop back to their starting point.

Two more Southites joined them, one bearing Ada and Dahlia, the other carrying the blanket. They covered the platform with the blanket then maneuvered their guests up onto it. Seth had almost grown used to being handled, but being raised above his bearer's head was terrifying. All he could do was brace himself and hope that the Southites' experience made it exceptionally rare for an adult of their species to destroy something of even moderate value by inadvertently letting it tip.

Once Ada and Dahlia were settled on the blanket in front of him, someone moved around the cart, sliding up safety rails along all four edges. This diminished Seth's anxiety considerably, but blocked his view of everything nearby.

"Please look for our friends!" he begged his hosts one more time, though no one could see him pointing to the river. The platform started moving; presumably a couple of drivers were dragging the cart, oblivious to his concerns. "What does it take," he muttered.

"For all they know, you could be expressing your undying gratitude at being plucked from the water," Ada said mildly.

"You have a better idea?"

"No. I'm just trying to be realistic."

"When you were in the water, I did everything I could to get them to find you."

"And did they understand what you wanted?"

"They didn't need to, but if they hadn't located you themselves so quickly, I think there might have been some kind of dialog." Seth wondered if he was fooling himself; he had no evidence that they'd read anything into his attempts to point to Theo's best guess of Dahlia's location. And Andre and Nicholas lay one level of abstraction beyond that: Dahlia's existence had been a given, but pointing vaguely at the now silent water could mean anything. Whether he'd been rescued out of compassion or mere curiosity, Seth didn't know how to summon a fresh object of interest into the minds of people with no knowledge of the expedition's size, and nothing with the immediacy of a screaming infant to make it obvious to them that their task was incomplete.

He looked up at the line of lights, and realized that the pattern of bright dots along its length was different now from the configuration he'd first seen. The Southites might know how to read this transformation as the lapse of some precise interval of time, or maybe they'd just measure the angle of the line against some fixed landmark, but he'd been spun around so much that he had nothing to compare it with. All he knew was that if he'd still been in the water at this moment, he would have been close to exhaustion, and close to death.

THE TERRAIN AROUND THEM changed very little as they moved along in the cart. Beside the river the land was covered in ice and rock, with patches of mud and still no vegetation in sight. There had to be trees somewhere, though, given that the cart Seth was traveling on and the boat that had come to his rescue were both made of wood. If there were paved roads in the southern hyperboloid, they'd yet to arrive at one; Seth could tell that the cart's drivers were steering it around small rocks, and despite their efforts the belts sometimes hit obstacles they couldn't be dragged over, forcing the drivers to backtrack and try again.

The lack of any clear grain to the land was exactly what Seth would have expected, but no less disconcerting for that. The idea of being able to turn horizontally through any angle at all was bizarre enough, but then doing so to such little effect felt like a kind of dream, where the thing that you supposedly knew was happening, declared as fact by an internal narrator, bore no relationship to the accompanying images. Seth tried thinking of the land around him as a giant, south-facing cliff, to which everything was drawn by a magical new force. That, at least, made some sense of his miserably impractical posture, and went some way toward assuaging his impossible desire to plant his feet on the ground and walk.

The cart turned toward a small settlement, with an open circle of half a dozen low buildings. Southites emerged and chatted with the drivers; a few raised themselves up for a better view of the contents of the cart. Seth was growing used to their short, broad faces, with bare wrinkled skin surrounded by orange fur, but this familiarity wasn't yet mutual: one glimpse of his body was enough to drive some of the onlookers into bouts of wild hooting. He hoped that they were merely expressing surprise and amusement; it was hard to believe that he was provoking fear, but if he was actually giving rise to disgust or revulsion that might influence the way the four of them were treated.

«Do you think they know that you're not actually part of me?» he asked Theo.

«Hard to tell. They have nothing like pingers themselves, so it might seem odd to them that one organism would make sound in two different ways.»

«No pingers, yet they can hear in your range. Are any of their vocalizations that high?»

«No.»

«Then why hear those sounds?»

Theo said, «There are plenty of natural sources pitched as high: grains of sand sliding over each other in the wind, chaff in the fields crackling when it rains. But maybe the reason *you* can't hear those sounds is to spare you from having to listen to me pinging all day.»

«What a deal: we gave up the power to hear sand squeaking . . . and you gave up the power to walk. No wonder your father thought Siders needed more experience in contract law.»

The cart stopped, a few paces from the nearest building. Seth still couldn't see what was happening around him, except when people jumped up to gawk.

Dahlia began wailing again.

Theo said, "Ada, you need to help comfort her. I'm doing what I can, but you're . . . the place where she needs to feel safe."

"Comfort her how? She won't understand a word I say."

"Just croon to her," Theo suggested. "Softly, but out loud." He wasn't cruel enough to start quizzing her as to whether she possessed any capacity for inspeech; that seemed unlikely, and even if she did it might be unreliable, or even stranger to Dahlia than everything else she was having to face.

Ada complied, though she sounded uncomfortable, and her efforts had no immediate effect. Seth could only wonder how much Dahlia was capable of understanding about her situation; it was unlikely that the drug had kept her silent her whole life but unimpaired in any other fashion.

"Should we give her something to ping?" he wondered. "Just to break the monotony?"

"It can't hurt," Theo replied. Seth waited to see if Ada would try the experiment herself, but when she didn't he reached over and waved his right hand above Dahlia's pinger.

The wailing changed, slowing a little. Seth made shapes with his hand, the way he had sometimes for his niece's adopted Sider, Leanne.

Dahlia began a kind of cooing. Seth was startled; it was so much like Leanne's response as to be eerie. But he persisted, and the soft murmurs that he took as signs of interest and amusement continued.

«Tell me if you ever want this yourself, to keep your pinger in shape,» he told Theo.

«Thanks, but I'd rather read a book.»

«I think your options might be limited there.»

They remained on the cart for what felt like hours, though now that he was motionless Seth could track the line of lights, which showed that his frustration and impatience were outracing the actual passage of time. Dahlia's moods came and went, but between the three of them they could usually find something that calmed her. Seth had given up shouting about Andrei and Nicholas; repeating the message more often and more loudly wouldn't make it any clearer, it would only risk making him seem like a lower-pitched version of Dahlia. He had to trust in the Southites' curiosity to lead them either to the missing pair directly, if they still had boats out on the water, or to a systematic attempt to communicate with their guests.

Finally, someone lowered one of the safety rails and reached up to take Ada and Dahlia off the cart. Seth was still struggling to distinguish one Southite from another, but when this one returned and took hold of him he was fairly sure that it was not the one who'd put him on the cart back at the shore: the scent, the grip, and some distinctive patches of mottled fur on the arms all seemed new to him.

«We need to learn to recognize individuals,» he said, as the Southite carried him across the open ground. It wasn't just a matter of courtesy—of avoiding the offense of misidentifying an interlocutor in some halting conversation once they'd started to make themselves understood. Different members of the community were likely to hold different attitudes to the guests, and if he couldn't learn to respond to different people in ways that accommodated that, any attempt to obtain the cooperation and resources that the expedition needed could be jeopardized.

«I haven't got much more to go on than you have,» Theo replied. «But I'll try to listen carefully to their voices.»

«We should start giving them names,» Seth decided. He'd have no chance of organizing his impressions without using some kind of label for each Southite, and there was no point waiting to learn what they called themselves. «This is Martha, holding us now.»

«What if you've guessed the wrong sex, and that's a grave insult in their culture?»

«How would he ever know?»

Theo said, «It's sure to slip out eventually.»

«I don't plan on being here that long.»

Martha carried them toward a small, rectangular enclosure that had apparently been prepared for them in the space between two of the buildings. Ada was lying on a blanket at one end, and Seth could see a water trough running alongside one of the low walls. There was even a sheltered area at the far end, with a wooden roof, large enough to offer protection from the rain.

Martha reached over the wall and placed him on a blanket of his own, then raised her head up and gazed at him from outside the enclosure. "Thank you," he said, hoping that the context might be enough to show her the meaning of the words. She, or whoever had built these quarters, had clearly put some thought into their guests' needs, and if the accommodation wasn't perfect, the real problems lay with the mismatch between their bodies and the local gravity. Seth had no idea what the best solution to his maladapted anatomy would be, so he hadn't been expecting anyone else to find a way to render him magically safe, autonomous, and comfortable.

Martha departed. The walls of the enclosure were low enough to let Seth look out across the settlement; beyond that, with the bowl of blue-gray land rising up in all directions and the line of lights stretching off to infinity, he did not feel boxed in at all.

Ada said, "I vote we shit at the point farthest from the water, given that they've made no other arrangements."

"All right." Mercifully, it had been so long since Seth had eaten that this wasn't a pressing concern. "How are you coping?" he asked. Dahlia seemed to be asleep.

"Don't worry about me," Ada replied, but her tone was listless.

"We're going to get through this," Seth promised her. "These people seem to have about as much good will toward us as we could have hoped for. It might take a while to learn to communicate with them, but if they were prepared to go out of their way to stop us drowning, I can't see why they wouldn't be willing to give us what we need for the journey back: a small boat, a few supplies, and local knowledge of the currents. And if they've mapped the edge of the hole we came through, we might even make it back to the surface with a definite answer as to whether or not the migration could pass safely around the chasm." If this catalog of wishes wasn't extravagant enough, in truth, he wanted even more: Andrei and Nicholas to turn up safe and join them; Sarah and Judith, Raina and Amina to be waiting in the camp when they finally returned to the steamlands. "We'll probably miss the hundred-day pickup," he conceded, "but they'll keep raising and lowering the basket long after that."

"Whatever you say." Ada curled up on her blanket, tucking her head close to her knees.

Theo said, «Nothing makes the hard times harder than having your slave wake up and start screaming in your skull.»

«No doubt. But we'd probably all be dead if that hadn't happened.» Seth couldn't deny that he'd felt an occasional twinge of satisfaction at Ada's plight, but in the circumstances gloating was neither morally laudable nor at all pragmatic. And if there was any question as to whether he really needed Ada as his ally, the fact remained that Dahlia needed all three of them.

Martha approached the enclosure again, carrying two net bags whose contents Seth couldn't make out. She began tossing the objects over the wall, and they landed near the water trough.

Black sapote. Eight in all.

Seth slithered toward the nearest one, learning how to move as he went. He soon realized that keeping his back curled actually made him quite stable; he could advance by sticking his knee and elbow out and then shifting his weight onto them and dragging himself forward.

It was laborious and uncomfortable, but when he arrived at the fruit it was worth it. The taste wasn't quite what he remembered, but it was still delicious; he devoured it, then started on a second one.

When he'd finished his share, he felt bloated; his stomach had probably shrunk from his long fast. He returned to his blanket to lie still and digest the meal.

«What do you think?» Theo asked. «A close cousin of the real thing?»

«Probably.» Seth took a moment to see his point: not only were there trees in the south, at one time there had to have been a tree that could grow in either hyperboloid—or seeds that had been shed in one but then sprouted, successfully, in the other.

Theo said, «The migration might not have witnessed another chasm anytime in recorded history, but in the eons before, there must have been others. Over time, there must have been all kinds of exchanges.»

«All kinds? What are the odds of anything bigger than a seed surviving?»

«Probably very small, on each occasion. But what if there were ten thousand opportunities? Or ten billion?»

«This from someone who's only just stopped claiming that the world is finite.»

«When the evidence changes, I change my mind.»

Seth said, «Why is it that I think I can guess where you're going with this?» Once Theo chose a direction, there was no such thing as pursuing it too far.

«If it's so obvious to you already, that probably means I'm right.»

Seth was too full of food, and too tired, to start arguing.

Theo said, «The Southites have no pingers of their own, because it's not worth it: they're low enough on the ground that they won't put a foot wrong using light—which is always present—and there's nothing to ping up in the sky. But if you grabbed one of them and took them to our hyperboloid, beyond the problems they'd have moving about, that cone of blindness around the axis would suddenly become a much more serious deficit. Maybe over the eons they could find their own way to deal with that—but making a bargain with a local might be a much faster solution.»

«You're saying I've come home to my ancestors?»

«To your cousins.»

«We don't even have the same number of limbs,» Seth protested sleepily.

«Limbs might come and go. You don't have a scamper's tails, but everyone thinks it's likely you're related to them. And all your limbs are *non-axial*, like a Southite's.»

Axial, non-axial: there was no more fundamental distinction. «So I belong here, but you're just an interloper? I can see by light all day and all night, while your useless pings hit the dirt or disappear into the sky?»

«Exactly.»

«All it would take to make me positively smug about that would be some prospect of actually walking.»

«Give it time.»

Seth laughed and closed his eyes. He pictured the line of lights wheeling around him, as the sun scoured the distant surface. «What a joy it is to be home,» he said.

15

SETH WAS WOKEN BY Dahlia's wailing. He tried to retreat back into sleep, but the glare of daylight was too strong. *Daylight?* He opened his eyes and looked around for the line of lights; it was pointing straight toward him. The distant chasms appeared no brighter than before—if anything, they seemed more subdued against the blue-white haze that now filled the air. But in a direction he had no name for, perpendicular to the line, that haze reached an almost painful intensity. It was like staring at the sun through a thin layer of cloud, except that the light was surrounded not by sky, but by land—as if the sun had risen, not over the horizon, but somewhere much closer.

«If they didn't get away from that, they're dead,» he realized. Up on the surface, the chasm's opening had started well clear of absolute summer, but Seth had no doubt now that the mouth of the thing stretched far enough south to be touched by the sun's cone. On the surface, being near to such a sun-blasted place could include being safely to the north of it—in the dark cone of any secondary, scattered light—but here, the rules were different: every point on the southern hyperboloid was visible from every other point.

«Nicholas and Andrei would have worked that out,» Theo said. «If they couldn't find a way north in time, they would have headed for the shore.»

Seth wasn't confident that that would have been far enough. Still, the Southites had left their boats moored there, so they couldn't have been expecting heat intense enough to ignite the wooden vessels, or to turn the water itself to steam.

«Fuck this place,» he muttered. He needed to defecate, and it wasn't going to be as simple as it had been on the slope.

When he was done, he approached the water trough. At first, he thought it would be impossible to drink without sticking half his head below the surface and immersing one of Theo's pingers, but eventually he found a way to lean against the side of the trough for balance, then position his right hand so that the water ran up over it and trickled into his mouth.

"Did you get any sleep?" he asked Ada.

She didn't reply. "Do you mind if we come over there and play with Dahlia?"

"Do what you like." Her tone wasn't sullen or irritable; nor was it distracted, as if her mind was busy elsewhere, or haughtily indifferent, as if such matters were beneath her. It was flat and dead, as disengaged from everything else imaginable as it was from the subject of their exchange.

Still, she'd eaten her share of the fruit they'd been given the night before—unless someone had taken it away, or she'd tossed it out of the enclosure herself.

Seth dragged himself toward her, self-conscious now about how filthy he was. In the not-quite-night the ground had been hard and icy, but in the not-quite-day the top layer had thawed into reddish brown mud, so splashing any of their limited supply of water onto his body would have been futile.

At first Dahlia was inconsolable, but whether it was Theo's inaudible baby-talk or Seth's hand-puppetry that did the trick, after a few minutes she became much calmer. Seth was beginning to think that the greatest mercy would be if the drug had left her incapable of understanding anything; that might be better than having to live with the knowledge of what Ada had done to her—and what Thanton had done to her relatives—let alone the implications of the fact that the world to the south of her had vanished.

"Did any of the Southites visit while I was asleep?" Seth asked Ada. He didn't want to needle her with constant small talk, but he wasn't going to close off all communication between them, however tempting she made that seem.

"No."

"Theo and I are going to try to give them all names. The one who carried us here from the cart is 'Martha' until we know better. Or maybe for a bit longer: even if she told us her real name, we might struggle to pronounce it straight away."

Ada said nothing. Seth looked out across the settlement; the open space he could see was deserted. Perhaps the Southites preferred the cooler hours; if so, he'd need to learn to adjust his own sleeping pattern.

The thought prompted him to spend a moment taking stock of the state of his body. He was hungry, but not ravenous, and he didn't think it would be a good idea to try to wake his hosts in the hope of being fed again so soon. His muscles felt both drained and disused; his left arm wasn't exactly in pain so much as in a state of perpetual, bewildered complaint at the way its motion had been unnaturally constrained while it had been forced, against all precedent, to bear most of his weight.

He was about to tell himself to get used to it, when his gaze fell on the sheltered section of the enclosure. He dragged himself over to the structure. The roof was high enough that if he lay beside it he could reach up and grip it, then use that handhold to lift most of his body off the ground, pivoting on the side of his foot—and by trial and error, he found a position where he didn't knock his head against anything in the process. Suspended, he could swing his left arm freely back and forth, while his left shoulder, blissfully, touched nothing but air.

"You have to try this," he told Ada. "That which spares you skin ulcers also makes you stronger."

Seth remained hanging for as long as he could, and when his right arm tired he used the left one to prop himself up, letting his forearm touch the ground. It was uncomfortable twisting his arm around to try to get the northern axial fingers of his left hand out of the way, so he dug into the mud and made a hole for them.

When he finally lay down on the ground again, both arms were aching, but he felt better than he had since his rescuers had dragged him from the water.

«You should do the same thing with your legs,» Theo suggested.

«So now you're an expert on other people's bodies?»

«I'm an expert on the downside of immobility. But if you think you can stay a Walker with no strength in your legs, go ahead.»

«Martha will carry me everywhere I need to go.»

«To Baharabad?»

Seth slithered around and got his foot up on the roof. Unlike his Southite cousins, though, he had no ability to grip anything with his toes. As he started raising his left leg from the ground, he felt his foot slipping. He stopped, then curved his upper body to make it harder for him to overbalance. Then he lifted his left leg, from the hip to the toe, and cautiously swung it back and forth. There was no doubt that it felt good, but it still felt precarious. «More next time,» he promised Theo. «Now it's your turn to practice pinging to the right, so Dahlia doesn't overtake you.»

Later, Seth lay on his blanket, waiting for the settlement to wake, watching the line of lights turning, trying to think his way more deeply into the rhythms of this new world.

«They must have their own migration,» he reasoned. «If they stayed in one place, eventually it would get too cold; the solar cone would keep sweeping over the nearest chasm, but it would do it faster and faster, until the 'days' only lasted a fraction of a second.»

Theo said, «So their habitable circle will correspond to the southern rim of our habitable zone. But they won't be restricted to a narrow band of longitude by the surface grain, like we are.»

«No, but if the chasms themselves are so far apart that you leave all the heat from one of them behind before you get to the next one, the region in which it's warm enough to raise crops might still be quite small. And when the time comes to move, it would be a long trek across cold ground.»

«That's true,» Theo conceded. «We complain about a few shifting rivers, but if we tell these people we can pick a mild solar latitude and then live at the same temperature every step of the way as we follow it south, they might go mad with jealousy.»

«What makes *me* jealous is the thought of planning the whole migration just by looking.» Seth waved a hand at the bowl of the hyperboloid, stretching out to the edge of his vision. «At all the same places where we'd risk stumbling over a cliff, with no idea what's ahead of us, they get the most prominent beacons imaginable, visible in advance for generations.»

«I told you this was your homeland.» Theo thought for a while. «It might not be quite that simple, though. A chasm might seem promising from a distance, but if the soil and the water and the climate don't work out, it could be a long trip to the second choice. I bet they have to send out advance parties to be sure that it's really worth bringing everyone.»

«So they might still have surveyors, of a kind.» Seth found the notion comforting. If the expedition's goals weren't entirely foreign to them, if they could understand what brought it here, surely they'd be willing to help the survivors return home with the information they needed?

AS THE LIGHT DIMMED and the air became cooler, the settlement came to life. Seth could hear the Southites conversing inside their houses; the sounds they made seemed so diverse to him that if he hadn't seen them with his own eyes, making all the same noises, he would have thought there were four or five different species contributing to the racket.

Shortly afterward, they began emerging from the buildings and moving briskly across the open space. Many were carrying small objects, but none of them wore clothing; apparently their fur offered all the protection they needed from the elements, at least at this hour, and the houses were mainly for shelter from the sun. Seth was hoping that there were no predators around; as yet, he'd seen no creature other than the Southites that was larger than an insect, and still not a blade of grass, so it was hard to imagine what anything capable of eating him would have subsisted on normally. But the sapote must have come from somewhere nearby—if not a jungle, at least an orchard.

He spotted Martha striding toward the enclosure, on just six legs, carrying more food. Witnessing the speed and economy of her motion could have just driven home his own incapacity, but instead it filled him with hope. However hostile this place seemed, it need not defeat him if he had the right friends.

«I think I'm in love,» he joked to Theo.

«Please don't ever tell her that.»

Martha reached the wall and tossed the fruit she was carrying into the enclosure. It wasn't sapote this time; Seth was excited at the thought of something new to try, but rather than rushing for the food, he wanted to take the opportunity to start engaging with his host.

"Thank you for the food," he said, enunciating as clearly as he could and looking at her directly as he spoke. Their eyes locked briefly, but her gaze slid over him, then she turned and walked away. "Thank you!" he called after her.

Ada started laughing.

"What's so funny?" Seth asked, glad to see her animated at last.

"We're just animals to them. A couple of strange, exotic specimens that they plucked out of the water. They're not going to learn our language and talk to us. Even if the possibility crossed their mind, why would they bother making that much effort? They must have a thousand better things to do."

Seth was stung, but he had to accept that some of what she was saying might be true. He and Ada wore clothes, but what did that mean to the Southites, who didn't? And they'd seen Ada's fragment of the boat, but even if they'd recognized it as part of a once-serviceable vessel, there'd been nothing to suggest that she'd built it herself, or even piloted it; she'd just been some wet, screaming creature clinging to a piece of flotsam that might have come from anywhere. What was there to point to the conclusion that these animals were capable of sophisticated thought, let alone conversation?

He said, "They might have better things to do, but we don't. We can learn their language, if we watch and listen carefully."

"Really?" Ada emitted some crude squawks and hoots. "We're never going to understand *that*, let alone speak it."

"We have to," Seth said. "Or we'll die here."

Ada smiled joylessly. "Which means we'll die here. Let's hope it's not from disease or old age; let's hope someone gets curious and cuts us open to see what's inside."

"And yet I see you're not starving yourself to death."

"That would have been my first choice," she replied. "But it's not worth the noise this blood-sucker makes when it feels the tiniest pang of hunger."

Seth was tempted to ask her why she hadn't silenced Dahlia for good, but then thought better of it. The idea must have occurred to her, but if he raised it that would only risk provoking her into action.

Theo said, "Suppose you're right about everything. The South-ites are preoccupied, at best. Seth and I are incapable of learning their language, however much effort we devote to the task. But even if I grant you all of that, it's still not reason to give up."

"And why is that?" Ada asked. "Do you think Andrei and Nich-olas are speeding back to the surface right now in their one-fifth of a boat, and when they get there they'll rally their friends to fly down in a balloon and rescue us?"

"I wouldn't rule out a word of that," Theo replied. "But it's not what I had in mind."

"Then . . .?"

Theo hesitated. "Tell me that you want to live. Tell me that you want to survive this, and get back home."

Ada snorted with derision. "It doesn't matter what I want; that won't make it possible."

"No," Theo agreed, "but it could make it impossible if you don't. If you want to wreck our chances, if you want us all to die here, just be honest and say so, and I'll leave you in peace."

Ada's face contorted with misery. "I'm the only one honest enough to face the truth."

"Maybe," Theo said calmly. "But you still haven't answered my question. When you tell us that we're going to die here, are you describing what you believe, or what you want?"

"Who could want any of this?" she replied. "I'm not insane. Of course I'd rather live."

"So if there was a way back, you'd do everything in your power to make it happen?" Theo persisted.

"Yes. But there isn't."

Theo said, "There might be, there might not. The drug you gave Dahlia might have damaged her brain, permanently and irrevocably, to the point where all she can do now is live out the rest of her life with no more mental capacity than an infant.

"Or, the drug might not have ended her development so much as held it in abeyance. And now that she's no longer receiving it, she might actually possess something even closer to the mental capacity of an infant: the power to learn by exposure and example faster and more efficiently than any adult. The power to acquire a language just by watching, and listening, and trial and error—and perhaps, like most Siders, two languages at once.

"In which case, Dahlia would be our best hope, our best chance to have a competent translator. But it's in your hands. Seth and I can talk to her, and she can probably hear the Southites shouting wherever she is in this cage. But you're her only real pair of eyes, her only chance to connect what she hears with what's happening around her.

"So that's what you need to decide. Are you willing to be her eyes? Are you willing to dedicate yourself to seeing what she needs to see, and making sure that she's sharing your vision? Because if you are, we might have a chance of surviving."

16

"**H**ERE'S MY HAND," SETH crooned, holding it above Dahlia's pinger, "and *here's* my hand," bringing it down in front of Ada's face. "Here's my hand . . . and *here's* my hand."

Dahlia burbled with delight as he spoke, but Seth was still not sure if she was being entertained by the experience of this one object manifesting through two modalities, or whether to her it was a simple hiding game. It was certainly true that any opportunity to use her pingers evoked a far stronger response than the most elaborate display of color and motion in Ada's field of view, but that didn't necessarily mean that she was light-blind. There was always something to be seen around her, even if it was only the walls of the enclosure, but anything intruding into the pristine space above was a novelty—at least for a while.

Seth kept up the game until Dahlia fell silent, either bored or exhausted. "She's asleep," Ada confirmed.

"Did she ever used to sleep while you were awake, back in Thanton?" Seth had got past the mixture of squeamishness and tact that might once have kept him from asking.

"Very rarely," Ada replied. "But it was rare that I'd be lying this still for so long unless I was asleep myself. As soon as I got up in the morning and moved around a bit, I could always see to the sides, though I never thought of that as someone else 'waking up.' If you lose sensation in your feet, you might say that they've 'fallen asleep'—but when everything works normally you don't say, 'I woke up, and so did my feet.'"

"Hmm." Seth maintained an expression of mild interest, but as much as he tried not to judge Ada, he still found himself unable to listen to a revelation like this without dissecting it, separating out threads of culpability and extenuation. To render her Sider invisible by picturing it as just one more part of her body seemed staggeringly crass—but if she'd been taught to think that way from the start, and her Sider had never been able to raise its voice to claim its own separate identity, what could be more natural?

At the sound of footsteps, Seth turned to see a young Southite approaching the enclosure. Many of the children in the settlement had displayed an initial burst of curiosity about the guests and then lost interest, but this was one of the more persistent visitors. Seth had named him Iqbal, after Amir's irrepressible younger brother.

Iqbal rose up as high as he could, bending all his legs, moving all his feet farther from his body so he could peer down over the wall at the inhabitants. Then he began hooting and shrieking, loudly and at great speed.

"Well, that woke her up," Ada muttered, but she dutifully turned to watch Iqbal as he spoke, imitating the Southites' grimace of attention in the hope of prolonging the interaction and making it more meaningful for both Iqbal and Dahlia.

«Is he inviting us to come out and play,» Theo wondered, «or telling us to crawl back where we came from and stop stinking out his town?»

«If he really despised us, there are plenty of things he could throw,» Seth reasoned. «So either he's afraid that the adults would punish him if he went that far, or he's actually being friendly.»

Dahlia babbled back at him, unintimidated by his exotic anatomy, if she was even aware of it, or his cacophonous voice, which she certainly heard. To Seth, her replies sounded nothing like Iqbal's language, or even his own, but Iqbal seemed to have more patience with this non-conversation than Martha showed when Seth tried to engage with her. Sometimes they talked over each other, but that had been happening less and less. It was not communication, but so long as neither of them were indifferent to the other's speech, Seth still held out hope that it could lead to something more.

When Iqbal departed—Seth thought he heard an adult calling him away, but he wasn't confident that the timing was more than a coincidence—Theo took over.

"Did you have a good time with Iqbal? He's such a nice friend to visit you." He went on like this, narrating the encounter for Dahlia in the Walkers' language again and again with slightly different words, for far longer than Seth could have done it. To Seth, the children's games came naturally, and he could play them without a trace of self-consciousness. But when he listened to these calculated language lessons, all he could hear was desperation.

When Theo finally stopped talking, Ada said quietly, "You know what today is."

Seth had tried to lose count, without success. "So we should celebrate," he said. "There's a chance that the others are on their way home."

"I hope so. But when they bring the basket down again, it's not going to be in the same position as before."

"Probably not," Seth conceded. "But it will be as close as the rope teams can make it. If it takes us a couple more days on the slope to find it, that's the least of our worries."

"A couple?"

Theo said, "When we get home and exchange stories with the others, even if they tell us that everyone else was riding the basket today, we'll still be counted as the lucky ones. Because when we get back to the slope, we'll be better fed, better supplied, and better prepared than anyone else was. We've all seen the Southites' boats. Which would you rather ride north: the brand new, two-tiered vessel that they'll build for their beloved cousins, as a gift to make up for all the time they unwittingly snubbed us, or those pieces of tat we rode down in, whose sole virtue was the fact that we could fit them in our packs?"

Ada didn't reply.

Theo asked anxiously, «Are we losing her again?»

«No.» Seth didn't begrudge Theo his ability to remain almost insanely resolute, but he was sure that it wasn't going to help

Ada if they started haranguing her every time her confidence wavered.

He said, "To Raina and Amina, Sarah and Judith, Andrei and Nicholas: we wish you a safe trip home."

IN A DAY, THE population of the settlement doubled.

Seth watched the people traipsing in, dragging battered carts piled high with what he supposed were their belongings. The new arrivals all looked exhausted, and some appeared injured, with limping gaits or limbs held strangely. The locals swarmed around them, vocalizing loudly, offering them food, taking charge of their loads, leading some straight into their homes.

"This must be a second group of migrants joining the outpost," Theo decided. "No wonder they're so bedraggled, if they've come all the way across the ice from another chasm."

"There's hardly room for them here," Ada said. She sounded as affronted as if it were her own hometown faced with an equivalent influx.

"Relax, no one's going to want to billet with us," Theo teased her. "Though I'm sure our ordure is the envy of the hyperboloid."

"They might build a second village, once they've had a chance to recuperate," Seth replied. "Prepare their own farmland, plant their own orchards." None of which would happen quickly. "This is what it will be like if we end up having to switch rivers back home." Despite the drought, he still hadn't witnessed an end to the luxury of incremental migration, where the farmers merely shifted all their fences a little to the south, and plowed a little more ground at one end of their fields while abandoning an equal amount at the other.

Theo said, "Switching rivers will be the least of it."

"Maybe." Seth wasn't ready to start debating the possibilities all over again, before they'd even acquired the one useful datum that they'd come here to obtain. "If we're right about these people, though—if they've come from far away—they must have seen this chasm the way we see the others: a light in the distance, small enough to take in at a glance."

Ada completed the thought. "Small enough to measure."

Theo said, "And all we need to do is ask them for the numbers. How hard can that be?"

WHEN MARTHA DIDN'T TURN up to feed them at the usual time, Seth supposed she was busy with the newcomers. Dahlia became irritable, wailing in protest at the declining nutrient level in Ada's bloodstream, but Seth played with her until she fell asleep.

Then the same thing happened at the second mealtime, and the third.

"They must have been expecting these people," Ada said. "Even if they didn't know exactly when they'd arrive. So they would have tried to plant enough fruit trees and crops in advance, to be ready to feed them; it's not as if they've been taken by surprise."

"While they waited, they would have had more food than they needed," Seth added. "Some of which they could store, some of it perishable. Throwing us the fruit that was going to go bad anyway would have cost them nothing. But now that the intended recipients have arrived, there's no excess any more."

"There must be a hundred people here," Theo protested. "How much would each of them have to give up, in order to feed us?"

"Not much," Seth conceded. "But if things are tight now, if they're all going hungry . . ."

Dahlia lost the energy to maintain her howling, and instead just made curt, disapproving noises which only became more vehement when Seth attempted to distract her. As his own strength waned, he stopped exercising, but it felt like a poor trade: within a day, he could feel the skin of his left shoulder burning from the unbroken contact with the ground. Rolling about on his blanket to shift his weight only ended up making things worse: the skin split open, creating a small wound that would have been tolerable if he could keep it in the air, but was excruciating when he lay on it. He dug a pit in the ground under his blanket, so he could position the wound directly over it and spare it most of the pressure. That helped for a while, but the pit kept filling up and needing to be re-excavated. And the circle of skin that was resting on the rim of the pit began to sting, then crack and bleed.

Iqbal came to visit Dahlia. His initial greeting was as loquacious as ever, but he quickly became more subdued. Seth looked on, trying not to over-interpret the exchange and raise his hopes too high. Even if this child understood his friend's plight—or his pet's suffering—what could he do? Dahlia's own vocalizations were more varied in his presence than they were when Seth tried to play with her; instead of just rattling her pingers in protest, she seemed to be making a genuine attempt to communicate. Whatever her limitations, perhaps she was observant enough to understand by now that Seth was not the kind of creature who had ever brought food for her Walker, so it really wasn't worth her time attempting to procure his assistance. But Iqbal, like Martha, had eight legs and orange fur. If she babbled at him in just the right way, anything might be possible.

TWELVE DAYS INTO THEIR fast, with the heat of the sun still lingering, Seth saw Martha approaching the enclosure, striding briskly across the open ground. People were usually indoors at this hour, and there was no one else in sight. She did not appear to be carrying any food, but Seth had stopped thinking of that as a serious possibility; now that the trough was almost empty, what he'd been hoping for was water. It was a long journey from the river's edge, but that had never stopped the Southites from sparing a little for their guests before.

Martha clambered over the wall and moved straight toward Seth. "Are you taking us somewhere?" he asked.

Ada said, "I think she has a knife."

"What?" Seth couldn't see it but he started to crawl away, dragging his burning shoulder over the rough ground. He'd barely moved before she was on top of him, gripping him with four of her hands. He tried to struggle, but he might as well have been wrestling with a boulder. Theo showed the underside of her torso above him, covered with loose, wrinkled skin; it looked soft and vulnerable, but he had no hope of landing a blow.

«Ping her harder!» Seth pleaded. If the Southites had heard Dahlia screaming on the water from afar, maybe a high-pitched sound this close could be painful. Theo's image of her underbelly grew brighter and wavered strangely, and Seth felt a shivering ache in his skull, but whatever Martha was perceiving, she was undeterred.

Seth saw the knife now; she was holding it, poised, just behind his back, as if she was trying to decide exactly where to plunge it in order to do the most damage. "Please don't," he gasped. Maybe this was meant as an act of mercy: now that she could no longer feed them, she'd decided to end their suffering. "Please don't," he repeated. His hunger was unbearable, but he didn't want this either.

Theo showed him the knife descending. Seth twisted away from it, contorting his body with all his remaining strength, but the blade sliced into his back. He bellowed with shock and pain, and as he struggled to free himself he felt his assailant's hands growing slick with blood, but she didn't yield.

As Martha raised the knife again, Dahlia started babbling: a string of strange, urgent noises. "You fucking animal!" Seth screamed. "You don't do this in front of a child!"

Martha was still, the knife suspended. Seth's body had been arched, but now his muscles turned to water and he flopped against the ground. Unwillingly, he closed his eyes, and a moment later Theo stopped pinging. The searing pain across his back confused him: it hurt his eyes too, like a bright light. Dahlia's protests rang in his head, but each time she paused now, another voice joined her, echoing back some of the same motifs with more authority and precision.

"EAT THIS," ADA URGED him. She was holding something toward him. Seth opened his mouth and let her put it in. It was a piece of spoiled fruit, with the flesh half rotten while the skin was hard and dry. Seth almost gagged, but he forced himself to swallow. She fed him another piece, then another.

Dahlia said, "Seth wake up."

"Yes," Ada agreed. "He woke up."

Seth wanted to ask for a second opinion on his sanity, but Theo wasn't awake.

"Have you talked to Theo?" he asked Ada.

"No. He's not talking to you?"

"Not yet."

"Give it time," she said. "You must both be very weak. I'll bring you some water."

Ada had nothing to use as a cup but a small piece of sapote skin, so the water came in tenths of a mouthful, but she kept ferrying it patiently from the trough to Seth's mouth until he told her he'd had enough.

His back was stinging, but when he moved, cautiously, to try to assess the severity of the wound he realized that the knife had only skidded across the skin and the damage was superficial.

"What happened, exactly?" he asked Ada.

"'Exactly'?" The stipulation seemed to amuse her, as much as if he'd asked for something truly impossible, like clean clothes.

"Dahlia talked her out of it?"

"That might be overstating it. But if she talked at all, in Martha's own language, the second part might be a tautology. I think they know now that we're not quite what they thought we were, and I think that was enough to change her mind." She held up a piece of rotten fruit. "If we're not exactly the beloved cousins, at least we're not animals to be slaughtered without compunction."

Seth slept again, woke and ate. The spoiled fruit they were receiving now was plentiful, and the sheer bulk of it filled his stomach, but it left him feeling weak. Dahlia might have spooked Martha out of using the knife, but this new regime was not the perfect solution that their hosts had been willfully ignoring; it was a gamble that they hadn't believed was worth trying, until the moral stakes suddenly shifted.

Theo still didn't stir. Seth was starting to worry that no nutrients were reaching him, but all he could do was eat as much of the disgusting mush as he could and hope that the quantity he ingested would make up for the fruit's deterioration. He knew that his body would put itself first: it wasn't going to cannibalize its own tissues just to feed its Sider. But nor would it treat Theo as dispensable and let him starve to death, if there was any way to avoid it.

FOUR DAYS AFTER THE stabbing, Seth woke to the sound of Dahlia and Iqbal talking. He lay still with his eyes closed and listened to the exchange. They were both being uncharacteristically quiet, and for a moment he wondered if they'd actually made an effort not to disturb him, but that seemed fanciful.

He could feel the heat in the air, and the glare rendered his eyelids translucent; this was not the usual time for Southites to be up. Just when he thought the conversation was over and that Iqbal must have left, he heard a succession of soft thuds: he was throwing something into the enclosure.

Dahlia spoke softly. Iqbal replied, more softly still. Then Seth heard him walking away.

Seth opened his eyes, and saw Ada crawling across the ground. One by one, she picked up the whole, fresh sapote and hid them behind the mound of rotten fruit.

He fell asleep again, and woke when it was cooler.

"Are you hungry?" Ada asked him.

"Yes."

"When you taste this, don't show any surprise." She fetched a handful of mush from the pile, but there was something more substantial in the middle of it.

Seth ate what she gave him, gratefully, though he would have preferred Iqbal's gift without the nauseating camouflage. "Do you really think anyone would notice?"

"Do you really want to take that chance?"

Dahlia said, "Iqbal brought food."

"Please don't tell Martha that," Seth replied anxiously.

Dahlia laughed, as if the idea was self-evidently preposterous. "No!"

"Do you think he's smart enough not to steal too much and give the whole game away?" Seth asked Ada.

"How would I know? Just because I'm there when they talk, it doesn't give me any special insight."

"Of course not." Seth hesitated, but he needed to know. "Do you have inspeech with Dahlia?"

"No."

Perhaps that depended too much on both Walker and Sider being at equal stages of development. "All right. But so long as the

Southites can't speak our language, we should still be able to keep a few secrets from them."

Seth had been letting Ada cosset him for too long; he crawled over to the trough to get a drink for himself. The wound on his back protested, but it did not tear open, and he managed to lift and lower his shoulder as he moved, instead of scraping it in the dirt.

As the water trickled into his mouth, he became aware of the ground below his head, and the emptiness above it.

Theo said languidly, «I dreamed we were back home. When I pinged to the south, there were rocks and mountains, and whole cities full of beautiful buildings.»

«We'll get there,» Seth replied. «But it's going to take a few more steps.»

17

SETH TURNED THE CRANK and the cart shuddered forward, but then something in the mechanism jammed. He tried going backward; the belts moved a little, but then they started to slip. He reversed direction again, and this time managed a full turn of the crank before another component began screeching in protest, loudly enough to discourage him from continuing lest he destroy the whole machine.

Iqbal approached, hooting with mirth, and reached into the interior of the cart.

"I did warn you that it's not perfect yet," Dahlia said. She and Ada were resting on a blanket, having had the first turn with the cart, until Ada, at least, had wearied of it.

"That's fine," Seth replied. "I'm happy to keep testing for as long as Iqbal wants to keep tinkering." He waited, stretching his left arm out as far as he could in the cavity around the crank. The couch that supported him on top of the cart was about the most comfortable thing he'd lain on since arriving in the southern hyperboloid, and it even offered Theo a view that included both the ground immediately ahead and a peek into the workings of the machine. For the rider to be able to fix a loose gear or a belt coming off its capstan, though, rather than just observe the problem, remained a prospect for the indefinite future.

Theo was growing anxious. «They're not going to let us join the expedition if they think we're going to hold everyone back.»

«No. But be patient.» Iqbal's efforts so far had been heroic, but from what Seth could gather through Dahlia, the twisted belts had been around for generations, and refined over that time for their one intended purpose: allowing the carts to be dragged along with ropes over difficult terrain. The idea that a passenger might ride on top and try to turn the belts by manually intervening in the action of the gear train had never occurred to anyone. What would be the point? And neither Seth, Theo, Ada, nor anyone in the settlement was enough of an engineer to be able to say, from first principles, exactly what ought to be changed to accommodate this new motive force smoothly and efficiently.

Iqbal withdrew, and gestured at Seth to continue.

"What did he change this time?" Theo asked. His view had shown three arms weaving between the belts, but the actual target of the intervention had been obscured.

Dahlia passed the question on to Iqbal. Seth listened carefully, in the vain hope that hearing the two versions one after the other might prove educational. "He tightened the . . . I don't know the word for it."

"In our language, or his?"

"Yours."

"Never mind," Theo decided.

Whatever Iqbal had done, the result was impressive. Seth turned the crank cautiously three times without incident, before daring to increase the rate and send the cart trundling forward at something close to his own walking pace. The belt rattled and shuddered as it ran over small stones, and slipped and stuck on patches of mud, but nothing in the mechanism was jamming now merely as a consequence of his efforts to propel it.

Seth followed the dirt track that led away from the main settlement, with the new orchards on one side, boasting rows of young trees crowded with fruit, and fields full of grain rising high on the other. He was surprised at how quickly his mind adjusted to the peculiar causality of the process: a *rotary motion* of one arm yielding an effect he was accustomed to achieving with his legs—or here, by flopping around curling his back and dragging his body. But within minutes it felt, if not natural, perfectly intelligible.

He heard Iqbal hooting triumphantly, and glanced back to see him a few paces behind. He was easily keeping up with the cart, but Seth still felt that his own speed was respectable. The crank was hard work, though, and it used his left arm in ways that he hadn't been able to exercise by other means. «I'm going to need to practice with this every day until we leave. I just hope our young genius can make a second one that's just as good.»

«He should make four: one for each of us,» Theo replied.

«Really? Even if you could regrow your lizard limbs, I'm not sure they could turn anything.»

«There might be some further tweaks required.»

Seth pushed the lever that disengaged and locked the belt closest to his feet, then drove the cart around in a circular arc. It reminded him of doing a forward-flip as a very young child, when his mother and father would squat on either side of him and guide his motion. When he re-engaged the second belt and started back toward the settlement, something wasn't quite meshing, and the disparity made the cart wobble from side to side. He stopped on a stretch of flat ground and drove back and forward a few times, until the two belts returned to synchrony.

As he came back to the place where he'd started, Dahlia cheered. "Our turn now!" she enthused.

"Do I have a choice?" Ada moaned.

"You'll love it," Seth promised her. "Once it's actually moving, it's glorious."

Dahlia spoke with Iqbal, and he lifted Seth off the cart and carried him onto the blanket. No Southite treated him with more respect, but after his spell of autonomy, simply being held and transported this way felt humiliating.

When Ada and Dahlia were back on the cart, they set off down the track, retracing his own journey. From his stationary vantage, though his excitement remained fresh in his mind, watching the rattling cart with Iqbal in leisurely pursuit made the modest scale of the achievement painfully apparent.

«Forget about a new design that Siders can ride,» he told Theo. «We need one that lets the Walker use their southern arm as well, somehow.»

«And while you're making wishes, both legs too.»

None of those refinements were likely, least of all in the short time they had to prepare. The third troop of migrants to the chasm had been due to arrive more than twenty days before, and while some variation in the time it took for each group to make the crossing was only to be expected, Seth understood that the people of the settlement were becoming anxious. The protocol—if he'd understood Dahlia's version of Iqbal's explanation—was that the search party would make their way back along at most the final third of the route; by carrying supplies for that limited journey, they'd trade range for speed. If they found nothing, it would be up to the next group coming through from the old chasm to lend assistance.

It was difficult for Seth to form a clear impression of the kinds of problems that could have befallen the latecomers. Surely it was hard to get lost when your destination was visible from all but the lowest ground, lit up like a flaming beacon? They could have run low on food, or been struck down by sickness, but even then it was puzzling that there hadn't been one or two among them still able-bodied enough to go for help.

When Ada and Dahlia came rattling back, Seth called out, "Well done!"

"That's me finished for the next ten days," Ada replied wearily.

"We should take it all the way back home!" Dahlia suggested. She conversed with Iqbal, then added disappointedly, "He says we're not supposed to use it where there are too many people. They're afraid we might hit someone."

Ada said, "*We're* the only people who couldn't get out of the way in time. But it's nice that they don't want us accidentally crushing each other."

As Iqbal lifted her off the cart, she asked Seth, "Are you sure you don't want to make this trip without me? You're the surveyor."

"You have noticed that I can't speak the language?"

Ada made a dismissive sound. "What will you need to say? You tag along, you make the measurements, you come back. Hopefully they find the stragglers safe and sound—and as part of the general rejoicing, they finally make up their minds to give us a boat and point us north."

"If it was that easy, I could do it on my own, any time at all."

"You need someone with you who can fix the contraption if it breaks," Ada conceded, "but if that happens, you won't have to explain anything: the fact that you're not moving ought to be eloquent enough."

"I need *Dahlia*," Seth replied, patient but adamant. "Have you really forgotten just how bad things can get when there's no way to communicate? This is all new territory to me. There's no point going out there with people who know it if I can't even talk to them when something goes wrong."

Iqbal placed Ada and Dahlia gently on the blanket beside Seth.

"Well, I gave you the choice," Ada said. "But if my arm gives out halfway, they'll either have to throw me on top of your cart beside you, or tie the two carts together with a rope so you can drag me along."

"If it comes to that, I'll do it," Seth promised rashly. "But only if you're serious about preparing." Though she'd joined him in his original exercise regime, her participation had been patchy. He couldn't blame her for a few lapses in enthusiasm when the prospect of having cause to use their leg muscles again kept receding into the distant future, but this was one journey the Southites weren't likely to postpone.

"All right," she agreed.

"So if I'm the one who needs towing . . .?"

"Don't push your luck."

Iqbal returned from having stowed the cart. He picked up Ada and headed for the settlement. Alone with Theo on the blanket, at the deserted junction between three dirt tracks, Seth felt the weight of his helplessness descend with a vengeance. The machine was glorious—when it worked, and when he was actually riding it. But he needed to be sure that he didn't let any momentary delusions of autonomy go to his head. Everything about their fate remained in the hands of the Southites.

Theo said, «Iqbal and Dahlia can't explain everything, but I've been watching what he does and building up a picture in my head of how he's solved different problems. It's not perfect yet, but I'm getting there. If the worst happens, and the others refuse to stop and help us, I think we'd still have a chance.»

Seth wasn't sure if he should feel relief at Theo's cautious optimism, or fear at the thought of being stranded in the icy wilderness, trying for days on end to slip a belt back onto a capstan.

Iqbal returned, shrieking cheerfully, and lofted Seth up into his arms. By any measure he was stronger, healthier, and more competent in this world than Seth and Ada—but his elders had ruled that the expedition was far too dangerous for him to take part.

18

SETH DROVE HIS CART out to the barren plain where the search party was assembling. It was easy to find the spot: the "old home" was lit up directly in front of him, a few degrees above horizontal. He was far from a seasoned navigator here, but this landmark was unmistakable; when the line of lights moved across it, it became brighter than anywhere else.

With Dahlia's help, Iqbal had told Seth that the chasm where he'd been born would remain habitable for thousands of days to come. The Southites' migration seemed to involve a relatively unhurried shift in population from a slowly cooling oasis to a slowly warming one, with a finely calibrated effort to match the numbers to the carrying capacity of the farmland at each end of the route. But if that part sounded manageable enough, the surveyors also needed to be planning a dozen steps ahead, to be sure that they weren't leading their people into a dead end. The most bountiful chasm would be nothing but a trap if it lacked a successor of its own that would emerge from the cold at just the right time. Seth had been curious as to whether the wild animals here possessed some instinctive grasp of that criterion, or just headed at random for the nearest bright light, but the question had defeated all attempts at translation.

"Seth!" Dahlia shouted. She'd lingered over her goodbyes with Iqbal, but now she and Ada weren't far behind. Seth stopped and waited for them to catch up.

"This is exciting!" Dahlia enthused, as Ada brought her cart along-side Seth's. "We're already farther than I've ever been from home!"

"Hmm." Seth had trained himself to resist the impulse to correct statements like this, but her words still pricked his conscience. He didn't know exactly what she'd heard from the Southites, but in the absence of any clear account of her origins from her own people, Dahlia had concluded that she'd been born in the river near the settlement, and that Seth and Ada were her parents. Theo, of course, was her brother. Seth had never quizzed her deeply enough to determine what kind of children she thought she might one day bear herself: Siders alone, or Walkers too? But though he'd long ago stopped clinging to the pretext that this lie of omission was no different than the customary delay in revealing the details of reproduction to a child, he had decided that it was up to Ada to choose when and how she explained Dahlia's history to her. They were the ones who would have to live with the truth.

The rest of the expedition had already gathered, but the nine Southites were still checking their supplies and redistributing loads from cart to cart. Mostly they were carrying food and fuel, but there was also a large wooden contraption that Seth had never seen before, occupying a cart of its own.

"Do you know what that is?" he asked Dahlia. He pointed to the device. "That thing on the third cart from your feet?"

"No. Do you want me to ask?"

She sounded a little shy about the prospect, and the Southites themselves looked busy. Seth said, "It's not important."

He had decided to stay at the rear of the expedition, so he could watch the routes the Southites took and follow whoever had the least trouble with their cart. There were small rocky outcrops everywhere, but he was hoping that the expedition leaders either had good memories or well-kept records from their own crossing to keep them on a path that had already proved viable.

"How's your arm?" he asked Ada.

"Why, do you want a race?"

"Maybe on the way back." Seth was glad that she'd overcome her misgivings about joining the expedition, but they'd been replaced by a ferocious competitive streak. Thanton's insular culture must have driven her mad, as it would any intelligent child, but it seemed to have left her with only two ways of dealing with obstacles: shrinking into herself in resignation, or setting out to conquer everything in sight. Seth much preferred the latter, in general, but not if she ended up stripping a gear.

"They're moving, they're moving!" Dahlia announced. In fact, only two of the Southites had set off, and they weren't dragging carts or carrying anything. Seth supposed they were scouts of some kind, who'd go ahead and check the route for problems.

But the others were finishing their preparations and securing their loads, and it wasn't long before they began trundling forward. The old home was growing dim now, but Seth trusted the Southites to keep their bearings; he'd learned to recognize many parts of the bowl himself, regardless of their state of illumination, and to anyone who'd grown up here, the more distant regions, which would look much the same from either chasm, ought to be enough to show them the way.

Ada moved first, then Seth followed her, and they soon settled into a position half a dozen paces to the rear of the Southites, who advanced with a fixed, methodical gait on six of their legs, using the other two to hold the towing ropes. Seth had been afraid that he and Ada might have trouble keeping up, but the Southites were held in check by their own carts; even if they'd had the strength to pull them along faster, a heavily laden cart hitting a bump at speed would be asking for trouble.

«I have a great idea for a scam when we get back home,» Theo said.

«I'm listening.»

«We go from town to town, offering to arm-wrestle the locals, and make sure that the bets are placed while people can only see you from the right.»

Seth said, «I'm not sure if the most optimistic part of that is assuming that I can somehow remain to the north of all our marks until the last moment, or assuming that my left arm will still be good for anything after its millionth turn of the crank.» All this talk of asymmetry wasn't helping; his neglected right arm, resting use-lessly along his side, positively ached to make a contribution, and his left arm really couldn't understand why it had to shoulder the entire burden.

«Rock,» Theo warned him.

«Sorry.» Seth had let his attention wander; he backed up the cart and steered around the outcrop. «I hope your pingers don't end up as unbalanced as my body.»

«Test me,» Theo replied. Seth waved his right hand above the side of his head; it appeared in Theo's view, as crisp as ever.

The line of lights swung slowly around the bowl, retreating into the distance. Seth drew his blanket tighter against the chill. Up on the surface, if the camp at the edge of the steamlands was still there, people would be sitting around listening to the evening rain.

«If this hole is too large to get around . . .» he began.

«Then the armchair surveyors will need to make a choice,» Theo replied. «Or maybe the logistics will make the choice for them.»

«Between the bridge of balloons . . . and what?» Seth had thought Theo had reconciled himself to the futility of trying to trap the sun.

«Between the bridge of balloons, and a journey like our own—only better prepared, and lasting much longer. If the migration's blocked in every direction, it will need to take a detour to the southern hyperboloid while the habitable zone passes over the chasm.»

Seth couldn't decide if he was serious. «Is this your idea of find-ing an alternative that makes building a mountain sound easy? I can't see how they'd get that many people down the cliff, let alone all the way down the slope. And once they got here, what would they eat? Four guests seems to be about the limit of the locals' hospitality, and even that's still touch and go.»

Theo said, «You're right about all of that, but if there's no other choice, there's no other choice. However hard it is, people aren't going to give up and die quietly: some fraction of them will make it down here, and some fraction of those will find a way for their fam-ilies to last out the wait.»

Seth still balked at the whole idea, but whatever the prospects were of it becoming a reality, the notion itself seemed dangerous.

«Don't mention any of this to Dahlia. If the Southites suspect that letting us go back could bring on an invasion from the other hyperboloid, then once they stop laughing at the thought of a million people flopping around on their sides, and picture them all equipped with armored carts instead—»

«I'm not stupid,» Theo said. «But nor are they. The fact that no one's ever questioned us deeply about why we were exploring the chasm, and why it's so important to us to know its size, has got more to do with Dahlia's limits as a translator than anything else. These people have been in a position to understand the shape of the world for far longer than we have. It might be a stretch for some of them to imagine life on our hyperboloid, and the nature of the migration there, but there must be a few who can work out most of it, without any help from us.»

«So . . .?»

«So whatever results we measure, if they ask, we tell them that the hole's small enough for the migration to detour around it. We can go back with the good news, and no one like us will ever bother them again.»

Seth laughed. «And we drop a subtle hint that, in the absence of any such confirmation, our people won't risk trying to go around the hole and ending up trapped. Keeping us here against our will starts to sound like the more dangerous choice—and anything less than giving us the best boat they can make to take us safely up the slope would be a false economy.»

«Yes.»

«I like that better than your arm-wrestling scam. But do you really think we understand these people well enough to fool them?»

«We won't need to lie about the measurements,» Theo stressed. «I'm sure they know how big the hole is, even if they don't know how to tell us. But the real question is, how big a hole does it take to block the migration? And that depends on something they've never experienced: the geology of a landscape where the axial direction is horizontal, not vertical. If we claim that we can go around the hole, most Southites would think: of course . . . what could stop you? But even the ones who've thought it through carefully, and are capable of carrying out all the purely geometric calculations, still won't be able to quantify the geological part of the problem. They can choose to doubt us, or they can choose to take our word for it. But there's no way they could know for sure that we're not telling the truth.»

WHEN THE SUN BEGAN shining from the chasm behind them, the expedition finally stopped to rest. Seth let his arm hang loosely against the crank and tried to find a position that took the load off his shoulder and elbow.

"This must be what it's like to try to tear your own arm off," he said.

"Really?" Ada replied. "I could easily keep going for another half a day."

Seth ignored her. "How are you feeling, Dahlia?"

"I'm all right. Do you think we'll find the missing people soon?"

"It's early days." Seth didn't want to raise her hopes too high, but it would be cruel to start speculating about how badly things must have gone for them if they couldn't send word of their plight, or even signal their presence. He hadn't been paying much attention to the land ahead, but if anyone had spotted a campfire or rising smoke, Dahlia would have been the first to know what they were rejoicing about.

"Iqbal wants me to meet all his cousins. He gave me a message to pass on to them if I see them first." Dahlia emitted a long string of squawks; Seth saw some of the Southites turn to stare at her. "He said they'll be surprised that I know so much about them."

"That might not be their biggest surprise," Theo replied.

A Southite approached, and spoke with Dahlia. "He wants to know if we're comfortable, and if there's anything we need," she said.

"Tell him 'thank you, we have everything.'" Seth didn't recognize him as anyone they'd named back at the settlement. "Can we agree that he's called Marco?" He wasn't sure that Dahlia could tell a Southite's sex any better than he could himself, either from their appearance or anything they said about each other, but he'd largely stopped caring.

Dahlia passed on the reply, including the adopted name.

"Nkko," the Southite echoed.

"We haven't insulted him, have we?" Seth asked anxiously.

"No," Dahlia assured him. "But see if you can say his real name." She uttered it, and Seth dutifully attempted to repeat it—leaving her helpless with laughter, and Marco apparently entertained. Theo tried as well, and did a slightly better job. Ada flatly refused. "I know my limitations," she said.

"Thith, Tho, Ata, Tatya," Marco declaimed proudly.

Another two Southites joined them; Ada named them Lana and Niall. Dahlia translated some of their banter, but it came too fast for her to explain everything. To Seth all three of them seemed friendly and curious; they might have been shy about approaching the guests back at the settlement, but now that they were traveling together they were less inhibited.

"They want to know if you and Ada are going to have more children," Dahlia told Seth.

"Not here and now," he said. "We'll need to get back home before we even think about that."

Dahlia translated his reply; the Southites jabbered and hooted back at her. "Lana said she doesn't believe you're my parents. She said I don't look enough like either of you." Dahlia sounded puzzled, and a little hurt by the suggestion.

Ada said, "Just tell her that things are different where we come from."

"Surely not that different," Dahlia translated.

"Tell her she's welcome to come and see for herself," Ada replied.

"She'd rather see the proof closer to home."

"Don't say any more about it," Seth interjected. "They're just teasing us. You should talk about something else."

Dahlia continued, offering no further translations. When the Southites finally went back to their group they seemed to be in the same good spirits as ever, but Seth couldn't help feeling a twinge of anxiety. If they knew that he and Ada had lied to Dahlia, or that Dahlia was lying to them, what would they think? It was impossible to be entirely honest with them, without being entirely honest with Dahlia.

Theo said, «So when will I have a little brother, Daddy?»

«Ask your mother.» Seth watched the Southites chatting among themselves as they lit a small fire. This close to the chasm it wasn't really cold at this time of day, but they were using the fire to melt some of the ice on the ground into drinking water.

«We need to be more careful,» he said.

«That's a nice sentiment,» Theo replied, «but I don't know what it actually entails.»

«Neither do I,» Seth admitted. Keeping more secrets? Telling better lies? «I don't know how much longer I can do this,» he said. «If I can't put my feet on the ground soon . . .»

«You're going to crawl inside a Southite's skull and start drinking their blood?»

Seth laughed. «Would that help? How do you live like this, and not lose your mind?»

«By getting my own way, enough of the time.»

«Yeah? But how do I manipulate these Walkers, when I can't even speak their language?»

Theo said, «By finding a way to convince them that their interests coincide with yours.»

TWELVE DAYS INTO THE journey, Seth could see the mouth of the chasm stretched out across the bowl behind him, a jagged ellipse that blazed and darkened as the line of lights swept by. But it was only on the fifteenth day that he was able to take his first measurements; before then, the angle that the chasm subtended had been larger than the maximum azimuthal span of the elegant Southite instrument that he'd borrowed.

Dahlia had done her best to translate the owner's instructions, but Seth would have had no trouble making sense of the device even if he'd found it discarded on the ground. The annotations on the calibrated plates for the alidade and plumb line weren't important in themselves; it was easy enough to guess, and then verify, what scheme of divisions had been used.

Seth chose a dozen points on the chasm's ellipse and measured, first, the angles between them, and then the angles from each sighting to the gravitational vertical. It was then an easy calculation to determine the angles between a line from the center of the world to his present location, and the corresponding lines from the center to the twelve points on the chasm's rim. Together, all of these measurements could tell him everything about the size and shape of the chasm's mouth—with one proviso. All of the results were expressed as fractions of the fundamental scale of the southern hyperboloid: the more-or-less constant distance from any point on the surface to the center of the world.

The equivalent measure of his own hyperboloid—the radius of the midwinter circle—had been established by the ancients and refined over generations. Seth gathered, from his tortured conversation with Siméon—as Theo had magnanimously dubbed the instrument's owner—that the same was true for the Southites. But whether it was due to some deep cultural fissure, or simply Dahlia's inexperience and limited vocabulary, Siméon had been unable to communicate this fundamental quantity in terms that Seth could understand. And Siméon's own measurements of the chasm, taken before he'd left the old home, were mired in even more opaque and bewildering conventions; Seth could have had infinite faith in his goodwill and technical prowess, but he still would not have trusted his own potentially garbled interpretation of the numbers to guide the migration and the fate of millions of people.

He had been on the verge of reconciling himself to returning home with all the crucial results expressed in an unknown scale, leaving it up to a second expedition to determine the missing parameter. But Ada and Theo had argued about the problem for days, and finally reached a solution.

Siméon—the original Siméon—had established a formula linking the period of a swinging pendulum to the strength of gravity. The period also depended on the length of the pendulum—and they'd lost all the calibrated objects they'd brought with them from the surface—but Ada insisted that she knew the length of the bone that ran from her wrist to her elbow with enough precision to use it as a standard. Seth had no reason to doubt her; the size she claimed looked plausible to his eye, and when Iqbal transferred it to a length of rope and used it to measure Seth's own height, the figure tallied with one he recalled from a surveying class when he'd needed it for an exercise in the geometry of shadows.

The Southites had no mechanical clocks, but the bowl itself made an exquisite timepiece. Once Seth had measured the angle between two distant chasms, he knew what the time between the line of lights illuminating first one and then the other would be, compared to the full circle of a day.

Iqbal had set up the pendulum for them, three Ada-forearms long, then Seth and Ada had taken turns with the observations, one of them counting the swings while the other watched the light come and go from the chasms. They'd repeated the experiment more than fifty times, then averaged all their measurements.

The final verdict had been uncanny: within the range of uncertainty of their method, the strength of gravity here was exactly the same as it had been back on the surface. So if the rock beneath them was of the same density, their distance from the center of the world was also the same. Theo had struggled to find an explanation for the coincidence—some kind of equalizing process that would have reshaped the world, over the eons, had the values not been identical. Seth had listened to all of his wild theories, but in the end he'd decided that it made no difference. If they'd found that gravity had been one-fifth more than usual, or one-twelfth less, he would still have trusted the method—and if Ada turned out to have been mistaken about the length of her forearm, they could easily adjust their results to account for that once they were back home.

As Seth took the measure of the chasm, he scribbled all the numbers onto a slate—another gift from Siméon. When he was finished he carefully packed the instrument away, then he stared at the figures, reluctant to proceed with the calculations.

Theo said, «I think I have the main results, but we should do this independently, then get Ada to check it as well.»

«All right.» Seth wrote out the geometric formulas he needed across the top of the slate, and began substituting the angles he'd measured. «When we were memorizing tables of hyperbolic functions for the surveyors' exams, did you ever think we'd be applying them to the southern hyperboloid?»

«I never even thought we'd need to remember them,» Theo replied. «How could anyone possibly lose their paper copies?»

Seth's concentration faltered. «Is that correct? Or have I lost the ability to multiply?» What if none of them could carry out basic arithmetic any more, let alone remember long lists of numbers from a lifetime ago? And Ada hadn't memorized those tables; to thoroughly check the results, she'd need to recalculate the values from first principles.

Theo said, «We're meant to be doing this independently, but I don't see any mistake there.»

Seth pressed on, converting all the angles into distances. When he was finished, he stared at the results. «Am I right?» he asked Theo. «Or have I dropped a digit somewhere and shrunk everything by an order of magnitude?»

«I think you made a small error in the fourth row.»

«How small?»

«Smaller than the precision of any of this, but you really ought to fix it anyway.»

Seth laughed. «I'll leave it in there, and see if Ada catches it. Or maybe she'll decide that I'm right and you're wrong.» Then without warning, he found himself sobbing with relief. What handful of numbers had ever cost so much to measure? And he knew now that if the answer had been different, he could not have borne it.

"What's wrong, Seth?" Dahlia called to him anxiously.

"Nothing," Theo replied. "We're happy."

"Why?"

"Because we think the hole in the world is small enough for everyone to walk around safely. No one else is going to have to make the hard journey we made."

EVERY TIME THE SEARCH party set up camp, Seth repeated his measurements. At first, Ada was willing to indulge him and check his calculations, but eventually she lost interest, and even Theo decided that any further repetition was pointless. «When you average all these results, you're reducing the effect of random errors—but there are sure to be a few systematic errors as well, which are the same every time. The instrument won't be perfectly calibrated. There'll be optical effects around the rim of the chasm. And the mouth of the chasm up on the surface won't be exactly the same shape as the mouth down here.»

«I wish you hadn't mentioned that,» Seth replied. The sense of gaining ever more precision, and ever surer knowledge of the migration's future, had offered a comforting antidote to the sense of panic he felt when his mind turned to all the delays they still faced before they could convey the news to the people who needed to hear it. «Am I crazy to think that we should head back to the settlement on our own?»

«Yes. I said we might be able to fix a broken cart on our own, if we absolutely had to. That doesn't mean we should risk going it alone just to get back a few days sooner.»

«All right.» Seth was still worried about the effect on Dahlia if they came across the bodies of the third group of migrants, but they couldn't shield her from everything. She'd survived watching Martha almost kill him; she was probably more resilient than he imagined.

He watched her and Ada, mingling with the Southites beside their campfire; she was chatting away like one of the locals. Seth hadn't asked her directly, but she had surely passed on the good news to them about the size of the chasm, and what it would mean to her people back home. The Southites could draw their own conclusions; he felt no need to belabor the point. By sending their guests home in a safe and timely manner, they would spare themselves the problem of any larger intrusion into their fragile community. Life here was hard enough already, without a horde of furless interlopers wasting their time over a question that had already been answered.

SETH SPOTTED THE SCOUTS in the distance, sprinting back across the icy plain. They usually stayed out in front until the main group set up camp, but that was hours away, and he'd never seen them returning with such haste before.

«Are they shouting something?» he asked Theo. He couldn't hear the faintest squawk himself, but if they were in such a hurry to tell the others what they'd found, it was hard to believe that they'd approach in silence.

«Not that I can tell,» Theo replied. «Why don't you ask Dahlia?»

«It's Dahlia I want to distract, if this is going to upset her.» If the scouts were carrying news of a gruesome find, at least he could insist that the four foreigners hang back and respect the Southites' privacy while they dealt with the dead.

Suddenly, Dahlia began yelling in the Southite language. Seth assumed that she'd heard something distressing from the scouts, and he waited for a chance to discover the details so he could try to comfort her, but then Theo interjected brusquely, «Do you fucking see that or not?»

Four or five long, thin objects were falling from the sky. For a moment, Seth could do no more than marvel that the emptiness to the south had been breached by what looked like a bundle of twigs. But as they dropped toward him, tilting wildly—revealing themselves to be stone, not wood—some part of his mind leaped ahead of his conscious reckoning, and he found himself turning the cart and pumping the crank with all his strength, moving toward the spot on the ground that his instinct told him would be farthest from any point of impact. The hyperbolas traced by the falling rods' lower ends raced ahead of the arcs of their descent, and they scraped into the ice and rock around him with a succession of bone-shaking screeches, sending debris spraying across the plain.

In the silence, he looked around. Ada and Dahlia were unharmed, but Niall had been cut in two: his body was literally bisected, with four limbs on each side of a deep, narrow gash that stretched for more than a dozen paces across the ground. Everyone else had been lucky: this trench, and the four others, had somehow spared them.

«More!» Theo warned him. Seth saw a cluster of specks descending; from below, the narrow, vertical rods were almost unnoticeable until they began to tumble. A part of him wanted nothing more than to move as fast as he could in any direction, but he forced himself to wait until he had a chance to extrapolate the way the rods would fall. Dahlia was shouting again, and he knew she must be terrified, but he wasn't going to try to second-guess the moves that would lead Ada to safety; all he could do was focus on his own fate. As the pattern above him became clear, he turned the cart, then turned it some more, and then at the last moment drove it backward into a gap between the falling blades.

The rods sliced into the ground, disintegrating as they struck. Seth stayed frozen until the sound of the last impact stopped ringing in his skull, then he turned his head to take in the latest damage. Furrows crisscrossed the plain, separating every member of the expedition from their companions. Two of the carts had been reduced to piles of firewood, and Niall's corpse had been mutilated further, but incredibly, no one else appeared hurt.

«Are you sure these people don't have pingers?» he asked. If the Southites were sky-blind, how could they have kept themselves safe?

Theo said, «Dahlia must be guiding them. She must be telling them where those things are going to fall.»

Seth had no time to take this in; a third cluster of rods was plummeting toward them. As he watched the weapons descend, not quite vertically, he realized that he'd noticed a glint in his own view, much lower down but from the same direction. As they were flung into the sky they must have caught the light before they'd crossed into his dark cone.

At some point he decided not to dodge the latest barrage: three rods were falling toward him on three sides, all closer than he'd wish, but it seemed more dangerous to try to get clear of all of them than to stay put. When they hit, none of them touched him directly, but the spray of dust and grit raised from their excavations pitted the side of the cart and punched through the blanket into his skin.

He looked to the Southites for some clue to their escape plans: he'd been expecting them to scatter across the plain, or to retreat at speed, to make for a more difficult set of targets. The scouts, wisely, had stayed away; Seth could no longer see where they were, but the attack had been focused tightly on the main party, so he had no reason to think that they'd been hit.

No one was scattering, though, or fleeing in any direction. Dahlia was still shouting to them in their own language—and now Lana was replying to her. He could tell that Dahlia was distressed, but the rhythms of the exchange struck Seth as equally urgent and purposeful on both sides; this was not the wailing of a terrified child seeking comfort, alternating with the soothing reassurances of an adult.

Lana moved toward one of the intact carts—the one carrying some kind of machine. A fourth group of rods was falling; Seth stopped worrying about the Southites' plans and concentrated on surviving. But as he watched the stone knives twirling down through the air, he felt a stab of empathy at the realization of how much more terrifying the attack would be to someone who couldn't even see the things approaching.

He swerved to safety, almost practiced at it now, but no less rattled as the rods carved a fresh set of furrows and another cart disintegrated.

"Are you all right?" he called to Ada, inanely, but he didn't know what else he could say.

"We'll be fine," she called back shakily. "This can't go on forever."

Seth looked around for Lana; not only had she moved to avoid being hit, she'd dragged the cart with the machine along with her. She shouted something, and Dahlia replied, then she reached into the device, made an adjustment, and pulled a lever.

A cluster of stone rods shot out of the machine. Seth followed them from his own view into Theo's and back as they arced into the sky, reached a high point and began to fall and tumble. He couldn't see a trace of the presumed enemy, but the rods disappeared behind some low, rocky hills that might have concealed anything.

Lana remained at the machine. In the silence between her curt exchanges with Dahlia, Seth could hear things clattering, squeaking, and rattling as she made her urgent preparations.

He caught a glint from the fifth cluster rising up from behind the hills, just as Lana released her own second barrage. The two passed each other with room to spare, still hanging in the air almost vertically, then they tipped and spread like two unfolding nets, imperfectly mimicking each other.

Seth froze, confused. His sense of the approaching rods' geometry had abandoned him; he had no idea how he should move.

«Forward!» Theo yelled. Seth pushed the crank; it made a quarter-turn, then jammed.

He brought his arm up from the crank to the top of the cart, raised himself out of the supporting couch, and slid down the front of the cart, thudding onto the ground. He felt the cart disintegrate behind him; he shielded Theo's pinger with his hand as chips of wood and shards of stone rained down on them.

"Seth!" Dahlia called out in distress.

"We're all right!" he yelled back. "Don't worry, we're not hurt!"

He cowered on the ground, waiting. How far and how fast would he be able to move, when the next attack came? Lana was loading the machine again, but the ambushers were ahead of her.

Someone ran toward him; Seth couldn't recognize the blur of furred limbs, but whoever it was scooped him up in two arms and gripped him tightly. Seth kept still and muttered in inspeech, forcing himself not to make a sound lest he distract his rescuer from Dahlia's instructions.

The sixth cluster fell as Lana's reply ascended. Seth watched helplessly, but when he saw that the incoming rods hadn't touched the outgoing cluster he felt a surge of hope: they weren't defeated yet.

But a rod was sweeping down toward him, perfectly placed to take three limbs off his bearer and excise his own head. Dahlia was shouting and shouting, but she had five falling rods and six blind companions to coordinate.

Seth bent his leg then straightened it emphatically, over and over in quick succession. The Southite deciphered his tic just in time, and leaped sideways as the rod whistled into the rock.

Seth started bellowing in shock and anger. When he stopped, he heard a familiar voice speak quietly, ending with a mangled attempt at his name.

"Marco?" Seth composed himself. "Thanks for that."

He could feel Marco tensed, ready for the next barrage. Lana sent off another cluster; Seth watched it rise then vanish behind the hills.

Nothing came back.

Silence descended; even Dahlia was quiet now. Seth called to her, "What's happening?"

She said, "We're waiting to see if we've broken their . . ."

"Catapult," Seth replied, though the word sounded far too innocuous for anything that could slice people in half. "The same thing Lana's using?"

"Yes."

After a few minutes, there was a discussion among the South-ites, then Ihsaq, Kate, and Reva set off toward the hills. Seth wished Marco would put him down and have a rest; he wasn't certain that the danger had passed, but if Marco grew tired from the load it could be bad news for both of them.

From the top of the hills, Kate shouted something back before the three continued on their way. Marco walked over to Ada's cart and placed Seth beside her, then he joined the others trying to clean up the aftermath of the attack. They left Niall's body untouched, working around it, salvaging food and other items that had fallen on the ground and piling them up on the remaining carts. Seth watched them in silence, feeling numb and battered. He wanted to be sure that he understood what had happened, but it seemed disrespectful to ask Dahlia to start quizzing their hosts while one of them lay dead.

The three who had gone over the hill returned, dragging two new carts and some meager supplies that they must have acquired from the enemy. Shortly afterward, the scouts rejoined the group. Everyone spoke together at length, sometimes including Dahlia. Then they set about their usual tasks: putting up tents, lighting a campfire.

"Did Lana kill all the ambushers?" Ada asked Dahlia.

"No," Dahlia replied. "One of them was trying to run away, but they caught her and she's dead now."

"Why were they attacking us?" Seth asked, though he believed he already knew the answer.

"They did the same to the people coming from the old home," Dahlia replied. "The scouts found what was left from the attack.

The ground was cut up in a hundred places, and everyone was dead." She spoke with a kind of reverent grief, as if she was not merely horrified by the idea of such a slaughter, but felt an intimate connection with the victims.

"But why?" Seth prompted her gently. "Why kill anyone?"

"Because they want the new home for themselves. They didn't reach it first, so they've sent people to hide along the route from the old home to the new one, trying to stop anyone else from joining us. They want to keep the settlement as small as they can, so in the end they can come and take everything away from us."

19

Despite Ada's offer to share her cart with Seth and keep on cranking it with double the load, Marco put him on one of the carts pilfered from the attackers, and then took turns with Ihsaq, Julia, and Kate dragging him back toward the settlement. Seth felt a twinge of humiliation at being helpless again, but he decided that petitioning Ada and his hosts to let him swap places with her and drive her cart for half the journey would seem petty. And the truth was, he'd badly bruised his left arm when he'd dropped from his own cart onto the ground; he believed he could still have worked the crank, but he would have been in pain all the way.

There were things he wanted to discuss with Ada, but although he was never out of shouting distance from her as the group made their way back across the plain, he was wary of attracting too much attention to their conversations. If one of the Southites asked Dahlia to translate what they'd said, Seth wasn't sure that he and Ada could rely on her to keep anything private.

«If only there'd been some kind of jumping predator here,» Theo lamented. «Some spring-toed lacerater that leaped right into its victims' dark cone before it struck. If these idiots had had to keep watch for dangers from above for a long enough time, they might have grown pingers of their own.»

«Wouldn't that mean that Walkers would have no need for Siders, either?» Seth replied. «I thought you believed that some ancient Southite fell through a hole and gave birth to my ancestors.»

«Do you really expect my counterfactual longings to be consistent with my merely hypothetical speculations?»

«No, you're right,» Seth conceded. «That's too much to ask.» He stared at the dark ellipse of the chasm ahead of them, with counterfactual longings of his own: if they'd left the search party and headed back to the settlement as soon as they'd made their measurements, everything might have turned out differently. «But un-counterfactually, how are we going to make ourselves less fucking useful?»

«Let's be precise here: you and Ada still aren't much use at all.»

«That's true. You haven't seen any puffballs around, have you?» Seth was half serious. «Maybe in the orchards?»

«No. But that would just switch the whole burden to the Walkers anyway. The Southites don't know a thing about Sider biology; if we feign a disease, we can make the symptoms worse than the effects of puffballs, and pretend the whole pair has ended up side-blind.»

Seth had been thinking of the puffballs more as a way of taking Dahlia out of the equation. «They'll know we're faking,» he said. «It's too convenient. We might as well be honest and just admit that we're not willing to do the job.»

Theo said, «At which point I expect they'll start threatening us. No weapon spotting, no food—or worse.»

«So what if we just agree to help them?» So far, none of the Southites had actually made any request—unless Dahlia was keeping that to herself—but it wasn't hard to anticipate what they'd want. «We escort as many tranches of migrants from the old home to the new as it takes to make the settlement unassailable. The Southites are grateful beyond measure, and offer to shower us with wealth, but we settle for a boat and wish them a fond farewell.»

«All of which takes . . . how long?»

«Too long,» Seth admitted. «Probably thousands of days.»

«And there'd be no guarantee that they'd set us free in the end,» Theo added. «If we never make it home with the measurements, maybe someone else will come after us—whether it's just a few more surveyors, or a whole horde of migrants taking shelter. The Southites aren't going to be afraid of an invasion; they'd welcome the chance to grab more sky-seers and make themselves permanently invulnerable against their enemies. This chasm is the only place in the world where they have a chance to get hold of an entire breeding population of magical slaves; once they leave it, the opportunity will vanish for however many thousand generations it takes for the migration on our hyperboloid to run into another hole. Why wouldn't they want to exploit that?»

Seth couldn't fault his logic, but he wondered if Theo was slandering these people. No one had actually treated them like slaves. Like animals, yes, but only when they'd known no better. As far as he could tell, Iqbal loved Dahlia as if she were his sister, and Marco had probably saved Seth's life—albeit at a time when Theo's potential utility was already apparent, but surely he deserved the benefit of the doubt.

WHEN THEY REACHED THE settlement, dozens of people ran out to meet the search party. Seth still had no talent for reading the Southites' emotions directly, but he could only assume that their vocalizations were suffused with grief and anger once they learned of the travelers' fate.

Marco took Seth and Theo straight to the enclosure, refilled the water trough, and brought some food. Ada and Dahlia had fallen behind, but then Seth saw Lana carrying them in, in her arms. At first he was afraid that she intended to take them to a different place, but once Lana had finished talking to someone who'd intercepted her as she crossed the open space between the buildings, she continued on to the enclosure and delivered her passengers to their home.

"Lana said she'd tell Iqbal about his cousins," Dahlia informed Seth, as Lana departed.

"Poor Iqbal," Seth replied. "It's a horrible thing to have to hear. It's going to be hard for a lot of people."

"I wish we'd got here sooner," Dahlia said sadly. "We could have helped. We could have stopped it."

"Maybe." Seth felt like a hypocrite; he shared her sympathy for the Southites, but he was also desperately searching for a strategy, if not to undermine it, at least to put it in the context of the risks that thousands of Walkers and Siders also faced. "But now that they know about the people trying to ambush them, they can be better prepared."

Dahlia said, "They still don't know about it at the old home!"

"No," Seth agreed. "But the people here will get a message to them as soon as they can. After that, all the travelers will know to take precautions."

"Precautions?" For a moment Seth wondered if the word was unfamiliar to her, but she seemed to catch his meaning anyway. "We're the precautions they need to take."

Ada shot Seth a glance suggesting that this was a conversation she'd already attempted. But Seth persisted. "What you did to protect our friends was amazing," he said. "They must be grateful, and I'm certainly proud of you. But they'd had no warning that the attack might be coming. If they'd known, there must have been other things they could have done to keep themselves safe: choosing a different route, or spreading out more to make it harder to be ambushed."

"But they already knew it might happen," Dahlia replied. "When the travelers from the old home didn't arrive, that's what everyone was afraid of."

Seth was taken aback. He looked away, out across the settlement, at the people gathering in mourning. Maybe it was pure hindsight, but now it struck him that they did not appear as shocked or agitated as they would have if the news had been entirely unexpected. "When did they tell you that? Before the attack, or after?"

Dahlia said, "After."

"All right." Seth wasn't sure how angry he should feel. No one had forced them to join the search party, and it had been his responsibility to ask the right questions before tagging along. For all he knew, the Southites might have thought it would be blindingly obvious, even to their guests, that if a group of travelers had gone missing, whoever went looking for them would be in peril too. In his conversations with Iqbal and Siméon, all his efforts had gone into making it clear how important the measurements of the chasm were to him. If they'd read that as an emphatic declaration that he was committed to the task despite the manifest dangers, who were they to argue?

"The only thing they told me before was to keep watch for anything from above," Dahlia added.

Seth needed a second opinion. «So they were using us all along?»

«It looks that way,» Theo replied. «But what else would you expect? They've lost more than a hundred people, and they're facing a war that might wipe them out completely. Thanton wasn't facing any kind of danger—and they still felt they had a right to make their Siders shut up and serve their masters in silence.»

«Yeah.» But if the Southites were understandably desperate, Seth took some hope from the fact that their reasons had not been petty or malevolent; it didn't follow that they'd be crueller than the Thantonites. «We know they put us in with the search party in the hope that we could protect them, but everything else is supposition. Until we've actually come right out and asked them to help us get home, we're just guessing as to what they'd say.»

Theo didn't reply, but Seth didn't need to be told that it was going to be a struggle to win Dahlia over to the idea, let alone anyone else.

He resumed the conversation with her. "You know that in the part of the world where Ada and I can walk, there's a migration too?"

"Yes." Dahlia was impatient. "That's why you had to find out the size of the hole. I understand that."

"The good news we found, though," Seth persisted, "won't do much good if no one else knows about it. What I did to measure it wasn't too hard—thanks to all the help I got from Iqbal and Siméon—but back where we came from, that would have been impossible. If we don't take the news back soon, people could die trying to get that information, and maybe from trying other things that they think they need to do, but we know they really don't." The last part sounded vague to the point of meaninglessness, but how could he explain the risks of building *a bridge of balloons over the node* to someone who'd only been conscious in this hyperboloid?

"Why would anyone die trying to find the size of the hole?" Dahlia demanded. "They can just come here like you did."

Seth said, "Coming here wasn't easy. When we started out, there were six other people with us. We got separated in the river; I don't know where they are now. I would have searched for them if I could, but the only way to travel is by boat, and the water moves so fast that you have no choice but to let it carry you along."

Dahlia hesitated. "Why didn't you tell me that before?"

Ada said, "We didn't want to make you sad."

Dahlia wasn't satisfied. "Theo?"

"It's true," Theo said. "Sarah and Judith, Raina and Amina, Andrei and Nicholas. We were all together at the start of the journey, but a lot of bad things happened along the way."

Dahlia lapsed into silence. Seth decided not to push her; she needed time to take this in. He crawled over to the pile of food that Marco had left; the pain this produced in his shoulder was even worse than he'd been anticipating. He tossed some fruit to Ada; she picked it up gingerly and started to eat.

Dahlia said, "I'm sorry about your friends. I hope they're safe, wherever they are. But if we don't help our friends here, all of them could die."

"They've survived without us for a very long time," Seth replied. "And we can't stay forever, you know that. They need to find a way to solve their problems on their own."

Dahlia was unswayed. "We can't stay forever, but we can't leave until we've done everything we can to protect them."

FROM THE ENCLOSURE, SETH watched the Southites preparing for a new expedition. Dahlia had explained its purpose, but it was exactly what he'd expected: the plan was to travel back to the old home in order to escort the next group of migrants on their journey to the settlement. In earlier times, they probably would have done the same thing in response to the attack, with the escort providing extra numbers to serve as scouts or soldiers, or whatever had been the best form of protection from being ambushed, before there were creatures who could see into the sky.

«Don't these idiots have diplomats?» Theo asked irritably. «We might kill each other over rivers sometimes, but at least we go through all the niceties first. And these chasms are visible for generations! They ought to have some protocol for deciding ownership, long before anyone actually makes the journey and tries to take possession of the land.»

Seth thought it over. «Maybe they do. But what if the land around some chasm that looked promising from a distance turns out to be unfarmable?» Predicting temperature and illumination might come down to pure geometry, but spotting soil types from afar was another question.

The reasons for the dispute didn't matter, though; if the Southites hadn't managed to make peace for themselves, Seth wasn't deluded enough to think that he was going to step in and resolve the conflict when he couldn't even speak the language.

He said, «There must be some way that they can travel safely, without dragging along a Sider to see into the dark cone.» He stared at the open carts, loaded with supplies; they looked absurdly vulnerable now. «If the fact that we come from such a different place is enough to give us a sensory advantage here, maybe we have some other advantage that has nothing to do with our bodies: something in our material culture that the Southites don't have, that we can hand over to them as a pure idea.»

«I want to steal the idea behind their carts,» Theo replied. «I bet we could make something that runs north-south on a belt, if we put our minds to it.»

«No doubt, but can we stick to ideas that *we* can offer *them*?»

«They don't seem to have balloons,» Theo observed. «If they were willing to try making the crossing through the air, their enemies would only be able to see them from afar. That might not make them invulnerable in the long run, but they could certainly get beyond the range of existing catapults.»

Seth wasn't going to dismiss anything out of hand. «They couldn't control the balloons with ropes over such a long distance, but there's no risk here of drifting into absolute summer; if you meander a bit, it's not instantly fatal. The question would be whether or not there are winds at some altitude that would carry them where they needed to go.»

«That, and whether they have the resources to weave that much fabric, and heat that much air. I doubt they could do it here, but the old home might have real forests and plantations.» Theo thought for a while, then added darkly, «Even if they could solve all those problems, though, they might want to hang on to our ability to see the ground directly below.»

«They could navigate without that,» Seth replied. «They'd still be able to see most of the bowl.»

«Yes, but I'm more worried that they'd want us to help them drop things on their enemies.»

Seth glanced at Ada; since they'd returned, she'd begun sinking back into the listless state he recognized from the time when they'd first arrived in the hyperboloid. He wanted to include her in the discussion, but it was hard to talk freely when Dahlia was listening.

«I suppose we could raise this with Siméon,» Theo suggested. «At least find out if it's an invention that they're aware of, and have already ruled out for long-distance travel, or whether it's an entirely new idea here.»

Seth had lost interest; he wasn't going to flop around in the dirt for another thousands days while the Southites improved their weaving skills. «This has gone on long enough,» he said. "Dahlia?"

"Yes?"

"You need to tell Lana that we're not joining the expedition to the old home. We're going back to our own home. They can help us or not, but as far as we're concerned what we did for the search party has more than repaid them for their kindness, and it's time we parted company."

"We can't leave!" Dahlia was horrified.

"We need to." Seth did his best to sound gentle but firm, like a loving parent correcting an errant child. "There's too much at stake for our own people for us to stay any longer. We've already helped our friends here understand the situation they're in, but now it's up to them to make the best of it. They need to find a way to protect themselves without us."

"I'm not telling Lana any of that," Dahlia replied vehemently.

"And no one can force you to," Seth conceded. "But Ada and I are the ones with limbs. We're not going to be turning any cranks, and if they try to carry us, we'll be struggling all the way."

Dahlia said, "You and Theo are useless anyway. You can't speak the language, so there's no reason to take you."

"Believe me, Ada has ways to make you every bit as useless." Seth had no idea what Ada could actually do to back up that threat, but the words had spilled out regardless, as if he could summon the spectre of Thanton without ever having mentioned the place.

"This is my family!" Dahlia's tone was anguished now. "I'm not going to leave them to die!"

"No one else is going to die," Seth assured her, summoning all the false confidence he could, thankful that she'd only seen one bisected body and not the mass carnage of the larger ambush. "Lana and her friends know exactly what the danger is—and it's something that their ancestors would have faced a thousand times before. Our families back home are facing a danger that no one's ever experienced. They're the ones who need us the most."

Dahlia fell silent, and Seth began to feel hopeful. The sheer numbers of the Southites and her immersion in their culture clearly carried a lot of sway, but she had to feel a special kinship with Theo, and a special bond with Ada. Once she turned her thoughts seriously to the unseen multitude of Siders and Walkers, she would understand where her loyalties belonged.

She said, "You and Theo should go, then. But Ada and I need to stay."

"No. That's impossible." Seth fought to keep the horror from showing on his face. "You've never seen a Walker where they belong, but you've seen the difference between us and the Southites. You can't expect me or Ada to stay here—even with the carts, even with the Southites doing their best to treat us well. We're in pain here, all the time. Our bodies aren't made for this place. If you care about Ada, you won't try to force this on her: you'll tell Lana that we're all going home."

Ada said, "And Lana will agree to that . . . why?" She sounded grimly amused at the absurd overreach of his ambitions. But then, she'd sounded the same when he'd first dared to claim that they had any chance at all of surviving here.

"I don't know what they'll agree to," Seth conceded. "But we have to ask. Dahlia has to ask."

"I'm not asking to leave!" Dahlia retorted.

"So you're going to torture Ada? Keep her where she doesn't belong, keep her away from all the people she misses?" Seth barely managed to stop himself before he embarked on a paean to all the love and protection that Ada had given her Sider. But however dishonest that would have been, Dahlia didn't know a thing about Thanton and the puffballs. Her cruelty was no less thoughtless than it would have been if Ada really had been her mother, or her most loyal friend.

"We won't have to stay here forever," Dahlia replied. "But I'm not going back until I know for sure that Iqbal will be safe."

Seth said, "You do know that you'll be dead long before the migration is complete?" He was guessing, but the prediction wasn't far-fetched; between the slow rate at which the land was thawing and the need to balance the workforce with the food supply, it could easily take a lifetime to increase the agricultural capacity to the point where everyone could come.

"It won't take that long to strengthen the settlement enough to make it safe," Dahlia replied, which was probably an equally plausible guess. Seth was tempted to ask her to bring in a Southite to adjudicate, but though he trusted Iqbal to be honest, his knowledge was patchy, and all the better-informed adults had agendas and a record of deceit.

Seth changed tactics. "The journey back is hard," he said. "Ada's had less experience as a traveler than I've had. If you and she try to come back on your own, and you get into trouble, the slope's an unforgiving place."

Dahlia fell silent again. Seth looked away, hardly daring to hope that he might finally have got through to her. What the Southites would accept was another question, but he could only face one obstacle at a time.

Ada said, "I'll stay. If the Southites give Seth and Theo a boat and show them the currents north, then I'll agree to stay here as long as we're needed, helping Dahlia to protect the migrants."

"Don't be ridiculous!" Seth wanted to slap her; they'd been so close to winning Dahlia over, and now she'd thrown that all away in a pointless gesture of self-abnegation.

"It's what I want," Ada said calmly. "There's nothing left for me back home." She met Seth's gaze directly as she spoke, and his skin tingled as he understood the message behind her words. No one would accept her in Thanton, with a Sider that had woken from its sleep. But whether she lived in Thanton or anywhere else, Dahlia would soon learn what her Walker had done to her, and that would be unbearable for both of them.

Ada smiled slightly, seeing that he understood. What did Seth expect her to do? Return to Thanton and send Dahlia back into oblivion? Or share her skull for the rest of her life with a Sider who had every reason to despise her?

"I'll talk to Lana, and ask her about the boat," Dahlia announced triumphantly. "I'm sure she'll agree, I'm sure!"

Seth lay staring at Ada, at a loss for words.

"I'll miss you and Theo," Dahlia said. "But I know you have to leave, to help all those people. This way, you can keep everyone safe back home, and Ada and I can help everyone here. I'm just so happy that we finally worked it out!"

20

SETH BORROWED ADA'S CART and drove it down to the river to watch the boat-builders at work. The line of lights had moved far away across the blue-gray bowl of the hyperboloid, but the dark water brought it back in broken, shimmering reflections, which stretched out into the distance until they vanished in the blackness of the chasm.

The two-tiered design being assembled on the scaffolding was a compromise between the demands of flat water and those of the slope. Seth had given up on the idea of trying to create a more robust version of the system of sliding modules used by the boat that had brought him here, but once he was sure that he and Dahlia had successfully described the vessel's needs he'd left it to the builders to choose the precise geometry, calculating buoyancies and ensuring that the whole thing would be stable throughout the journey. No one could promise that they'd survive every waterfall and every dunking, but he believed they'd stand at least as good a chance as they had in the flimsy box that they'd ridden on the way down.

Four of the builders were laboring away now, shaping the boards of the timber hull; Seth stopped the cart and observed them in silence. It felt chilly by the water in the not-quite-night, but the Southites preferred it that way.

He said, «As soon as it's complete and they've loaded the supplies, we just need to find a way to get Ada and Dahlia down here alone, while the Southites are sleeping.»

«They're not going to let that happen,» Theo replied.

«Are you sure? Because I have no idea what they'd do if we tried.» That was the most hopeful, most maddening part of it. Dahlia had flatly refused to translate anything that went beyond Ada's proposal; the Southites had agreed to it, apparently quite willingly, but no alternatives had ever been raised. It was obvious where their self-interest lay, but they'd never been given a chance to demonstrate whether or not they were willing to rise above it.

Still, Seth could see one benefit from Dahlia's censorship: it might have saved him from revealing just how fervently he was wishing for a better outcome. If the Southites believed that he was content with the deal, there was still a chance that he could take them by surprise.

Theo said, «But we do know that it's not what Ada wants.»

«If she's here beside the boat, if there's nothing to stop her, do you really think she'd turn down the opportunity?» Her relationship with Dahlia would be difficult, but when she weighed that against the misery of being trapped here, Seth couldn't believe that she'd choose a life of suffering. «You and I should fight more, in front of her. Let her know that it's perfectly normal for Walkers and Siders to have to patch up their differences.»

«It's not what Dahlia wants, either,» Theo added.

Seth said, «Dahlia's a child who's never even seen her real home. She's in no position to decide whether to go or stay.»

«And when the Southites catch us trying to renege on our agreement, you're certain that they won't punish us by refusing to allow anyone to leave?»

«I never said I was certain about anything.» Seth backed the cart away from the water, and started to turn it around.

Theo wasn't finished. «Dahlia's not a child any more, in any sense of the word. If there are places she hasn't seen and things we haven't told her, that's no reflection on her own powers of judgment.»

«All right, she's not a child,» Seth conceded. «But that doesn't make me any more willing to give in to her. She's used her access to the Southites to get her own way on everything, but just because Ada's resigned herself to that, it doesn't mean I'm going to do the same.»

AS HE DROVE BACK into the settlement, Seth passed the stationary convoy of carts, still loaded with supplies in readiness for the expedition to the old home. «They'll choose an unpredictable route,» he suggested. «It might take a bit longer, but it'll make things much harder for anyone who's trying to cut them off. And if they stay away from places where people can hide a catapult, they won't need to see into the sky to avoid surprises.»

Theo was skeptical. «If it were as simple as that, no one would ever get ambushed. But it's not me that you need to convince.»

Seth drove the cart all the way up to the enclosure, and then lowered himself slowly down the three narrow stairs that Iqbal had attached to the front of the vehicle after Dahlia described his painfully abrupt dismount during the attack on the search party.

"How's the boat looking?" Ada asked. She was curled up on her blanket, and covered in a second one to keep out the cold.

"It's going well," Seth replied, crawling over onto his own blanket. "I think they'll be done in a few more days."

"Good."

Seth was surprised that Dahlia hadn't greeted him. "Is she asleep?" he asked quietly.

"Yes," Ada confirmed.

"Then try not to wake her. I want to talk to you without her."

Ada said nothing, but Seth took her stillness as assent.

"I'm going to find a way to get us all home," he promised. "I know it will be hard for you and Dahlia, when she learns the truth. But did I ever tell you that my sister almost murdered her Sider? And they got over it, eventually. You'd be amazed what people can forgive, when they're stuck with each other."

"I know you mean well," Ada replied. "But you need to understand that this is something you can't change."

Seth was about to respond, but Ada's face tightened in a warning.

"Hello, Seth," Dahlia said sleepily. "What's happening?"

"I was looking at the boat," he said. "It's beautiful. I want you to thank the builders for me, next time you get a chance."

"I will."

SETH WAS WOKEN BY Theo's voice in his skull.

«We need to try something different.»

He opened his eyes, squinting against the glare from the chasm. «What, exactly?»

Theo said, «You seem to be willing to risk everything to help Ada. What I'm going to suggest involves a risk, too, but it's a much smaller one.»

«I'm trying to help Ada *and* Dahlia,» Seth replied irritably. «Why don't you just tell me what your idea is, and then we can argue about the relative degrees of danger?»

«I want you to press one of the northern fingers of your right hand against the rim of my right pinger, as hard as you can.»

Seth looked across the enclosure, checking to see if Ada was awake, but she was huddled motionless in her blankets. «Why would I want to do that? If we're going to fake a fight, shouldn't we have an audience?»

«I don't want you to fake anything,» Theo insisted. «I want you to break the seal.»

«Have you lost your mind?» Seth rubbed his eyes. «I don't mind a bit of blood, but that would be ridiculous.» As he moved his arm, he realized belatedly that Theo wasn't pinging in either direction; he was holding both membranes tensed and still, in the same protective configuration he would have used if he'd actually been under attack.

«We need to show Dahlia what's possible.»

«Dahlia?» Seth was lost now. «Ada's the one who needs convincing that reconciliation is possible.»

«But it's Dahlia who gets her own way,» Theo countered. «So we need to show her another possibility, for what *her way* could be.»

Seth was finally beginning to see where this was heading. «No, no, no. We can't do that to her!»

Theo said, «It's not our decision. Show her, and let her choose for herself. I told you, she's not a child.»

Seth felt nauseous. «Show her *what*? Even if I can pry you loose, what then? I can cut myself to feed you, but then what's the point? Apart from the fact that we'll have half-blinded each other, you'll still be relying on a Walker to survive.»

«I've heard people say there was another way,» Theo replied tentatively. «When a Walker died and the Sider was separated, sometimes the Walker's relatives would bleed themselves, but sometimes they'd chew up food instead and offer that to the Sider. Any Southite could do that much—and for the magic weapon that's going to save them from their enemies, they'd hardly begrudge her the effort.»

Seth said, «She'd be light-blind and naked. Do you think you really know what that would be like?»

«No,» Theo replied. «But I'm willing to find out.»

«And when you're back inside my skull, what then?» Once the connections that enabled shared vision and inspeech had been severed, how long would they take to be reestablished?

«I don't know,» Theo admitted. «We're not so young that everything's guaranteed to sort itself out, like it did for Leanne and Patricia, but the fact that it's the same pairing, not a new one, has to count for something.»

«Does it?» Seth wished Theo could see his scowl of disbelief. «Did I blink and miss it when you studied medicine?»

«If *your* plan goes wrong,» Theo replied, «the Southites sink the boat to punish you for trying to spirit Ada and Dahlia away. Don't try to tell me that's not worse than us ending up incommunicado.»

Seth felt his courage faltering. If Ada was intent on staying, why should he risk going side-blind just to stop her? He should have agreed from the start to go along with her plan, and let her have exactly what she claimed she wanted.

«Are you playing me?» he asked Theo suspiciously. «Hoping I'll give up on Ada, if you can make the price as unpleasant as possible?»

Theo said, «What I'm hoping for is that you won't get everyone stranded, along with the measurements.»

«But you really want to try this?» Seth pressed him.

Theo hesitated. «Can you think of a better way? Not counting scenarios where the Southites turn a blind eye, Ada does whatever you ask her to, and Dahlia doesn't scream for help when we try to kidnap her and take her down the river?»

«Fuck.» Seth put his finger in place, and applied as much force as he could muster.

The pain fell far short of being stabbed, but his protective instincts compounded the raw unpleasantness of the sensation; it was like trying to poke himself in the eye and then dig deeper without flinching. He could feel the ridge where his skin joined up with Theo's membrane warning of the danger, then protesting at the damage, and then finally starting to yield. And he could feel Theo shivering—but apart from his own labored breathing, they both succeeded in remaining silent even as he broke through the seal.

Seth knew that if he stopped to take stock of what he'd done he might not be able to bring himself to continue; the warm dampness on his skin and the scent of blood were still abstractions whose meaning he could hold at bay, but only for so long. He kept his finger pressed against the bony wall on his side of the wound, and forced it around the edge of the circular aperture, tearing through the seam more readily now that it had been breached. At the halfway point some part of him rebelled in panic and revulsion, summoning up mental images of the difference between a cut that left a flap of skin attached, and one that excised it completely to leave the flesh unprotected. But he stared through the visions of flaying and persisted.

When his finger came full circle he flopped down against the blanket. Blood was trickling over his face and the back of his head, but he kept his hand out of sight so he wouldn't have to look at it.

«Can you hear me?» he asked Theo.

«More or less.» Theo's inspeech was muffled; they'd already disturbed something deeper than the pinger itself.

«If I do anything that feels like it's going to injure you, yell out loud.» On the rare occasions when he'd thought about the anatomy of the connection, Seth had always imagined that the intertwined tissues linking Walker and Sider would be weaker than anything in the interior of either. But that was just a guess, without even a trace of folk-wisdom to back it up; the only time most pairs were separated was when one member had already died.

The bottom pinger was much harder to attack, with his left arm confined between his body and the ground. It was difficult to control the angle his finger made with the membrane, and it kept slipping out of the wound. He heard himself emitting brief, quiet sobs, as much out of frustration as pain, but he did his best to stifle them. Any chance of selling the endpoint to Ada and Dahlia would vanish in an instant if they had to witness what the process entailed.

With both seals broken, he lay still for a while, breathing slowly, trying to marshal his strength. But then he felt Theo squirming, shifting inside the tunnel. There was no room for him to thrash about, but waves of contraction were moving along his skin, tugging at Seth's flesh one way then the other, pulling on a thousand tiny connections like an animal snagged in a patch of thorns patiently working itself loose.

Seth wanted to ask if he needed help, but he couldn't bring himself to speak, even in a whisper. When he'd started this, it had felt like a contained, self-inflicted mutilation, but now his perception of the act kept switching between amputation and expulsion—as if the thing in his head, having ceased to be a normal, welcome part of him, desperately needed to be driven out, but at the same time the idea of its loss was as horrifying as the prospect of a limb breaking free and crawling away.

"Can you give me a push?" Theo said quietly. His words sounded as odd as if they'd come from some other Sider whose invisible host was lying so close to Seth that their heads should have touched.

Seth brought his right hand to the side of his head and gently pressed all three axial fingers against Theo's pinger. Immediately, it started to yield—and he froze, as shocked and revolted as if he'd prodded his own side and the flesh had begun to give way like rotten fruit.

"More than that," Theo begged.

Seth increased the pressure, and he felt Theo tensing so as not to damp the force on its way to the connective tissue. For a moment there was no more play; it was almost as if they were back to normal, if not for the fact that his right hand was farther to the left than had ever been possible when he'd held it beside his skull before. Then the taut membrane began retreating from his touch and he forced himself to follow it down, until his fingers could reach no farther, their target slipped away and they were hanging in the air.

He heard something drop onto the blanket beside his left shoulder. The upper part of Theo's body would still be in the tunnel, but once he emerged fully he'd need something else keeping him upright. Seth hurriedly rearranged the blanket, gathering it up to form a supportive pit, but that felt precarious so he reached beneath it and scooped soil into place under the ridges. Then he raised his head and let Theo slide out completely.

"Are you all right?" he asked.

"I think so." Theo's voice sounded stranger than ever.

Seth moved away from him slowly, taking care not to disturb the mound that was supporting him. When he'd gone far enough to shift Theo out of his dark cone, he still found it hard not to avert his eyes, afraid that the result of their rash experiment might resemble an organ ripped from his body, with no chance of surviving on its own.

But the pale gray cylinder standing on the blanket was only bleeding in a couple of places, and though Seth could see tears in Theo's skin, they did not look like serious wounds. The muscular wall of his body appeared perfectly capable of maintaining its posture without the usual jacket of bone; Theo might never have needed to move more than a finger's width in his entire life, but pumping out sound waves every waking moment clearly required more strength and rigidity than Seth had appreciated.

"Have you got . . . *two* mouths?" The small apertures, each bearing four tiny teeth, were widely separated, but Seth couldn't discern any difference between them.

"No. One's for waste."

Seth pondered this revelation. "Are you saying that you've spent your whole life pissing into my blood?"

"Where did you expect it to go?"

"I'm not letting you back."

"It might not end up in your bloodstream," Theo decided. "There might be a different vessel that transports nothing but urine. As you keep reminding me, I'm not a doctor. I just know that I have to latch on in two places."

"What's going on?" Ada demanded.

Seth turned toward her; she'd barely raised her voice, but he could see the shock on her face. "Don't panic," he said. "We're just trying out some different living arrangements."

"But how's he going to eat?" Dahlia asked, more fascinated than concerned.

"Toss me some fruit," Seth instructed Ada. He took a small bite and chewed it for a while, then spat it out onto a finger and approached Theo. "I'm going to try feeding you; just don't stick those teeth into me."

"All right."

Seth hesitated. "Which one's your mouth?"

"The left one."

He dabbed some of the mush directly into the tiny hole. Theo did something and the food was drawn in deeper. Seth had imagined his blood spurting freely into his Sider's mouth under pressure, as it would from a wound, but maybe it wasn't like that at all; maybe his body measured out and partitioned its offerings, giving Theo access to a small reservoir to draw on, rather than a continuous stream. "I'm really starting to wish I'd studied anatomy."

"What does it taste like?" Dahlia wondered.

"Strange," Theo admitted. "But not terrible. Can I have some more?"

Seth complied. "Tell me if you feel in danger of toppling."

"You'll be the first to know."

"What's wrong with you idiots?" Ada was moving from incredulity to anger. Seth couldn't blame her; no one liked being ambushed.

"We're just gathering information," Theo replied innocently. "How could anyone not want to know what it's like for a Walker and Sider to live apart?"

"Everyone already knows that they'd live badly."

"There are degrees of bad," Theo retorted. "I'm sure you can think of some worse arrangements, can't you?"

Ada fell silent. Dahlia said, "I'm worried about Theo falling. Can I ask Iqbal if he could bring something, or make something . . .?"

Theo said, "A surrogate skull, with a stable base?"

"Yes."

"So long as there are gaps for my mouth and urethra, that would be perfect."

IQBAL KEPT COMING BACK to make more measurements of Theo, and to converse at length with Dahlia. Half a dozen other Southites gathered around the enclosure to gawk at the strange new development.

Seth was tired, and all the noise from the spectators was wearying. "It's like arriving all over again," he complained. "They did know all along that there were four of us, didn't they?"

"Yes," Dahlia confirmed. "But they didn't know that we could live this way."

Ada said bluntly, "We can't. I'll give him three days before he starts to get sick." Seth wasn't sure why she remained so hostile. She must have guessed what Theo was hoping for, but it was hard to see why she found the plan so objectionable. Given a choice between living side-blind back home, or confined to lying on a cart while she and Dahlia went into battle with the Southites, the first option sounded more like a reprieve than a maiming.

After half a day of to-ing and fro-ing, Iqbal finally brought his construction. It had a broad, square frame as its base, and three smaller squares that acted like collars for Theo's body, connected to the base by short, inclined beams. Iqbal held it above Theo so he could ping it and decide if he was happy to make it his new home; Theo gave his approval, with Dahlia translating.

Seth helped Iqbal slip the thing into place; Iqbal had more than enough hands for the job, but Seth would not have forgiven himself if anything had gone wrong.

"Is it comfortable?" he asked Theo.

"Comfortable enough. And at least I can't fall over in my sleep now."

Iqbal wasn't finished; he returned with a solid square of timber, which he slid carefully under the existing base—with Theo squirming up to raise his lower pinger off the blanket—and then secured with eight pegs. Now it would be possible to lift the whole thing without any danger of Theo sliding out.

Lana had joined the crowd beside the enclosure, and Dahlia translated a question from her. "She wants to know if this is an ordinary part of our . . .?"

"Life cycle," Seth suggested. "Tell her it's not very common. Some of us never do it."

"Some?" Ada interjected.

Seth listened to Dahlia's exchange with Lana, reconciled to the fact that he'd never learn to extract any meaning from the noises themselves, but still hopeful that he could glean some small insight from the length of the conversation.

"What else did she say?" he asked. The discussion had almost certainly moved beyond a translation of his answer.

"It's not important," Dahlia replied.

Seth didn't push her, but he could guess Lana's next question: *It's not an ordinary part of the life cycle, but now that this one has done it, will you?*

Theo said, "There's a game I want to play."

SETH TAPPED THE SIDE of his cart. "Four, minus seven!" Theo shouted.

"Close," Dahlia declared encouragingly.

Seth made the sound again.

"Four, minus six," Theo decided.

"Exactly!" Dahlia started squawking, explaining the outcome to the crowd of spectators. Seth started moving the cart again, backing it up and turning it before driving it forward, so as not to make Theo's task too easy.

Iqbal had marked out the grid by scraping lines with a stick on a patch of open ground in the middle of the settlement, then he'd placed Theo at the center. Seth had shouted out the coordinates from two of the corners to get him oriented, but after that it had been up to Theo to judge the positions of every sound that followed.

"So where am I now?" Seth asked.

"Two, zero," Theo said confidently.

"Two, zero!" Dahlia confirmed, and translated.

Ada said, "This is ridiculous; he can hear the cart moving from place to place."

"So how should we be doing it?" Theo asked mildly.

"Get three or four Southites on the grid. They wander about at random, then one of them makes a sound, and you have to place it."

Seth said, "I'd be happy to withdraw. Dahlia? Can you ask for volunteers, and explain the new rules?"

He drove the cart off to the side. Iqbal ran in and touched up the grid, repairing the lines that the belts had scuffed, while Dahlia conversed with would-be participants.

Eventually, Iqbal, Marco and Lana took to the grid. They scuttled around Theo in all directions, throwing up dust and immersing him in a confusion of eight-legged footfalls. Then Dahlia called out to them, they froze, and Lana emitted a brief hoot.

"Five, three?" Theo said tentatively.

"Exactly!"

Dahlia translated the verdict, and the game continued.

Sometimes Theo was off by one grid square, but never more. Seth was astonished; he'd always known that his Sider's hearing was superior to his own, but it had never occurred to him that the ability to locate an object in the dark cone by its echo would extend to objects outside the cone that were emitting sounds of their own. However helpful it was for Walker and Sider to share each other's vision, apparently the Siders had never entirely lost their ancestral talent for deducing the position of anything that made a noise, in any direction.

Dahlia said, "I want to try it!"

Ada grumbled, but didn't refuse. Iqbal took Theo aside, and swapped Ada onto the cart where Seth had been lying; she drove herself to the center of the grid, then Iqbal fetched a small timber screen with one axial edge and propped it up in front of Ada's face to block her view.

The Southites went to three corners of the grid and called their positions, then continued the game as before. Dahlia gave her answers in both languages, and at first she did much more poorly than Theo, but by the ninth or tenth try she began to improve.

"This might actually work," Seth said quietly. As relieved as he was that the ordeal hadn't been for nothing, the truth was he felt almost as bad at the prospect of leaving Dahlia alone here as he had at the thought of abandoning Ada. "Could you live with the Southites, as the only one of your kind? Never speaking your own language again? Never having a family? Never sharing the view by light?"

"No," Theo admitted. "But my history's very different from hers. What's 'her own' language: ours, or the Southites'?"

"If Ada was staying, at least they would have had a chance to come home eventually."

Theo said, "Don't underestimate the power of curiosity, on either side. Just because we've got all the measurements we need, it doesn't mean there might not be another expedition here eventually, if we can think of ways to make the whole thing safer. Or the Southites might decide that they want to go and meet a few more of their cousins, while they still have the chance."

"Good luck to them getting up the cliff." At least their feet would be in the right place to make contact with the surface, even if the direction of gravity was less than helpful.

Dahlia was shouting out the coordinates exuberantly, right every time now. But the happier she sounded, the more Seth ached at the thought of walking away without her.

SETH HAD EXPECTED THE novelty of Theo's separation to wear off quickly, but the Southites seemed to find his emergence as fascinating as if they'd stumbled upon an entirely new creature. Seth's skull throbbed as much from the noise of all the squawking onlookers as it did from the aftermath of the act. Once or twice, while everyone else was sleeping, he inserted his fingers into the empty tunnel and probed the wall. It wasn't bleeding anymore, and when he touched the skin—or whatever it was that lined the tunnel—he felt no pain, but the act was repugnant in a different way, imbued with an overpowering sense that he was violating the proper disposition of things. He was afraid that the ruptured surface might become infected, but equally afraid that it would heal in the wrong way: so successfully, so thoroughly and hermetically that when Theo returned, there'd be no hope of reconnection.

Whatever pain or doubt Theo was feeling, he kept it to himself. When the glare from the chasm filled the enclosure, Seth watched him sleeping in his strange wooden frame, and wondered what it would be like never to be woken by brightness.

Dahlia said nothing about her plans, but every day she challenged Theo to another round of the grid-location game, as if she was intent on convincing herself that she'd still be able to help her Southite friends if she chose this new condition. As Seth watched her playing, with Ada's eyes covered for the duration of the game, it struck him more forcefully than ever just what Dahlia would be giving up. If the glorious panorama of the hyperboloid was mere scenery, light also offered the most natural way to perceive her companions.

On the fourth day, as usual, Theo played first, standing inert in the middle of the dusty ground. It didn't seem fair for Dahlia to judge his calls when they were competing, so Seth took on the role, watching from atop a cart so he could see the grid properly.

Iqbal was joined by two new grid-runners, Reva and Julia. Seth was always amused by the efforts the Southites put into complicating their paths between calls, circling the caller multiple times then spiraling back again, as if the whole trick depended on tracking their motion in detail. Seth would not have put it past Theo to announce the locations of all three runners even if they'd stayed silent when they stopped, but the people on the expedition who were going to be relying on Dahlia's protection would surely be willing to call out their names to her periodically as they marched across dangerous terrain.

The runners stopped, and Reva hooted.

"Six, seven," Theo called.

"Not even close!" Seth ruled, surprised; Reva was at four, one. Dahlia spoke to Reva, who hooted again.

"Six, seven!" Theo insisted angrily. "No. Six, seven, eight, nine, ten."

"Theo?" Dahlia sounded hopeful that he might be joking with her.

"Six, seven, eight, nine, ten," he repeated.

The players and spectators grew silent. Seth said, "We need to get him away from here. Take him to the enclosure."

Dahlia translated, and the Southites acted swiftly; Iqbal carried Seth, and Reva carried Theo. In the enclosure, Seth used a scoop to bring water from the trough and pour it into Theo's mouth. The tiny muscles worked to draw some in, whether by will or by reflex. The chewed mush he'd been imbibing for the last four days had been moist, and he'd never asked for it to be supplemented with water, but he might not have been fully aware of his own thirst, or understood its remedy, the way a Walker would have.

"Is that better?" Seth asked.

Theo emitted a long string of gibberish, but the nonsensical words did nothing to diminish the utter weariness in his voice.

Ada and Dahlia arrived, driving the cart up to the side of the enclosure. Ada said, "You know what he needs."

"Yes." Seth wasn't going to risk harming him by trying to get him back inside his skull in this state. "Does anyone have a knife?"

Dahlia hesitated, then called out to the group of Southites who'd gathered nearby. Someone ran off. Seth lay staring at Theo, at a loss as to how he could comfort him without inspeech; ordinary language felt inadequate for the task, like trying to comfort a fellow Walker in distress without laying a hand on them.

Lana approached, holding a knife. Seth waited for her to pass it to him, already thinking through the geometry; the shaft wasn't axial, which was a nuisance, but he'd still be able to grip it between his fingers and poke the tip into some part of his skin. But Lana entered the enclosure and walked past him toward Theo.

"What's she doing?" Seth demanded, suddenly recalling Martha's attempt to euthanize him. "Dahlia? *What's she doing?*" He crawled after her and grabbed at one of her hind legs, but she pushed him away effortlessly.

She picked up the water scoop that was sitting on the ground, held it against one of her front legs, and then cut herself with the knife. Seth saw blood trickling out of the wound, red as his own, leaving its color on her matted fur as it flowed down into the scoop.

"No!" he protested. "He needs mine!" He looked to Dahlia, and she translated his words, but Lana ignored him. When he tried to move between her and Theo, she grabbed him with two free hands and held him at bay.

Theo started muttering again, his pinger shuddering out confused fragments of words. Lana raised the scoop to his mouth; Seth couldn't see if he was accepting her offering, but only a few droplets spilled down his body.

Lana held the scoop to her leg again, and squeezed the flesh to make her blood run out faster.

"Why won't she let me feed my own Sider?"

Dahlia put this to Lana, then replied numbly, "She needs to know what's possible. If this doesn't work, then she'll let you feed him."

Seth watched, angry and helpless, as she tipped more blood into Theo's mouth; all he could do was hope that she didn't poison him before she accepted that she'd failed.

Theo shuddered strangely, but then he spoke. "Where the fuck am I? Seth?"

"We're in the enclosure. What do you remember?"

"We were going to play the grid-running game," Theo replied. His words were a little slurred, but he seemed lucid now. Lana was still pouring from the scoop, oblivious to the meaning of their conversation. "Then I started to feel dizzy. But . . . if you're over there, who's giving me this blood?"

Seth said, "Someone who's just proved that she really is my cousin."

THREE DAYS AFTER THEO returned to the tunnel, Seth was woken by the sound of Ada and Dahlia whispering to each other. He couldn't tell whether Theo was awake too, so he lay still and tried to fall asleep again. They were both going to need their rest, if the torn connections were ever to be rejoined.

He succeeded, but only for a while.

"Seth?" It was Dahlia's voice, quiet but insistent.

"Yes?"

"Will you help us? Please?"

His eyes were still closed, but the gray light penetrating his eyelids seemed to shift in front of him.

"What does Ada say?" he asked.

"We need your help," Dahlia replied.

"And I need to hear that from her."

Ada spoke haltingly. "I want to stay here with Dahlia." Seth had never heard so much pain in her voice.

He said, "You need to agree on this, between yourselves."

"She can't live here!" Dahlia protested. "It's too hard for her. I understand that now; her body needs to move the way it can in her old home. I'll be all right. Everyone here is good to me."

Seth felt his own body start shaking, but he forced himself to speak calmly. "I understand, but it's not my choice. You need to agree."

Theo said, "Ada?" She didn't reply. "I can promise you this much: without you, Dahlia will still receive nourishment, and she'll still always know exactly who's around her. I might not be smart enough to learn the language, or strong enough to offer to take her place, but I know it won't be hard for a Sider in the way it would be for you."

Ada remained silent.

Seth wished he had some way of untangling all the things that might be driving her to stay: the bond she'd formed with Dahlia, the guilt she felt about the way she'd lived before, some sense that this was the only way to atone. He said, "Do you want Thanton to change, or do you want life there to go on as it is?"

"I want it to change," Ada replied angrily.

"Then come back, and help to make that happen. Because I doubt there's anyone in the world more able to do that than you."

Ada said nothing, but Seth heard Dahlia whispering to her, repeating one phrase over and over. He couldn't make out the words, but the rhythm alone was one of reassurance, like a parent soothing a child. Seth clung to the sound, trying to reconcile himself to what was happening.

Ada let out a cry of anguish, but then she replied to Dahlia, quietly and calmly.

Seth waited.

"We need your help," Ada said. "We need you to help us separate."

21

"IS EVERYTHING SECURE UP there?" Seth asked anxiously. He glanced toward the line of lights; it was getting close to the departure time.

"Yes!" Ada called back. "And you can't fault the Southites for their carpentry. I'd bet you anything that when we disembark, the fruit won't even be wet."

Seth cranked his bench up, away from the storage lockers at the bottom of his box-like section of the hull, raising his body high enough to let him look straight out toward the shore. Dozens of Southites stood by the water's edge: Lana, Siméon, and Martha were among them, along with all the boat-builders, but many were curious spectators that he had never had reason to name.

"Do you ever think about the Southites from the other chasm?" he asked Theo. "If our lot win, what happens to them?"

"They'd better get creative, and learn to negotiate. They must have something to offer a collaboration."

"I hope so." Seth could only wish them well, with no sense that he was leaving the problem behind. His own hyperboloid was going to have to deal with the same kind of competition for resources, as the migration squeezed past the hole.

He described the crowd to Theo. "Iqbal and Dahlia are at the front; she's in that tall frame that holds her up above his back."

"There's something I can be thankful for," Theo replied.

"What?"

"At least I don't have to stare at your body all day long."

"It's her choice," Seth said. "Orange fur, or a tiny patch of dirt." He laughed. "I think Dahlia must have overheard you."

"Why do you say that?"

"Iqbal's started juggling stones." He was tossing them high into the air with one hand and trying to catch them with the opposite one. He wasn't doing a bad job—and whether or not Dahlia had found some way to give him cues fast enough to help, it would certainly break the monotony of her view.

"Are we going?" Ada asked impatiently.

"We're going." Seth gazed at Dahlia for a moment, glad that she couldn't see his face. "Be happy!" he shouted. "Be safe! Stay warm!"

"You too," she called back.

Seth waited to see if Ada had some last words for her, but the two of them must have said their goodbyes. He reached over for the lever that engaged the runners, and lowered them into the water. The flow started up, brisk and steady, and the boat began moving away from the shore.

He looked up at the blue-gray bowl, hunting for the navigation cues he'd need to find his way to the northbound current. Then he looked back to the shore, where the Southites were hooting and squawking. Dahlia was almost invisible now; he could just make out the slender beams of the pyramid that held her.

He raised one of the runners, letting the boat turn three-quarters of the way toward the blackness of the chasm. The journey ahead remained as daunting as ever, but they were as rested and well supplied as they could have been. "I can't wait to fucking walk again!" he called up to Ada. "Even with a stilt."

"Yeah." Ada's voice was somber.

"Are you all right?" Seth asked.

"I'll live."

Seth didn't have it in him to keep insisting that she'd done the right thing. "Dahlia will be happy," he said. He believed that much. Even if most of the Southites thought of her as merely useful, at least one of them genuinely cared about her.

"She told me she knew we weren't her parents," Ada said. "She made it sound as if she was the one who should have been embarrassed, for ever assuming something so childish and naïve."

"But it's good she's clear about that." Seth watched the chasm growing nearer, as the last traces of light abandoned it. "Did she ask about her real parents?"

"I told her that they were like her, with the same kind of bodies. She said that was obvious now, but she didn't ask anything more."

Theo said, "Giving her the whole story just as you were leaving would have been worse."

"I know," Ada conceded. She was silent for a while, then she said, "If I'd stayed, I would have tried to find a way to tell her, and then hope she'd be able to forgive me. But I couldn't do that and walk away."

Seth could feel the northward current tugging on the boat. "Let's hope this river's long and fast," he said. They'd have less than a day to get far enough back along the slope to escape the heat of the sun. "They'll all be waiting for us, wondering where we've been: Raina and Amina, Sarah and Judith, Andrei and Nicholas."

Darkness rushed forward across the glimmering surface of the water, then the boat descended into the chasm.

Afterword

A Note on the Translation

If you could listen to the speech sounds used by the characters in this novel, not only would you hear no words in your own native language, you would not hear any of the proper names employed in the story, such as "Seth," "Theo," "Baharabad," or "Sedington." The actual sounds that played the same roles as these words would not consist of anything a human would recognize as a string of phonemes, so it would be pointless to attempt to render them phonetically. Like every other word, they need to be translated.

Words such as "smile," "laugh," "groan," and so on are used to indicate the nature of the emotions that elicit these acts, rather than any anatomical or phonetic similarities to human utterances and gestures.

While numbers as such are a universal concept, several kinds of measurement have been converted into familiar units, where it makes sense to do so. Angles are translated into degrees, not because the people of this world would have chosen to divide a circle into three hundred and sixty parts, but because "ninety degrees" immediately tells the reader what proportion of a circle is involved, which is all that matters. Similarly, periods of time less than a day are translated as seconds, minutes, and hours, because these words convey the appropriate proportions, regardless of the particular scheme of diurnal subdivisions actually employed.

The word "year" is not used at all, since the world of the novel neither orbits its sun nor experiences cyclic seasons. The names of our own, chronological seasons have been repurposed as names for different solar latitudes, which determine the angle at which the sun crosses the sky, and hence the average temperature—albeit in a contrary fashion to the way this works for us. The region where the sun passes directly overhead at noon is colder than any other, hence "the midwinter circle." Odd as this sounds, it would be odder still to use "winter" for the zones of scorching heat to the north and south, where the sun never rises as high.

Colors have generally been translated on the basis of the kinds of common objects that bear them. I have written other novels with non-human characters where the most crucial thing a color conveyed was the wavelength of light observed in a star trail or a laboratory experiment, but in this case there was no need to tie the names of colors to any particular physical quantity. For most purposes, to a human the word "green" means "the color of certain kinds of foliage," "red" means "the color of one's own kind of blood," and so on, and the translation here aims to preserve those kinds of associations wherever possible.

Similarly, "water" here is a ubiquitous liquid upon which life depends, and "air" is a substance (in this case, a liquid not a gas) that covers the world. They are not—and could not be—precisely the things that bear these names in our own world, since there are no atoms of hydrogen, oxygen, or nitrogen in the universe of the novel, but the translation reflects the roles they play. "Steam" is what "water" becomes when it is heated and turns invisible; the fact that it has dissolved and dispersed into the more abundant liquid, rather than evaporated into a gas, is a distinction worth keeping in mind, but not one that merits a neologism.

A Note on the Geometry

The events of this novel take place in a universe where the usual three dimensions of space and one of time have been replaced by two dimensions of space, and two of time. Instead of 3+1, we have 2+2.

What does it mean to have two dimensions of time? It does *not* mean that any one observer's experience of time becomes two-dimensional. Seth has a linear stream of consciousness, with a sense of history in which events follow one after another, rather than being spread out over a two-dimensional plane. The presence of a second dimension of time offers more directions in space-time with the *potential* to be someone's arrow of time—but each arrow still points in a single direction.

Perpendicular to an observer's arrow of time are the three dimensions that they experience as "space"—and this is where the difference between 3+1 and 2+2 is most apparent. "Space" with 2+1 dimensions is like a pared-down version of the full 3+1 dimensions of our own universe, with the behavior of ordinary objects displaying the kinds of exotic effects that we would only see in relativistic physics.

For example, any distance that Seth measures obeys an altered version of Pythagoras's Theorem, in which the square of the overall distance is found by summing the squares of two ordinary distances (such as east-west and up-down), then *subtracting* the square of the north-south distance, rather than adding it. If the result is positive, it is the square of an ordinary distance. If the result is negative, it is the opposite of the square of an "axial" distance—a distance whose square is always subtracted in this kind of calculation, just like a distance measured directly along the north-south axis.

A similar rule governs the notion of "spacelike" and "timelike" separations between events in our own, (3+1)-dimensional universe. Events that happen at different places at the same moment are said to have a *spacelike* separation, while events occurring at the same place at two different times have a *timelike* separation. You might wonder if relativity could blur this distinction by asking, "The same according to whom?" But assuming you can't travel faster than light, your locations at noon and at one p.m. can never be my idea of two different places at the same moment in time, whatever our relative state of motion.

The corresponding prohibition in (2+1)-dimensional space is that an object that lies along an axial direction can never be rotated in such a way that it ends up aligned in an ordinary direction, or vice versa. If a stick starts out pointing due north, turning it to the east will cause the distance it spans in both the north-south and the east-west directions to increase, but the difference of the squares of the two numbers will remain constant. For example, the individual measurements might change from five meters north-south and zero meters east-west, to thirteen meters north-south and twelve meters east-west, because thirteen squared minus twelve squared is equal to five squared. If this sounds odd, compare it to the situation in our world, where a five-meter stick could end up spanning three meters north-south and four meters east-west, because three squared plus four squared equals five squared. That's just Pythagoras's Theorem, with the usual sum of squares rather than the difference. But in Seth's world, the stick's north-south span will always be greater than its east-west span, so it can never end up pointing due east.

What if the stick *starts out* pointing due east? East-west is just one of two ordinary dimensions, so this kind of stick can end up perpendicular to its original direction: say, pointing straight up. But any attempt to rotate it toward the north or the south must still follow the rule that the difference of squares is unchanged, so the stick can never end up pointing *more* to the north than in the other directions.

In our universe, if we fix one end of a rod to a pivot then swing it around freely, the other end traces out the surface of a sphere. But in the universe of the novel, the same kind of rod will trace out either a one-sheeted hyperboloid—an infinite saddle-shaped surface that wraps around the north-south axis—or an infinite bowl-shaped hyperboloid that faces north or south.

Between these hyperboloids sit a pair of cones, facing north and south: these are surfaces where the difference of squares of the distances from the pivot is exactly zero. Within these cones, the difference will always be negative.

It is the nature of light in our universe—and by analogy, what we choose to call light in the universe of the novel—that any portion of its world line through the full, four-dimensional space-time has a difference of squares that is precisely zero. If a beam of light were to follow a trajectory through (2+1)-dimensional space for which the difference of squares was negative, the final quantity pertaining to the world line would have yet another square (the square of the elapsed time) subtracted from it . . . which could never bring it up to zero. So light can never travel within the two cones, and no one can see (by light) in these directions.

However, there is nothing to prevent material objects, or vibrations within a material medium, from traveling either inside or outside these "dark cones." The rule that applies to the world lines of material objects is that the difference of squares must be negative: this is obviously true for the case of an object standing still, when there is zero change in position, minus the square of the elapsed time. And for any trajectory within the dark cones, the overall difference of squares will again be negative.

Outside the dark cones, the trajectory through space starts out with a positive difference of squares. To bring this down to a negative value, the elapsed time for the object must be greater than the length of the trajectory itself. In other words, the speed of the object must be less than 1, in units where the speed of light is also 1. So in these ordinary directions, as in our own universe, nothing can travel faster than light—but within the dark cones, where light itself can't travel, no speed limit applies.

More details can be found at www.gregegan.net.

GREG EGAN is a computer programmer, and the author of the acclaimed SF novels *Diaspora*, *Quarantine*, *Permutation City*, and *Teranesia*, as well as the Orthogonal trilogy. He has won the Hugo Award as well as the John W. Campbell Memorial Award. His short fiction has been published in a variety of places, including *Interzone*, *Asimov's*, and *Nature*.

Egan holds a BSc in Mathematics from the University of Western Australia, and currently lives in Perth.

Find out more at www.gregegan.net.